Books by T. A. Belsi

Tracy's Hot Mail

Tracy's Celebrity Hot Mail

Out of Control

www.trevorbelshaw.com

Unspoken

By

T. A. Belshaw

Many thanks to my editor, Maureen Vincent-Northam without whom this book would never have been completed.

For Doreen. I miss you.

Copyright ©2020 T. A. Belshaw

Cover design by: J.D.Smith Design
http://www.jdsmith-design.com

ISBN: 978-1-8383202-0-1

Chapter 1

Jess

'Darling, I'm home.'

Calvin's cheery voice wafted across from the front door through the passage and into the open plan lounge/diner where Jessica Griffiths was just finishing washing up last night's dinner plates. She heard the cupboard door in the passage slam shut as Calvin deposited his golf clubs. A few moments later he breezed into the lounge.

'I made two over par today.'

'Well done!' said Jessica with more enthusiasm than she really felt. 'You'll hit that level par score before too long.'

Calvin almost purred.

'That bloody Liam Watt put me off by coughing on the last tee or I might have made it today.'

A look of searing anger appeared across his face. 'I'll get my own back next time. Two can play at that game.'

He stood behind Jessica, put his arms around her waist and nuzzled her neck.

'Perfume?'

'It's only a dab,' said Jessica defensively.

'What are the rules, my darling?' Calvin's voice dropped an octave.

Jessica held her breath.

The rules?

'I don't wear perfume unless we're going out together,' she replied.

'That's my girl.' Calvin's hands ran over Jessica's stomach and up to her breasts. He kneaded them softly.

'Come on, love, on the sofa, let's have some fun.'

Jessica broke free and turned to face him.

'I don't have time for that, much as I'd like to. I have to go out.'

Calvin stared hard at her, his voice stern.

'Out? Where is out?'

'It's Wednesday, Calvin. I always go to Nana's on Wednesday. You know I do.'

His face softened.

'Ah, of course, got to keep on the right side of the old gal eh? She can't have that much time left and she's worth a small fortune.'

He patted her on the backside. 'Go and sow the seeds, my darling. We might get the flat bought for us and a bit to spare.'

Jessica said nothing. She picked up her cardigan and car keys and walked across the lounge.

'See you in a couple of hours.'

'Oh, Jess,' he called.

'Yes?'

'Wash off the perfume before you go.'

Jess drove across town wiping her eyes every few minutes. The tears were a mixture of embarrassment and anger. Why did she allow herself to be treated like this? She was, in every other aspect of her life, a strong, intelligent, independent woman. When it came to Calvin however...

She loved him, he was handsome, he was clever, he possessed a quick wit, in fact that was the thing that had drawn her to him initially. Nowadays though, he saved it for friends, strangers and acquaintances, and used it less and less in her company.

He was a narcissist; she was almost certain of that. Everything was always about him. Nothing was ever his fault. Every misfortune he suffered, no matter how trivial (the golf story from this morning for instance), was a personal slight on him, his character, or, it was an underhand attempt to make him look stupid or to stop him succeeding in life.

Jess tried to drag her thoughts away from her own personal misery and settled them on Nana, Alice, her soon to be Centenarian Great Grandmother.

Alice was, to an outsider, grumpy, self-centred and aloof, but Jess knew a different side to her.

'We are two peas in a pod,' Alice told her frequently. 'My mirror image, my Doppelganger.'

It was true. They were extremely alike, when you took into account the generation gap. Alice had shown Jess some old black and white photographs from the nineteen-forties when she was in her early 20s, pretty much the same age as Jess was now, and the likeness was remarkable.

Alice, at ninety-nine and eleven months, was as age-worn as she should be but that classic beauty still remained. The bone structure, the smile (when it reluctantly appeared) and the eyes, flashing with annoyance or lighting up with a joyous glint, that she was sure, her own eyes couldn't match.

Nana lived in a two-hundred-year-old farm house that nestled snugly in an acre of overgrown land.

The farm had once covered a hundred acres but Nana had sold plots off over the years to builders, the council (for a football pitch), and some individual buyers who fancied a self-build.

All of this had brought in plenty of money but had also brought suburbia into what was once an expanse of greenery. Alice would have been condemned by the environmental lobby for enriching herself by such means and indeed, Jess herself would not have been happy with the result, but this was all history. Nana wouldn't give a damn for the Green lobby anyway. She appeared, on the face of it at least, to be an old-fashioned woman, with outdated views. Not that they had ever discussed modern day concerns. Jess thought it might be time they did.

She left the main road that ran through the town, turned left down a narrower road with bungalows, the sports field and a few larger, modern family houses and pulled off the road onto an asphalt drive. She sat silently for a moment then gave herself a mental slap.

Come on, Jess, pull yourself together. Happy face for Nana.

She got out of the car, took in a deep breath, put on her best smile and headed for the front door.

Chapter 2

Alice

The ray of late autumn sunlight eased its way through a narrow crack in the vertical blind and reflected itself via a polished, metallic likeness of Marylin Monroe, onto the sleeping face of Alice Mollison.

The old woman screwed up her face, blinked a few times, then called to her carer, Gwen, who was busying herself making sandwiches for Alice's lunch. Gwen called in twice a day; morning, to get Alice out of bed, dressed, watered and fed, and in the evening to get her tea and into her night clothes.

Alice slept in a bed in the corner of the room, the stairs being a mission too far nowadays for the soon to be Centenarian.

Gwen came through from the kitchen.

'What is it, my lovely?'

'Can you shut that bloody sunlight off? It's burning out my corneas.'

Gwen stepped across the room and adjusted the blind.

'How's that? We shouldn't really be complaining about the sun coming out. We've had weeks of rain. I'm taking my Gareth out for a walk in the park this afternoon. You don't know when we'll see it again. I think—'

'It felt like a laser beam on my eyelids,' Alice interrupted. 'It's still hot now; here, feel.'

Gwen went back to her sandwich making.

'Jessica will be here soon, won't she? It's Wednesday.'

Alice brightened. Jessica was her great granddaughter, a kindred spirit. She was a clone of Alice when she was that age. She always looked forward to her company. She was bright, engaging, and an aspiring novelist to boot. She read pieces of her work in progress to

Alice at least once a week. Sadly, the novel that Jessica knew was inside her had yet to surface. Her laptop was filled with half-finished manuscripts, story ideas and plotlines. She liked to be called Jess but Alice wouldn't comply with her request.

'Jessica is the name on your birth certificate, so Jessica, you remain,' she had said.

Alice turned to her left and took a small make-up mirror from the drawer in the narrow, walnut, side table. She studied her face intently.

'Not bad for almost a hundred,' she mused. She turned her head this way and that. 'If you can see past the folds of wrinkles and liver spots.'

In her youth, Alice had been a beauty. Everyone said so. Not the filler-assisted beauty of the present day, more of a classic beauty, like the wartime film star Rita Hayworth, with whom she had been favourably compared.

'Good legs, good bust, nice arse and a face to die for,' as Ada Blunt, the landlord's wife of The Old Bull, had once described her. 'She'll come down to earth with a bump,' she had added, as though she was a clairvoyant.

Alice still had a good head of hair, albeit an almost translucent white. It fell to just below the nape of her neck and was swept back at the sides, held in place with hairpins. She patted it into shape and returned the mirror to the drawer.

She sighed. She hated old age and everything it brought with it, even though she had been extremely lucky with her health. There had been no major illnesses, no cancers, no eye problems, not since she had had the laser surgery at least. There had been no hypertension, no real problems with osteoarthritis, and thankfully, best of all, no Alzheimer's or Dementia. Alice's mind was sharp as a tack. When she was awake that was. Her 'forty winks' were becoming more and more frequent.

She eased herself up in her chair, reached behind and adjusted the two cushions that had become a permanent feature as Gwen returned to the room carrying a plate of sandwiches and a flask of tea.

'There you go, my lovely. That should see you through to this evening. I'm sure Jessica will get you anything you need in between.' She pointed to the commode that sat in the corner opposite the bed. 'Would you like to go before she gets here?'

Alice grimaced. The commode was the thing she despised most about old age. She'd give half of what was left of her life to be able to use a proper flushing toilet. She had a stairlift to get upstairs but no longer had the strength in her legs to get her there, even with her walker.

'Have you ever seen me on the commode, even once in all the time you've been coming here?' she asked.

'No, but I just thought I'd ask. Just in case. There's a first time for everything,' Gwen replied.

'I'm neither immobile nor incapable,' Alice retorted. 'Even Jessica doesn't get to see me defecate or urinate. I do have some private moments, few as they are.' Alice continued as though Gwen hadn't spoken.

The carer picked up her bag and walked to the lounge door.

'See you tonight then. I'm off to see old Mr Hathersage now, bless him.' Ben Hathersage was bedbound. Gwen always added the epithet whenever she spoke about him. 'Bed bath today.' She shuddered. 'That won't be pleasant, he's incontinent.'

'Well, you always seem to want to watch me poo,' said Alice, with a little glint in her eye.

Gwen turned away. 'See you later then.'

She stopped and turned as Alice called her name. The old woman smiled a short smile and nodded to the carer. Gwen winked, nodded back in acknowledgement and walked along the passage towards the front door.

'Cranky old bugger,' she said, chuckling to herself.

Alice adjusted the cushions again and looked up at the clock. She despised that almost as much as the commode. All too frequently these days, she'd sit and watch it tick her life away as she listened to Classic FM on the new DAB radio that Jessica had bought her for her ninety-ninth.

'Damn clock. Damn time.'

The clock was saved from further abuse when Gwen suddenly appeared again.

'Look who's here,' she announced, her voice full of surprise.

'Clark Gable?' Alice asked.

'No, silly.' Gwen gave a little laugh. 'It's Jessica.'

Gwen backed away and Jess appeared in the doorway. Her chestnut curls fell around her shoulders. She wore mid-blue skinny jeans, a black top covered with a thigh-length cardigan. On her feet were open toed sandals, and a large canvas shoulder bag sat against her hip.

Her face was clear of make-up. Not even a hint of mascara. Alice noted that her eyes were puffy. She had been crying. Again.

When she smiled her blue eyes lit up. She turned her head back as the front door closed. 'Bye, Gwen,' she said, and waved.

Jess almost bounced into the lounge, dropped her bag at the side of an old-fashioned, lion's-foot, coffee table and stepped quickly to Alice's side. She put her arm around her shoulders and gave her a kiss on the cheek.

'Mmmm, you smell of lavender. How's my favourite Nana,' she asked.

'I'm the only Nana you have, dear. The other one couldn't last the distance.'

Jess laughed. 'You're a wicked old hag. Would you like some tea, I'm parched.'

Alice pushed herself up from her chair and grabbed at her walker. 'Close the kitchen door behind you and give me ten minutes, will you, Jessica. I'm desperate for a pee.'

Ten minutes later, Jess tapped on the door and eased it open an inch.

'Have you finished?'

'For now, but I'll be going again soon if you keep forcing all this tea down me.'

Jess pushed open the door with her knee and carried in a tray holding a flowered china tea pot and a matching china cup, milk jug, sugar bowl and a brightly coloured mug. She set it down on the table and sat in the arm chair opposite Alice.

'I've never once heard you refuse a cup of tea,' she said. 'I think you have PG Tips in your veins, not blood. That's why you've lived so long.'

She leaned forward, poured the tea, added two heaped spoons of sugar, a dash of milk and handed it to Alice with a courtesy.

'Tea is served, Ma'am,' she said.

Alice took a sip and nodded approvingly. She looked over her cup at Jess.

'Have you been crying, young lady?'

Jess bit her lip. Nothing got past Nana.

'It's just a silly thing,' Jess replied. 'An old song on the radio, I always get emotional when I hear it.'

Alice decided to let it go.

'No story today? Weren't we riding aboard an old tea clipper last week? I want to know what happens to Abel and his intended. They've been apart too long. It's time they were wed.'

Jess studied her mug intently. 'I've sort of shelved that. It wasn't going to plan.'

Alice laughed and choked on her tea. Jess was at her side in an instant, hanky in hand, wiping the tea from her chin, the other hand reaching behind to pat her back.

Alice waved her away. 'Don't fuss, I'm fine.'

As Jess returned to her seat, Alice returned to the subject of the book.

'That's a shame, I quite liked Abel. You will have to finish one of these tales, Jessica. The publishers won't print half a book.'

Jess sighed. 'I know, Nana. I just keep thinking there's a better story somewhere, one with utterly believable characters. A story that everyone can relate to.'

'Most of us have one of those in our past,' said Alice. She hesitated for a moment and then continued.

'Who are you going to spend all of your Wednesdays making tea for when I'm gone?' she asked.

Jess frowned. 'What a topic of conversation, Nana. Gran says you'll outlive us all.'

Gran was Martha, Alice's eldest daughter. Alice was Nana, because Great Gran never seemed right and Nana was a lot more familiar. Apart from Gran there was Great Aunt Marjorie, Alice's second daughter. Jess's mother was Nicola, Martha's only child. Alice had little if anything to do with any of them. Jess was Alice, reborn and they both knew it.

'What a notion,' said Alice. 'I'd still be sitting on that blooming commode when I was a hundred and seventy, perish the thought.'

'You must be looking forward to next month, Nana. Not too many people get a telegram from the Queen.'

Alice shook her head, her crystalline hair coming to rest a full second later.

'I won't get to read it, Jessica, I'm coming towards the end, a little bit more of me fades away every day.'

'Oh, Nana, don't say such things,' said Jess, a tear sliding down her cheek. 'You'll still be here next Christmas, you're as tough as old boots.'

'I mean it,' replied Alice. 'When I sleep, I see the blackness now, there are no colours anymore. Every time it's the same. It's like I'm looking into a pitch-black tunnel. It was like that for weeks, but then, a few days ago, I saw a pinprick of light, only just bright enough to make out. Over the last few days, it's grown larger. The light isn't daylight or anything like that, it's a brilliant white light, but it's soft, if you see what I mean? The pinprick has grown bigger every day and now it's about a quarter of the size of the tunnel. I'm being called, and I'm ready to go.'

Jess wiped her eyes with her tea-stained hanky. 'Don't, Nana, please. I don't like you talking like this.'

Alice leaned forward and patted Jess's proffered hand.

'It comes to us all sooner or later, my dear, and now it's my turn.'

She waved away Jess's fretful protestations.

'Listen, my sweetheart. I have something to tell you, a secret I've not shared with a living soul for eighty years.'

Jess wiped her eyes again and blew her running nose.

'Not even Gran or Mum?'

'Especially not your Gran or Mum,' said Alice. 'It would hardly be a secret if they got hold of it and, well, they wouldn't be able to cope with the knowledge anyway. No one knows, Jessica. I'm the sole bearer of the secret, but I'd like to unburden myself of it before I go, a sort of confession if you like. Will you be my priest?'

Chapter 3

Alice

Jess shifted in her seat and leaned in towards Alice.

'You can tell me anything, Nana, you know that. I promise not to tell a soul.'

'I know that, Jessica,' replied Alice, 'and I'm sorry it's you who will have to carry the burden of that secret... well, there are quite a few secrets if I'm honest.'

'I can handle it, Nana. It can't be that bad.'

Alice pushed herself back onto the cushions.

'You'd be surprised at the things that have happened to me, the things I've done. I have not led an ordinary life by any standards, Jessica. I've had to learn to live with things I still regret and things that I'd do again tomorrow if I had to.'

Jess took hold of Alice's hand again as she continued.

'You know, I'm really glad I don't believe in St Peter, Heaven and Hell, all that malarkey because I would be judged harshly.'

'Well, you know I don't believe in all that angelic choir stuff myself, Nana,' Jessica replied. 'But I do think there's something; that spark of life, soul, whatever you want to call it, has to go somewhere. I was reading an article about Quantum Physics the other day and the writer said that they're on the verge of proving that alternative universes actually exist. There could be millions of them, and that's where you pass to when you leave this place. There's also an argument for thousands of dimensions which we could pass through. That's why some people think they've seen ghosts, it's just a tear in the dimensional wall.'

'That sounds all right,' said Alice brightly. 'But I don't want to spend the next million years passing through dimensions, universes etcetera, looking like this.'

Jess chuckled.

'Oh, Nana, you do make me laugh sometimes.'

'Good,' said Alice. 'Now tell me the real reason you were crying. You had been crying last Sunday too. You can't fool me with your forced smile. Your eyes give you away, even without the puffiness. I can always tell when you're unhappy so, come on, out with it.'

Jess let go of Alice's hand and held hers together as if in prayer.

'Me and Calvin, we've just, well, we've got a few issues to sort out. We're having a lot of fights lately.'

Alice looked hard at her.

'Fights? Fight's as in violence? Or is it this American term that's corrupted our wonderful language. Fights as in arguments?'

Jess hesitated a second too long.

'Get rid of him, Jessica. Don't tell me it's a one-off incident. Because they don't exist. A one-off incident leads to two, three, then it's a weekly occurrence, then a nightly one. I know you love the man but believe me, for the sake of your own sanity and for the safety of any children to come, get out now. He's never going to change.'

Jess pulled a face.

'It's not like that, really, Nana. He just likes to be the man of the house.'

'Abject nonsense,' spat Alice. 'I've met these men, Jessica, I know how they operate. They're a type, and sadly, you, my dear, just like me, are attracted to them.'

'You mean you had an abusive relationship? Not that ours is,' she added hurriedly. 'He's really not that bad.'

She looked away and tried to move the subject matter on.

'You were the lucky in one respect, Nana; Great Grandad was the love of your life, wasn't he? Everyone in the family talks about how you could never take another man after he died fighting in the war. You've spent a lifetime alone, mourning him. He must have been some kind of man. You never seem to talk about him. Does it still hurt too much?'

16

'He was a special kind of man all right,' replied Alice. 'And yes, I remember the hurt as though it was yesterday, but it's not the heartache sort of hurt you're thinking of. I was glad when he was gone. Ecstatic in fact.'

Jess frowned.

'But Gran said—'

'What would my daughter know? She was only a baby when he disappeared out of her life. She only has made-up memories about him. She's never seen a picture of him. I wiped him from her life, and mine.'

Jess tipped her head to one side and said quietly.

'All right, Nana, I'm intrigued. I'd like to hear your story, but only if you're sure it won't upset you too much.'

'I won't be upset or overly emotional about any of it,' replied Alice. 'I've lived with it all for eighty years. It's high time I got it off my chest. Now, do you want to record this, or will you rely on your memory, there's a lot of it and you might wish I'd kept some of it to myself.'

Jess tried to make light of Alice's chilling words.

'Careful, Nana, I might turn it into a novel.'

'I hope you do,' said Alice. 'I won't be here to read it. Just make sure you protect yourself, change the names and the locations. You should get away with it then. As I said, our family knows nothing of it, they'll think you just have a very vivid imagination, and even if one or two of them do make a connection, they'll think that you thought the worst of me too. It's how they are.'

Jess got up and lifted the tray from the table.

'A good story is always better with a cup of tea,' she said.

Chapter 4

1919-1937

I was born on the twenty-fourth of September nineteen-nineteen in the family farmhouse, on the night of the first violent weather event of the autumn. The winds were so bad they took half the roof off our barn and deposited it onto the flock of sheep that were huddled down in a pasture a hundred yards away. We lost ten ewes and thirty barn-dwelling chickens that night. My father later told me if I had been born a dog instead of a child, I would have been named Storm.

We owned a hundred acres at that time. The rain had a devastating effect on our newly harvested crops. It was a bad end to the year and not an auspicious start for a new arrival.

I was, to say the least, a difficult birth. My mother was in labour for forty hours, she lost so much blood it was a miracle she survived. The local doctor and the midwife who supervised the birth thought my father was about to lose both of us. When I eventually arrived, the trauma had been so great that I refused to cry, even after five upside-down bottom slaps. I was breathing fine, but I was stubborn and wouldn't give in to their demands, even at that age. It was to be a trait that has stayed with me all of my life.

My father was frantic about the state of my mother. They were soul mates, in love from the first class they attended at the local school. He would have laid down his own life if it meant she would live.

As it was, she did survive. Just. She was never the same woman after, she was weak and prone to every infection going. Luckily the Spanish flu had almost burnt itself out the year before so she was spared that.

Growing up on a farm in the nineteen-twenties gave me a far easier childhood than most working-class children. I was well fed, I got plenty of fresh air and was mostly isolated from some of the nastier bugs that infected the town children. I did get chickenpox at four and a quite severe dose of measles at six, but the sporadic epidemics of the deadly scarlet fever disease weren't really seen in our neck of the woods.

I always felt loved, despite my mother's near-death experience, though at times I did catch her regarding me with a strained look in her eyes as if she was remembering those horrendous two days. Dad loved me unconditionally. I was half my mother and that was always going to be enough for him. I looked a lot like her and he would often sit in his huge high-backed armchair watching me play with Betsy my rag doll and remark that it was just like watching my mother play at school.

We had ten farm workers and a few casual ones who would come in for seasonal work. The wages weren't great and the days were long; some of the work was backbreaking but they were a happy crew. Twice a year – at Christmas and on my mother's birthday – my father would invite them and their families around to the farm for a celebration party. The farm workers' wives used to come around to help my mother prepare the food. Dad provided a barrel of ale and a few bottles of gin to help the party swing. We children had bottles of fizzy lemonade to sate the thirsts we worked up playing tag around the farmyard buildings.

We had a few cows at that time and the villagers would bring pails every morning for milk squeezed fresh from the cow. They could buy pasteurised milk from the local shop but old habits, as they say, die hard. No one to my knowledge was ever taken ill drinking our raw milk. Indeed, we used to drink it ourselves. It was much tastier than the small bottles we were given at school.

The farm's main business was wheat, corn and pork. We had twelve big sties, each holding a boar and ten sows. Occasionally we'd have two boars who had been raised together in with the sows, especially if they weren't breeding too well. The sows were isolated when their time came and reintroduced to the boars a few weeks later. The piglets, to my huge disappointment and frustration, were bulked up for slaughter.

One night in the autumn of nineteen twenty-five, I was woken from my slumbers by a loud shout. My father had leapt from his bed, hared down the stairs, grabbed his shotgun and ran out into the yard. I rushed to my window. The moon was full and I had a perfect view of the farmyard and my father blasting the head off a young fox that had snuck out of the barn with a chicken in his mouth.

The next morning Dad kept me well away from the barn, a place I used to love to play in, while he carried out the twenty, headless, legless, dead and dying chickens that were the victims of the fox's frenzy. Thankfully, my own pet chicken, Dolly, had survived the carnage. My father had found her on one of the barn beams. How she got up there we'll never know.

Having not seen the bodies of the poultry, I found myself feeling sorry for the fox. I sat on the back step and cried at the sight of its poor carcass, lying where it had died. My father knelt in front of me and explained in quite stark terms for the ears of a five-year-old, why he'd had to do it. Then he dragged the fox by its brush, around to the pig pens, and hurled it over the wall of the largest of them.

I can still remember the sound of snuffling and scuffling that followed as the excited porcine sounder attacked their surprise dinner.

He looked at my puzzled face as he walked back towards me.

'Pigs will eat anything,' he said.

As I grew up, I began to understand the harsher aspects of farm life. I remember my father's tears after he had to put down his favourite dog.

I myself had to perform the same heart-breaking task, and I shot a fox and disposed of it in the same manner. Neither my father nor I fed the dogs to the pigs. They had their own personal space at the bottom of the vegetable garden.

The dogs were workers and not really pets, but old Billy was allowed to sleep in the kitchen next to the pot-bellied stove and he always loved a tummy rub and a back scratch.

I did have my own pet. A cat I called Jemima though everyone else called it Slasher. Dad carried it out of the barn one day after it had been abandoned by a feral mother. He was about to kill it and chuck it in the pig pens when I spotted it and after vehement protestations and a long lecture about whose responsibility it was to feed and look after the creature, I was allowed to adopt it.

Feeding was the first problem. We ended up giving it creamy, raw cow's milk, filtered through a rubber teat on my old baby feeding bottles.

The practice of giving cats cows' milk is frowned on today, but Jemima thrived on it and soon moved on to the daily minced beef or pork that my mother used in her award-winning pies.

Jemima was half feral. No one could get close to her but me without almost losing an arm. She was a wonderful mouser and could have been a champion ratter if such a title had existed. She was never quite part of the family but I loved her. She lived until the end of the war and was still catching vermin up until the day she died.

In nineteen twenty-six, the country was riven by the General Strike. Though the majority of strikers worked in the mines and docks, some farm workers were encouraged by activists in the Communist party to hold sympathy wild cat strikes.

The issue never surfaced on our farm, even though the agitators tried to persuade some of our workers at The Old Bull in the village. My father never forgot their loyalty. Our workers didn't need to hold wild cat strikes anyway. Jemima performed wild cat strikes every day of her life.

Nothing much happened over the next few years and our farm life went on just as it always had. Then, in nineteen twenty-nine, Wall Street in America suffered a catastrophic crash and the economies of the entire world went into meltdown. What followed was known as the Great Depression. Millions of workers lost their jobs, wages were cut across the board and most working-class families suffered immensely.

My father did his best to help our workers. He never forgot the loyalty they showed to us a few years earlier and now he repaid that debt. He kept their wages at the same level but all had to work an extra hour a day, especially at ploughing, sowing and during the harvest. We still kept the rituals of mother's birthday and Christmas where, as an added bonus, my father produced a couple of giant turkeys.

Old Joshua Cohen, who had worked well past his retirement date and who my father had put on light duties some years before, had finally thrown in the towel at the age of seventy-one, his arthritic hands not able to hold a cup, let alone a scythe. He was left with only a pittance of a pension and no way to pay the rent on the cottage he had lived in with his daughter and three grandchildren.

My father, in his usual way, quietly sorted things out. He bought the cottage from the landlord for one hundred and ninety-five pounds and gave Old Joshua a rent-free contract for the rest of his life. His daughter was given a job at the farm helping my increasingly fragile mother perform her tasks.

So, the farm survived the Great Depression though my father did have to sell off ten acres from the top fields to the owner of the neighbouring farm to get us all through a bad patch in the winter of nineteen thirty-three.

In the winter of nineteen thirty-seven, my mother's strength finally ran out and she died in my father's arms whilst the doctor was hurrying towards us. She had been bedbound since the previous autumn. My father and I, along with Old Joshua's daughter, Miriam, used to spend hours reading to her. She'd drift in and out of consciousness but my father insisted we read on. Amazingly, when she woke up, she'd be in the same place of the story as the reader.

My father bore her death badly and he took to drink. I was seventeen at the time and I found myself running more and more of the farm's affairs. It wasn't a problem as I helped my father with so many things over the years. I could start a cold engine on the old truck that was parked up in the barn to protect it from frost. I had already learned to do the books (my father checked them religiously every week and seldom found an error). I had worked in the fields with the farm hands, I could talk to the foreman without him getting uppity about things. I actually think he respected my knowledge. He called me The Corn Dolly, as they all did, because of my habit of hiding in the cornfields when I was dodging some task I didn't fancy performing.

So, although my father's absence didn't make the running of the farm any easier – we were one man down after all – we did manage to get by. For the first few weeks after my mother's funeral, he spent most of his time at The Old Bull, drinking pint after pint of dark beer. I used to drive up in the truck to find him if it ever got too far past closing time. I found him in hedges, in a field and even propped up, fast asleep against an iron lamppost.

Soon though, he became a home drinker. He sat in the armchair in the living room looking out over the distant hills, a bottle of whisky on the table at his side, another bottle on the floor.

The landlord of The Old Bull dropped them off on a daily basis. I got the bill once a month. Dad hardly uttered a word. I did my best to try to coax him off the spirit but I was wasting my time. He wanted to be with my mother again, nothing else mattered.

By autumn nineteen thirty-seven I had my own, life-changing, problems to worry about. I was pregnant and the father wasn't around.

Chapter 5

Alice

'Oh, my goodness!' exclaimed Jess, one hand over her mouth. 'You really got dragged through the mill, Nana. I don't know how you coped.'

'I didn't really,' replied Alice, that's how I ended up pregnant. I was still mourning my mother and I was under a lot of stress worrying about my father.'

Jess leaned back in her chair and blew out her cheeks.

'I don't know what to say.'

'Neither do I, but I know what you ought to do,' said Alice pointing at the clock. 'I'd love you to stay longer, but you really ought to go home. You've been here for four hours now.'

Jess almost fell out of the chair in her hurry to get to her feet. She pulled her phone out of her bag and checked for text and voicemail messages. There were none. This was odd. Usually if she was late, he'd be texting every five minutes asking where she was.

'Oh my God, he'll be angry,' she said aloud. 'I've got to do a bit of shopping yet.' She smiled at Alice. 'Will you be all right on your own?'

'Of course I will, silly child,' retorted Alice. 'I do it every day, remember?' She wriggled into her cushions. 'Gwen will be here at six to feed me, empty my disgusting commode and get me ready for bed.'

Jess grabbed her things and hurried to the door. She spun around, blew a kiss and disappeared down the hallway. 'Bye, Nana, see you on Friday,' she called.

Alice blinked as the front door slammed.

'Cheerio, Jessica,' she said.

Gwen arrived in a fluster, fifteen minutes late.

'I'm so sorry I'm late, Lovely, but I got stuck at poor Mrs Swinston's. She had an accident just as I was leaving and I had to change her.'

Alice shuddered and raised a silent thank you to whichever deity had delivered her from incontinence.

'You haven't had your flask, and you haven't eaten your sandwiches,' chided Gwen.

'Jessica was here for longer than expected, we forgot all about them. Leave them where they are, I'll have them for tea,' Alice replied.

'Speaking of tea,' said Gwen raising the tea pot from the coffee table and shaking it. 'I'm ready for one, are you?'

'All right, I'll have one,' replied Alice, 'but if I'm up all-night peeing, you'll be held responsible.'

She reached out for her walking frame. 'Shut the door, Gwen, I'm just about ready to burst.'

Later that evening, after an hour staring at the clock whilst listening to News Hour on the radio, Alice shuffled across the room behind her walker and with several grunts, eased herself into bed. She picked up the novel she had been reading, opened it at her bookmark, then shut it with a snap and returned it to the table.

She lay on her back, her head propped up on soft pillows and stared at the cracked plaster on the ceiling. Within seconds she was back in the autumn of 1937.

'Damn you for all eternity, Frank Mollison,' she uttered.

Chapter 6

Jess

Jess jumped into the car and drove far too quickly to the Tesco Direct in town, taking no notice of any other road users. She bought ingredients for a quick stir fry and grabbed a mid-range bottle of white wine. As she reached the checkout, she changed her mind about the wine, rushed back and picked up a bottle of Calvin's favourite, but much more expensive, wine.

Outside the store she checked her phone again. No messages, what the hell did that mean? She was about to cross the road back to where she had parked, when a man's voice called to her.

'Jess? Is it really you?'

Jess turned back to see a youngish man of about six-two in height, he had rugby player's shoulders with a football player's waist. He wore a brown leather jacket, white t-shirt and light jeans.

'Ewan? Good God, it's been years. How are you?'

Ewan had been a member of her group at school, never a close friend but frequently on the fringes of the crowd. Always there but never really a part. It was the same at the local Uni which they had both attended. Ewan was in the rugby team but again, had been on the fringes of her group of friends. Drinking with them, fooling with them, attending demos with them, but no one knew that much about him.

'You won't have seen me around, Jess. I went to Africa volunteering with MediAid for a couple of years. I'm back for good now though. I've got a job at the local paper, reporting on environmental issues.'

'Well done you,' said Jess hurriedly. 'Look, I'm sorry, Ewan but I've got to rush, I'm seriously late.'

'Oh, don't mind me,' said Ewan with a big smile. 'I'll, erm, see you about the place.'

He waved as Jess sprinted across the road and hurled herself into her car.

'Hopefully,' he said.

When she arrived home, Calvin's BMW was parked in its usual spot in the forecourt of the block of flats. Jess parked alongside, grabbed her bags and fumbled nervously with her keys at the front door. It opened before she could insert the key in the lock.

'Hello, Jess. You decided to come home after all then?' Calvin stepped aside to allow Jess to get by with her bags.

'Sorry, Calvin,' she blurted out as she hurried up the stairs. 'I was having a serious conversation with Nana and forgot the time. I've got dinner.'

'I hope you were discussing her will,' said Calvin. 'Time well spent if so.'

Jess couldn't understand why he was being so pleasant. Usually she'd be interrogated if she was even fifteen minutes late.

'It was nothing to do with money.' Jess sighed and put her bags on the table. She fired up the hob and took down a wok from the shelf above. 'It was a private matter, a personal thing she wanted to discuss with me.'

'Christ, she hasn't started shitting herself, has she? Keep well away from that, Jess. Leave it to her carer, that's what she's paid for. Don't come back here with your hands stinking of shit.'

Jess glared at him.

'It's nothing to do with her health, well, not directly. She was telling me about her past. Wartime and all that. It was really interesting; I'm thinking of basing a book in that era.'

Calvin groaned. 'Not another bloody wild idea? Can't you just finish one project, sell it, and make some money so we can have a decent holiday?'

Jess ignored him. 'Anyway, that's why I was late.'

'I know,' replied Calvin. 'I saw your car parked outside her house about an hour and a half ago.'

'Have... have you been following me?' Jess blurted out.

'Don't flatter yourself,' replied Calvin. 'I just fancied a drive that's all, some fresh air.'

'But there's nothing on that road past Nana's except another farm. It's a dead end,' said Jess, puzzled.

'Well, I know that now,' Calvin replied with a laugh. 'Who was that bloke you were talking to outside Tesco?'

Jess concentrated on keeping her hands from shaking. 'Bloke?'

'Yes, bloke. The tall dude with the big chest, you were talking to him.'

'Oh, you mean Ewan?' He used to be in my class at school, I haven't seen him for years. Since school actually.' Jess decided not to complicate things any further by mentioning Uni.

Calvin came up close behind her.

'And you're sure you haven't seen him since. Like recently perhaps?'

'Hardly,' replied Jess. 'That's what the conversation was about. He's just come back from four years in Africa, volunteering.'

Calvin turned away and sat on the sofa.

'More fool him, that's all I can say. Why waste your life like that? Is he gay?' he added. 'He looked gay.'

Jess swore under her breath.

'I really have no idea,' she said.

As they sat down to dinner Jess's phone rang.

'Hi, how are you? Really? I'm not sure to be honest, I'll ask Calvin, he might be doing something on Saturday.'

She took the phone away from her ear.

'Calvin?'

'No, I'm not interested whatever it is,' he said sternly. 'I was going to shoot some pool at the Crown.'

Jess returned to her conversation.

'Sorry, Sam, Calvin is—'

'Sam? Is that the lovely Sam? Of course we'll come, what are we doing?' Calvin beamed across the table.

'Make your mind up, Calvin,' shouted Sam down the phone so that Calvin could hear.

Jess explained the situation.

'Sam has a new bloke in tow, she's been out with him a couple of times this week and now she wants to know what he's like in civilised company. So, she wants us to make up a foursome on Saturday.'

'I'd happily make up a threesome,' snorted Calvin. 'Yes, tell her yes. We'll be there.'

Jess cut off the call.

'It's the Venetian restaurant. Eight-thirty, sharp.'

Calvin took a forkful of stir fry.

'Sam,' he whispered, then louder. 'Sam.'

That night, in bed, they had their usual post wine sex.

Jess could feel something wasn't right. She looked up at Calvin as he slid back and forth. His eyes were closed tight and he had a dreamy look on his face. She dug him in the ribs with her elbow.

'Hey, I'm here too you know.'

Calvin took a few moments to respond.

'Sorry, babe, I was just concentrating on you.'

It took Jess two hours to get to sleep that night. Calvin snored his usual light snore alongside her as she thought about Nana and what it must have been like back then for a pregnant seventeen-year- old in a society that just would not accept it.

Chapter 7

Alice

On Thursday, Gwen left on time as usual and went to sort out Mr Hathersage's mess. Alice listened to classical music for a while on the DAB, cursing everyone who dialled in to request music the station played every day, sometimes twice. She resisted the urge to pick up the phone and request Rachmaninov's Sonata for Cello and Piano, switched off the station, leaned back in her cushions and stared at the clock, willing it to stop.

After another thirty minutes of her life had ticked by, she began her usual abuse.

'Stop, Damn You, I have little enough time left as it is.'

She looked around for something to throw at the clock but found only her empty tea cup and the TV remote, none of which she could realistically use to find the target.

Alice closed her eyes and dozed for a while. When she awoke, the filtered shadows had moved across Marylin's silver image to the Turner prints further along the wall.

She yawned, her jaw making a slight cracking sound, and focussed on the clock again.

'Is this to be the remainder of my life?' she asked aloud. 'Come on, God, if you're there, help me out here. There's plenty of time for Purgatory after I'm gone.'

As if to answer, the phone rang. Alice reached across and managed to grip the handset at the second attempt. As she lifted it, she noticed that her hands were gradually taking on a vellum-like texture. She sighed; she had always looked after them, using only good quality hand creams. After a hard day on the farm, she looked forward to a hot bath, and a bit of indulgence, spending her meagre 'me time' on her face and hands. Even at seventy her hands looked good, despite all the years out in the cold, wet weather.

She held the phone in front of her and pressed the green, answer button.

'Yes, hello. I'm sorry but I'm afraid I do not require assistance with the virus that has infected my computer as I don't possess a computer. However, my granddaughter has a computer. No, she's not here at the moment. She's at work, she's a detective inspector in the police force, shall I get her to… Oh, you've gone.'

Alice put down the phone.

'That's a shame, I was enjoying that. Back to Purgatory practice.'

She nestled back in the chair and studied the clock face again.

At six, on the dot, Gwen arrived. She warmed up a frozen meal of Risotto in the microwave and gave it to Alice on a tray. The meals were delivered by an online company that Gwen had organised to save her cooking fresh food every night.

'This tastes like cardboard,' complained Alice.

'I'm sorry, Lovely,' said Gwen with a frown, 'I'll ring them tomorrow and put in a complaint for you.'

'Don't bother,' replied Alice. 'Everything tastes like cardboard these days, even the tea. I think my taste buds have been nuked by all the microwaved meals.'

Gwen shook her head slowly and laughed.

'You are a one at times.'

Alice's gaze once again settled on the large, round, antique wall clock as Gwen emptied the commode and had a general tidy up. There was never much to do, Alice only ever got out of her chair to answer nature's call or go to bed.

Alice was her last call of the day. A colleague had volunteered to see Mrs Swinston allowing Gwen to get off early. She had organised a baby sitter so that she could go to the cinema with her husband, Gareth.

'What are you going to see,' enquired Alice, whose last visit to the cinema was to see The Sound of Music.

'It's a war film, dear. Dunkirk I think it's called. Gareth does like his war films.'

'I remember it the first time around,' said Alice. 'I wouldn't like to sit through it again.'

Gwen picked up her coat and bag of essentials.

'Is there anything else I can do before I go, Lovely?'

'There is actually,' replied Alice. 'Could you take that bloody clock off the wall and smash it with a hammer?'

Gwen chuckled as she walked down the passage.

'But how would you know what time it is? Goodnight, my dear, see you tomorrow.'

The door slammed shut leaving Alice staring forlornly at the clock.

Chapter 8

Alice

On Friday morning, Alice ate a late breakfast; she had felt a little nauseous earlier. Gwen had been concerned but Alice admonished her and told her not to fuss.

'It'll no doubt be that cardboard curry you served up last night,' she said.

'I'm going to have a word with that company,' replied Gwen. 'I know you're half joking but you should be able to taste the meals. You're okay with my scrambled eggs, aren't you?'

The question came with a look of concern that Alice dismissed with a curt reply.

'The eggs are fine.'

Gwen relaxed.

'But then again you don't blast them into the cosmos with radiation.'

Gwen turned to hide a smile.

'All right, Lovely, you win. No more microwave meals. I'll cancel the order.'

Alice thought for a moment.

'If you look inside the store cupboard in the old pantry, you'll find a three-tier veggie steamer. Some fresh veg would be nice. It might help with the bowels too. As you are fully aware, I haven't been in a couple of days.'

Gwen disappeared and came back with the dusty, three tier, stainless steel steamer.

'I'll give this a good scrub. It'll only take fifteen minutes to cook the veg tonight, that's only a little bit longer than the microwave really. What would you like with it?'

'Gravy,' said Alice. She licked her lips. 'Thick gravy, so thick you can almost chew it.'

'No meat? A pie? I could do one in the oven and freeze half for another day.' She warmed to the task. 'Or I could cook a couple at home then bring them here and—'

'Warm them up in the Hadron Collider?' Alice interrupted.

'Warm them up in the oven,' continued Gwen with a curt nod. 'How come you know so much about science anyway?' she asked.

'Radio Four.' Alice pointed to the DAB radio. 'It's amazing what you can learn when it's going to be of no use to you whatever.'

Alice watched Gwen busy herself cleaning areas that didn't really need cleaning, mainly to avoid watching the clock. She was becoming increasingly worried about how quickly time was passing. The dreams were increasing in their intensity and the white light now covered an area larger than the blackness in the tunnel. In recent days she had closed her eyes and tried to will the tunnel into her mind to see if she could see anything beyond the light, but she only ever had flashbacks of her dreams, not new connections.

At nine-thirty, Gwen stopped, looked quizzically at Alice and asked.

'What time is it, Lovely? Am I late for Mr Hathersage, bless him?' She hurriedly pushed the vacuum into the cupboard beneath the stairs. 'Goodness me, I haven't made your tea and sandwiches yet.'

'What are you panicking about?' asked Alice, frowning. 'There's a blooming great big clock on the wall here, my only friend in the evening hours.' She looked at it and flipped a V sign. 'You have a watch, don't you?'

Gwen's head appeared around the kitchen door frame.

'I forgot it this morning. I'm a bit confused, Lovely, because Jessica is here. She never arrives until I'm about to leave.'

As if she had just been announced at a regency ball, Jessica stepped into the lounge.

'Hello, Nana. Hello, Gwen.'

Alice studied Jess closely. There was no redness around her eyes and her demeanour was far more relaxed.

'Good morning, Jessica.' She motioned her to come close and whispered, 'you're early.'

'I know,' whispered Jess. 'Calvin has an IT course and he's out of the flat until about six tonight, so I can stay all day if you like? Why are we whispering?' she added.

Alice pointed towards the kitchen.

'You've confused Gwen by arriving early. She thinks it's ten o'clock or later.' She chuckled to herself.

'Nana, you're incorrigible.' She called to Gwen in the kitchen. 'Don't rush, Gwen, I'm early.'

'Thank goodness for that,' Gwen called back, a note of relief in her voice. 'I didn't want to leave Mr Hathersage lying in his mess longer than I have to, bless him.'

Jess wagged a finger at Alice, who was biting her lip trying not to laugh.

'Nana!'

Gwen left at her usual time, leaving Jess and Alice in the lounge with a fresh pot of tea, some wrapped sandwiches for Alice, and a plate of digestive biscuits.

'I don't know why she keeps leaving those out for me,' said Alice. 'The crumbs make me choke.'

'She's being thoughtful, that's why,' chided Jess. 'You are mean to Gwen at times.'

'She knows I don't mean it,' replied Alice. 'It's just banter.' She moved in her seat and stretched out one leg. 'Ah, that's better. I thought I was seizing up for a minute.'

She returned to the subject of Gwen.

'The Social Services, in their wisdom, decided that I needed a full-time carer a couple of years ago. I gave them short shrift. NINE HUNDRED POUNDS A WEEK! I'd be flat broke inside a month.'

Jess shook her head.

'Nana, I saw your bank statements don't forget. That time you thought you were being overcharged for gas? You could pay for a full-time carer for the next ten years and still not have to sell the house to pay for the care.'

Alice sniffed.

'That's neither here nor there. I didn't need a full-time carer then, and I don't need one now. Gwen's hours are quite sufficient. Especially on the days when you come around.'

She bent her knee again and relaxed.

'Which reminds me. I'd like to talk to you about that. Time's running short, Jessica. The light is getting ever closer and brighter. Do you think you could add another day or two to your visits, or stay longer when you do come around? I'm worried that we won't have enough time to get through my story. We've hardly started yet.'

Jess nodded.

'Yes, I'm sure I can, Nana, I can definitely do Monday as well as the usual Sunday, and I could come around one or two evenings too perhaps, but please, don't talk as though this is the last few days we'll ever have together.'

'What about Calvin?' asked Alice.

'What about him?' replied Jess. 'He'll just have to put up with it.' She looked at Alice closely. Her confession that she felt she was fading a little more every day had worried her. She was looking frailer, a little weaker, her voice didn't have the strength it held a few short weeks ago and her skin was taking on a paper-like appearance.

'I'll see about sleeping over a couple of times a week too if you like?'

Alice smiled and stuck up a thumb. 'Thank you,' she said.

She leaned back into her cushions and, deliberately ignoring the clock, focussed her mind on the past.

'Right,' she said. 'Nineteen thirty-seven. Now, hurry up and pour that tea before it gets cold.'

Chapter 9

Calvin

Calvin climbed into his BMW and drove through the town and out into the countryside, past the Mollison farm, then turned around to face the way he had come at a gravel-strewn passing point, about fifty yards beyond the farm, on the narrow lane, the hedgerow protecting him from view.

He pulled on the handbrake and settled back to wait.

Twenty minutes later he spotted Jess's car pull into Alice's drive. He waited ten minutes, then pulled out and drove back into town, stopping at the off-campus Uni building where the IT lecture was to take place.

He looked at his watch.

'Thirty minutes to go. May as well grab a coffee.'

Calvin walked across the campus car park, crossed the road and pulled open the door of Coffee Express. There were a few customers littered about, sipping on lattes or tending to business on their laptops.

In the corner, by the window, was a blonde girl, idly stirring her coffee as she gazed out of the window. Her short skirt showed off a pair of athletic looking legs.

Calvin ordered an espresso and sauntered across to look out of the window himself. His eyes lingered on her legs for a second too long.

'Haven't you seen a pair of legs before?' the girl asked, a smile flickering across her lips.

Calvin's hand swept through his immaculately groomed hair.

'Not like those I haven't.' He smiled, showing off his perfect teeth. 'I'm Calvin,' he said, with all the charm he could muster. 'Do you mind if I join you?'

The girl smiled again and opened her hand, aiming it towards the seat opposite.

'I'm Tania, and I'm bored witless. Take a seat, I could do with some entertainment.'

Calvin pulled out the chair and sat down.

'I can do entertainment,' he said.

She smiled again and sipped her coffee, the tip of her tongue ran over her lips.

'Don't you have something better to do?'

He flashed his teeth again. 'What could be better than this,' he said.

Chapter 10

1937

I was still mourning my mother's passing by the time my birthday came around in the September. I had been busy through the summer looking after the farm. In July we lost the other half of the barn roof in a storm that was almost biblical. Luckily, this time, the gale was early and there wasn't a lot of stored hay or crop seed to lose. We didn't lose any sheep this time either, although three of the pig sties flooded pretty badly.

The farm lads repaired the barn roof so we didn't need to get any outside companies involved, thank goodness. It had been a pretty dreadful year so far. The news from abroad wasn't so good either. Hitler was threatening everyone in sight and the Spanish were fighting each other to the death. Never had I been so grateful to live on an island.

My father's depression was worse than ever as he sank further and further into his alcohol addiction. As we approached my birthday, he became increasingly agitated and fixated on those awful days, seventeen years before. Even in his almost paralytic state, he assigned my birth date to the beginning of my mother's decline.

'But for you, she'd still be here,' he slurred one night as I took him a meal of stew and dumplings that I knew he wouldn't eat. I left without saying a word.

I passed a lot of the spare time I did manage to snatch, with my best friend, Amy, who lived about half a mile away on the outskirts of what used to be a large village, but was now increasingly becoming a small town.

Amy was a year older than me but as in most country schools of the day, we sat in the same classroom with the same teacher, learning slightly different subject matter. I missed her terribly when she left education at fourteen to join her mother at the cotton mill on the river about a mile outside of town.

Amy was a pretty girl with hair the colour of flax. Girls today could never get that shade in a bottle. She was fair-skinned, blue eyed and had (in my opinion and many of the village boys) the best figure of any girl/woman for miles around. She was unaffected by it too and just laughed as the boys, and men, wolf whistled or called out some innuendo laden comment to her as they passed on the other side of the road.

She was a fun, happy go lucky girl. If she ever suffered on her period, she never let it show. I had never seen her in a bad mood. She loved life and helped me enormously through the weeks after my mother's death. She could make me laugh in an instant. Her impression of our old teacher, Mrs Blount, used to have me in hysterics. She could even do a passable impression of the landlord of The Old Bull, a man who never missed the chance to sell a pint. He knew exactly how old Amy and I were, but he allowed us to sit in the snug and drink port and lemons if no one else, such as a courting couple, wanted to use it. She was my favourite person on earth.

It didn't take much to get us tiddly and well before closing time we'd be on our way home laughing or singing one of the tunes we'd heard on the radio show, Bandwagon. Amy had a wind-up gramophone that I was insanely jealous of. Her uncle sold sheet music and records imported from America. These things would have been prohibitively expensive but Uncle Maurice, like everyone else, was totally captivated, and her collection grew every birthday and Christmas. We would regularly sit in her front room singing with Al Jolson, Bessie Smith and Bing Crosby.

Some nights in the summer, Amy would walk down to our farm and we'd drag a couple of chairs out onto the back yard overlooking the fields and imagine our futures. I always said that Amy would end up being a film star but she'd laugh that off and call me Rita Hayworth, an American actress who would become a major film star during the war years. We had seen her in one of her early roles at a rare visit to the cinema in nineteen thirty-six. Amy had nearly got us thrown out by exclaiming, 'What are you doing up on the screen?' when she appeared in her first scene. She kept looking at me, then the screen, open-mouthed throughout the movie. I started out giggling but quite enjoyed it when a young man in the seats behind, leant forward and agreed with her.

Rita's hair was, in fact, dark red, not chestnut like mine, but the rolling, shoulder length curls looked identical when seen in black and white.

One warm night, as we sat under a star strewn sky, drinking lemonade, I told her that she'd end up marrying Clarke Gable. Amy laughed, looked at me seriously, studied me for a moment or two and said that she didn't think I could ever give myself to just one man for a lifetime. She said she'd stake her beloved record collection on the fact that I'd never marry.

As it turned out, her collection was safe.

On the night of my birthday I pulled on my favourite floral-print frock and my only pair of going out shoes. They were a black Oxford style with a laced-up front and a pretty bow at the top.

For one night only, according to the landlord of The Old Bull, we were allowed into the public bar. Several of my friends were invited and we had a wonderful time, laughing, and dancing to Amy's gramophone that her father had set up for us on a table near the bar.

As the night progressed, we escalated from tiddly, to drunk, to very drunk and I began to flirt with some of the men in the bar. One man in particular took a real shine to me. He was a lot older, about thirty or so with untidy hair and a day's worth of stubble on his chin, but he had a rugged charm and a quick smile. He was funny and complimentary in equal measure. We danced, we laughed and towards nine-thirty, after I had staggered drunkenly back from the Ladies, almost clearing a table of empty glasses, he took me to a quiet corner and we sat down and chatted.

Amy's father twice came over to see if I was all right. The second time he had a quiet but stern word with Frank, as I now knew him to be.

Frank assured Mr Rowlings that he was a friend of my father and had done some work for him on the farm. I was way too out of it to contradict this wanton lie and when I was asked to verify the story I just smiled, nodded and he went back to the party and left us alone.

When the landlord bellowed 'Time' the party broke up and Frank took my arm; we stood in the small pub garden saying goodnight to everyone. Amy, who was as drunk as me, leaned on her father for support. He asked me if I wanted to stay over but I remember muttering something about 'cows' and declined. I brazenly took Frank's arm and we all walked together for a few hundred yards until we reached Amy's house. Once again, a worried Mr Rowlings asked if I wanted to stay, but again I declined and we left them waving to us, and Frank half walked, half carried, me along the lane that led to the farm.

About half way along was a gap in the hedge and as we reached it Frank stopped and said he'd like to give me a birthday kiss. I was all for it. I'd never kissed a man properly before and I was desperate to try a movie style snog.

I tipped my head upwards (he was a good foot taller the me), and Frank pushed his stubble strewn face onto mine. Our lips collided, rather than brushed against each other and before I knew it a beer-soaked tongue was sloshing around inside my mouth. I nearly gagged and tried to pull away but he was too strong. Eventually he came up for air.

'Let's just get off the road for a moment, Alice,' he said. 'I've got something I'd like to give you for your birthday.'

I allowed him to lead me into the field and we sat down on the still-dry grass. The autumn dew hadn't yet settled. He put his arm around my shoulders and began to undo the buttons at the back of my dress.

'Hey,' I said, turning towards him. 'What's your game?'

'Snakes and ladders,' he replied and we both laughed.

I don't remember my brassiere being unhooked but it must have been because a couple of minutes later I was on my back with my breasts exposed to the world. Frank was ever complimentary, telling me they were the loveliest things he had ever seen. He ran his hands over them and squeezed them and I must admit I found the experience very pleasurable. When he sucked on my nipples I moaned, lay my head to the side and began to fall asleep.

The next thing I remember my knickers were being pulled over my ankles. I kicked out a bit and asked him what he thought he was doing, but seconds later, my legs were spread and his hand was between my thighs, stroking and exploring. I tilted my head back and enjoyed the feeling. I had never felt anything quite like it before. Then he rolled on top and entered me. I tried to sit up and shove him off but he was too heavy. As he began to push, I gave in, lay back and just let it happen.

And that was my first experience of sex. It was short, rough and ugly. Afterwards, even in my drunken state, I felt used and ashamed.

Frank rolled off. Pulled up his trousers, walked back to the footpath and lit up a cigarette.

'You'd better get yourself home,' he said. Then he turned and walked back the way we had come leaving me half naked and crying.

Chapter 11

Jess

'Oh my God, Nana. What a terrible thing to happen. He should have been ashamed of himself, the brute.'

'It was my own stupid fault,' said Alice. 'I shouldn't have got so drunk and I should have put up a struggle. I just let it happen really.'

'Nana, you were only just eighteen and totally inexperienced, he was a fully grown man of how old, thirty, thirty-one?'

'He was twenty-nine when it happened, but he was almost thirty by the time I clapped eyes on him again.'

Jess wouldn't be mollified. 'It's disgusting. If that happened now, he'd be outed by the feminists in the town.'

'There was no feminism then, Jessica. Women were second class citizens, even in law. We couldn't do half the things men could do; we'd only been able to vote for nine years. It was a different world. Men were the breadwinners; women were supposed to stay at home and bring up the babies. What was the saying, women were supposed to be maids in the living room, chefs in the kitchen and whores in the bedroom. There was no justice for women. Men hit them with impunity. If the dinner wasn't up to their high standards, they got a thump. When they came back from the pub, drunk as lords and couldn't perform in the bedroom, it was the woman's fault and they got a thump. If they did perform and the sex wasn't as good as expected, they got a thump for that too. Life was one long rollercoaster of black eyes and busted lips.'

'Something should have been done about it,' said Jess angrily.

'Well, nothing was done,' said Alice calmly. She glanced at the hated clock. 'It's four o'clock, shouldn't you be somewhere else?'

'I'm okay this afternoon, Nana, Calvin's at a lecture off-campus. I don't know what else he can learn about computers; he's been working from home as an advisor on them for four years. You'd think he knew it all by now.'

The mention of Calvin's name made her automatically reach for her phone. There were two text messages from eleven-thirty that morning. She opened the first with growing anxiety.

'Hi, Jess, are you still at your Nana's? What time are you home?'

Nervously, she opened the second.

Don't rush to get back, this bloody lecture will go on until seven at least. The whole computer system went down. See you later. XX Calv.

Jess re-read the texts with a puzzled look on her face. This was the Calvin of old. The caring Calvin. The Calvin who let her know what he was doing without demanding to know what she was up to all the time.

She texted back. *Sorry, Calvin. I was engrossed in Nana's story; I've only just read your texts. I'm really sorry. Honestly, so sorry.*

Thirty seconds later another text arrived.

No worries, Jess. Look after your Nana, things are hectic here.

She heaved a sigh of relief, slipped the phone back into her bag and got to her feet.

'I'm just nipping to the loo then I'll make us another cuppa, Nana. There's no rush to get home today so I'll stay until six-ish. I'll talk to Calvin about staying over a night or two. It will be fine.' She hesitated. 'I'm sure it will.'

Chapter 12

Calvin

Calvin propped himself up on one elbow and watched the naked Tania get out of bed. With her back still facing him she took a white satin blouse from the back of a chair and slipped it on. Calvin took in the long legs, the curve of her bottom beneath the white satin and he became aroused again.

'Come back to bed,' he said huskily.

Tania turned around; she had fastened just one button over her navel. Calvin blew a wolf whistle and patted the bed.

'Come on, I'm ready for more.'

'You've had more than enough for one day, we've been in that bed for over four hours,' said Tania. 'Anyway, I have to go to work, I need a shower so you'll have to go soon.'

Cavin wasn't used to being ordered around but he bit his lip.

'Where do you work?'

'I'm a waitress at a restaurant,' she said. 'I work eight to midnight.'

Excellent, thought Calvin. She's home in the day, busy at night. Perfect.

'I bet you're a fabulous waitress too,' he said. 'I can see you being good with people.'

'I am,' she said.

Tania pulled the cover off the bed and shook her thumb towards the door.

'Come on, Casanova, I've got to get ready; I don't want to be late.'

Calvin slid off the bed and turned his back to her.

'It was good though wasn't it? The sex I mean.'

'It was passable,' she said.

He spun around, a look of incredulity on his face.

'PASSABLE?'

She giggled.

'Okay, it was really good, I'm only teasing. What is it with you men? You always have to be the best performers. It's not a competition you know? Women have different moods, sometimes we like it soft and gentle other times we want to be rammed into the middle of next week. It's different every time. Don't take things to heart so much.'

Placated, Calvin pulled on his socks and slipped into his pants. He turned towards her and posed. He looked good in his pants.

Tania threw a pillow at him. 'Come on, Tarzan. Go.'

Calvin finished getting dressed and she walked him to the front door of the flat.

'Do you, um, shall we err...?'

'Do this again?' She thought for a moment. 'Why not.'

'If you're not sure, don't bother about it,' said Calvin huffily.

Tania giggled again.

'You are easy to wind up, I must say.'

She kissed him on the cheek and straightened his collar.

'Look, I enjoyed it. It was very nice and I'd love to do it again. Same time, same place?'

'I'll give you my mobile number,' said Calvin eagerly. 'I'll call you in the week.'

'I don't have my phone with me,' said Tania, looking down at her blouse for effect. 'Give it to me next Friday. I'll be in the café, same time as today.' She blew him a kiss and ushered him out of the door.

Chapter 13

Jess

Jess arrived home at six-twenty. She had just begun to wash the salad when Calvin arrived twenty-five minutes later. Jess dried her hands and held her arms out towards him. He stepped into her embrace but just held his cheek against hers instead of kissing her. She let it go.

'Did you manage to fix the crash?'

Calvin walked across to the sofa, picked up the evening paper and sat down.

'Well?' asked Jess.

He looked up and frowned.

'Well, what?'

'The computer problem at Uni. Did you manage to fix it?'

'It wasn't my job to fix it.' He returned to the paper.

'I see. And how was your day, Jess? Oh, it was fine thanks, I ran over an escaped polar bear outside Tesco and they had to get a zoo vet to treat it.'

'Really?' he muttered.

'NO! Not really. You haven't listened to a bloody word I've said since you walked in the door, Calvin. Firstly, I'd have had a warmer greeting from that sodding polar bear and secondly, you're just an ignorant pig.'

Tears welled in her eyes but she managed to hold them back, just.

Calvin tossed the paper aside and got to his feet, his face a mask of concern.

'I'm sorry, Jess. I was miles away. I've had a stressful day.'

He wandered across and took her in his arms. He kissed her lips, softly, then her cheek, then he held her so close she could hardly breathe.

'You do still find me attractive, don't you, Jess?'

Jess managed to pull away far enough to be able to take in some air.

'Of course I do, you're my handsome man, the handsomest man I've ever seen.'

He pulled away and stared at her intently, looking for any trace of mirth or lies.

'Really?'

'Really,' replied Jess.

'And... This is going to sound ridiculous. You, you, still think I'm good in bed?'

Jess nodded. 'The best I've ever had. I can't speak for anyone else.'

He screwed his face up.

'I wish you hadn't mentioned the others,' he said. 'You know I like to think that I was your first.'

'I'm sorry,' said Jess. 'What's brought this on?'

'Brought what on?' Calvin looked puzzled.

'These questions about your manliness; you don't need to ask. You know how I feel about you. I've never looked at another man since I met you and I never want to. You're perfect for me.'

Calvin pulled back and gave her a beaming smile.

'How's your ana?' he asked.

Jess blinked. 'Nana? You never ask about Nana.'

'Well, I'm asking now. How is the old girl?'

'She's not so good to be honest, she thinks she's fading fast and I tend to agree with her, she is.'

'That's good then,' Calvin replied.

'Good? GOOD! What do you mean, GOOD? She's bloody well dying for Christ's sake.'

Calvin was full of remorse.

'I only meant, it's good that you're with her, Jess. For pity's sake, I didn't mean anything horrible. You should be spending time with her, in fact spend as much as you want. I've got to work from Uni a couple of days next week so I won't even be around much.'

Jess was mollified.

'I was going to ask what you thought about me spending a couple of nights over there for the next two weeks or so. I'm worried about her being alone when the carer goes home. It's only two nights,' she added quickly.

Calvin gently moved her away from the sink.

'I don't see why not if you're that worried,' he said. 'Spend as much time as you like with her.'

He rinsed his hands and started tossing the salad in the cullender that Jess had just put down.

'Now, sit down and relax. It's Friday, I always cook on Friday.'

Jess sat in her favourite armchair and stared at the blank TV screen.

What the hell was wrong with him? So frosty one moment and so full of concern and affection the next. She had seen him like this before, she racked her brains to remember.

Of course! Alisha and Jeremy's wedding. Calvin was best man and his speech hadn't raised more than one or two laughs although he'd spent a month working on it. Jeremy had said, 'never mind Calv, you can't be good at everything.' It had really hit home. His confidence, which normally bordered on arrogance, was shot to pieces. He had been in exactly the same mood tonight. Aloof, cold, then in desperate need of reassurance. She wondered what could possibly have happened to have shaken him so badly. It must have been this incident at work. Maybe he couldn't fix the problem but someone junior to him had. That wouldn't have gone down well at all, and if it had been jokingly remarked upon by his colleagues, it would have made it worse, much worse.

Jess decided she has solved the issue. She knew how to bring him out of it too, at least for tonight. It would have to be compliments all the way followed by as much sex as she could manage.

After dinner, which Jess said had been the best he had ever served up, they watched TV for a while, then she cuddled up to him and whispered, 'how about an early night?'

Calvin stretched, yawned and said he was going to sleep alone as he was tired, stressed, and needed a solid night's sleep and probably a lie-in tomorrow morning.

He gave Jess a perfunctory kiss on the top of her head, stretched his arms again and went through to the spare room.

Chapter 14

Jess

Jess got up at seven on Saturday morning, but Calvin was nowhere to be seen. The door to the spare bedroom was open and the bed had been made. She checked the cupboard at the bottom of the stairs, there were no golf clubs.

Jess wasn't too concerned. Calvin often spent his time on the golf course working out things that were troubling him.

She gave the flat a quick going over with the cordless vacuum and dusted in the lounge and bedroom. She was about to start on the bathroom when her phone rang. It was Calvin.

'Hi, Jess. I'm not going to get away from here for hours yet. I'm in a four ball and we're stuck behind the slowest pair I've ever come across. I'm in the last sixteen of the club stroke-play this afternoon so I doubt I'll be back until five-ish.'

'That's okay. Thanks for letting me know, Calvin,' Jess replied.

'Erm, that's not the reason I called,' said Calvin, quickly. 'Could you run an iron over my best white shirt and check my navy suit for creases? I don't want to look a slob tonight. Oh, and give my brown Chelsea boots a rub over while you're at it? Right, got to go, it's my shot.'

Jess threw her phone onto the sofa and swore at it. Then she went back to the bathroom and scrubbed the bath and sink to within an inch of their lives.

After lunch, Jess read her Writing Magazine for an hour and then opened up the laptop and resumed the article about pollution levels and its effect on children's health that she had been commissioned to write by Environment UK, magazine. The research was tedious, but it was an important topic and she was fully onboard with the ethics of the magazine. The article wasn't due to be sent until the following Friday but she liked to be in front with things.

At four, she made coffee and grabbed a cheese sandwich then, with a sigh, dragged the ironing board and steam iron out of the cupboard and set about Calvin's shirt. When that had been draped over a hanger and hung back up in his wardrobe, she brushed down his suit and checked the boots. They were perfectly clean, so she just waved his can of spray polish at them and put them back on his shoe rack amongst the dozen pairs of shoes. 'Shh,' she said to the boots. 'Don't let on.'

I always thought shoes were a woman thing, she thought. She only owned six pairs herself, if you didn't count the trainers. She didn't bother choosing a tie for him. Whichever one she went for he'd select a different one anyway.

Calvin arrived home at five-thirty, just as Jess was settling into the bath. He sat on the toilet seat and grinned.

'Guess who's in the last eight of the stroke-play?'

Jess tried to hide her annoyance at being disturbed. Bath time was meant to be a solo pleasure.

'Hmm, let me think,' she played along. 'YOU!' she cried out. 'Well done! When are the quarter finals? Is it the quarter finals next?'

Calvin nodded vigorously. 'It is, and I've only gone and drawn Liam Watt, remember him? The guy who ruined my chance at getting a par round last week. I'll show the rotten sod. He's only a twenty-four handicapper so I'll have to give him a fair few shots advantage, but I can wipe the floor with him still, and I WILL!' he shouted triumphantly.

Jess didn't understand the intricacies of the golf club rules but she clapped anyway. Her reaction did the trick and he left the bathroom swinging an imaginary golf club.

'I've ironed your shirt and checked the suit,' she called after him.

'Thanks,' he called back, 'but I'll give it a once over myself anyway. I've got time.'

Jess flicked a soapy V sign at the bathroom door and slid down into the bubbles.

'I hope you lose your little balls,' she said.

After her bath, Jess dried her hair and brushed her curls while Calvin had a shower. She applied her make-up with a mirror propped up on the dining room table as he pampered himself with body spray and post-shave balm. She had time to slip into her favourite black dress, hold up stockings and heels before he came out of the bathroom.

He snuggled up behind her and nuzzled into her neck.

'No scent?' he asked.

'I wasn't going to bother,' she lied.

'You must,' he said. 'You're never fully dressed without perfume.'

Jess was ready to go for seven forty-five. Calvin came out of the bedroom a full ten minutes later. She always had to wait for him. He eased up close so that she could smell his aftershave.

'Is that the Tom Ford? I thought you only used that for special occasions?'

'But this is a special occasion,' he replied. 'We're meeting Sam's new boyfriend. We have to make a good impression.'

Jess looked to the ceiling and shook her head. The smell of his aftershave lingered even though he had gone back into the bedroom to retrieve his wallet. She could buy half a dozen bottles of her favourite perfume for what one bottle of his cost. It was extortionate and she could never afford to buy it for him, even for Christmas and birthdays. Calvin seemed to relish that fact. He liked to think of himself as exclusive.

The Uber dropped them off outside the Venetian at eight twenty-seven. Sam was already there. She wore her blonde hair down over her shoulders. The red dress was so short that the cream jacket was only an inch shorter. She wore red Italian leather ankle boots and had a Gucci bag under her arm. Sam could look good in a sack but tonight she had outdone herself.

She squealed when she saw Jess and rushed forward to hug her. Calvin waited impatiently until the pair had exchanged pleasantries, then he stooped to kiss her, she turned her face so his lips brushed her cheek, then she stepped back and took him in.

'Wow, look at you, Calvin. It's a good job you're with my best friend or I'd whisk you off to bed. You look good enough to eat.'

Jess smiled. She knew Sam of old. She'd flirt with the Duke of Edinburgh if he happened to be passing.

Calvin preened and looked around. 'Have you been stood up?' he asked, with a hopeful tone in his voice.

'He wouldn't dare,' said Sam. 'Jamie's had to nip back to the car. He left his phone in the cradle, he's from out of town so he used it as a Sat Nav. Shall we go in?' she added. 'I'm bloody freezing, he'll find us.'

She led them into the plush restaurant. The head waiter saw them arrive, checked their reservation and showed them to a table close to the bar. Calvin played the gentleman and pulled out the girls' seats before sitting down himself next to Jess and directly opposite Sam.

Sam slipped off her coat revealing her magnificent bosom. More chest than dress, as Jess had remarked on many an occasion. Sam loved to show off her assets. She was one of those rare women who could wear anything, no matter how outrageous, and never look tarty. She hung the jacket on the back of her chair despite the head waiter's offer to take it in the cloakroom.

'I've got a spare pair of knickers in the pocket in case I lose mine tonight.' She winked at Jess. 'I wouldn't want them to fall out while he's carrying it.'

'Good call,' said a smiling Jess.

'Ah, here he is.' Sam waved as Jamie came into the restaurant and looked around for them. He arrived at their table full of smiles.

'Hello, I'm Jamie,' he announced.

Jess stood up and he pecked her on the cheek. He was tall, well dressed, as handsome as Calvin and had an easy-going air about him. His dark-brown hair was cut in a fade style, swept forward on top and shorter at the sides. His charcoal suit, which fitted well, was definitely off the peg. He wore a light blue shirt and a black tie. As he leant in for the kiss, Jess smelled Hugo Boss, Orange. He might look like a rival to Calvin in the good-looks stakes, but his tastes were definitely more affordable.

He held his hand out to Calvin who remained in his seat until he noticed Jess's glare.

He stood up slowly and offered his hand. 'I'm Calvin, pleased to meet you, erm... Jimmy, was it?'

'Jamie.'

'Jamie, that's right.' Calvin sat down again and picked up the wine list. 'Shall I order?'

'Calvin's our wine geek,' Sam explained to Jamie. 'Are you a white or red man?'

'I have no idea about wine,' he replied. 'I'm more of a beer man really.'

Calvin shot him a glance and smirked.

'No beer tonight, Ji...Jamie.' He raised his hand, clicked his fingers and a waitress strolled slowly over to the table.

'Don't go overboard for me,' quipped Jamie. 'I wouldn't know a hundred-pound bottle from a bottle of Tesco value brand.'

'Don't panic,' said Calvin. 'I won't break the bank.' He pointed to a fifty-four-pound bottle on the wine list and the waitress went off to get it. 'The mark up on this wine is unreal. You can buy this stuff at Waitrose for eighteen quid.'

When she returned, Calvin made a fuss of sniffing the small amount the waitress poured into his glass. 'Seems fine,' he said, then took a sip. 'Lovely. I'll pour, shall I?'

Calvin ordered another bottle of cheaper wine to go with their meals, and another when the desert arrived. Jess didn't refill her glass at all after the first drink, nor did Jamie as he was driving, but Calvin and Sam poured each other top-ups at regular intervals. As the night went on their flirting became ever louder and the innuendos ever more obvious.

After one particularly raucous exchange, Sam got out of her seat, leaned over the table towards Calvin and jiggled her breasts. 'I'm off for a pee,' she announced. 'I'll need to wear those spare knickers if I hang on much longer.'

She tottered off toward the Ladies. Calvin watched her every step.

Jess dug him in the ribs.

'What?' he asked with a frown.

Jess narrowed her eyes at him and tipped her head towards, Jamie.

'He's her date,' she hissed.

'Oh, I'm sorry, my darling,' Calvin slurred. 'Are we feeling a little left out?' He wrapped his arm around Jess's shoulders and pulled her to him. 'Diddums,' he said.

Jess pulled away and glared at him.

'You're showing us all up. Stop it.'

'Don't be a party pooper, Jess.' Calvin got to his feet unsteadily. 'I think I'll join Sam,' he announced to the room. 'I could out-pee a dray horse.'

As he staggered off towards the Gents, Jamie puffed out his cheeks and then let the air escape.

'Are they always like this?' he asked.

'Pretty much,' replied Jess. 'At times, when these two get together it's like there's no one else in the room. There's nothing in it though, they just like to bounce off each other. Don't worry about it. He's my partner. Sam knows that and she knows where the limit to this sort of thing is. Unlike Calvin, who is too drunk to care.'

Sam and Calvin arrived back together, leaning on each other and whispering conspiratorially.

When they were seated again, Calvin sipped his wine, looked challengingly at Jamie and asked.

'Do you play golf?'

Jess groaned. She'd rather he flirted with Sam than talk golf.

Jamie nodded. 'I do as it happens.'

'Great,' said Calvin. 'What's your handicap?' He eyed him up, silently appraising him. 'I'd say, twenty-two, twenty at a pinch. Come down to Fairgreens, it's only ten minutes from here. I'm a member. I'll give you a few tips.'

Jamie smiled.

'I'm the club pro at Lakefields course,' he said lightly. 'I play off scratch. I was going to join the pro tour at one time but life got in the way.'

Calvin's face went the colour of Sam's dress.

'Lake...Lakefields.'

Lakefields was a championship course, it had held the British Open on three occasions. The green fees were astronomical and although it was less than twenty miles away, Calvin had never played it.

'Come over one afternoon,' offered Jamie. 'I'll show you around and you can give me those tips.'

Calvin hardly said a word for the next fifteen minutes. As Jess said, he could sulk for England when he was in the mood. Sam brought him out of it by playing footsie with him under the table. When he looked across at her she winked.

'What was it you were saying about trouser snakes?'

At eleven, Sam called for the bill. She insisted on paying it in its entirety, telling them all, 'I'll text you my bank details, you can pay your share in the week.'

Jess pulled on her jacket and chatted to Jamie while Sam and Calvin tottered off to the toilets again.

Sam came back a few minutes later but Calvin was nowhere to be seen.

Jess gave him a couple of minutes, then went to look for him.

'He's probably throwing up,' she decided.

As she walked around one of the screens that marked off a private dining booth, she saw him next to the emergency exit, leaning on the wall, talking to a very leggy and very attractive blonde waitress. He seemed very animated. Jess stepped back behind the bamboo screen and watched through a gap in the weaving. There wasn't much left to witness. Calvin said something to the girl and they both laughed, then she shrugged, smiled at him, and walked off towards the kitchen area.

Jess quickly returned to their table where Jamie was helping Sam with her jacket. She managed to get one arm into a sleeve but the coat got snagged on the top corner of her chair and a pair of skimpy, white knickers fell onto the timber floor. Jamie looked shocked but Sam just burst out laughing.

'Those are my just in case knickers,' she announced. She crouched down to pick them up while half the diners in the room looked at her in varying shades of surprise and disgust.

She stared them out and waved them in the air.

'I'll put them on later,' she told them.

Outside, the temperature had taken a tumble. A still giggling Sam gave Jess a big hug.

'That was fun,' she said in her ear.

'It was a memorable ending,' said Jess. 'You outdid yourself tonight, Sam.' She laughed and looked for Calvin.

'He followed Jamie round to the car park,' Sam said. 'They'll be talking golf. I'll send him back in a minute.'

Sam gave Jess another quick hug and disappeared around the corner.

Jess shivered as she waited, then she heard her friend's voice, faint but still audible.

'Don't be a prat, Calvin. Go home.'

Thirty seconds later, Calvin appeared. He looked up and down the street.

'That bloody Uber is late,' he said.

Chapter 15

Jess

They stood in silence until their Uber cab arrived ten minutes later. Calvin got into the front and Jess climbed into the back and carefully slid across the seat as the driver adjusted his rear-view mirror to see if he could see up her skirt.

When they arrived home, Calvin got out first and headed for the flat. He opened the front door as Jess was paying the driver.

'I'll put a tip on the app,' she lied.

You're unlucky tonight, she thought. No upskirt and no tip.

When Jess arrived in the kitchen, she found Calvin waiting for her. He looked angry.

'Don't ever, ever, talk to me like that in public again,' he said, his whole body shaking with anger.

'What do you mean, I didn't—'

'You announced to the entire restaurant that I was showing you up.' He grabbed her arms just below the shoulders and shook her violently.

Jess's head cracked against the wall. She tried to lift her hands to push him away but he held on.

'Do you *UNDERSTAND*?'

Tears flowed down Jess's face.

'I'm sorry, I won't do it again. I'm sorry, Calvin.'

Calvin shook her again, the back of her head slammed into the wall.

'Ow, Calvin, please stop, you're hurting me.'

Calvin let her go and paced the kitchen, back and forth.

'You did it twice, you pulled me up about that bloody know it all, Jamie.'

'Oh, Calvin, I was only pointing out that she was his date,' Jess said through her tears.

'I know he was her fucking date,' spat Calvin. He approached her again. Jess held her arm in front of her face and cowered.

Calvin stopped ranting. He stood still for a moment and began to stroke her hair. It was like someone had pulled a switch.

'I'm sorry it's come to this, Jess, I really am. I don't want to be harsh, but you put me in an impossible position.' He slowly removed the arm that was protecting her face and pulled her to him, her head rested on his chest. She sobbed uncontrollably as Calvin stroked her hair, her neck and her shoulders.

'There, there, Jess. I love you. You know I do. I didn't mean to hurt you.'

Jess looked up at him through tear-soaked eyes. Her mascara had run and her make-up was smudged.

Calvin tilted his head to one side and studied her wet face.

'You look a right mess. Go and clean up, I'll make us a milky nightcap.'

Jess snuffled her way across the flat. As she reached the bathroom door, Calvin called to her, his voice soft, almost sympathetic.

'I hope you've learned something from this, Jess. I really do.'

Chapter 16

Alice

'Right then, Lovely, that's you sorted. I'll get you some breakfast now.'

Alice settled herself into her chair. She felt better after her shower. Gwen understood her need for privacy as she bathed, and she always kept her eyes averted and always looked at the floor, or wall as she passed Alice a huge beach towel at the end of her ablutions. When she had wrapped herself in it, Gwen helped her off the shower seat and walked her slowly to the stair lift. Once downstairs she dried her hair and brushed it into Alice's favoured style. Then she disappeared while Alice got into her underwear and appeared again, like magic, to help her dress.

'Does your family ever object to you working a seven-day week, Gwen?' Alice asked.

Gwen didn't answer.

'Gwen?'

She came to the kitchen door, holding a whisk and a bowl of whipped eggs.

'No, they don't mind. I only do for you Saturdays and Sundays anyway, it's only a couple of hours really.'

She turned to go back to the cooking.

'Wait, Gwen.' Alice was suspicious. 'When you say you only ever come to me at weekends... are your employers all right with that arrangement? It seems to me like I'm getting special treatment that I'm not paying for.'

Gwen studied her mixing bowl.

'They're okay with it,' she mumbled then turned away again.

'Gwen?' Alice called her back again. 'You're not being paid for this, are you?'

'I, err, look... I don't mind, I, err, I don't mind looking after you, honestly.'

'Oh, Gwen,' Alice's face softened. 'You really are a dear. I'm going to make this right. I can easily afford to pay you for these extra hours. You've been doing it for weeks now. How much do I owe you? I'll pay the going rate, more as it's weekends. I really do appreciate what you do for me, even if I don't show it all the time.'

'There's no need,' said a clearly embarrassed Gwen. 'I do it because I want to. I like caring for you. I wish the others were as easy.'

'You're not looking for something in my will, are you?' Alice narrowed her eyes.

'Of course not, what a notion,' replied Gwen. 'I've never considered such a thought. I—'

Alice's eyes were bright, 'I'm only teasing you, Gwen. Please don't take that remark seriously.' Alice beckoned her to come closer. 'Now, listen. I am going to pay what I owe and there will be no argument about it. I'll work it out with Jessica when she arrives. You've done so much for me and that effort has to be recognised.'

Gwen opened her mouth to protest but Alice was having none of it.

'Go and finish my breakfast, woman, I'm starving to death here. I don't want to have to report you to the council for neglect.'

Gwen gave up and returned to the kitchen.

Jess arrived at ten. She was relieved to see that Alice was looking a little better. Her skin didn't look as papery, she wasn't slumped into her chair like she had been on Friday, she looked alert. Her eyes had regained that glint of mischief. Maybe Alice's gloomy prediction was wrong after all.

'You're looking a lot better today, Nana,' she said with a smile.

'You're not,' replied Alice. 'You look like you haven't slept for a month. Come on, out with it. What's wrong?'

'Nothing.' Jess looked away. 'I didn't sleep very well that's all.'

'What's he been up to now?' Alice demanded to know.

'Nothing... well, not much. We went out for dinner with Sam and her new man last night. It was fun...

Look, all it is... I've been working on a new article and it's such hard work. It's all boring research, I don't think I've done a very good job so far and it has to be submitted by Friday.'

Alice didn't believe a word of it.

'Since when have you ever been worried about writing an article. You can do them in your sleep. When you do sleep that is. Now, what's been going on? It's him, I know it is.'

'Oh, we just had a big row that's all, Nana. It will all be forgotten about by tomorrow.'

Alice let it go, for now. There didn't seem much point in pushing her. She'd talk about it in her own time.

'All right, seeing as you're not going to let me in on the secret, get the tea made. I want to talk to you about Gwen, she's been working weekends for nothing, the silly woman. I want to make it right.'

'Oh, bless her,' said Jess. 'I've got a calculator on my phone; we can work out what you owe on that.'

'Add some extra too,' said Alice. 'She's worth every penny.'

Thirty minutes later, with Gwen's remuneration worked out. Alice resumed her story.

Chapter 17

1937-1938

Through the final three months of nineteen thirty-seven, and into the January of thirty-eight, I was in denial. Although I obviously noted my missed periods, I put it down to stress. The harvest, whilst a bumper crop, was a difficult one to manage. We usually had extra casual labour to help out, but this year, as the Great Depression came to an end (in our neck of the woods at least), men were finding full time work in the local factories. There were some older ones who knocked on the door of the farm, cap in hand.

'Do you have any work, Missus?'

Some of them were so worn out after a lifetime of heavy labour that they looked as though they had used up all their strength getting out of bed, but Barney, the foreman, never refused any of them. I had to rubber stamp the decision of course but I didn't have it in my heart to refuse any of them either.

One eighty-year-old, called Thomas, was employed carrying enamel buckets, filled with tea, out to the fields to keep the reapers hydrated. The weather was exceptionally warm for the first six weeks of autumn. We took full advantage of it, although I excused myself from the early part of the day, as my stomach tended to rid itself of the breakfast I had burdened it with.

I found myself spending more and more time hanging around the pig pens. They were close to the farmhouse, therefore close to the outside lavatory we had at the time. If things were really bad, I could just lean over the wall of a nearby sty and throw up into that. The pigs never complained. As Dad said, they would eat anything.

Apart from meal times, and when Miriam called into the front room to empty his chamber pot, my father remained alone, brooding and drunk. We set up a camp bed for him so that he didn't spend twenty-four hours a day in his chair but he seldom used it.

At Christmas, we had the usual party for the farm workers' families but no one's heart was really in it. Things had changed. My mother was gone and my father was well on his way. I tried to keep the atmosphere light but I had my own worries. The weather remained kind and we lit torches around the farmyard. John Postlethwaite fired up his accordion and there was dancing, singing and, as usual, plenty of drinking.

Christmas Day was, as customary, a day off for all the workers but two or three came in early to milk the cows and pick up their own pails of milk.

I wasn't well in the morning and with no company, I didn't celebrate. In the afternoon, I walked up to Amy's house but they had gone to a relative for Christmas lunch. The pub was open but I doubted my stomach could take a port and lemon, so I went for a walk up to the station and from there around the old part of the village. I got home just before dark to find Amy waiting in the kitchen.

'Merry Christmas,' she said, handing me a piece of fruitcake wrapped in a flowery paper napkin.

I hugged her and a sudden rush of tears ran down my face onto her neck. I had kept my problems from her although I usually shared everything.

'Alice, whatever is the matter?' Amy was full of concern.

'Oh, it's nothing,' I lied. 'I'm just a bit emotional, you know how it is? It's the wrong time of the month and I've been on my own most of the day. I've missed out on all the family fun and frolics.'

'I did invite you to ours,' Amy reminded me.

'I know you did; I didn't think it was right to impose myself on someone else's Christmas lunch,' I replied.

'Alice, you're almost family. You know that. Dad asked where you were. I told them you'd have second thoughts about it.'

I opened a bottle of gin, amazingly left over from the workers' party, and we sat in the kitchen and talked about the year just gone and our hopes and dreams for the one to come.

Even as the effects of the gin took hold, I still kept my guilty secret. In normal circumstances the losing of my virginity would have been something I'd have been eager to tell Amy all about. It should have been a time for much mirth, feigned shock and sharing of intimate details and feelings. We had a pact, made years before, that the first one of us to do the deed would confess as soon as possible so that the other would know exactly what to expect when her turn came. I felt guilty about breaking our covenant but I was embarrassed by the way it had happened. There was no true love, no sweeping me off my feet. The act had been a humiliating moment that I wished I could forget.

Although I wasn't yet willing to admit to my pregnancy, I was fast beginning to realise that stress, emotional turmoil, caused by my father's increasing dependence, and my continuing morning sickness (I had convinced myself that it was caused by the unpasteurised milk that I still drank every day), were not to blame for the missing periods. I was also finding it increasingly difficult to squeeze my breasts into my brassiere.

Amy went home at eight-thirty. I had one more gin as a nightcap, then I went upstairs and fell into a dreamless sleep.

By January, my denial had morphed into the terrible realisation that I had a child inside me and it was beginning to show.

I had to let out the seams of my weatherproof work trousers and I took to wearing baggy, woollen jumpers, even inside the house. I couldn't talk to my father about it, I'd get no reaction anyway and I couldn't let Miriam into the secret either, although I began to suspect that she had guessed anyway. Women who have been though a pregnancy always seem to be able to tell.

The farmworkers were now employed maintaining machinery, fixing gaps in barns, disinfecting the pig pens and keeping their eyes out for foxes that were increasingly desperate for food over the freezing winter months. There was snow in the second week of January and that put a stop to a lot of the work. I sent the lads home at ten, most days, and I looked after the pigs myself. As my pregnancy went on, I designated the upkeep of the pigs as my personal responsibility. I spent so much time with them I even gave some of them names.

During the third week I decided it was time to confess to Amy. At her door, I hesitated and almost went back home but I eventually summoned the courage, and knocked.

She was, as always, delighted to see me. She took me into her room to show me a Sealed With A Loving Kiss, embossed letter that had been pushed through her letterbox. Thankfully for Amy, she had found it before her father.

'Who is it from?' I asked, almost as excited as she was.

'Barry Tomkins.' She held the letter over her breast. 'Be still my pounding heart,' she said.

'Barry Tomkins? Isn't he the lad with the droopy eye?'

'One and the same,' declared Amy. 'In this letter, he professes his undying love for me. He promises that one day he'll have improved his station and will have a far better job than he has now, an income that will provide for me and our five children.'

'FIVE! He's got everything mapped out then,' I said, laughing. 'Isn't he the junior attendant at the men's toilet up at the station?'

'He is that very man,' said Amy, pretending to be serious. 'To think, he would give up a glittering career like that just for little me. My heart is full to bursting.'

'Have you replied to him yet?' I asked.

'No, I only got it this morning. I'll let him down gently,' she said.

I knew she would, there wasn't a bad bone in her body, as the saying went.

'Five babies though...' Amy stuck a pillow up her jumper. 'I'd be permanently pregnant with droopy eyed babies.'

I tried to laugh but burst out crying instead.

'Alice, whatever is the matter?'

I tried to speak but nothing but sobs and choking, sniffling and gasps for air would come out. Eventually I pointed to the pillow that was still cocooned in her jumper.

Her face fell.

'Oh, Alice, no.'

I nodded, looked at her helplessly, then more sobs came. 'What am I going to do, Amy? I've been feeling so alone. I couldn't tell anyone, not even you.'

Amy put her arms around me and held me until my wailings had subsided. When it had reduced to snuffles, I told her all about it. She was incandescent with rage.

'The pig, the brute, the absolute swine.'

'A pig and a swine are the same thing,' I said, trying to be funny.

'A total bastard then.'

That shocked me; I had never heard Amy swear.

When she had calmed down, she told me to sit where I was while she made us both a cup of calming tea. Her father was at work and her mother was at the afternoon market shopping for bargains.

We sipped our tea in silence, then Amy spoke.

'Right, we need a plan,' she said.

I was so glad she was with me; I knew she would stick by me whatever I had done, but it was soothing to know she would do everything she could to help.

'I don't know, I'm totally stuck,' I said.

'Well,' said Amy. She pursed her lips. 'We know that half the men in the town would jump at the chance of marrying you. You're Rita Hayworth, and you have a farm, which beats Old MacDonald into a cocked hat.'

I laughed at the joke.

'No one will want me now though, not in this condition. What man would want to take on some other bloke's kid?'

'Plenty,' replied Amy. 'As I said, not only are you stunning, you have collateral.'

'I have what?' I asked, puzzled.

'A bloody great big farm,' replied Amy. 'Who wouldn't want to get their sweaty hands on that?'

'They're not having the farm,' I said. 'It's a family concern. I'm not going to be the one to hand it over to a stranger.'

'Right then, that just leaves plan B,' said Amy.

'What's plan B?' I asked. 'I couldn't even come up with a plan A.'

'We find this bastard, Frank, and we blackmail him into marrying you,' said Amy, slapping her right fist into the palm of her left hand. 'The poor man won't know what's hit him.'

Chapter 18

Alice

'Oh, Nana, you poor thing, what a position to be left in. I'm so glad you confided in Amy, she was such a good friend to you, wasn't she?'

'She was the best friend anyone could ask for. I helped her out with her own problem a little later on, but that's a story for another day.' Alice yawned. 'I think I'm going to take a nap, Jessica. Will you still be here when I wake up?'

Jess nodded.

'I'll stay as long as you need me, Nana. I brought my laptop with me so I'll do a little bit of work while you sleep. That was an emotional story, no wonder it tired you.'

By the time Jess put the laptop on the table and opened it up, Alice was quietly snoring.

Jess spent an hour editing her article. It was frustrating because she had to rely on memory for the relevant facts. Alice had no Internet provider. Had Calvin been around he would have found a 'tethering' solution, using her mobile phone, but she couldn't remember how to set it up. Jess had often tried to persuade Alice to have broadband installed but she was adamant that she didn't want emails and pornographic videos popping up on her TV screen in the middle of Countryfile.

Jess smiled at the memory of that conversation. She had explained to Alice that it was impossible, but Alice was sure she had seen a BBC Panorama program about illegal, pornographic internet sites, spreading viruses and child pornography all over the planet.

When Alice woke, Jess made a pot of tea and took two cream cakes from the fridge that Gwen had put there that morning. There was a note on the plate alongside the cakes.

No crumbly digestives left to choke on. Hope these go down better. Gwen. xxx

Jess sat with Alice, chatting about trivial everyday topics until Gwen arrived at six. She handed her a cheque for five hundred pounds that the carer at first refused to accept, threatened to tear up, then, after a candid lecture from Alice, decided to accept.

She wiped away a tear as she stuffed it into her bag.

Jess got her things together, gave Alice a hug and a wet kiss on the cheek and left to go home.

Gwen busied herself warming up a beef and onion pie she had made that afternoon. She whipped up some instant mash and warmed up a small tin of mixed vegetables before making a third of a jug of the thickest gravy she could manage. Alice was delighted and ate every last morsel.

When Gwen came back in from tidying in the kitchen, she sat on the arm of Alice's chair.

'Jessica did say you were looking better today and it's true. You are. Your appetite is back too. Long may it continue.'

Alice smiled thinly as Gwen stood up and carried the dinner tray to the kitchen. When she was napping, the tunnel had appeared during the daylight hours for the first time. In the soft white light was a figure and it was beckoning her towards it.

Chapter 19

Jess

When Jess arrived home, Calvin ushered her to the dining table and a few minutes later produced a homemade pizza and a bottle of decent wine.

They made small talk during the meal, just as they had when Calvin had first moved in, some six months before.

When they had finished, he insisted on clearing the table and washing the plates.

Jess sat on the sofa, sipping her wine staring at the TV but not taking in what was on the screen. She wanted to bring the events of last night up, but she was unwilling to risk changing his mood.

It can't go on like this, she thought. It was like walking on egg shells all the time.

Calvin came through from the kitchen, stood between Jess and the TV, leaned forward a little and gave her a half smile.

'How's Nana? ... do you know, Jess, thinking about it, that's a really childish name to give someone of her years. Wouldn't great gran be better or maybe just call her Alice? That is her name after all.'

Jess frowned. How can a person's mood change so quickly? He had gone from loving partner to nasty git in the time it took to toss a coin.

'She's Nana because she's been Nana ever since I was a toddler, what's more, she'll always be Nana.'

Calvin slapped his forehead.

'But it's so bloody childish.'

'I don't care what you think it is, Calvin. She's my relative not yours. Do I tell you what to call your gran?'

'No,' he replied, 'and that's because I call her Gran, not bloody Nana.'

Jess looked away.

'I've had enough of this. It's ridiculous.'

'Here we go again,' Calvin jeered. 'Jess loses an argument and goes off in a sulk.'

'I am not sulking,' Jess replied, wondering how the conversation had managed to turn so quickly. 'You're just being mean. I do have feelings you know?'

'So do I,' said Calvin, 'not that you ever notice. It's always, Me, Me Me.'

He began to pace back and forth. Jess shrank back into the cushions on the sofa. This was never a good sign.

'It can't always be about you, Jess.' Calvin's voice raised a level. 'You seem to think you're the only person with feelings, but you're not, you trample over mine whenever it pleases you.'

He stopped pacing and leaned towards her.

'I've been under so much pressure recently, my confidence has been shot to pieces, but do you care? Just take last night for instance. In the space of a few minutes, I was embarrassed by you on two occasions and insulted by a man I don't even know, then we get back and you can't even give me a proper apology, it had to be forced out of you.'

Jess said nothing, she put her wine on the side table and waited for the storm to ride out.

Calvin began to pace the room again.

'You really will have to start thinking about other people, Jess. Their lives matter too.'

'I do,' said Jess quietly. 'I think about Nana all the time. Then there's my family—'

'You never talk about your family,' shouted Calvin. 'I can't remember the last time you bought any of them up. It's like they don't exist, the only one you ever mention is your precious bloody Nana.'

He spat out the word Nana like an abusive term.

'That's because you always mock them when I do,' said Jess. 'You don't like any of them.'

'Well, that's hardly surprising, they're the most unlikeable bunch of misfits I've ever met.'

'I'm not going to argue with you there,' said Jess, trying to lighten the mood a little. 'I love them all, they're my family after all, but I don't actually like any of them.'

'You never talk about my family either,' said Calvin, moving the argument along. He only had two surviving relatives: his mother and his gran, who he hadn't seen for months. 'Mum may as well not exist as far as you're concerned.'

Jess and Calvin's mother hadn't hit it off from the start. She thought her son was wasting his time on Jess, a failed writer and a girl with no breeding to boot.

'I sent your mother a birthday card only two weeks ago. And I rang her to wish her a Happy Birthday, which is more than you did.' Jess wasn't going to let him get away with that one.

'Don't try to turn this around to me,' Calvin spat. 'We're discussing your behaviour.'

He stood in front of her again.

'Why didn't you stick up for me when Jamie was having a go at me last night?'

'Did he have a go?' Jess looked puzzled.

'About the golf. The bastard set me up good and proper. Why didn't you tell me he was a golf pro? I offered to give him tips for Christ's sake.'

'I didn't know he was a golf pro and I don't think he was offended by anything you said,' replied Jess. 'He offered you a free round on that posh golf course, didn't he?'

'He was taking the piss,' moaned Calvin, 'but of course you didn't notice.'

'I've had enough of this.' Jess got to her feet and moved towards the bedroom. Calvin got hold of her arm as she passed and swung her back around. Jess grabbed at her shoulder and screamed.

'Ouch! Calvin, that hurt. Stop this nonsense now, I've had enough. I don't know what's come over you lately.'

'Disappointment,' said Calvin. 'Total bloody disappointment. I thought I knew you, Jess, but you're not the woman I was hoping you'd be.'

'You're definitely not the man I thought I had met,' said Jess through gritted teeth. She turned and attempted to walk away, but he swung her back around by the injured shoulder. Jess cringed but Calvin held her by her biceps just as he had the night before.

Jess glared at him, willing him to shake her again. Calvin noted the hostile look and stared down at his own chest, breathing hard. After a few seconds he let her go.

'Jess, I—'

'Do that one more time and we're finished.' Jess turned and stomped off into the bathroom. She locked the door behind her, sat on the toilet and began to cry.

'What the hell has happened to us,' she sobbed.

Chapter 20

Calvin

Calvin slept in the spare room again on Sunday night. He crept in to speak to Jess at two o'clock in the morning but she had just called out, 'Don't even try,' so he had gone back to bed and spent the entire night staring at the ceiling trying to work out where it had gone wrong.

He heard Jess moving around the flat at seven but he stayed where he was. He didn't want to risk another argument while she was being so emotional about everything.

He got out of bed when he heard the front door slam. She had left a note for him on the coffee table.

Off to NANA'S. Back this evening. No more arguments, PLEASE!

Calvin ate a bowl of cereal, showered and pulled on a clean pair of jeans, a pale blue t-shirt, a navy bomber jacket and a pair of white Nike shoes. He brushed his hair carefully and rinsed his mouth with Corsodyl.

He picked up his work attaché case and skipped down the stairs. It was a warm day, so he dropped the front windows of the BMW, fired up the music system and set off for town. He parked in the off-campus car park, stooped to check his hair in the driver's side mirror, then he walked across towards town, aiming his key fob blindly over his shoulder to lock the car.

Five minutes later, he arrived at the door of Tania's flat. He checked his breath in his cupped palm, then rang the doorbell. Getting no response, he rang it again, then a third time.

Tania opened the door and squinted in the sunlight. She blinked twice and sleepily said, 'Calvin?'

Calvin eyed her from top to toe. Her hair was messy, her eyes, sleepy. She wore a man's shirt fastened by two buttons above her navel. He could see her white knickers between the undone bottom two buttons.

Come to bed eyes, thought Calvin. He smiled his best smile.

'Hi, Tania, I was just passing and thought I'd drop in on you.'

Tania yawned. 'It's er... what time is it?'

'Nine, just after,' answered Calvin.

'Bloody hell, that's the middle of the night,' replied Tania. 'What do you want?'

'I, erm, well, I thought we might carry on from where we left off on Friday.' Calvin raised his eyebrows. 'I've thought about nothing else all weekend.'

'You were thinking about something else on Saturday night,' said Tania, 'that little blonde with the big tits. The one who waved her knickers in the air?'

Calvin shook his head. 'She wasn't with me... not as such. I tried to tell you on Saturday in the restaurant, but you were busy.'

'Tried to tell me what?' Tania tipped her head to one side. 'This should be interesting.'

'I was asked to make up a four at short notice,' said Calvin, who had rehearsed the speech in the car. 'Jamie, my mate, had a foursome organised with his partner and her friend, but the other guy backed out, so Jamie asked if I'd step in. I was reluctant, but he's a mate, so what can you do?'

'It looked like you'd known her for ages,' said Tania. 'Look, Calvin, I'm not the jealous type and we've only just met, really, but don't tell me you weren't having a good time whichever one was your date, they were both stunning.'

'They were okay,' said Calvin, 'not my type really. You're more my style.' He gave her a lecherous look.

'Do you know, I think I actually believe you,' replied Tania. 'When I saw you at first on Saturday night, I thought you might have been with your partner, wife even, but then I thought, no, this man will never settle down. It isn't in him.'

Calvin was about to argue the point but thought better of it.

'I'm not sure that's quite right, I guess I just haven't met the right girl yet.' He took a step forward. 'You could be that girl,' he said, winking.

'Not this morning I can't. I didn't get home until two o'clock. It was Sunday, I'm supposed to be home by twelve-thirty.'

'What were you up to? Did you meet someone?'

'No such luck. The till was down so we had to go through every transaction until we found the error. I'm knackered,' she said, yawning again.

'I know something that will relax you.' Calvin placed his right foot inside the lobby.

Tania closed the door on his foot. 'Sorry, luv, but I'm just too tired. Another time. I'll look forward to it. Promise.'

'When?' asked Calvin a little too eagerly.

'When can you make it?' She stopped and thought for a moment. 'I thought we'd settled on Friday morning.'

'I can't wait that long. I'm driving myself nuts thinking about you,' said Calvin. 'Tell you what. Why don't I bring a bottle of wine around tomorrow evening? We could make a night of it.'

'Works for me,' said Tania. 'I'm off Tuesday and Thursday night this week.' She smiled at him seductively. 'Make it two bottles eh? Let's get pissed.'

She leaned forward, giving him a glimpse of that wonderful cleavage, then she pecked him on the cheek and with a curt, 'bye now,' closed the door in his face.

Calvin smiled to himself as he walked back to the car and retrieved his attaché case. Things couldn't have worked out better. Jess wanted a couple of nights with her bloody Nana, well, she could have them.

He walked into the Uni building whistling. Things were looking up.

Chapter 21

Jess

The drive to the farmhouse seemed to take longer than usual, though there was little traffic. Jess's mind was in turmoil over what to do about Calvin.

She loved him still, there was no doubt about that, but she couldn't and wouldn't take much more of this. She wondered what had happened to make him change so much in such a short space of time. He did say he was under pressure, but from what? It could be work, though they gave him as much leeway as he wanted. He worked remotely a lot of the time so he didn't even have to go into an office, lab, or whichever area he covered. Maybe that was it. Because she worked from home too, maybe they were spending too much time in each other's company. Everyone needed a break in a partnership. Most couples only ever saw each other in the evenings or at weekends. She decided that she'd talk to him about it. She could work from a café some days or the local library. That would be good for her really as all the research tools she would ever need would be at her fingertips and she liked books much better than the world wide web, amazing as that was.

As she waited at the traffic lights near Tesco Direct. her thoughts turned to his accusations. Was she really as innocent as she was trying to make out? Had she been a bit selfish? She couldn't remember any real instance of it, though if he was so utterly convinced that she was, there had to be a reason, hard as it was to fathom.

Calvin had always been sensitive to criticism; she was well aware of that. She wasn't sure where that had come from. Had he been brought up doted on and spoilt, or had he taken more than his fair share of put downs as a child? It was hard to say. He never talked about his father other than to say, 'he left us'; maybe there was a connection there. Had his father been a bit of a brute, or had he been a loving father that had left them suddenly, leaving Calvin bereft? She couldn't talk to him about that topic, she had tried a few times early on in their relationship and he'd just clammed up.

She did worry that he was a narcissist; he was showing all of the classic traits. She wasn't sure if there was any way to bring someone out of that condition. She doubted it, but maybe it could be held in check. She decided to do some research later.

Jess pulled the car into the farm's drive, grabbed her bag, checked her face in the rear-view mirror, forced a smile and got out of the car. She slammed the door shut and walked up to the front door crossing her fingers and hoping that Nana looked as good as she had the previous day. Then she did something she had never done as a life-long unbeliever. She offered up a short prayer.

Chapter 22

Alice

Alice sighed and stared at the clock as it ticked another two minutes of her life away.

Last night's dream had been vivid. The dark part of the tunnel had shrunk back to leave just an outer rim, while the light in the middle was both brighter, yet somehow, even softer. The figure in the light was getting clearer, the shape larger and the beckoning motion, surer.

She wasn't frightened of the prospect of meeting whoever, or whatever, it was in the tunnel, she had always wondered what lay beyond death's final embrace and now, unlike the vast majority of healthy people, she was getting closer to discovering exactly what secrets lay ahead. The figure in the light surely meant there was some sort of existence beyond this earth. She was both intrigued and excited at the prospect.

She wasn't quite ready to explore the unknown yet though, she still had things to oversee in this lifetime. She could do without the clock's unreasonable theft of her time. The story had to be told before she passed on. She owed it to Jessica, herself, and the people who were no longer around to speak for themselves.

Her thoughts were interrupted when Jess walked into the lounge.

'Hello, Nana, how are you today?' She studied Alice carefully, she looked pretty much like she had yesterday. Her skin had a little colour and her eyes were bright. She looked to the ceiling and silently thanked whichever deity had answered her prayer.

'Hello, Jessica. I'm as well as can be expected for someone of my great age, and I do feel quite spoiled seeing you so often.' Alice studied Jess in exactly the same way that she had just been appraised herself. She didn't look as washed out as yesterday, though there was a hint of redness around her eyes. She decided not to pry today.

'Where's Gwen?' Jess asked.

'She's off to the shops. Apparently, I have run out of gravy salts or whatever they call them nowadays.'

'Granules,' replied Jess.

'Granules,' repeated Alice. 'Whatever next?'

Jess laughed.

'They've been around for years, Nana. You've been buying them without knowing it.'

'Do you know, I thought it looked a bit lumpy for gravy salts, it used to be like powder.'

Jess took off her jacket, put down her bag and gave Alice a big hug. She turned away, then turned back and hugged her again. Alice looked surprised.

'Now I'm worried. Why am I treated to two hugs?'

'Because you're worth two hugs,' Jess replied. 'You always have been.'

Alice cleared her throat.

'Can I smell the kettle?' she asked rather croakily.

Gwen came back just as Jess was pouring boiling water into the tea pot.

'Hello, Jessica,' she said. 'Here, I'll do that.' She whipped off her coat, laid it across the back of a kitchen chair, put the bag of shopping on the table and picked up a tray from the work surface. 'You get yourself sat down. I'll be through in a moment.'

'Did you find some gravy salts?' Alice called from the lounge.

Gwen looked worried.

'No, Lovely, they only had granules. The same sort you had in your cupboard, do you want me to take them back and see if I can find some... salts, was it?'

Jess put her hand on Gwen's arm. 'Ignore her,' she whispered. 'She's just teasing you again.'

Gwen shook her head slowly. 'She gets me every time.'

When Jess was seated and the tea had been poured and distributed, she told Alice and Gwen her good news.

'I'll be staying over tomorrow and Thursday night, plus I'll still be here all day Wednesday and Friday. I'll come on Sunday as usual.'

Alice was delighted. Gwen gave a little clap and disappeared back into the kitchen.

'But, have you discussed this with Calvin?' Alice asked, a puzzled look on her face. 'I wouldn't have thought he'd be too enamoured with the idea.'

'It was his suggestion actually,' replied Jess. 'We've probably been spending too much time together with us both working from home. I think that's what's behind our recent trials and tribulations.'

'That and the fact that he's a one hundred percent, top-drawer, unredeemable, narcissist,' said Alice.

Jess pulled a face at her.

'I'm not convinced. He has a soft side, and it's a beautiful thing to experience. Even you would fall under his spell, Nana.'

'I've been under many a spell woven by men like him, Jessica,' Alice replied. 'Not one of them was worth the effort I put in. You can't change them; you can't understand them. They're never happy until they've sucked every last drop of emotion out of you. Then, when the job is complete and your last vestige of self-respect has been trodden underfoot, they move on.'

Jess shuddered. An icy shiver ran down her spine as Alice laid out her own fears for her relationship with Calvin in such stark terms. She pulled a small, rechargeable, digital voice recorder from her bag.

'I'm going to record your story today, Nana, if that's all right? There's been so much detail that I'm scared of forgetting parts of it. I'm going to make some notes of the story so far when I stay over tomorrow.'

'Record it any way you like, Jessica,' said Alice, still staring at the tiny gadget. 'I thought you were going to take my temperature with it for a moment. I was a bit concerned where you were going to stick it.'

Jessica almost choked on her tea.

'Nana, you get worse,' she said.

Jess pushed a button on the machine and spoke into it.

'Monday, ninth of September twenty-nineteen. Nine forty-seven AM. Subject. Alice Mollison. Review date. January, nineteen thirty-eight.'

'That all sounds very formal, Jessica,' said Alice.

Jessica flapped her free hand, put her finger to her lips and pointed at the machine. *'It's recording'* she mouthed.

'Oops,' said Alice. 'I'd better get on with it then.'

Chapter 23

January 1938

It was a further two weeks until we could put Amy's plan into operation. Frank had done a runner. There had been no sight of him since my birthday party at The Old Bull. Amy made a few discreet enquiries through some acquaintances who lived near him, but it was like he had vanished from the face of the earth.

Amy embarked on the first part of her Plan B by seeking out a few trusted old school friends, implying that Frank owed her father a fair amount of money and she wanted to know the moment he returned to town. Despite the best endeavours of Edwin, Bernard, Josie and Kath, who knew everything there was to know about everyone in the town, there was no news of him.

Then, at the end of the month, he appeared in the railway station's foyer, looking out into a near blizzard.

What follows is what I was told, first hand, by the protagonists, Edwin, Kath and Amy.

Edwin, who sold newspapers in the station lobby, spotted him as he strolled across the stone floor and stood in the station's entrance, obviously deciding whether to risk the snow or wait it out to see if it eased.

Edwin crossed immediately to the ticket office and beckoned the teller towards him.

'Could you do me a favour, Colin? Can you call Mrs Parsons on two-eight-six and ask to speak to Kath? She's her daughter. Just tell her, the homing pigeon has returned to the loft, please.'

Colin glared at him. 'Are you taking the piss? You aren't a spy, you're a bloody newspaper seller.'

'Please, Col,' said Edwin urgently. 'It is important. I can't tell you why, but it really is.'

'Ring her yourself,' said Colin, who wasn't a bad sort despite his permanent grumpiness. He opened the door to the ticket office and beckoned Edwin inside.

'The telephone is on the desk over there. It's brand spanking new so don't bloody break it.'

Edwin crossed to the desk and picked up the handset from the base. The telephone was one of the new Bell system models with a dial on the front.

'Where do I put the tuppence in?' he asked.

'You don't need bloody tuppence. It's not a public call box. Just dial the sodding number,' replied an increasingly irritated Colin, who still thought Edwin was messing him about. 'And hurry up, I'll be bloody well sacked if the station master catches you in here.'

Edwin picked out the numbers with his index finger and spun the dial three times. After a few seconds he was connected.

'Hello, Cranstone two-eight-six.'

'Erm, hello, Mrs Parsons, it's Edwin, from next door, is your Kath there?'

'Edwin, do you have a telephone now? Wouldn't it be cheaper to just nip round?'

'I'm at work, Mrs Parsons. In the ticket office. Is Kath there?'

'She's just this minute come in. She looks like a snowman...woman...girl.'

'Could I speak to her please?' Edwin could feel Colin's eyes burning into the back of his head.

'Hello, Edwin, it's Kath, isn't the weather foul? Hope you're nice and dry where you are.'

'Kath, I need you to get a message to Amy. Can you tell her that the homing pigeon has returned to the loft?'

'Is he back?' asked an excited Kath. 'I'll go now, shall I? It is snowing though; Mum might have something to say about it.'

'Tell her you forgot something,' said a panicking Edwin. 'Please, Kath, hurry.'

'Shall I tell Amy's dad. He'll be pleased to know—'

'NO! the message is for Amy's ears alone, Kath. Have you got that? It's important, our secret.'

'Righty ho,' said Kath, conspiratorially. 'Message received and understood.'

Edwin put the receiver down and thanked Colin for the use of the phone.

'That call cost more than tuppence,' Colin moaned. 'You owe me, lad.'

Edwin nodded and looked past the ticket master to the station entrance. Frank was still there, leaning on a pillar reading a newspaper he hadn't yet paid for. Two other men were waiting to be served. He stuck up a thumb to Colin as he opened the door for him.

'Afternoon Post,' he yelled as he ran across the stone tiles and back to his pitch.

When Kath told her mother that she had left a glove at Amy's house and she wanted to return immediately to retrieve it, she was more than a little confused.

'Didn't you have them on when you came in?' she asked. 'I'm sure I saw them.'

'I had one on,' said Kath feeling seriously guilty. She hated lying to her mother but her gang came first. This was an emergency.

'Didn't you feel the cold when you left... and I thought it was Rita you were going to visit.'

'I did, but I called in at Amy's on the way back. I kept my hands in my pockets,' she said.

'Amy's house isn't on the way back, it's further away,' said Mrs Parsons, suspecting something was awry.

'Not much further,' Kath replied. 'Can I go to get it? they're my favourite furry ones, the pair you got me last Christmas.'

Mrs Parsons gave in. Amy only lived a couple of hundred yards away. 'Be quick then.' She looked out of the window at the thickening snow. 'And come straight back once you have it.'

Kath stepped out of the house onto a path covered in six inches of snow. She looked back to see her mother watching her from the kitchen window, so she waited until she was out of site before pulling her gloves from each pocket of her coat. She was glad to put them on; her hands were already feeling the cold.

She arrived at Amy's house a few minutes later and knocked on the door. Amy answered.

Kath cupped her hand to her mouth and said quietly. 'I have a message from Edwin. The pigeon has returned to the loft.'

Amy made a fist and punched the air. 'Thank you, Kath, and thank Edwin if you see him before I do. Please, don't tell anyone about this. It's our little secret.'

'Guides honour,' said Kath, making the three fingered salute. 'Got to go, Mum's watching out for me.'

Chapter 24

1938

The news that Frank Mollison was back in town sent shivers down my spine but also made me determined to seek him out and see what he had to say for himself. Amy thought this should be done at the point of a knife, or the farm's shotgun but I was slightly more down to earth about it all.

There would be talk in the town, especially in The Old Bull and amongst the market shoppers, but that was inevitable. I was already four months' gone, if I had got married at that stage no one would have believed I'd only carried for five months when I gave birth. It would die down eventually and I could live with it. Had my father been well, or my mother still alive, it would have been a different story, but as it was, I thought I was strong enough to bear it.

We decided to stake out The Old Bull.

Amy and I wrapped up against the cold and trudged our way up to the town through the deep carpet of snow.

The lane was still covered, as hardly any traffic used it. Even the main road only had a few tyre tracks running along it and there was very little by way of footprints, until you got around the area of the pub. It would take more than a blizzard to keep the working men from their beer. On the way home there would be many a slip and fall, but they wouldn't feel much pain in the state they were in.

We were lucky, as it happens. We'd only been there for about twenty minutes when we saw him plodding towards the pub from his mother's house on Elm Lane. He was with an older man I'd seen before, but couldn't place. When they were close enough, Amy nudged me but I found I couldn't speak, so being the best friend she is, she spoke for me.

'Scuse me, Frank, have you got a minute?'

The old man with him smirked and offered to help Frank out if he couldn't handle both of us.

Frank forced a smile and the old man went into the public bar entrance.

'What's up?' he asked, looking guiltily at me.

'I think you know what's up, Frank.' Amy stood, legs slightly apart, and stared him down.

'Can you remember back to last September? Alice's party night?'

Frank looked abashed. He nodded but said nothing.

'Well,' Amy continued. 'Alice would like a word with you about that, wouldn't you, Alice?'

I looked at my boots and nodded at them.

Amy stepped away but fired one last salvo.

'You ought to be ashamed of yourself, Frank Mollison. You took advantage of her. It's hardly the thing a real man would do.'

Frank held my arm and took me to the railings at the side of the road.

'Your mouthy friend's right of course. I should be ashamed, and I am. I was drunk, I was randy and I was wrong. That's why I've been away. I'm not proud of myself.'

I was shocked. I expected him to either deny it, or say I had it coming. I said nothing, so he carried on.

'I can't give you back what I've taken, I know that. But I can say I'm sorry, I regret it and I hope that one day you'll be able to forgive me. You'll obviously never forget.'

He half smiled at me, when I didn't smile back, his vanished.

'I won't ever be able to forget it, Frank, not because it was so memorable, I can't remember most of it to be honest, but, well, the fact is... Look, I'm going to have your baby, I'm pregnant.'

Again, I half expected him to question whether I was a virgin at the time, or if I'd been with other men since, but he didn't. He just looked, stupidly, back at me.

'Jesus,' he whispered.

'No, it's not him,' I said. 'I was the virgin: Alice, not Mary.'

He thought for a moment.

'I'll face up to my responsibilities, Alice,' he said eventually. 'I'll pay you some of my wages every week, once I can find another job that is. I'm a worker, not a shirker, I've always worked, always paid my way, always paid my debts, and I'll do it this time too.'

Amy had crept closer and had been listening.

'That won't help her when the rumours start, Frank. It won't help her when the tongues wag and her name is dragged through the dirt. You'll just be seen as a bit of a lad, a lady's man, but Alice will be branded a slut, a prostitute, a lush...' She ran out of epithets, so she decided to challenge him head on. 'Are you going to be a proper father? Ask her to marry you, Frank. That's what a real man would do.'

Frank had had his turn, now it was my turn to be shocked.

'I don't want to—'

Amy dug me in the back with her fingers, so I shut up.

'I need to think about this,' said Frank. 'It's one thing helping pay for the young 'un's, upkeep, it's another thing again marrying someone, especially someone so young. You say people will call Alice names, but I'll be branded a cradle snatcher. She's only a kid.'

Amy stared at him, wide-eyed.

'She was bloody well old enough to shag, wasn't she? You didn't think about her age when you were ruining her did you? Go on then, have a good think, Frank, but don't take too long over it,' she pointed to my stomach. 'The secret will out before too long.'

I felt the decision on my future was being taken without me having any say.

'I don't want to ma—'

Amy poked me again, harder this time.

Frank sighed heavily.

'I'll think things over,' he said. 'And I'll talk to my mum, she'll know what to do.' He turned away but instead of entering the pub, he walked back the way he had come.

'You shouldn't have to think about it at all, Frank,' Amy yelled after him. 'Grow up. Be the man your mother thinks you are.'

Chapter 25

1938

The answer came much quicker than either of us had anticipated.

I had said goodbye to Amy at her gate. She was still under the impression that Frank was a snidely, underhand, midget of a man, but I reminded her that he had offered to help with the baby's upkeep.

'But for how long, and can you trust him to keep paying, Alice? It wouldn't surprise me if he was on the first train out of town in the morning.'

When I got home, I made myself a hot cup of cocoa, looked in on my father, and settled down in front of the pot-bellied stove in the kitchen.

I had just turned to the romance story in the nineteen thirty-six copy of Nash's magazine that I had found buried in a pile of farm-related papers in my mother's bedroom, when I heard the back gate open. Puzzled as to who would come calling at nine-thirty at night, I picked up a sharp kitchen knife and crept to the back door. A few seconds later, someone rapped on it, hard.

I took a deep breath, brandished the knife in what I thought was a threatening manner, called out, 'I'll get it, George,' to let any would-be attacker know that I wasn't alone, and opened the door an inch.

Frank stood on the top step; cap grasped tightly in his hands. He nodded to me as I opened the door wider.

'Frank? What on earth...'

'Can I come in, Alice? It's bloody freezing out here.' He looked down at my hands where the long, sharp, boning knife was still pointing at him. 'You won't need that,' he said, calmly.

I opened the door, he stepped inside and waited as I closed it again.

I walked over to the kitchen table and waved my hand towards a seat near the stove.

'Get yourself warm, you've got an icicle hanging off your nose.'

Frank sat down and rubbed his nose between his finger and thumb.

'I've erm, talked to my mother. It wasn't a long conversation,' he mumbled.

I waited; I wasn't in the mood to help him out.

He wrung his cap in his hands like he was preparing to hang it on the washing line.

'She says I should beg your forgiveness and ask you to marry me,' he blurted out.

I still said nothing.

'Well,' he asked after an aptly named, pregnant pause.

'Is that your mother asking, or you?' I said, answering a question with a question.

'Me,' he said, meekly. 'Me.' He hesitated for a moment, then obviously decided to do it properly. He got down on one knee in front of the stove and asked, with the utmost sincerity. 'Will you marry me, Alice?'

I didn't really have to think about it.

'No, Frank, I can't. You're being a gentleman, and I really think you deserve a lot of credit for that. I wouldn't like to be you when you get home to your mother, either, but I'm afraid the answer has to be no.'

I smiled at him gently. 'Please, get up,' I said.

Frank got to his feet. He didn't look relieved, he didn't look angry, he just had a look of total bewilderment on his face.

'But your friend said—'

'She's my best friend and she's trying to look out for me,' I replied. 'However, she isn't the one who's pregnant. I am, and I'm sorry, but I don't want to marry you, Frank.'

He sat down heavily.

'Let me make you some cocoa,' I offered.

'That's kind of you,' he muttered.

I poured some milk into a pan and put it on the stove to warm up.

'Why not?' he suddenly blurted out. 'Why won't you marry me? What's wrong with me? Aren't I good enough?'

'You'd be a fine catch for someone, Frank, there's nothing wrong with you. You're a good-looking man. I just don't want to get married, that's all.'

'But what about the baby?'

'It's good of you to offer, but I'm sure I can bring up my own child. Plenty of other women have managed it.' I replied.

'It's my child too,' he said, stubbornly. 'The way it happened... well, it wasn't right, I admit that, but I'm still the father. Don't I get a say?'

I have to admit I was quite taken aback by his insistence on being part of the baby's life.

I tipped two teaspoons of cocoa powder into a tall mug, took the pan from the stove and poured in the milk. I put it on the table at the side of him, with the sugar bowl and a spoon.

'I have to say, I'm quite taken by your attitude, Frank. I really didn't expect it.'

'We have to do something, girl,' he said. 'Amy was right, tongues will wag and I'll only get the good end of it all. You'll get the bad.'

An Idea suddenly lit up like a roman candle in my brain.

'I have an idea, and it might just work out for the both of us,' I said.

Frank scooped two spoons of sugar into his drink and stirred it. He was about to put the wet spoon back into the sugar bowl, but catching my look, he quickly changed his mind, sucked the moisture from it and placed it on the table instead. He put both hands around the mug, took a sip and leaned forward.

'What do you have in mind?' he asked.

'Move in here,' I said. 'Not in my bed,' I added quickly. 'We can put you up on a foldaway trestle bed in the parlour for now. Later, we'll see how it goes, perhaps you could move into one of the unused bedrooms. People will perhaps see that as an acknowledgement of your parenthood,' I answered.

Frank wasn't convinced.

'I'd much rather do the right thing. I'm a good worker, Alice. I won't let you down, there are jobs going at the mill.'

'Work here,' I said.

'Here?'

'Why not? There's always work on the farm. It will be a proper job, with proper wages. But you'll have to work your way in with the lads. They won't just accept you because you're living in the big house. I'll pay you a bit more than they're on, but you must never let them know.'

It was Frank's turn to think.

'It's a plan, of sorts,' he said. 'What about later on – if it all works out, and we get on really well? How about marrying me then?' He looked around the kitchen, its warm hearth, the horse brasses on the wall and the feeling of permanence that went with it. 'I quite fancy myself as a farmer.'

Alarm bells rang. I was adamant that I wasn't going to hand the farm over to a stranger, it had been in my family for generations, and once my father had gone, if I married Frank, the farm would be pretty much his. The law didn't care about women. Justice was a device for men to utilise.

'I'm not saying, no, Frank,' I said carefully, 'and I won't rule the idea out completely. Maybe in a few years? As you said, we will have to get to know each other.'

'A few years?' Frank thought about it. 'I think we should at least pretend we're married. To the locals if no one else.'

'We could,' I agreed. 'I've no problem with that.'

'Let's go away for a weekend,' he suggested. 'We could come back and say we got married while we were at the seaside or something. Maybe Gretna Green? that really would get their tongues wagging. No bugger will ever ask to see the marriage certificate.'

'Now you're getting it,' I said. 'That's a masterstroke.' Another idea came to me, but not one I was certain I wanted to take up. I looked at Frank, sitting on the chair warming his hands in front of the boiler, and stupidly, felt sorry for him. 'Tell you what? Wait until just before the baby is here and I'll change my name by deed poll. That way all three of us will have the same surname. That ought to convince the most ardent of doubters.'

Frank finished his drink and got up from the chair.

'When do I start?' he asked.

'Monday?' I suggested. 'Bring your stuff over at the weekend.' I hesitated a moment and then spoke in the firmest voice I could muster. 'Frank, never forget, I'm the boss here?'

I'm not sure he really liked that idea much. He walked to the back door before turning to face me.

'That's reasonable, for now, but don't show me up in front of the other lads by ordering me about,' he said. 'Let me have a modicum of dignity.'

'The other lads don't have a problem with it, but I'll do my best, Frank,' I replied. 'One big thing to remember though. I've got a foreman, and until he retires, foreman he stays.'

Frank nodded and leaned towards me; his lips pursed.

'Good night, Frank,' I said, stepping aside to avoid his overfamiliar gesture. 'Good luck with your mother.'

Chapter 26

Alice

'What an interesting solution to your problems, Nana. I really disliked Frank, but it seems he did have a good side to him.'

'He did his duty by me, there's no disputing that,' replied Alice. 'A great many men would have just denied any knowledge. It would have been my word against his, really. There was none of this fancy hi-tech DNA thingy back then. A blood group was as close as you got to identifying someone. He was honest enough to admit it and he couldn't really deny the confession once he'd come clean in front of Amy.

'He may have only disclosed it in shock when the two of us confronted him, but once he'd told his mother, there was no going back. She held seriously old-fashioned attitudes. I met her a while after he moved into the farm. She was a cold woman who had taken a lot of hard knocks in life. She brought Frank up on her own after his father did a runner during World War One. He wasn't in the army fighting in France or anything. He was a reserved occupation, coal miner. As soon as he found out Nancy was pregnant, he was off. She found out later that he was hanged for the murder of another woman who fell pregnant by him, so, she had a lucky escape really. She raised Frank to know the difference between right and wrong and he must have had the story of how she was left in the lurch, drilled into him over the years.'

'So, he wasn't such a bad man then, Nana?'

'Oh, he was a pleasant enough man,' replied Alice, 'He had a dark side when he hit the bottle though.'

'Was he a big drinker, Nana?' asked Jess.

Alice shook her head. 'Not at first. He'd have a few beers with the lads from the farm on payday but that was about it. I never begrudged him that. Farming is hard work and they all deserved a drink at the end of the week. I'd have gone with them sometimes, but it wasn't the done thing back then. After my father died, that all changed. But, that's a story for another time. We're getting too far ahead of ourselves.'

Jess packed away her things and checked her phone for messages. She had muted the usual message alert because she was recording and she didn't want Alice's thought stream interrupted by pings and dings from her mobile. There was one message from Calvin. It said simply, *Get coffee. Not the cheap crap.*

'Do you want me to stay until Gwen gets here, Nana?' asked Jess.

'No, get yourself off home, Jessica. I don't want you getting on the wrong side of that man again.'

'Oh, don't worry about him,' replied Jess with more confidence than she felt. 'We just need to talk things through, that's all.'

Jess gave Alice a hug, then one more for luck and kissed her on the cheek. When she straightened up, she ran her tongue over her lips and felt a cream-like substance on them. She ran a finger over her bottom lip and studied it.

'Nana, are you wearing make-up?'

'Just a little bit of rouge cream,' replied Alice. 'We girls have to make an effort.'

'We do.' Jess smiled. 'See you tomorrow evening then, Nana.'

'I'll be here,' promised Alice. 'My diary is empty.'

Jess looked at her watch. 'Gwen shouldn't be long.'

'Go,' said Alice forcefully. 'You have a life outside of here.'

When Jess had gone, Alice cursed the clock for ten minutes before slipping into a troubled sleep.

This time she didn't go straight into the tunnel. Instead she was back on the farm in the winter of 1938. Building contractors were preparing the base for a large milking parlour. She stood with the farm foreman, Barney, and watched the men dig out the foundations. Barney was speaking, but Alice couldn't hear the words. Then the image faded and she was at the entrance of the tunnel again. The darkness was now reduced to a tiny, almost pencil-drawn line around the circumference. The light itself was even softer than usual and a swirling mist had formed inside. Out of it came a male figure, still too nebulous to make out a face, but he was walking slowly towards her, arms outstretched. There was sound this time too, a voice that became louder as she

99

watched. The voice, deadened by the fog, spoke to her from the depths of time. It was last voice she wanted to hear.

'Alice...Alice...'

Alice blinked twice, then looked around the room to confirm that she was still in her armchair at the farm.

'You were having a bad dream, Lovely. I thought I'd wake you.' Gwen removed her hand from Alice's forearm. 'How about a nice cup of tea to help you wake up properly?'

Alice nodded, weakly. Anything to keep her awake. She considered ringing Jess and asking her to stay over tonight as well. She was dreading going to bed, she didn't want to face the night alone.

She remembered the part-used pack of sleeping pills in the bedside drawer. The doctor had prescribed them months ago when she had bruised her hip after a fall. The hip cramped overnight causing her to lie awake in pain for hours. The pills had worked. For two solid weeks she had slept soundly and dreamlessly, or at least she couldn't remember any dream she may have had.

Gwen came back with her tea.

'I'm just going to put dinner on. 'Ham and eggs tonight. Your favourite.'

Alice sipped her tea and stared at her bedside cabinet drawer. She hoped to God that Gwen hadn't thrown them away.

Chapter 27

Jess

Jess fired up the engine of her little Toyota and eased out onto the narrow lane.

As she approached the T junction, she braked hard and looked back over her shoulder towards the farm.

'That's why she's looking a bit healthier,' she thought. 'Bloody rouge, the crafty old...'

Jess parked outside Tesco and crossed the road to the store.

'We'll have to stop meeting like this.' Ewan came out of the shop as Jess was about to step in.

'Hello again, Ewan.' Jess smiled as he held the door open for her. 'Africa hasn't called you back then?'

'Not yet,' said Ewan. 'Though there's time still. I would like to go back one day, I've only seen the middle bit so far. It's a fascinating continent.'

'I can imagine,' replied Jess.

'Look, erm, I don't know if you're interested, but I'm giving a talk on my experiences at Mondale House, the off-campus Uni place in town this Friday afternoon. I'd love it if you came... That's if you want to of course?'

'I'm sorry, Ewan, but I'm looking after my Nana at the moment. Friday afternoon is one of our together times. She's a hundred years old the week after next. She's telling me all about her wartime memories.'

'Not to worry,' said Ewan, obviously disappointed. 'Maybe we could meet up for a drink sometime or coffee if you prefer?'

'Again, I'm sorry, Ewan, but I do live with someone. I don't think that would go down very well.' She stepped past him into the shop. 'Nice to bump into you again. Take care.'

'I saw you with him the other, week,' Ewan called after her. 'It's you who should take care, Jess. You can't trust him.'

Jess grabbed a pack of Taylor's filter coffee and a jar of her favourite instant. At the checkout she thought about Ewan's warning. What did he mean by that? Was it just down to jealousy? Probably, but he did seem extremely earnest.

Calvin was in one of his better moods when she arrived home. He seemed overly delighted when he saw the coffee.

'You got my text then? That's good.'

Jess ignored the urge to tell him that his messages always got through. She wanted his mood to last as long as possible, she knew only too well how quickly it could change.

'Pasta tonight? Or would you prefer something else?'

'Pasta's fine,' he said. 'Is there any of that wine left?'

The evening passed quietly. Calvin worked on his computer on the coffee table. Jess set hers up on the kitchen counter and finished her article. She proof read and filed it onto her computer desktop, ready to send. Then she checked her email and discovered a new offer from The Feminist Age magazine requesting an article on the increasing demand for women's rights in Central Africa. She frowned. That would be hard to research; there wouldn't be a vast amount of data at the library. The money was too good to turn down though; The Feminist Age was one of the better payers.

Jess doubted she could gather enough relevant information to make the job into a quality assignment, so she reluctantly replied to the email advising the editor to try to get a journalist of African heritage to take it on. She was just about to click send when she remembered Ewan. Three years working with a charity in Africa that helped women and families sort out their medical and social problems would have given him a mountain of experience. How would she go about finding him though? She couldn't just wait outside Tesco Direct until he turned up. Then she remembered his invitation. She couldn't let Nana down on Friday afternoon, but she could ring the Uni, someone there would have contact details.

Jess deleted the email and closed the lid of her laptop.

Next month's rent coming up, she thought.

Calvin looked up from his own computer. He took a sip of wine and smiled at Jess.

'You look rather pleased with yourself,' he said.

'I've just landed a plum assignment,' she replied. 'I need to interview someone to do a proper job of it though.'

'Will I do?' he asked, seriously.

'Sorry, darling,' Jess said. 'In normal circumstances I wouldn't look any further, but this time you'd have to be an expert on the subject of the political motivations of Rwandan women.'

'Bugger that,' said Calvin. 'English women are still a mystery to me. One in particular.'

'Sorry,' said Jess, 'I don't mean to be unfathomable.'

'Oh, not you,' said Calvin.

'Who else do you need to understand intimately?' asked Jess, only half-jokingly.

'Tania at Uni,' said Calvin with feeling. 'I never know where I stand with her.'

'Don't worry about it,' said Jess. 'Some people are too deep to really get to know.'

'I'll keep working at it,' said Calvin, more to himself than Jess.

Chapter 28

Jess

Calvin had always been an early bird but just recently he had gone beyond that and had become the worm that was up and about before the bird.

When Jess woke on Tuesday morning, Calvin had showered, eaten a morning breakfast of muesli and was now on his third cup of coffee. Jess couldn't keep up with him on that front. More than three a day gave her the shakes. Calvin seemed to be able to drink it like water. Maybe that's why he got so hyper.

He waved the coffee pot at her as she left the bedroom. She shook her head, yawned and accepted his offer of a peck on the cheek as she passed. She patted his shoulder in response.

'Are you on Nana duty tonight?' he asked, as if by way of small talk.

'Yes, I'm going over for tea and I'll be back some time tomorrow afternoon, depending on how she is. She's started putting rouge cream on her—'

Calvin cut in.

'Okay, well I might be out late myself. I'm playing squash with some of the lads from work, then we're going to the Manvers Arms over at Lanersby. If it's a lock-in, it could be a very late one.'

Jess bit her lip and managed to avoid responding to his interruption. She put two slices of thick bread in the toaster, poured herself some fresh orange juice, and perched herself on a tall, kitchen stool.

'I've been thinking,' she said.

'I thought I heard something clanking,' he replied with a smile.

'Do you think we spend too much time together, Calvin?' she asked.

'How do you mean?' He frowned in response.

'Well, most people only ever see each other in the evenings, and at weekends. We're cooped up here together all the time. No wonder we get crabby with each other.'

'I don't get crabby. When do I ever get crabby?' he asked.

Jess didn't bite.

'I've been thinking really hard as to why we've suddenly started arguing, sometimes over nothing, or things so trivial they shouldn't matter. I came to the conclusion that we ought to be apart a little bit more, so we look forward to seeing each other later in the day.'

'What are you suggesting, Jess?' Calvin got slowly to his feet and walked to the kitchen.

Jess held her breath but he was just waiting for her to continue.

'Well, for a start, I could work out of the library. It's full of all the resources I need, I can get Internet, and the research section is excellent. I could also work out of the café near the Uni, if I fancied a change.'

Calvin wasn't sold on that idea.

'I'd miss you too much.' He kissed Jess on the top of her head. 'Besides, I don't want you to become the fantasy of every young, male Uni student off-campus. They all hang around that café.'

Jess stood her ground.

'I want us to be happy, Calv, but at the moment I don't think we are. There seems to be something coming between us and I'm not sure what it is, so I thought this might help. We don't have to be apart every day, but a couple of times a week or so wouldn't hurt.'

'I'd hardly see you at all if we did that, Jess, what with your Nana and all that nonsense.'

Jess did bite at that.

'It isn't nonsense, Calvin, she's nearly a hundred and she needs my help.'

'Aren't you just using her to get her story?' Calvin paused. 'I didn't mean it to come out like that.'

'She's old and I don't know how much time I have left to spend in her company. Her story is just something we're sharing between us. That's all.'

She threw her toast in the bin and headed for the shower.

'Okay, I agree,' Calvin called after her. 'We'll sort out a work at home roster. I can do my thing at the Uni or in that café, some days. It would be handy if I needed to nip into the office for anything.'

Jess stopped at the bathroom door.

'I really do think we need to do this, Calvin,' she said softly.

'I thought only old married couples did this sort of thing. We'll be having date nights next,' replied Calvin. 'I'll go along with it for now, but don't go thinking it's permanent, and don't go talking to any men while you're running back and forth. I wouldn't be happy about that at all.'

At four-thirty, Jess picked up her bag, kissed Calvin and hurried to her car. She had packed an overnight bag, her unfinished Writing Magazine and a fantasy novel by Robin Hobb. She wasn't really a fantasy sort of person but the Farseer trilogy had her hooked.

She opened the front door to be greeted by Beethoven's Ninth blaring out across the house. Fearing the worst, Jess dashed along the hall into the front room. Alice was sitting in her chair swinging her arms as if conducting an orchestra.

'What on earth,' Jess raised a hand and waved to Alice. 'Nana?'

Alice stopped the conducting immediately and waved back.

Jess stepped across the room and turned off the DAB radio.

She cupped her hands over her ears for effect.

'Wow! That was loud,' she said.

'It had to be,' replied Alice. 'I was making sure I stayed awake.'

'But why, Nana? Are you having trouble sleeping at night so you're trying to stay awake in the day?' That made sense, of sorts.

'The opposite. I sleep far too easily at night, but I don't want to, Jessica.' Tears welled in her eyes.

'The dreams are too horrible.' She stared at Jess, wide-eyed. 'Someone's coming for me, and I don't want to go with him.'

Jess rushed to her side to comfort her.

'No one's coming for you, Nana. I won't let them.'

Alice patted her hand.

'Sadly, you can't stop him, Jessica. I wish to God you could, but no one can.' She began to shake. 'I know what's coming out of that tunnel. I see it every time I fall asleep now. It's my destiny.'

'We don't believe in fate, destiny, Heaven and Hell, remember?' Jess tried to soothe the obviously terrified woman. 'Dreams mean nothing, Nana. Nothing.'

Alice hung her head.

'A few short weeks ago I'd have totally agreed with you, my darling. But these aren't just ordinary bad dreams. This is one dream... no, one vision, and it's continuous, like it's played back on a video recorder, over and over again, but it subtly changes every time, the light takes up more and more of the tunnel, there's a thick mist in the centre now and someone is coming out of it to claim me.'

'Honestly, Nana, it's just a dream, albeit a recurring one. I used to have one about an attic,' Jess loosened her hold on Alice. 'I think you ought to be the novelist, Nana, not me. You'd have a best seller with this one.'

Alice tried to laugh but only succeeded in making a gravelly sound in the back of her throat.

'You probably won't believe me until you get a similar experience yourself when you're coming to the end, my dear, but I won't allow you to have as bad a time of it as I'm having. I'll be there already, wherever "there" is, and I'll ensure that I'm the one waiting in that tunnel. I won't allow anyone to get in my way.'

Alice pushed herself back into her cushions. Even through the dab of rouge, Jess could see her face was ashen. She wiped away tears as she heard Alice's words. She put her arm around her again.

'I know you'll always be watching over me, Nana,' she whispered.

Chapter 29

Alice

By the time Gwen arrived, Alice had calmed down.

'Hello, Lovely,' she said, removing her coat. 'I've got a treat for you tonight seeing as how I've got two to cook for. It's my speciality,' she preened. 'Spag Bol, in my own recipe sauce.'

'That sounds right up my street, Gwen,' said Jess.

Alice nodded with what she hoped looked like enthusiasm.

'Double helpings for me,' she said.

Alice ate sparingly, despite her boast about seconds. She wasn't as tired as she thought she might be. She was pleased about that because she wanted to take Jessica through the next part of her story and she didn't want to nod off in the middle of it and have a heart attack or something worse. She hoped that Jessica would sit up late with her tonight, so she could get the double helping of dinner she couldn't manage, out in story form.

When Gwen had washed the dinner plates, she took off her apron and came into the lounge.

'Shall we get you washed and into bed, Lovely?'

'I'll do all that tonight, Gwen,' said Jess. 'Get yourself off home early. Give your family a treat.'

'Oh, they won't notice if I'm there or not,' said Gwen with more feeling than she meant to display. 'I really don't mind staying, Jessica. I like to care for Alice.'

'I know you do, Gwen, and bless you for it,' said Jess. 'But, if you don't mind, I'd really like to do it myself on the nights when I stay over. Come in late in the morning, I'll get her showered and dressed.'

'You'll be putting me out of a job, soon.' Gwen forced a smile. 'Right, I'll be off. I'll see you in the morning for breakfast, Lovely.' She dropped her head and let herself out.

'What time do you normally go to bed, Nana?' asked Jess, when Gwen had closed the door.

'About now, usually,' replied Alice. 'But, as you're here, I'd like to stay up a bit later tonight.'

'Of course, Nana. I'll help you into bed whenever you're ready to go.'

Alice smiled and her whole face lit up.

'Break out the booze then, Jessica, we're in for an all-nighter.'

Jess grinned. 'No booze, Nana, you'll be on the commode all night.'

'I don't mind that,' replied Alice. 'I'd welcome it.'

'Tea will have to do for now, although I'll make you some cocoa before bed,' said Jess. 'We're not at a student's party, you know?'

When the tea had been poured, Alice took a sip, then placed the mug on the small table at the side of her.

'How far had I got in the story, Jessica?' Alice asked as Jess set up the voice recorder.

'Frank had just moved in, Nana.'

'Oh, yes. There was fun and games on the farm after that.' Alice looked at the ceiling while she collected her thoughts. 'The farm hands didn't take kindly to Frank moving onto their turf. Not in the beginning at least.'

Chapter 30

1938

I sometimes forgot that I was still only eighteen and getting more and more emotional as my pregnancy progressed. On the Monday after Frank moved in, I ordered the first man to arrive, to ask his workmates to wait in the yard because I had something important to say to them. I had often seen my mother and father address the men when some project or other was beginning, or the prospect of a shortage of work required a comforting, reassuring speech. In my teenage arrogance, I thought I had the same magic touch. I was wrong.

I had the respect of the lads, I knew that. I had often heard one or another of them say, 'she's her father's daughter all right,' and that sort of throwaway remark gave me the false belief that I could do, or say, anything I liked and they would accept it.

This was going to be a tricky one, however I approached it. I should have thought a little deeper about how my father would have handled it, after all, I was about to add a newcomer to the workforce at a time when there wasn't enough work for the men we already had, and the younger ones among them might well have thought that layoffs were imminent.

The older men wouldn't have seen it that way. After my father kept them on during the early years of the Great Depression, they would be fairly confident that layoffs were not about to happen. They knew that just as the days were short in the winter months, work was too. But they also knew they would be paid, even if they were sent home mid-morning. I was my father's daughter after all.

I stood in the kitchen with Frank, watching them gather. In my own mind they would just accept the situation and get on with the day's meagre work allocation. I had an idea for the summer that meant a square of land would need to be cleared in readiness for a new section of the piggery. I wasn't sure the ground could be dug in these snowy conditions but we could try.

Barney was always the last to turn up – being the foreman, he felt he had the right. I had seen him hiding in the front garden on a few occasions waiting for the stragglers to arrive before he put in an appearance.

When my entire workforce was gathered, I looked at Frank and tipped my head towards the back door. We stood on the top step, side by side as the men muttered among themselves.

'Good morning, lads,' I began.

'Who's that?' asked Simon Humphreys, one of the younger workers.

'I've seen him in The Old Bull,' shouted someone from the back of the crowd. 'What's he doing here?'

I allowed my arrogance to get the better of me. My mother would have calmed them with soothing words. My father would have just stared at them and they would meekly quieten down.

I took what I thought to be a banter-like stance.

'If you'll bloody well shut up, I'll tell you.' I waited for the laugh. It didn't surface.

I decided to start again.

I motioned to my left where Frank was standing.

'This is Frank,' I said. 'Frank Mollison, and he's going to be starting work here from today. I hope you will all welcome hi—'

'What's he going to do here?' asked Benny Tomkiss, the last person we took on. 'It's not one in, one out, is it?'

There were angry mutterings, Benny was a popular lad, he would be on full wages in a couple of months when he reached eighteen.

'Frank will be doing the same work as you,' I said. 'He told me he's done farm work before, so he knows how to go about it.'

'He told you that did he?' said Alfie Brown, a regular at The Old Bull. 'As I remember, he's a builder's mate.'

Frank nodded. 'Yes, I was a builder's mate for a couple of years, until the work dried up. But I've also worked at the mill. I've worked in the concrete pipe plant, I've worked as a stable boy at the big house, I've worked as a house painter and I've worked on a farm. Three farms in fact. I've worked the harvest; I've worked planting and I've been laid off in winter on all three occasions. That, thankfully, appears to be something that doesn't happen here.'

The men listened to him in silence. Then Alfie Brown spoke up again.

'Are there going to be layoffs this winter, Girl?'

I felt the challenge in his words; I also felt anger at the disrespect in his use of the term 'Girl'.

'Alfie,' I replied with a steely look. 'This "Girl" is your boss, your employer, the person who pays your wages, the person who finds work for you when there's none to be found.'

'You're not long out of nappies,' Alfie replied, getting a mutter of agreement from certain quarters.

I felt I was losing them but Barney came to my rescue.

'Right, Missis, I know you have the right to set on who the hell you want to set on, but I think the lads need a cast iron guarantee that no one currently employed, will be laid off.'

'I've just given them that,' I said, a little testily.

Barney stepped forward.

'Could I have a private word, Missis, on behalf of the men?'

I nodded, grateful for the respect he had shown me. Barney was the only one to call me by the title my mother held through sickness and health. I opened the back door, and stepped inside, Barney followed. I crooked my finger and beckoned towards Frank. 'You too,' I said. 'We don't want a murder on our hands.'

Frank gave me a stern look; it was obvious he didn't like being summoned by the crooked index finger of a spoilt young girl, potential employer, or not. I realised later how demeaning it must have looked. Yet another mistake to add to the catalogue of them that day.

I offered Barney a seat at the table but he declined.

'Missis,' he began. 'I know you're running things at the moment and that there's little chance the Master will come back, but you can't treat the lads like this. They deserve better.'

'Better,' I said, puzzled. 'How can I treat them better? I'm telling them what's about to happen. This hasn't been planned, there's no agenda. It's just another worker joining the farm.' I looked Barney straight in the eyes. 'There will be no layoffs.'

'I believe you, Missis,' Barney held out his hands, palms facing up. 'But it's hard for some of those lads out there to take you at your word. No disrespect, but you're only a young girl. What if you suddenly fell for a young man and sold up? Where would they all be then?'

My mind reeled. Did Barney know about me and Frank? He was hardly young and he certainly hadn't swept me off my feet. Pulled me off them, yes. I felt a huge wave of relief when Barney spoke again.

'Sorry, Missis, that was just an example. Young girls do that sort of thing all too often. Their hearts rule their heads.'

'Not this young girl,' I said with spirit. 'This is a family farm, I'm aware of its history and its traditions.' I crossed my heart. 'Barney, I make this promise now. While I'm alive, this farm will never be sold off. It will remain in my family for my lifetime and hopefully, the lifetime of any offspring I produce. Most of you will be long gone by the time that happens.'

Barney looked at Frank, who had stayed sulkily quiet.

'Is it true, he's moved in here with you?'

I hesitated, but decided to tell some of the truth at least. The rest could wait for now, it would come out pretty soon anyway.

'I won't deny it, Barney. He moved in at the weekend. BUT! He is not sharing my bed. Do I make myself clear?'

'He's still under your roof and you're a single woman. People will talk, and it won't be pleasant.'

I took hold of Barney's arm and led him to the parlour where a trestle bed was covered in neatly folded blankets. Frank's case stuffed down the side of it.

'Happy now?' I asked.

As Barney pulled his arm away his hand brushed against my stomach. Although it was covered in a thick, baggy jumper, there was no hiding what was underneath.

He looked at me, then Frank, and nodded in understanding.

'So, pretty soon we'll have a new boss. Married rights and all that.'

I shook my head vigorously and leaned in close to him.

'As I said in there, Barney. This farm will never leave my family. If it means me taking out a covenant, or placing it in a trust, I'll do whatever it takes. There will be no married rights, or any other sort of rights for anyone on the outside of my immediate family.' I looked back at Frank who had a look on his face that clearly said, watch this space.

The vehemence of my statement went a long way to convincing Barney.

'I won't say a word about this, Missis, it's a personal matter after all. I'm more concerned with how Frank will fit in here.'

'He'll fit in with you and the lads, if you give him a chance. I don't want to hear tittle tattle, accusations of favouritism, or made up stories about his performance. You will be the arbiter of all that sort of thing, his judge and jury. If he slacks, or if he's a shirker, come to me and he'll be out of work as quickly as he found it. You have my word.'

Barney gave me a half smile, just as the door to the front room opened and the wretched, rake-like figure of my father shuffled into the kitchen. When he spoke his voice was slurred, his eyes were like black slits.

'Barney?' he said. 'Is it you? I heard a voice...'

'It's me, Master,' replied Barney, his eyes welling up. 'It's so good to see you.'

'Who's this?' My father looked at Frank. He staggered as he did so, and fell against the wall.

I rushed across before he went over completely, Barney was only a footstep behind.

'This is Frank,' I said. 'He works for us now.'

'Hello, Frank,' said my father. 'Welcome to the family.'

I was sure he meant our farm-family, but Frank beamed. As Barney helped my father straighten up, he threw his arms around him.

'Barney,' he half whispered, half hissed. 'Look after her, she'll make mistakes, but she'll learn.'

Barney touched his forelock, gave my father another big hug, nodded to me, and left the house.

Two minutes later the farmyard erupted in a cheer that was followed by a rousing chorus of, 'for he's a jolly good fellow.'

I helped my father back into the front room just as Miriam stepped through the back door.

'What are they all cheering about? I was going to join in,' she said.

'They're cheering Dad,' I told her. 'But I'd hold back on the cheering if I were you. There's a pair of piss-stained trousers that need changing, and my stomach isn't up to it today.'

I walked back outside, holding my hands across my stomach, the way pregnant women do. I hastily adjusted my stance when I realised what I'd done, and clasped them in front of me instead.

'Well, lads,' I said, feeling a lot more confident. 'Is the meeting over, or are there any more concerns that need airing?'

'I've got one, Missis,' said Alfie Brown. A few moments ago, I was Girl.

'What's that, Alfie?' I smiled now the tension between us had dissipated.

'Could we have a hot brew before we start? I'm frozen to the marrow.'

I leaned back inside the door and instructed Miriam to boil the urn when she'd finished changing my father's clothes, then I turned to Frank.

'Here's your chance to integrate, Frank. Fill those two large, aluminium tea pots, grab a dozen of the big metal mugs, and pour them a drink. You'll be their best mate by lunchtime.'

I thought he was going to argue the point at first, but in open view of the workforce, he touched his forelock, pulled on his flat cap and went to help Miriam with the tea.

Chapter 31

Alice

'I didn't realise you went to bed so early, Nana.' Jess slipped her voice recorder into the pocket of her cardigan and settled back in her chair.

'Six-thirty, at the latest,' replied Alice. 'It's a bit silly really but that's when Gwen goes home. I could stay up a bit later if I paid for another carer to come around to tuck me in, but I don't see the point. I may as well be in bed propped up on the pillows as in my chair propped up with cushions. I watch TV for a while, or I'll get Gwen to bring the radio over to my bedside and listen to that. I read... It's pretty much the same as in the day really.'

'It does seem rather early though, Nana. How about we stay up late tonight? Shall I get you ready about nine-ish?'

'You can make it midnight for me,' replied Alice. 'Where are you sleeping?'

'Gwen has made a bed up for me in your old room,' said Jess.

'Watch out for the lumpy mattress,' warned Alice. 'I've been meaning to get a new one for years, but, well, it's one of those things you never get round to doing. I don't need a new one now anyway.' She pointed to the single, hospital style bed in the corner of the lounge. 'I've got that beast of a bed, now. There are so many buttons on the controller thingy, I'm sure it would stand on one end if I pressed the wrong one.'

Jess laughed. 'I don't think they tilt quite that far, Nana.'

Alice shrugged. 'I only use two or three of the buttons anyway. God knows what the rest do. There's even an alarm you know? A panic button, thingy. Not that there's anyone else to hear it. I pressed it once to see what it would do, it beeped right through the night until Gwen switched it off when she got here in the morning. I had to wear ear plugs all night. Good job I had some in the bedside drawer.'

Jess shook her head. 'Honestly, Nana.'

'Would you like some more of the story this evening?' Alice asked suddenly.

'Are you sure you're up to it?' asked Jess.

'It's only talking, I'm not doing the fifty-yard dash,' replied Alice.

Jess took the voice recorder out of her pocket, pressed the on switch and went through her cataloguing routine.

Alice stared at the far wall and began.

'Frank settled in quickly enough in the end...'

Chapter 32

1938

We didn't get the expected bad weather in February. It was the mildest one any of us could remember. There were no bad frosts and not a lot of rain, so much of the work that would have been done in March was done early.

Frank and Benny dug out the earth on the piece of ground I'd earmarked for the extension to the piggery. Frank, who had worked with builders before, measured out the plot and even worked out how much concrete and hardcore we'd need for the base. Mathematics wasn't Benny's thing and he began to show a little more in the way of respect for Frank, who had done a bit of college after work when he was a teenager.

The two of them were getting on quite well, which is why I chose to partner them. Benny was an easy-going sort of person and Frank had a similar disposition. He was good in a crowd as long as it was male (he was more awkward with a group of women). He came up with some genuinely funny jokes and could keep a conversation going with anecdotes from his working past.

It wasn't the same with all the men. Barney had to sort out a few quibbles and complaints from a couple of the farm hands who still harboured suspicions about Frank. In general, though, he slotted into the system well. He was hard working, respectful, especially of Barney, and he was the first to volunteer for any job that needed doing urgently. Even clearing the blocked drains in the pig pens or, on occasion, the drains of our outdoor toilet.

All the bickering about him stopped when he became the hero of the day, after a wagon, pulled by Bessie, our shire horse, tipped over, trapping Alfie Brown's legs underneath. Frank was working in the next field but heard the shouts and rushed across to help.

The two Georges, Foulkes and Foulds, stood around, uselessly flapping their arms and arguing with each other over what to do.

The trailer was full of thick planks and sturdy railway sleepers that were to be used to ford the perpetual quagmire that made up the eastern side of the bottom acre, and to build a reliable, all year round, platform to enable access to the farm lane.

Frank assessed the situation in seconds and selected two sleepers and one of the shorter planks that had fallen out of the trailer during the accident.

He snapped orders at the almost shell-shocked men, telling them to stack the sleepers about three feet away from the toppled wagon. He picked up the chosen length of timber himself, slid one end under the trailer next to Alfie's shoulder and using it as a fulcrum, ordered the two men to bear down on the raised end.

In what must have seemed like a miracle of engineering to the two Georges, the trailer was eased up by about a foot, and Frank dragged a grateful Alfie to safety.

Alfie was off work for eight weeks in total. The doctor at the hospital informed him that he had been lucky. Had he stayed under the trailer for too much longer, the blood supply would have been cut off and he may have lost a leg. There was no such thing as sick pay back then, but I paid Alfie's wages anyway. I paid for the doctor who looked after him when he left hospital too. He was my responsibility after all.

Frank was toasted time and again at The Old Bull on the following Friday evening, and again, when Alfie was well enough to attend himself. After that, there was no backbiting or complaints about him. He was one of them.

After work, Frank would strip to the waist and have a flannel wash at the kitchen sink. He was a well-built man with a thick, but solid, waist and a broad chest. I must admit there were times when I made an excuse to be in the kitchen while he was washing. I would even carry some item or other in there with me and pretend to be looking for it.

Frank didn't pester me, or hint at any carnal relationship at that time. Mind you, I was five months' pregnant and the bump was getting bigger by the day. I doubt I was the most alluring woman in the town. Miriam was in far better shape, and she was a good twenty-five years older than me.

I'll even admit that I felt a little jealous when I overheard him talking to his workmates about some woman or other he had been chatting up in the town.

'Tits like melons, I'm not kidding.'

I could sympathise with that woman. Mine were beginning to look like melons by then.

After dinner, on weekday evenings, Frank and I would listen to the radio or we would sit opposite each other by the boiler and read. He would always have a thriller by the likes of Graham Greene or Raymond Chandler. I'd be reading library copies of Agatha Christie's crime novels. One night, Frank complained that he'd finished his stack of books and had nothing left to read. I offered to let him borrow my, as yet, unread copy of Agatha's, Death on the Nile, but he refused on the basis that it had been written by a woman and he didn't like romantic fiction. He was steadfast in his refusal, even after I read him a few paragraphs and explained that she was one of the best-selling crime writers of the day and didn't actually do romance.

On Monday evenings we always listened to Monday Night at Seven, where we could pitch our wits against Inspector Hornleigh of the Yard who would spend fifteen minutes interrogating witnesses to a crime. The audience was encouraged to try to pick out the mistakes made by the suspects and guess who the perpetrator of the crime was. Frank and I had quite a few arguments during the program. To his horror, I was correct on far more occasions than he was. I explained that was because Agatha Christie was a better writer then Graham Greene and he should really read her books instead. He said I was just lucky.

One night, in late February, I was feeling a bit down and more than a bit emotional. I had just read an article in Woman's Own about a woman who had suffered fourteen miscarriages and had been unable to adopt because she couldn't afford the agency fees.

I felt so sorry for that woman. She had been trying for a child for over fifteen years without success and there was I, five months' pregnant after one drunken fumble in the long grass. It didn't seem fair.

As I sat snuffling in my chair, Frank came in from a visit to the outside toilet.

'What's wrong, Alice?' he asked.

'Oh, nothing, I've just been reading about a poor woman who can't have children and there's me, who didn't want one...'

I began to sob, uncontrollably.

Frank walked slowly round to my side of the table, crouched down at the side of me and gently took my shaking hand in his. It was rough, calloused and weather worn, but it felt so reassuring that I turned to him and threw my arms around his neck. He held me close while I sobbed, my head on his chest.

'There, there, Alice. You can't hold yourself responsible for everyone who is having a bad time. It happens, it's life, and there's nothing you can do to change it. All right, that poor woman would swap places with you in an instant, but would you really swap places with her?' He stroked my hair and held me tighter with his free arm. I pulled my head away from his chest and looked up at him through bleary eyes. My face red and wet.

'I don't want this baby, Frank. I'd give it away now if I could.'

I half expected a lecture on his paternal rights but it didn't come. Instead, he made soothing noises and assured me that when the baby finally arrived, I would love it unconditionally.

'I know this to be true, because my mother was in exactly the same position as you at a very young age. She felt scared and uncertain about her future too. She had the opportunity to be rid of me at an early stage, but she didn't take it. She gave birth to me and she loved me. You'll do likewise. It's what mothers do.'

At nine o'clock, Frank kissed the top of my head, said goodnight and went to his bed. I trudged upstairs to mine but at half past nine I came back down and tapped softly on the door of the parlour.

Frank opened it, squinting into the light of the kitchen.

'I don't want to be alone tonight,' I said, quietly.

Frank followed me across the kitchen and up the stairs to my room. I got into what used to be my parents' bed and Frank lay down on the covers alongside. He held out his arms, then wrapped them around me as I snuggled into his chest.

When I woke up in the morning, he was gone.

Chapter 33

Calvin

As soon as Jess closed the door, Calvin headed for the bathroom. An hour later he felt he was looking and smelling good enough to charm the knickers off a nun.

He dressed in jeans, a white tailored shirt and a navy suit jacket, then he reached into the dark recess of the built-in wardrobe to retrieve his secret pack of ribbed condoms. He shoved three into the pocket of his jacket then, on reflection, added another just in case the night was as wild as he hoped it would be.

As he left the bedroom he blew into his cupped hand and sniffed at it, as was his custom before any date. Frowning, he went back into the bathroom and swilled out his mouth with Corsodyl. He checked his breath again, then his watch. He was too early. He couldn't really rock up at Tania's at six o'clock. He would look far too eager, even needy.

Calvin decided to drive to the Wine Cellar, in town, and take his time choosing which bottle he would treat her to. He was a regular customer in the store and he and the owner could talk for hours about different wines, regions and vintages. He wouldn't need to spend hours talking tonight. One would suffice.

He settled on a couple of bottles of Blackbook Chardonnay, sold at a very reasonable twenty pounds a bottle. He thanked the shop owner for his advice, and left to walk the short distance to Tania's flat.

Calvin was about to press the doorbell when the door flew open and a scraggy haired man with three days' worth of stubble, almost fell out into the street. Behind him, with a look of fury on her face, was Tania. She was dressed in her customary men's shirt and white knickers.

'Don't show your face round here again,' she screamed.

The man turned his head to Calvin as he hurried away.

'Don't go in there, mate, it isn't safe.'

Tania threw a V sign after the retreating figure, then stared at Calvin with a surprised look on her face.

'What the fuck do you want?'

Calvin tried to hide his annoyance. How could she forget?

'We had a date?'

'Oh shit, so we did,' replied Tania.

Calvin wasn't impressed. 'I think I'd better go,' he said, grumpily.

'No, it's all right,' said Tania, recovering her poise and looking at the labelled carrier that Calvin was holding. 'Is that wine I see before me?'

'It was,' said Calvin, turning away.

'Oh, don't sulk, Calvin, life's too short,' said Tania, breezily. She looked up and down the street to ensure no one was in sight, then undid the two buttons of her shirt that were holding it together.

'Calvin,' she purred, opening the shirt.

Calvin turned around, blew out his cheeks and stepped smartly into the lobby of her flat.

Tania laughed. 'Men. You're so easily won over,' she said.

Chapter 34

Jess

At nine-thirty, Jess helped Alice get ready for bed. She brought in a bowl of hot water, soap, a flannel and towel and sat them on the overbed table that had been sent with her hospital style bed.

She helped Alice strip down to her underwear, then sat on the sofa while she had a rub down with the flannel. Jess helped her dry the hard to reach bits, then slipped her nightdress over her raised arms. Alice wriggled to allow the nightie to fall down over her frail body, then she sat on the bed and applied her hand and face cream that she kept in the drawer at her bedside.

Jess offered to put the cosmetic items back into the drawer for her but Alice refused. 'I'll see to it,' she said, firmly.

When Alice requested a glass of water, Jess took the washing items back to the kitchen and returned with a tall glass, half filled. She placed it on the overbed table and helped Alice climb into bed before sliding the table across.

'Are you going to read tonight, Nana?' she asked, picking up the book that lay on top of her bedside cabinet.

'No, thank you, Jessica. As you're here, I thought we'd just chat for a while.'

Jess noticed Alice take a quick glance at her bedside drawer.

'Oh, I haven't cleaned my teeth, yet,' Alice said suddenly. 'My brush and toothpaste will be in the kitchen cupboard I expect. Gwen keeps them out there somewhere.'

Jess got to her feet and went to search for the items. Gwen had left them on the work surface near the microwave along with a small, Pyrex bowl, presumably for Alice to spit the residue into.

When she returned to the lounge, Alice was leaning over the side of the bed desperately trying to get hold of something she'd dropped on the floor.

'I'll get that, Nana, don't you go falling out of bed trying to pick it up.'

Alice flapped her hands at the fallen object a couple of times before leaning back into her pillows with a resigned sigh.

Jess put the teeth cleaning equipment onto the overbed table and bent down to retrieve whatever it was that Alice was trying to recover.

'Nana!' Jess read the label on the box of tablets that Alice had dropped. 'Sleeping tablets? And they were issued last year: they could even be out of date.' She slipped the foil strip out of the box. There were only a few pills left. 'Are you having trouble sleeping? I thought you said you dropped off easily at night.'

'I do, that's the trouble,' replied Alice. 'I go to sleep and the first thing I see is that dreadful tunnel with those ghostly hands reaching out towards me. They're coming to take me, Jessica, but I don't want to go, not until I've finished my story. I don't want to go with the person that's waiting for me either.'

'These tablets are no good for you, Nana,' said Jess, reading part of the leaflet that came with the tablets. 'It says not to be used long-term.'

'Come on, Jessica,' said Alice with a frown. 'I don't have a long term. I could start smoking forty cigarettes a day and it wouldn't have a detrimental effect on my longevity. I had one last night, and I'd like to keep taking them until they're all gone.'

'But why, Nana, if you can sleep anyway?'

'When I take these, I don't dream,' said Alice quietly. 'I just go to sleep then wake up in the morning. There's no tunnel, no arms reaching out to pull me into it and no one calling my name, trying to trick me into venturing inside.' Her eyes closed and tears ran down her cheeks. 'Please give them to me, Jessica. I'm sure I'll die in my sleep if I don't take one. I'm so frightened.'

Jess sat on the edge of the bed and gently eased Alice towards her. She held her close for a minute until her body had stopped shaking, then she popped out one of the tablets and picked up the glass of water.

'There you are, Nana. No bad dreams tonight.'

When Alice had settled down, Jess went to the kitchen again and came back with two steaming mugs of milky cocoa.

She handed one carefully to Alice, then went back to her seat on the sofa.

'How long do the pills take to work, Nana?'

'Half an hour or so,' Alice replied. She held the mug in both hands and sipped at the cocoa. 'What shall we talk about in the meantime?'

'Anything you like,' replied Jess. 'There isn't enough time for another excerpt from your story, that will have to wait until tomorrow.' She thought for a moment. 'I, I, erm, I would like to know why there's so much hostility towards you in the family. If you don't mind discussing it that is.'

'I don't mind at all, Jessica. It's about time you heard my side of the story. You've only ever heard theirs. What have you been told?'

'Only that you refused to help Mum and Dad out of a mess when they came begging for your help. I've never believed it though.'

'It's partly true,' replied Alice. 'I'll explain it all shortly.' She took another sip of cocoa. 'What about my children, Martha and Marjorie?'

'Gran and Marjorie have never had a good word to say about you in all the time I've known them,' Jess replied, thoughtfully. 'Marjorie always seems to agree with whatever Grandma Martha says.'

'She always has. Martha dominated her from the day she was born and there was only a couple of years between them,' said Alice.

'So, how did all the bad feeling start?' asked Jess.

Chapter 35

Alice

Martha disliked me from the day she was born. She took one look at me when she came out and screamed the house down. She didn't stop screaming until the midwife took her off me. Once she was handed back, she screamed again. I think she'd been listening in when I told Frank I didn't want the baby. She was fine with him by the way. Night time feeds were easy for me. He had to do it or she wouldn't drink.

Right from feed one, she decided that my breasts weren't suitable. We even tried to syphon the milk out of them and feed her in a bottle, but she wouldn't have anything to do with it. She had to go straight onto the formula milk.

Marjorie fed on the breast for her first feed. Then, Martha must have garbled a warning to her in toddler speak, because from the moment those two were introduced, Marjorie refused to breast feed. Again, it was good for me, because I didn't have to spend half the bloody day expressing.

As they grew up, Martha took complete control over Marjorie. She used to copy everything Martha did, every little quirk, every action, even the speech patterns were the same, she became a clone of her sister. I didn't think it was healthy, nor did Miriam, who took on the extra task of looking after them in the daytime while I was out on the farm.

We tried to isolate Marjorie but she just screamed the place down until we let Martha into the room. They shared a bed when Marjorie was old enough to leave her cot. She had her own bed but she'd get out of it as soon as the light went out and climb in with her sister.

Martha was married twice, how she managed to snare two men with her personality, I'll never know, but she did. The first one was a tubby, balding man called Thomas, and he married her at twenty-five. He had a good job in a bank and they were very comfortably off. Martha never needed to demean herself by having to take a job, she thought she was the Queen Bee. They bought a house with a cheap, bank employee mortgage. It was a nice one too, detached with a big garden. They had just the one child. Your mother, of course.

Thomas died of a heart attack in nineteen seventy-five, but Martha didn't seem to mourn his passing that much. The house was paid off by that time and he'd left her a decent amount in the bank account. She was only a widow for six months. She met a man called Roger at Butlins, where she'd taken Nicola on holiday. Marjorie was there too of course. She had never married. Martha hadn't approved of any of the few men she had met.

Roger was younger than Martha by a good few years; he was a serial adulterer, a lousy husband and an awful step-father. He refused to work, and spent Martha's money like water. Although she worried about the drastically dwindling bank account, she refused to take my advice and throw him out. She accused me of never liking him and that was true. I told her not to marry him at the start and I'd never even met him.

Marjorie backed her up of course. In a rare moment of singular thought, she told me that I had cursed her sister's marriage. Anyway, I refused to get involved after that, and when Roger announced that he wanted a divorce, as he'd met someone younger, I wasn't the slightest bit surprised.

Martha was. She was grief stricken; it was as though she had suffered another bereavement. Marjorie moved in with her and nursed her through the divorce proceedings, giving up her own rented bungalow in the process.

Because she'd been stupid enough to marry him, and live together for eight years, Roger was able to claim some of her assets. The divorce court judge awarded him a quarter of the current value of the house, but she was allowed to keep its contents and the paltry amount of money left in her bank account.

Martha loved that house, it enabled her to look down her nose at the ordinary people of the town who struggled just to pay their rent, but she couldn't afford to remortgage as she didn't have a job, and even if she got one, she wouldn't be able to earn enough to cover the monthly payments. The only income she had was her family allowance and the inflated rent that she charged Marjorie.

So, the pair of them came cap in hand to me.

I had not long sold off a couple of acres of land to a house builder, and the farm was still ticking along nicely, so I had a good income and money in the bank to spare. When they knocked on my door, I had just finished wrestling with a boar so that I could get to a hen that had somehow found its way into the sty. I was aching, wound up and grumpy. Not in the best of moods to receive a cry for help.

Martha and Marjorie sat facing the window in the front room, I sat opposite them in pretty much the same spot, though thankfully, not the same chair, that my father had sat in during his drunken sojourn. They didn't waste time on pleasantries.

'I need twelve thousand pounds, and I need it this week,' Martha said, flatly. It was a demand, not a request.

Marjorie repeated part of it like the parrot she was. 'This week.'

I didn't reply. I had seen this coming, just not the extortionate amount.

'You owe me,' Martha said. 'I'll get the farm when you die anyway, let's call it an advance.'

'An advance,' repeated Marjorie.

I pursed my lips as if I was considering the ridiculous request. I hadn't offered them so much as a cup of tea and I wasn't about to agree to this.

'Martha,' I said firmly. 'I advised you to get rid of that leech of a man a long time ago. Had you taken that advice he wouldn't have been in the position to fleece you like he has.' I looked out of the window to the neatly kept front garden. 'So, because of that, I'm not going to give you the money. You can quite easily sell your house and buy a smaller one. You don't need all that space. Why do you need four bedrooms? You can buy one of the new builds on the other side of town for the money you'll make. Have you seen them? They're quite nice.'

'So, my house is too big, but it's all right for you to rattle about in a huge old pile like this?' Martha spat.

'There's a difference,' I said evenly. 'I own this house and all the land around it, I don't have to sell to pay off some disgusting lothario who has swindled me out of my life savings.'

'You couldn't get a man, you dried up old crone.' Martha was incensed. Marjorie opened and closed her mouth like a goldfish. I glared at her until she stopped.

Martha was on a roll now. 'You couldn't keep the only man you managed to hold on to for more than a fortnight. He ran away to war, ran away to die, because it was better than living with you.' Martha took a breath then ranted on. 'You call me a desperate woman for still loving Roger, but look at you. You've spent your whole life pining for Frank, and we all know why. He was the only man stupid enough to take you on. He was my father, but you drove him away before I could get to know him properly.'

I thought she was going to burst into tears over a man she couldn't even remember, but thankfully, I was spared that performance. She just took a deep breath and went back to the subject of money.

'I own part of this place, because I'm Frank's daughter. I want part of my father's share. It's my right.'

'Frank and I were never married,' I said coldly. 'You didn't know that did you?'

Now it was Martha's turn to do the goldfish impression.

'We lived in sin,' I continued. 'I changed my surname to Mollison by deed poll just before you were born so that you'd have his name on your birth certificate. The truth is, Frank could be sitting here today, and he wouldn't own a blade of grass belonging to this farm. He was under the impression that I'd placed it in a trust.'

'I had a lawyer draw up the trust documents, but in the end, I never signed them. The money, the farm, everything here, plus an extraordinary amount of limited company shares, belong solely to me. I won't tell you how much I'm worth, because it would make you even more jealous, but I will tell the pair of you this. Neither of you will ever get your sweaty hands on this farm or any of my assets. I'll be seeing my solicitor tomorrow. I would rather leave everything to a cats' home than to you, Martha. I disown the pair of you. Now, get out!'

I got to my feet and pointed to the kitchen. 'Leave via the back door. I don't want anyone to think I invited you here.'

Chapter 36

Jess

'So, that's what it was all about. I suspected money had something to do with it. Every time your name was mentioned it had tight, or miser, added to the sentence.'

Jess searched her memory for any sign of love or affection showed towards Alice from any of her relatives. She could find none.

'Well, they got what they deserved after that performance, Nana. Absolutely nothing,' she said.

'Nothing was too much to give them,' said Alice, sleepily. 'Will you stay with me until I'm properly asleep, Jessica?' she pleaded.

'Of course, Nana, I'll stay on the sofa if you...'

There was no reply. Alice was fast asleep.

Jess looked up to the big clock for the time; it was just coming up to nine-thirty. She checked her phone for messages but there were none. She thought about Calvin, alone in the flat, and decided to send him a text.

Sorry you're all alone. Love you to the moon and back. Jess.

She waited for ten minutes for a message then remembered he was out on a pub crawl with his friends so she sent another.

I've just remembered you're going at it hard tonight. See you tomorrow evening. Love you. Jess.

Jess pulled the Robin Hobb from her laptop bag and settled down to read for an hour.

At eleven o'clock, she put the book down and stepped over to see how Alice was doing. She was breathing softly, but regularly. 'No sign of the night terrors, my Lovely.' Jess smiled to herself as she slipped into Gwen mode for a moment. She leaned forward and kissed Alice on the forehead. 'Sleep tight until morning, my darling.' Jess stepped away, but as she walked across the room she looked back over her shoulder towards the bed. 'Press that alarm button if you need me.'

Chapter 37

Calvin

Calvin followed Tania up the stairs, ducking slightly to get a better view of her tight buttocks.

'Seen enough?' she asked, half way up the staircase.

'I'll never see enough of that backside,' Calvin replied. He lifted the tail of the shirt and wolf whistled.

Tania shook her head. 'Men, you're all the same, wasn't the tit flash enough? Your brains are kept in your trousers, I'm sure of it.'

Calvin grinned. 'Well, you can make as much use of my brains as you like tonight. Who was the bloke rushing away just now?'

'No one you know,' Tania replied. She opened the door to the lounge diner and stepped inside.

'He was a scruffy so and so,' said Calvin, not giving up on the subject.

'Put the wine in the fridge,' ordered Tania, 'let it chill a while. I'll ring for the takeaway shall I, what do you fancy, Indian, Chinese?'

'Chinese might be best,' said Calvin. 'We don't want to be sharing curry breath later on.'

He opened the small fridge door and slipped the wine carefully onto the empty top shelf.

'There's no food in here,' he said.

'I'm on hold,' said Tania. 'No, I tend to live day to day. I get meals from the restaurant when I'm working and warm it up the next evening... Hello, yes, I'd like to place a delivery order please.'

'The wine won't take long; it was in the chiller cabinet at the Wine Cellar.'

'Wine Cellar?' Tania winked at him. 'Posh. You're not a supermarket wine drinker, that's for sure,' she winked again. 'Or is this just to impress me.'

'I use the Cellar a lot,' Calvin answered, defensively.

'I'm sure you do,' said Tania. 'I'm only pulling your leg, Calvin.'

Calvin sat next to her on the sofa and stroked one of her long, shapely thighs.

'So, who was he?'

'Calvin, you're getting boring now, leave it alone will you?'

He couldn't.

'It's just that, well... You dressed like that when there's a bloke in the flat.'

Tania looked down at her chest. 'I always dress like this when I'm home, it saves a fortune on the launderette.'

Calvin rubbed his chin. 'I was beginning to wonder if...' he broke off.

'You wondered if I was on the game?' Tania glared at him.

'No! No, nothing like that, I just... well, I wasn't expecting to see another man here, that's all.'

Tania brushed away Calvin's wandering hand and got to her bare feet.

'I don't see why you deserve an explanation, Calvin, I've only known you for two minutes, but, as it happens, that was my ex.'

'Your ex, why was he—'

'He was trying to borrow money. He has recently developed a drug habit which is why we broke up,' said Tania. 'Now, is that enough for you, or do you want to follow him out of the door?'

Calvin shook his head, slowly. 'I'm just fine where I am, thank you.'

After the meal, Calvin topped up Tania's wine glass again but didn't bother with his own.

'Are you trying to get me drunk?' she asked with a giggle. 'If so, you've succeeded.'

'We've still got half a bottle to go yet,' replied Calvin. 'What do you think, nice, isn't it?'

'It's very nice. Much better than the Asda fiver specials I usually drink.' She smiled at him. 'Thank you.'

'I'll bring a different vintage next time. Wine is my thing. Do you like red?' he asked.

'I like anything as long as it's alcoholic.' Tania giggled again. She looked at Calvin seductively, undid her shirt again, pushed Calvin back onto the sofa and straddled him. 'The wine has gone straight to my head, let's see if it's gone straight to yours.' She undid his belt, the top button of his jeans and carefully eased down his zip. 'Oh, I see it's gone straight to yours too. Goody.'

Chapter 38

Jess

Alice hadn't been joking about the lumpy mattress. Jess wondered how old it was. Every time she turned over another spring pinged out of place. Eventually she found a more comfortable spot right in the centre of the double bed. It sank in alarmingly when she rolled onto it but at least the springs stayed quiet.

She lay on her back and made patterns out of the cracks in the ceiling plaster. She was sure there was a face up there looking down at her. Jess twisted her body and heard another spring go ping. How old was this bloody mattress? She wondered if it was the same one that Alice had lain on as a worried, pregnant eighteen-year-old, wrapped up in Frank's reassuring arms. It couldn't be that old, surely? Mattresses didn't last that long.

Jess got up twice in the night to check on Alice, but she needn't have bothered. She hadn't moved from when she first fell asleep and she was breathing softly and regularly.

She was still fast asleep when Jess got up at five-thirty. The mattress had finally beaten her. She showered, dressed into the clothes from her overnight bag, cleaned her teeth, and dragged her long-suffering hairbrush through her tangled mass of curls, then went downstairs to make tea.

To her surprise, Gwen was in the kitchen, wiping down the surfaces with a new kitchen cloth dampened with an anti-bacterial spray.

'Gwen, whatever are you doing here? It's the middle of the night.'

'Hello, Jessica, did you sleep well? I've checked in on Alice, she's fast asleep still.'

'Yes, I looked in too, but what are you doing here, Gwen? I said come in late.'

'I just wanted to be here, in case I was needed,' Gwen replied. 'Would you like an early breakfast? I'll do Alice's later.'

'No, it's too early for me,' said Jess. 'I was just going to make tea. Would you like one too?'

Gwen grabbed the kettle before Jess could get anywhere near it.

'I'll do it,' she said.

Jess sat with Gwen at the kitchen table, drinking tea and chatting about Gwen's other clients, all of whom had now claimed the epithet of 'poor thing'.

At six forty-five, Jess allowed Gwen to check on Alice. She was awake and sitting up in bed, demanding tea.

While Gwen made a fresh brew, Jess stepped brightly into the lounge. 'Good morning, Nana. I hope you slept well. I checked on you twice and you hadn't moved an inch.'

Alice yawned. 'The pills did the trick. They always do,' she said.

Jess gave her a hug and a peck on the cheek. 'We seem to have a problem. There are two of us vying to get you up to the shower this morning. Shall we toss a coin, draw lots, or fight to the death for the honour?'

'Let Gwen take me up, Jessica. She was rather put out last night when you said you'd get me ready for bed. She needs to feel wanted.'

'I know, Nana, I was only joking. I was going to suggest it myself.'

When Gwen came in with tea, Jess asked her if she would take care of Alice while she answered some urgent emails. Gwen tried to hide her delight.

'Of course, yes, of course I will, It's what I'm here for.'

Jess settled down on the sofa and checked her phone for messages. There was nothing from Calvin but she did have an email from The Feminist Age, editor, Melanie, querying whether Jess was interested in the African assignment. She replied that she would like to do a little research and would let her know by the end of the week.

Next, she sent a text to Calvin.

Hope you enjoyed your boozy night. See you later today. Love you.
Jess.

When Gwen had gone, Jess sat in her usual armchair, opposite Alice, and realised with a shock how parchment-like her skin was without the rouge that she had been applying over the last few days. She hadn't been able to rub it into her cheeks that morning because she had never been out of sight of Jess or Gwen.

Her eyes were dimmer too, that famous glint of mischief was no longer there. Her forearms were thin, the skin hanging off them, the hands that she had spent so much time on over the years, had the look of chicken's feet. Jess reeled. How could she have deteriorated like this in such a short space of time, and why hadn't she, the one who loved her so much, noticed it happening?

When Alice returned her stare, Jess retrieved her voice recorder from the bag and was about to press the on switch when Alice asked her if she knew the story behind her own parents' antipathy towards her.

Jess shook her head. 'I assumed it was the same reason Gran and Marjorie had.'

'No, although it's not all that different a story.'

She stopped suddenly.

'Are you sure you want to hear it, Jessica? You will almost certainly be shocked by it. I don't want you to be upset.'

'Tell me, Nana. I want to know. It's always been a puzzle and they'd never tell me when I asked.'

'I'm not surprised to be honest,' said Alice with a shake of her head. 'I wouldn't want anyone to know either.'

Chapter 39

Alice

Your mother and father were, on the surface, a relatively happy couple. Martha despised them for it. In her mind they had somehow stolen the happiness that she and Roger should have been enjoying.

When you came along in the summer of ninety-four, there were no joyous visits to the hospital from a loving, first-time grandmother, no excited telephone calls and demands for photographs when your mother took you home. Instead, all that was sent was a cheap, supermarket card, with one word scrawled across it. *Congratulations.* Marjorie treated your birth in the same unforgivable manner.

I, on the other hand, visited you at the hospital every afternoon. I had my picture taken with you and handed over a generous donation to your – what was the term, some Americanism that doesn't make sense... Baby ... Bath? ... No, Shower. I have no idea where Nicola got the idea from, possibly the American pen pal she had written to for years. Anyway, she had this big party and just about every woman she had ever spoken to in her life, was invited. Only half a dozen turned up though. Martha and Marjorie declined, but I went.

The money was supposed to be placed in a bank account that your father claimed to have opened in your name on the day that your birth had been registered, but I later found out, from your mother, that he used most of the money to pay off one of his debts and he gambled the remainder away. Your mother wasn't happy about it and I was furious. I ended up setting up an account for you myself that you could access at twenty-one. You were at Uni at the time it matured and it turned out to be very timely, what with fees and what have you.

Anyway, I'm waffling now.

Your father was a salesman for an office supply company and he was very good at it, but he was also a heavy gambler. When he was away from home, visiting out of town clients, he used to seek out illegal poker games, or he'd go to the dog track or horse racing meetings. Sadly, he wasn't as good a gambler as he was a salesman, and he was soon in serious trouble with money lenders.

When you were eleven, you moved house. Your father told you it was because he needed the money from the house sale to invest in a new project that his colleague at work was setting up.

The rented house was smaller, older, shabbier, and not a patch on the one your parents had just sold, but luckily you could still go to the same school. That was the only good thing about the whole episode.

Now, enough history, you know all that. Here's what really happened behind the scenes.

Your mother came to see me in a blind panic one Friday afternoon.

'Gran, I'm desperate, I need your help.'

I took her through to the front room where I had denied financial assistance to Martha all those years before.

I cut straight to the chase.

'How much and what for?'

'Twenty thousand pounds. I can't tell you why, Gran. It's too painful.'

I told her that if she didn't spill the beans there wasn't a hope in hell of her getting anything out of me.

'It's Owen. He's been gambling again.'

This news wasn't a surprise to me after the way he'd stolen the money I'd handed over at your Baby...thingy, so I sat there, said nothing and waited for it all to come out.

'He's got big debts, Gran.' Her hands were shaking. 'We've never had much money to throw about, what with the mortgage rate being as high as it is, but we did have enough to get by on. After he stole Jess's baby fund money, I laid the law down. He had to stop gambling or I would sue for divorce. I also told him that he had to visit Gamblers Anonymous sessions. I used to drive him there every week, and pick him up afterwards. I know he stayed for the duration of the meetings because I'd sit in the car park for two hours and watch the exit in case he sneaked out.'

141

I began to develop a modicum of respect for Nicola. She had come down hard on him. It's what I would have done too.

She went on. 'The sessions appeared to have worked. Over the next five years we managed to pay off most of the debts he'd accrued and there was hope on the horizon. We even started to plan for a holiday abroad. Then I got a letter from the building society, demanding the last three months' mortgage payments or they were going to send in the bailiffs to recover the sums, and if that wasn't possible, they would seek a repossession order.'

She passed the letter to me.

'I got one from the bank as well, asking me to pay off the unauthorised overdraft charges that were accruing at ten pounds a day and had built up to the sum of nine hundred pounds. They also demanded that the overdraft itself, along with a substantial loan, which amounted to six thousand pounds, should be paid back within the next calendar month or, just like the building society, they would send in the bailiffs.

'I rang them to say this wasn't reasonable and they had to give us time to sort out the problem. The manager told me that they had written to us on seven occasions over the last month.

'Bloody Owen had been getting to the post first and filtering out the letters. When I confronted him, he burst into tears and begged me to forgive him. I asked him where he thought we were going to find over eight thousand pounds in the next month. He just sobbed and said he didn't know.'

I asked her why, if the debts were between eight and nine thousand pounds, she was asking me for twenty thousand.

'Because, Gran, he's maxed out five credit cards that I had no idea he had... and...' She began to cry. 'He's been to the bloody money lenders again.'

I admit to feeling sorry for her, and I allowed that sympathy to cloud my better judgement. I asked for her bank details and told her that I'd go to my bank that very afternoon and get the money transferred over. I also told her that this was a one-off favour and if he had any more problems with gambling, she'd have to look elsewhere for help.

She almost fell over in her haste to hug me. She was still sniffling when she left five minutes later.

'This afternoon, for sure?'

I told her the money would be transferred today, but I wasn't sure how long it took to clear at her end so I advised her to give it until Wednesday to be sure. I also mentioned that her bank would probably clear their own overdraft and charges before anything else could be taken out.

She blew me a kiss and departed. I looked out of the front window to see her run across the drive. Owen was hanging out of the driver's side of the car. She shouted something to him and his face erupted into a gash of a smile.

Two weeks' later I received a telephone call from your mother, requesting a loan of ten thousand pounds, and could she have it immediately.

'He withdrew a lot of the money that was left after the bank had taken its share and he wrote a stack of cheques that pretty much cleared the rest of it. The bloody fool gambled it all away in one crazy night at the Grosvenor Casino in Maidstone. He claimed he was four thousand pounds up by midnight, but his luck turned. I asked him why he didn't leave when he had four thousand pounds in his pocket. He said, *because I was winning.*'

I told her that I was going to refuse the loan because I couldn't trust them. I was sure he'd find a way of getting hold of the money, or some of it at least and I wasn't about to fund the local loan sharks. I did offer to look after you while they found somewhere else to live.

They wouldn't make any money from the sale of the house. It was mortgaged to the hilt. I thought Nicola had been strong and had tried to curtail his spending, but I was wrong. She had no sort of control over his habit at all. He didn't care whether his own daughter starved, providing he could get his fix. She had done little to rein him in this time around.

So, they went to Martha, who at first told them where to go, but then, after hearing how I had flatly refused to help them out, gave them a couple of hundred pounds which your mother used to pay the removal company's fees.

Your father left not long after that and your mother got a job at, of all places, the local bookmakers. She needed benefits to top up her earnings so the rent could be paid.

I never heard from her again, but I did hear the rumours of my miserly nature. Of how I refused to help out my own family in a time of crisis. Twice!

Your mother has never bothered with men since. She is a one-man woman, just as I am, allegedly, just as my mother was. Martha has had two, but only really cared for one. As for Marjorie, well, she wasn't allowed to have one at all.

Don't be a one-man woman, Jessica.

Chapter 40

Calvin

Calvin woke early as he usually did. He checked his watch, six thirty-seven.

He had slept facing away from Tania, just as he did with Jess. He eased himself onto his back and watched the rise and fall of her breasts under the single white sheet. Watching her face closely, he took hold of the seam of the sheet and inched it down, leaving her chest exposed. As he slid his hand across her arm to fondle her breast, she opened one eye.

'Not a chance, Mister. Can't you ever get enough?'

Calvin grinned. 'Not of you. I'll never get enough.'

Tania looked at the clock. 'Christ, Calvin, do you suffer from insomnia or something? The sun hasn't taken its pyjamas off yet.'

'I'm an early bird,' replied Calvin. He lifted the sheet so she could see his naked body. 'Looks like my brains were awake before me.'

Tania snorted. 'You won't let that joke go, will you?' She slid out of bed and with her back to him, slipped on the man's shirt that was draped across the arm of a chair. She fastened the customary two buttons and stepped away from the bed.

'Where are you off to?' asked Calvin.

'I'm bursting for a pee if you want the sordid details,' replied Tania.

'Hurry up back,' he said lasciviously. He pulled off the sheet to show her his erection.

'Sort it out yourself,' she said seriously. 'I'm too sore.'

While she was in the bathroom, Calvin pulled on his black boxer shorts and studied himself critically in the full-length mirror that was fixed to the door of Tania's wardrobe. He breathed in to expand his chest and pull in his already flat stomach. Satisfied that he hadn't put on weight overnight. He walked over to the kitchenette, filled the kettle and switched it on. He picked two mugs from the branches of the mug tree and looked in the cupboard for coffee. Finding only cheap instant he pulled two tea bags from the half-full box of eighty, and dropped them into the mugs.

Tania came back as he was pouring boiling water over the tea bags.

'You can have a job here if you like,' said Tania. 'I could use a Chai Wallah.'

'A what?'

'Chai Wallah. Ah, you've never been to India. They're all over the place there. They make you a cup of tea on demand.'

'Never been, never want to. It's too hot, too sticky and the smell in the towns must be horrendous. The poverty there is appalling.'

'It is, but it's beautiful too,' replied Tania. 'I'm going back next summer. I've already booked. I want to see the—'

'I'm going to the States when I can get the money together.'

'You really can be quite ignorant at times you know.' Tania stared at him, legs slightly apart, hands on hips.

'Ignorant? I was about to tell you about my planned trip to the USA, that's all.' Calvin looked genuinely puzzled.

'You cut me off, mid-sentence,' said Tania. 'Other people have hopes and dreams too, Calvin. You should listen to them sometimes. Don't be so selfish. It can't always be about you.'

'I'm not selfish. I do things for people too,' complained Calvin. 'I just made you a cup of tea.'

Tania blew out her cheeks and slowly shook her head. 'Thank you,' she said, taking the proffered mug from him.

Calvin sat on the end of the bed and sipped at his tea. He pulled a face; it wasn't the brand he liked.

'I'll bring you some decent coffee the next time I come,' he said.

'I like the instant in my cupboard,' said Tania. 'There's nothing wrong with it.'

'Wait until you try the Whittard's,' he replied. 'Have you got a proper ground coffee maker?'

She shook her head. 'No, it's all too messy. I'll stick with my instant thanks.'

'Suit yourself, but you don't know what you're missing. It's like the wine really. You get what you pay for.'

Tania leaned forward to look at her phone that sat on the bedside table and her tea spilled onto her shirt.

'Damn,' she said and walked over to the sink to try to wash out the stain before it set.

Calvin put down his tea and stood close behind her. He put his hands on her waist and pulled her back towards him.

'So, how was it for you last night?'

She sighed.

'It was fine, Calvin. What do you want, a score out of ten? Okay it was a seven point five. How's that?'

'Is that all? What was wrong? I thought you were really into it. How many blokes give you three sessions?'

'It was fine, as I said, Calvin, and I'm already fed up with having to repeat this conversation.'

'What was wrong?' Calvin persisted.

'All right, seeing as you asked.' Tania dropped the wet cloth she'd been sponging her shirt with and turned to face him. 'You're not very... adventurous, are you?'

'How do mean, adventurous?' Calvin stepped away and looked at her quizzically.

'Well, you seem to love the missionary position. When I tried to climb aboard you turned me over again and whilst I admire your endurance, there's no variety; it's missionary or doggy all the time. You always have to be in control. You should loosen up. I like to be boss sometimes.'

'You didn't complain last night,' he said sulkily.

'No, I didn't, it was nice, as I said. Look, Calvin, I'm getting really bored with this. I told you before, I'm not into comparing lovers. I don't hand out medals.'

'You think I'm boring. I've never had any complaints.'

'I'm not complaining, Calvin, just pointing something out.' Tania walked towards the bathroom. 'I'm going to shower now; I've got things to do this morning.' She opened the bathroom door, looked back towards him and smiled a half smile. 'Let yourself out.'

Chapter 41

Jess

'When my father left, I wasn't too upset at all as I remember, Nana. I hardly missed him to be honest. He often worked away and when he came home it was only for a few fleeting hours. I used to think he worked twenty-four hours a day at times, but after listening to your story, I now know that he was only coming home to get himself smartened up for whichever gambling joint he was visiting that night.

'I never had much in the way of treats when I was growing up, not from my parents at least. There were no day trips, no holidays, the only time I got out of my own street was when I was allowed to come and stay with you for a weekend, or a whole week in the school holidays. You can't even begin to guess how much I looked forward to those visits. Looking back, they always seemed to happen at a time when Mum and Dad had been arguing a lot. I used to lie in bed listening to their raised voices from the room below. I only picked up a few words and none of them made sense to me. Many was the time I'd go to sleep and dream that they had died suddenly and you had claimed custody of me. I wasn't wishing them dead, but I would dearly have liked to move in here with you.

'I used to wonder why the other kids at school seemed to have so much while I had so little. I always looked forward to a parcel or a letter from you. You saved my birthdays and Christmases for years. I never got much from them. A book here and there, and a lot of those were second hand. I didn't complain too much, I just thought that's the way life was and that was it.'

Jess paused as she thought.

'I used to think you were a millionaire. Mum never spoke of you without the word 'money' in the sentence and when Gran and Marjorie came around it was never long before the conversation worked its way around to you. They really despised you. Martha used to say you'd got a secret stash of cash and gold trinkets hidden on the farm somewhere, and they'd sit around discussing where it could be. They even drew plans of the farm buildings and the inside of the farm house.

'Martha's best guess was under the parlour floor. She said there was a secret trap door there that led down to a dark cellar. She claimed to have been down there once when she was about ten, but Miriam had found her and dragged her out before you discovered her. She said that Miriam had told her you'd tie her up and leave her down there for eternity if you ever found out.

'Marjorie agreed with that and claimed that she had observed it all happening. Martha turned to me and warned me to stay clear of that parlour, as she didn't want to hear that I had suddenly disappeared. She really does hate you, doesn't she?

'One night, around Halloween, she claimed you were a witch and you held coven meetings in the loft. She said there was a chest full of money up there too.

'Mum and Dad must have known it was all nonsense but they never contradicted her. They were either frightened of her, or reliant on her to help out with money maybe.

'I used to love listening to her go on about the scary old crone in the big house. It didn't make me scared of you as I'm sure the stories were intended to do. They made me think of you as someone I'd like to hang around with. Someone who led an exciting life. The witch and cellar tales were just like stories I'd read in books. I really wanted them to be true.'

Jess looked up and caught Alice's dull, almost grey eyes. She missed that glint of mischief.

'The stories weren't true, were they?' she asked with a glint in her own eyes.

'Of course they were,' replied Alice. 'But sadly, we had to seal the cellar up before Martha was born. We had rats in there, some as big as cats, and my mother refused to go down. As for treasure in the loft... well, you'll be able to find out for yourself soon enough. It isn't treasure of a monetary kind though, so don't go getting your hopes up.'

Jess laughed. 'Damn! And there was me planning on bringing a lorry round to cart off the gold and jewels.'

Alice smiled; thick folds of skin appeared across her face. Only a few days ago there had been none.

'I didn't know about the witch's coven story. I'd have played up on that one, believe me,' she said with a throaty chuckle. 'Alice Mollison, the Wicked Witch of the West.'

She chuckled again, then settled back in her cushions as though the effort had tired her.

'Now we've done with the family history, are you ready to hear some more of my story?' she asked.

Jess picked up the Dictaphone and spoke into it, setting up her cataloguing system before giving Alice the thumbs up to begin.

Chapter 42

March 1938

The early months of nineteen thirty-eight seemed to be all about claiming territory.

Adolph Hitler took over Austria, Mussolini took over Ethiopia and we finally got back the strip of land that bordered the lane that led to our farm. The land was one-hundred-and-fifty yards long and about twenty-five yards deep. We had lost it back in the twenties when a useless, obviously blind, council surveyor misread a map and pronounced that the border of our farm was a lot further back from the road than it actually was. So, for some fifteen years, there had been a strip of overgrown land lying on the edge of our "official border" that was of no use to us (unless we took up the council's generous offer to rent it), nor was it any use to them, as there was nothing on that part of the lane except our farm.

This bureaucratic cock up annoyed my mother. She had long harboured plans to build a dozen cottages on the land that would bring in rents when times were hard, but we could never get the council planners to consider it. Although it was private land the cottages would need to be attached to the sewers, water main and so on.

One day in late March, a man in a pinstriped suit strode self-importantly into the farmyard clutching a leather briefcase. He cursed as he stepped onto the detritus left behind by the farm livestock. He grabbed a handful of straw from the barn and began to wipe off the mixture of chicken, pig, and cow manure. We hadn't yet hosed down the yard.

He was in a foul temper as I let myself out of the new pigpen. I'd been attempting to separate two bad-tempered sows. Barney had heard me yelling at them to stop biting each other and arrived in the yard to help me. If the suited man's mood was dark, mine was black. I was six months pregnant, sweating, and feeling as fat as the sows I'd just tried to placate.

The man checked his shiny patent leather shoes were clean, then began to berate me about the state of the farmyard. I say began, because he had only got five words into his rant when I let him have my own opinion.

'It's our farm, our yard, our dung. We clean it up when we have time. Next time you visit, I suggest you wear rubber boots, like these.' I lifted my booted foot to show him. 'Now,' I said, 'WHAT THE HELL DO YOU WANT?'

He scaled back his temper and replaced it with an air of boring officialdom.

'I'm Mr Glasscock,' he said, looking at both of us, daring us to laugh. 'Seymore Glasscock, and I'm from the council.'

I bit my cheeks and did my best to control the giggle that was welling up inside. He managed to do that for me by producing a folded-up surveyor's drawing. 'It's about that unkempt, overgrown, unsightly, disgracefully tended strip of land just up the lane there.' He turned and pointed in its general direction.

'But the council told my parents that the land wasn't ours, so I don't see why we—'

'Do you think I would come all this way and wade through shi... and waste my precious time for no reason? That land is a disgrace and the ratepayers of the borough want it cleaned up.'

To be honest the grass and bramble mess had grown to an unsightly five-feet but how it impinged on the ratepayer's sensitivities, I couldn't work out.

Once again, I asked why we should clean it up if it didn't belong to the farm. He pointed to a strange looking boundary on his map which, to my eyes at least, seemed to take in the lane and the verge on the far side too. I was puzzled; the lane had been there ever since I was a child.

'Wait there,' I said, and waddled into the house.

I found the deeds in the drawer of the tallboy along with some other farm related documents and waddled back out to the yard again.

When I got there, Frank had joined the fray, although he didn't know a thing about the farm.

153

I showed Mr Glasscock my drawing and he compared it to his. I showed him where our boundary should lie, alongside the lane. He dismissed it as though it was a forgery, and said he'd have to take it back to the surveyor's department to have it verified.

Back in the day, another council official had come to see my parents regarding the disputed land and had shown them a different official land registry drawing, with the retracted boundary. It was signed in the bottom right corner by a surveyor called Batley, or as my father had nicknamed him, Blind as a Batley. I mentioned this to Mr Glasscock and advised him to seek it out.

The official wasn't moved. He had the genuine copy in his hands, and that was it as far as he was concerned. Barney tried to reason with him. He worked on the farm when my grandfather ran it and the land was ours back then. Mr Glasscock folded away his drawing and stuffed it back into his briefcase.

Frank had his say then. He wasn't a fan of officialdom at the best of times, and he told Mr Glasscock where he could stick his document.

I stepped in, pushed Frank away, and told him in no uncertain terms to get back to work. Barney pointed to the fields and said that the lads needed an extra hand in the middle acre.

If looks could kill, I'd have been lying in the chicken muck breathing my last, but he stomped off muttering to himself anyway.

I told Mr Glasscock that I would bring our drawing to the planning department in the morning, and he left, stepping gingerly across the yard. 'We open at nine,' he said, curtly.

The next morning, Frank had recovered his lost dignity and as I was feeling ill, he drove me up to the council offices in our old truck.

To cut a long story short, the surveyor we spoke to initially refused to acknowledge the validity of our claim, so Frank put in a complaint (written out on a sheet of council headed notepaper that he lifted from one of the desks) alleging negligence by the council with regard to the upkeep of the unsightly plot of land that ran parallel to the farm. The official almost fainted when Frank handed the sheet of paper to him. He rushed out of the room clutching it as though the angel of death had handed him his ticket to the afterlife.

The next thing we know, the Borough Surveyor put in an appearance. He looked at all three documents, and then dressed down a shaking Mr Glasscock, pointing out that the date in the bottom right hand corner of the drawing he had brandished the day before, read eighteen thirty-six.

He tore up the newer drawing by the infamous Mr Batley and ordered Mr Glasscock to take the hundred-year-old document to the council archives and file it as an historical map.

Finally, with an air of arrogance and annoyance, he announced to the whole department that the strip of land belonged to us. I almost cheered. I had sorted out a dispute that had gone on for fifteen long years. Me, an eighteen-year-old pregnant girl.

When we got back, I thanked Frank for his quick thinking and rushed through to tell my father. Whether he heard or not I'll never know. I hope he did, he'd waited long enough for the news.

In bed that night, I thought about my mother's plans for the freshly returned land. We couldn't really afford to build one house, let alone twelve, not without a hefty bank loan and I wasn't about to put the farm into debt before it was mine.

The next morning, I asked for volunteers to clear the reclaimed land. Frank, as usual, was the first to put his hand up. Benny was second and while he went off to get the scythe, shears and rakes, Frank got the keys to the truck and turned it around to face the lane. Benny loaded the tools on the back and climbed into the passenger seat. Frank hung out of the front window and asked me something I didn't catch over the noisy, irregular chugging of the old engine.

I shook my head. 'I can't hear you.'

'I said, do we take the dividing hedge up too?'

I thought about it. The hedge had been planted a couple of years after we lost the land. It would leave the field open to the lane if we destroyed it. I hadn't given up on my mother's plan to build on the land either.

'No, leave the hedge, Frank. I've got an idea for the new bit. Just clear it please.'

Frank drove off tooting the horn to scare away a couple of hens that were pecking at the dust in front of the truck. I had a chat with Barney about the middle acre, then I got on with my own job. Cleaning out the pigs.

In the lunch-break, Frank appeared at the back door as I was tucking into a thick sliced, ham and cheese sandwich that Miriam had made for me. It was cut into two halves and I knew I wouldn't be able to manage it all. I wasn't eating for two as the saying went. I could hardly manage enough for one, especially if I wanted to keep it down.

Frank stepped into the kitchen. 'Could I have a private word?'

Miriam disappeared into the front room to collect my father's uneaten lunch and make sure he was comfortable. I waved my hand towards an empty chair at the table and pushed the plate with the other half of the sandwich towards him. He picked it up, took a huge bite and nodded at me. 'Thanks,' he mumbled through the mouthful of thick bread.

I made us both a mug of tea and waited for him to finish his unexpected lunch.

'I was thinking it was about time we took that weekend away,' he said when he had finished eating. He pointed to my bulging stomach. 'That belly will be empty in three months. We ought to get the sham wedding done well before then.'

'I haven't forgotten, Frank,' I said, 'it's just that with the good weather we had over the winter months there's been a lot to organise. I agree though, we had better do it soon. Where do you suggest we go?'

'Sheppey isn't that far and no one will know us there,' he replied. 'We can get the train from here to Sittingbourne, and the connecting train from there to Sheerness on the island. It will only take us a couple of hours altogether, and we can get back quickly if there's an emergency.'

I had never been to the Isle of Sheppey, though my mother and father had often talked about taking me.

'If it's an island how does the train get onto it?' I asked.

'There's a rail and car bridge,' he said. 'Big boats can go under it.' Frank took a gulp from his mug of tea. 'There are a couple of nice beaches. It will be a bit cold for a swim at this time of year but we can have a paddle at Sheerness, or Leysdown-on-Sea. There's a bus every couple of hours from Sheerness.'

'That sounds really nice, Frank,' I replied. I hadn't seen the sea in years although we were only a few miles away from it. Kent's western fringe was all coastline from Essex in the north right down to Sussex.

'There's a place called Minster with a pebble beach, and the cliffs there are full of fossils that date right back to pre-history.'

I was impressed with Frank's geographical knowledge.

'How come you know so much about Sheppey?' I asked.

'I worked there, building the sea defences for a while. Sheerness has always been prone to flooding.'

'Where will we stay?' I was getting excited by the idea now.

'There are a few hotels in Sheerness and some people offer lodging in their homes,' Frank replied.

'Let's go for a hotel,' I said quickly. 'I don't want to doss down in someone's spare room. I'll pay for it all.'

'That's settled then.' Frank grinned at me. 'We'll set off early Saturday morning.'

Chapter 43

April 1938

At six-thirty on Saturday morning, I struggled into the passenger seat of our old truck with my weekend bag, which was actually a medium sized suitcase. Frank asked if we were going for a fortnight and wondered if he should get more clothes himself. I had hardly slept I was so excited.

There wasn't enough room in the front for Frank, so he sat on a dirty, oil stained tarpaulin that lay in the back of the wagon. Barney was the designated driver. He didn't ask us a single question about why we were going to the station at that hour of the morning, nor why I had asked him to get one of the lads to look after the piggery while I was gone.

Miriam had volunteered to stay overnight on Saturday. Her father had died a year before and she was alone in her cottage now that her children had all flown the coup. Her husband had left her years before, straight after the birth of their fifth child.

We got to the station in good time and stood around on the platform making small talk while we waited for the Sittingbourne train.

I bought us third class, return tickets to Sittingbourne. Once there we'd have to get another pair of return tickets to Sheerness. For some silly reason you couldn't get a second-class ticket. It was either first or third, and even though I wasn't exactly poverty-stricken, I refused to pay the highly inflated price for a better seat on a fifteen-minute journey. It was only twenty-five minutes for the second leg too.

The train huffed and puffed into the station with a blast of the hooter and a squealing of brakes. The strong breeze that swirled across the platform blew east to west, so we were spared the choking, thick puffs of smoke that rose from the stack.

There weren't a lot of people about at that time of the morning so we could pretty much choose where we sat. Opposite us was a young couple with two, highly excited, children who ran up and down the carriage for the whole journey. Further along the carriage was an old lady wearing an acorn hat. She had a parasol with her, I hope she wasn't expecting blazing sunshine if she was heading for the coast. Both Frank and I wore thick overcoats.

We reached Sittingbourne bang on time, and as we had forty minutes to wait for our connecting train, we went to the station café and ordered tea and toast. The tea was strong, as the navvies like it. The toast was chunky, a good shade of brown and was topped with a thick layer of butter.

We weren't quite as lucky with seats on the Sheerness train. It had come from London and was carrying workers home for the weekend. A young man, noticing my bump, offered me his aisle seat and Frank stood alongside until the conductor came along. Frank took an instant dislike to him and to be honest, I didn't think much to him either. He punched our tickets, instead of tearing them in half as he would have done for a single journey, then told Frank he would have to move because he was blocking the aisle.

Frank told him the journey was only twenty-five minutes long, and we were half way there already. The conductor didn't seem to care.

'What if someone needs to get by?'

'Then I'll move,' said Frank, giving the man a hard stare. 'I haven't had to move as yet. No one has asked to get by.'

'I want to get by,' said the conductor. 'Now, please don't make me stop the train and call the railway police.'

Frank looked like he was about to give him an earful, but I tugged on his sleeve and shook my head. Frank sighed, and attempted to squeeze past the conductor to an area where the embarking door was.

The conductor spread himself across the aisle.

'That way,' he said, directing Frank along the full length of the carriage to the toilet area.

Frank glowered, but did as he was told. He kept an eye on the official as he clipped tickets in the next carriage. When he moved on from there, he came back.

'Officious, little...' He looked at me. I frowned. '...so and so,' he finished.

Sheerness station looked pretty much like our local one, with a signaller's building, a ticket office and a waiting room come café. The wind, however, blew the train's smoke into our faces as we traversed the platform. We pulled our coat collars over our mouths and hurried to get out of the station.

'I feel like I've just smoked a whole packet of fags at once,' said Frank, hoarsely.

Outside the station we turned onto the aptly named Railway Road. About half way along it we found a pub, not surprising called The Railway. In the window was a sign advertising rooms with breakfast. Six shillings, double. Four and six, single.

'What do you think?' he asked.

'Won't it be a bit noisy?' I said. The pub looked in good condition, on the outside at least.

'It'll be fine at this time of year,' said Frank. 'I have stayed here, but only for one night. I couldn't afford nearly five bob a night out of the wages I was earning. I had to go into lodgings. It was a right flea pit too.'

He shuddered at the memory.

'Let's have a look at the room first,' I said. My scalp started to itch. I resisted the urge to scratch it.

The pub was clean, and the landlady was friendly. She ordered a scrawny-looking man with a thick head of tightly curled, ginger hair to take my case and show us up to the double guest room. She noticed the anxious look on my face as he opened the door to the stairs.

'I'd sleep in it,' she said with a smile. 'You'll both be cosy in there.'

I was glad she didn't use the phrase, snug as a bug in a rug.

Robert introduced himself as he led us up the one, steep flight of stairs. 'I live with Irene,' he announced, in a matter of fact way. 'We're not married or anything.'

I pulled my left hand up my sleeve so he couldn't spot that Frank and I weren't married either. I hadn't even considered bringing a ring with me.

The room was nice, bright, and had a window facing the street, not the railway line that the rooms at the back of the pub must have overlooked.

It had a large, enamel basin and water pitcher on a shelf in the corner, clean towels, and a newish-looking double bed on the wall opposite the window. There was a single wardrobe and a round, oak table surrounded by four, rickety looking chairs.

'The bathroom is at the end of the corridor. Just turn left, you can't miss it.' Robert hung around waiting for a tip, so I gave him a threepenny bit and he turned away.

'Payment is in advance,' he said suddenly. He spun around and looked at Frank. 'Shall I show you the way down?'

Frank looked at me and shrugged.

'We'll be back down in a moment,' I told him. 'My husband will pay you then. Just the one night.'

When we returned to the bar, we found that Irene was in a far more business-like mood. The friendly smile had gone, and had been replaced by a steely-eyed stare.

I'd given Frank a ten-shilling note before we came down. He produced it with a smile.

'There's a five-bob deposit,' said Irene. 'In case of breakages. It will be refunded when you leave.'

I wondered what there was in the room that could be broken. There was only the bowl and pitcher and they looked sturdy enough.

'Five bob?' Frank exploded.

'It's the new rules,' said Irene. She leaned over the bar towards us. 'I'm already breaking one rule by letting you stay here at all. We don't usually allow unmarried couples into our rooms.'

I pulled the extra shilling from my purse and handed it over. I leaned forward myself and whispered. 'Where do you and Robert sleep then?'

Irene stuffed the money into a pocket in her apron and looked smug.

'We don't sleep here,' she said.

We gave up arguing and went for a walk up to the town.

The High Street was a mix of Victorian and Edwardian buildings with faded, washed out shop fronts, but for someone like me, who lived in the country, it was a treasure trove of modern consumerism. On the High Street was a Boots store and behind it, a brightly painted clocktower that stood out vividly alongside the dull expanse of grimy, red brick and mortar.

We stopped for tea at a café in the town centre, but we had to drink it in a breezy garden at the back, because the café itself was under renovation. A waitress, wearing a uniform better suited to Lyons tea rooms than a tiny, underused little café in Sheerness, took our order and apologised on behalf of the café owner. The tea was well brewed and the waitress helpful, explaining to us the quickest way to the sea front. I left her a threepenny tip for her trouble.

After tea, we retraced our steps until we came to Broadway. A few minutes later we arrived at Sheerness beach, which was empty apart from a couple of dog walkers and two children hunting for shells. We walked along the Marine Parade until we reached the pier which the people walking just in front of us had called 'the jetty'. It was built as a place for boats to unload passengers, but at this time of year there would have been little in the way of business for the boat owners. At the end of the pier was a pavilion. We never found out what entertainment it provided because it was closed, and wouldn't open again until May Day.

We walked back along the pier to the Marine Parade, past the silent, unoccupied bandstand and headed further down towards Minster. The sea air had really worked on my appetite, so we bought fish and chips and sat down on the sea wall to eat them. A chilly wind came off the sea and seagulls raided inland looking for easier pickings than the hard to find fish in the Medway Estuary.

It was only about two and a half miles back to Sheerness, but it seemed more like five. Although it was March, we both removed our coats and allowed the shrill wind to cool our bodies. I was tired, even though I was a fit eighteen-year-old farm manager, who worked a fourteen-hour day, month in, month out. Babies tire you out even before they are born.

Frank didn't even get out of breath. At one stage he jokingly asked me if I wanted a piggy back ride.

Back in Sheerness, Frank led me to a shabby-fronted jewellers with a torn, washed-out, awning that flapped about in the stiff breeze.

There were a number of new and second hand rings in the window.

'You have to be wearing one when we go back or we won't get away with our little subterfuge,' said Frank, who surprised me at times with his intelligent conversation. He'd been well schooled by his mother, that was for sure. I was pretty well educated myself; I'd been awarded the National School Certificate when I was sixteen, and I had achieved credit passes in Mathematics and English, but I had never heard of a 'subterfuge'. I assumed it meant a crafty plan.

Inside, the shop was dimly lit. The stock was displayed in smeared, glass cabinets along one wall. We walked along them slowly, examining the price labels on each of the worn velvet pads that the rings were seated on. He finally spotted one priced at one pound, seven shillings, and eleven pence.

Behind a desk, at the far end of the shop, sat a white-haired, bespectacled jeweller who had been watching us like a hawk, presumably in case Frank produced a hammer, or worse, a gun.

Frank called him over and asked to look at the ring we had picked out. The man produced a bunch of about ten small keys and immediately found the right one. He passed the ring to Frank who lifted my left hand and slipped it easily onto my ring finger. It felt strange, I had never worn a ring in my life. it was slightly too big, I could spin it around quite easily, but I doubted it would fall off.

'I'll give you fifteen shillings for it,' said Frank.

I thought the jeweller was going to have a heart attack. 'The price is on the label,' he said.

Frank tried again. 'Seventeen and six,' he offered.

'I can't take anything less than twenty-five shillings,' said the man.

Frank screwed up his face and shook his head. 'It's tarnished,' he said. He held up my hand to show him. 'I'm beginning to wonder if it's brass, not gold.'

The jeweller produced his little magnifier and offered to show Frank the hallmark on the inside of the ring. He pointed to my bulging stomach. 'You'll need it quite soon by the looks of her, so you shouldn't quibble too much about the price.'

I thought Frank would take umbrage at that remark, but when he spoke again, his voice was calmness personified.

'A guinea... Twenty-one shillings. My final offer.'

'I can't, I paid more than that for it.' The old man wrung his hands. If he was looking for sympathy, he'd picked the wrong man.

'Sorry, love,' Frank said, softly. 'It looks like we'll be using that brass curtain ring you found at your grans.' He turned his back on the jeweller, pulled a sad face, and pointed at mine. I got the idea straight away.

I slipped the ring from my finger, and wiping a fake tear from my eye, I handed it back to the jeweller. As we walked slowly to the door, Frank slipped his arm around my shoulders.

'Never mind, love. I bet there's something in the junk shop.'

I made a noise I hoped sounded like a sob as we reached the door.

'One moment.' The old man walked towards us; the ring nestled on the palm of his right hand as if to display it in its best light.

'Twenty-two shillings and eleven pence,' he said. Shopkeepers have always loved to price things one penny short of a shilling. I suppose it was to make an item look somewhat cheaper than it actually was.

'I gave you my final offer,' said Frank. 'We've only got enough left to pay the registrar, and if we don't hurry, he'll have gone home. We got the last appointment of the day.' He looked at me and winked. 'As you said, we're pretty desperate to get it done.'

'All right, all right. Twenty-one shillings, but I'm robbing myself,' said the jeweller.

I turned my back on him, so he couldn't see the folded money in my purse, and produced two ten-shilling notes and a single silver shilling. He gave us a hand-written receipt, and Frank slipped the ring into his pocket.

'Hurry now, My Sweetness,' he said. 'The registrar is waiting.'

Frank had no idea where the registry office was, but he asked a local passer-by, who gave him the name of a street that he had no idea how to find.

'Why do we need the registry, Frank?' I asked, puzzled. 'We're not getting married.'

'I know that,' Frank replied. He grinned at me and took hold of my hand. 'Come on,' he said, 'I know where we'll go. We passed it earlier on.'

'Where are we going?' I asked as he pulled me along the street back towards the Marine Parade.

'You'll see soon enough,' he replied, still wearing that stupid grin of his.

When we were outside the door of a Catholic church called The Saint Henry and Saint Elizabeth, he suddenly produced the ring from his pocket and got down on one knee.

'Will you bloody well marry me, Alice?' he said with a chuckle in his throat.

'No, I bloody well won't,' I replied.

He got back to his feet and slipped the ring onto my finger again.

'I now pronounce us man and wife,' he said.

We got back to The Railway at about five o'clock, walked past the all-seeing eyes of Irene, and climbed the stairs to our room. I immediately threw off my coat, kicked my shoes across the threadbare carpet, and sat on the end of the bed massaging my swollen feet.

I looked at the foreign object on the finger of my left hand and laughed. I can guarantee no other girl has ever had a wedding ceremony quite like that one.

Frank picked up the battered enamel bowl and carried it out of the room. When he came back five minutes later, he placed the now full, steaming basin at my feet.

'There's an Ascot boiler in the bathroom,' he said. 'No bath, sadly.'

I eased my aching, swollen feet into the piping hot water and sighed with contentment. Frank could be a really thoughtful man at times.

Chapter 44

April 1938

At six-thirty, Frank disappeared downstairs again. Twenty minutes later, he came back with a large plate of freshly made sandwiches.

'They only had fish paste or potted meat, so I got some of each.' He placed them on the round, oak table and returned to the door. 'I've got us a pot of tea too.'

He reappeared a couple of minutes later carrying a tray laden with tea, sugar and milk.

I picked up the milk jug and looked at the watery, white liquid. 'Not a patch on our creamy, farm milk.'

Frank agreed through a mouthful of fish paste sandwich. 'These are all right though. The bread is fresh.'

'How did you persuade the Lady of the Manor to provide this lot?' I asked.

'I mentioned money to her,' Frank replied. 'One and ninepence for this lot. Robert made it anyway, she's glued to her seat at the till.'

Although we had eaten fish and chips earlier, I tucked into the sandwiches like I hadn't eaten for weeks. I wished we had sea air at the farm, maybe I'd be able to eat properly then. The odd thing was, I hadn't felt the slightest bit sick since we left home. Maybe it was the smell from the piggery?

After tea, Frank suggested that we go down for a few Saturday night drinks. He'd missed his Friday night session with the lads at The Old Bull, choosing to sit up late with me in front of the stove.

Friday night was bath night for me and I used to boil the copper and fill the bath whilst he was at the pub. This week he had to sit in his room as I bathed. When I had dried myself off and dressed, I tapped on the parlour door and asked if he wanted to use my bath water.

I went into the front room and sat with my father for twenty minutes as Frank bathed. When I heard him shout, I went back through to the kitchen to find him standing stark naked on the mat, rubbing his backside.

He turned around as he heard me enter, then cupped his hands over his private parts.

'Sorry,' I said, turning my head away. 'I heard you shout and thought you'd done.'

'I burnt my arse on the stove as I stood up,' he moaned. 'You'd have shouted too.'

I did my best not to laugh but it came out anyway. A few seconds later, Frank joined in.

I went back into the front room, my head still full of the vision of the naked man in my kitchen. Strangely, his manhood didn't look anywhere near the size it felt in the field on the night of my birthday. I knew all about erections, Amy and I had discussed them since we were young teens.

I put the disparity down to my drunken state and it being my first sexual encounter, but having witnessed his naked form for the first time, I couldn't help feeling rather disappointed.

I told Frank I'd come down for a couple, but I doubted I'd last the night out, what with the baby and the sea air. I was already yawning as we walked down the stairs to the bar.

I found a seat away from the door, and the icy blast it sent through the pub as another Saturday night drinker came in. Frank bought himself a pint and a double gin for me.

'No tonic water, they've run out,' he said.

'Run out?' I looked around the bar and its all-male clientele. 'Who the hell would drink tonic water in here?'

'There's a lounge area if you'd rather sit in there,' Frank said, as the door opened and the cigarette smoke swirled around the bar like a clearing morning fog.

We took our drinks and walked through the door marked 'Snug'. The air was cleaner in there and there was no outside door to let in the cold air. There was a young couple sitting at a table near the window and an older pair on the table next to the door. I nodded to everyone and took a seat opposite the older couple. When I took off my coat, both women had a good look at my swollen belly. The older woman smiled at me. The younger one, a couple of years older than me, looked scared. The men, having seen my chestnut curls and my pretty face as I walked in, looked disappointed.

Frank and I made small talk for half an hour, then he went to refill his glass. I refused his offer of a second drink, mostly because the gin was making me feel a little tipsy already, and it had rekindled the sickly feeling that had been absent all day.

Around eight-thirty my stomach had had enough of gin and was threatening to expel it.

I apologised to Frank, who really didn't seem to mind at all, and the two of us left the snug. The older woman smiled sympathetically at me.

'It'll be over soon,' she said.

Back in the bar, Frank made a show of kissing me on the cheek and wishing me a good night.

'I'll be up later, Sugarplum,' he said lovingly.

The men in the bar winked at each other and some of them, at me. I left the bar as quickly as I could and rushed up the stairs. I needed to pee and be sick and I didn't know which one was going to come first.

The toilet on the landing was old but clean and had a chain hanging from a wooden box above. On a hook on the wall were squares of cut up newspaper. I cringed. The toilet squares we used at the farm came in a box and although they weren't exactly silky, at least they were covered in aloe oil to make them softer. I refused to use the Izal paper that had been in use in my schooldays. It never mopped up moisture, it just seemed to move it around. You could cut yourself in half with the edge of it too.

Having said that. I'd have happily wiped myself with a few sheets of the much abused Izal rather than use the torn-up strips of yesterday's newspaper.

Thankfully, the nausea had abated and I returned to our room to retrieve the flannel and towel that I'd packed, before walking back to the, laughingly named, bathroom. I ran water from the hot tap until the Ascot kicked in, then I put the plug in the basin and half-filled the sink. There was a bar of soap in a dirty dish on the shelf next to the sink, so I lathered up the flannel and gave myself a strip wash, making sure I had totally removed yesterday's headlines from my lady parts.

Back in the room, I stripped to my undies, pulled on a flannelette nightie (not the ideal garment for a bride on her 'wedding' night), switched out the light and, by the glow of the streetlamp outside the window, made my way to the bed and slipped under the covers. Ten minutes later I was fast asleep.

I was woken a couple of hours later by the sound of men's laughing voices. I thought it was a dream at first but then I heard our room door close and the laughing became louder. I poked my head out from under the covers as the light came on. I blinked, shook my head and blinked again as four male faces blinked back at me.

'Here's the blushing bride,' slurred Frank.

'She's bloody gorgeous, mate, you ought to be in bed with her, not standing over her with us,' said a scrawny-looking man with thin, fair hair and bad teeth. He showed them off to me as he grinned.

'Evenin, Missis,' he said. He didn't appear to be quite as drunk as Frank, but he swayed as he spoke.

The other two were equally drunk, one touched the peak of his flat cap and the other just nodded. Suddenly their attention was elsewhere.

'Where's the beer gone? I'm parched,' said the fair man with the bad teeth.

'It's by the table there,' said Frank. He looked at me drunkenly. 'Go back to sleep,' he said.

The men wobbled off to the round table, dragged out the chairs and settled themselves down. Frank took bottles from the crate, whipped off the tops with an opener he carried on his keyring and passed them around.

'Right, where were we when that bitch turned off the taps?'

The man with the cap reached into his pocket and pulled out a handful of notes and coins. He deposited them in the centre of the table. The others leaned over and counted it. Satisfied that flat cap hadn't come up short with the stake, they pulled playing cards from their pockets and studied them intently.

'Your call, Charlie,' said Frank.

'Excuse, me?' I called from the bed. 'I'm trying to sleep.'

The men waved at me, one said 'sorry', then they went back to their game. When one of them spoke a little too loudly, the rest made shhhh-ing noises that were actually louder than his voice.

I ducked down under the covers again and tried to sleep.

About an hour later, I woke again. Someone had apparently told the world's funniest joke. The laughter was riotous. I sat up in bed again, thankful I had chosen the thick flannelette nightdress, although I still shivered.

'Haven't you got homes to go to?' I asked, quite reasonably.

Flat cap stood up.

'I have,' he said.

'Is that the time?' said the blond man.

The man called Charlie threw his cards on the table and began sorting the cash into four piles.

'What are you doing?' asked a distraught Frank.

'Game's over for the night,' said Charlie. 'I agree with your missis. We've outstayed our welcome. I'll get it in the neck from my old girl when I get in.'

The other two friends laughed and took back their share of the stake.

Frank sat, motionless, with a thunderous look on his face.

The men called goodnight to me, patted Frank sympathetically on the shoulder, and departed.

'How will they get out?' I asked Frank.

'That bitch Irene will let them out,' spat Frank. 'We paid her five bob to let us bring the game up here.'

'You shouldn't have done that, Frank,' I said quietly. 'I was in bed.'

'I fucking KNOW THAT!' Frank shouted, his face a seething mask of anger. He rushed across the room, bounced off the wall and came to a swaying halt at the side of the bed.

'YOU JUST COST ME TWENTY FUCKING QUID!' he yelled. 'TWENTY FUCKING QUID.'

'I heard you the first time,' I said. 'Now, please stop shouting before the landlady comes up.'

'FUCK THE LANDLADY,' he shouted. He swayed and steadied himself by putting a hand on the bed next to my hip. He glared at me. 'I'm not at work now,' he hissed. 'So, don't think you can tell me what to do.'

His chin dropped to his chest. 'Twenty, fucking quid,' he whispered.

'Will you shut up about the bloody card game,' I said. 'I'm tired and I want to go back to sleep.'

I turned away from him, but before I could get back under the covers, he grabbed me by the shoulders and swung me around. He pushed his face close to mine, the smell of warm beer assailed my nostrils. 'You need a sharp lesson in manners, my girl, and I'm just the man to give it.' He straightened up and pulled back his right hand. I screamed and threw myself across the bed as his fist came sweeping down, clipping my ear, before it crashed into the pillow. He pulled his arm back again and made ready for a second attempt.

'No, Frank,' I pleaded. 'Don't, please think about the baby.'

It was probably the only thing I could have said that stopped me receiving a black eye, or worse. Frank stood stark still, his arm still raised, then his head dropped to his chest and he began to weep.

'Frank,' I said. 'Get some sleep.' I tried to make light of it. 'We're on our honeymoon, remember?'

Frank continued to snuffle. He walked across the room and pulled our two overcoats from the hooks on the door. He placed one on the floor, lay on it, then covered himself with the other.

I thought about telling him to switch out the light, but as I needed to pee again, I got out of bed, picked up my still-damp flannel and revisited the toilet. When I returned, I picked up a spare pillow and tossed it onto the floor at the side of Frank's head. The gas streetlight was flickering like an empty Ronson cigarette lighter, so when I turned off the bedroom light, I had to gingerly tip-toe my way across the pitch-black room, to the bed.

Chapter 45

April 1938

Surprisingly, after the events of the early hours of Sunday morning, I slept quite well.

I woke up to find that Frank had returned the overcoats to the hooks on the door, which told me he hadn't done a runner at least. My bulging bladder forced me out of my warm bed, so I grabbed the flannel and towel and headed for the bathroom. When I came back, Frank was sitting at the table with our promised full English breakfast of sausage, bacon, two eggs, tomatoes, fried bread, toast and tea.

Had I been at home, I'd have been running for the lavatory again as the smell of the bacon hit my nasal passages, but here, it just made me hungry.

I didn't speak to Frank; I just dived in, cutting a chunk of sausage and dipping it into the soft yolk of one of the fried eggs. Frank poured me a cup of tea and I took a huge mouthful before attacking the bacon.

When we had finished eating, I belched and apologised out of habit. Frank nodded in acknowledgment and piled the empty plates and cups in the centre of the table.

'Last night,' he said.

I stood up, picked up my overnight bag and began to pull out the change of clothes I had brought with me. Frank had already changed into a clean shirt and a hand knitted, V-necked jumper. I waited for him to apologise. He didn't. Instead, he cleared his throat and said, 'It won't happen again.'

'You're damn right it won't,' I replied.

'It was the drink, I was tired, there was twenty quid on the—'

'Mention that blood twenty quid once more, Frank, and I swear it will be the last thing you ever say to me. I'm sick of hearing about it.'

Frank bridled, but then saw sense and bit his lip. 'Okay, I understand it must be getting boring by now. I won't mention it again.'

'Good,' I said, gathering up the bloomers and woollen knee length socks that had fallen to the floor. 'I'm going to get dressed. Will they give us more tea or do we have to pay for it?'

I had a strip wash in the freezing cold bathroom. The Ascot seemed to have given up the ghost and the water was tepid, at best. I got dressed quickly and returned to the room where Frank sat with a grin on his face.

'I couldn't find anyone to ask, so I made it myself. We finally got something for free.' He pulled half a dozen biscuits from his pocket. 'I found these too. I'll save them for the train.'

I folded up my dirty clothes and put them carefully into my case. Frank just stuffed his shirt and jumper into his bag before wrapping the stolen biscuits in a printed sheet of paper that lay on the shelf, informing us about the rules of the house. He placed the stolen treats carefully on top of his clothes and fastened the buckled straps.

Our train wasn't due until two o'clock, so we stayed where we were as long as possible. We sat at opposite ends of the room, me on the bed and Frank at the table. We didn't utter a word to each other.

The rules, that Frank had just packed into this bag, stated that customers must vacate their room by twelve PM so at three minutes to twelve, we got to our feet, checked we'd left nothing behind, and descended the stairs, Frank carrying my suitcase.

At one minute to twelve, we presented ourselves at the bar. Irene looked distinctly disappointed as we approached. She checked the clock twice, obviously hoping for it to magically jump forward by a couple of minutes.

'Can I help you?' she asked.

'Yes,' Frank replied. 'We'd like our five-bob deposit back please.'

'It's only refundable if there are no damages or complaints, and the rules of the house have been strictly adhered to,' she reminded us.

'There have been no complaints and there are no damages and we broke no rules that I can remember,' said Frank.

'What about all the shouting and screaming at one o'clock in the morning?' she said.

'There was no one else here to complain,' said Frank. 'We're the only customers.'

'Read the small print,' smirked Irene. 'Excess noise and the use of profanity, is a sub clause of Rule six.'

'Come on, be reasonable,' I said. 'It lasted all of five minutes. It was me on the receiving end of the profanity after all, and I'm not going to make a complaint. We spent a fair bit of money too. Frank virtually emptied a barrel of porter by himself, last night. We'd really like to come back again in the summer with our friends, but we can't really do that if you're going to be so mean.'

Irene sniffed and dipped into the pocket of her overall. She fished out four, shilling coins and a threepenny bit, and tossed them onto the counter.

'The deposit was five shillings,' said a puzzled Frank.

'You had extra tea, and took some biscuits from the tin on my shelf this morning,' she said smugly.

I pocketed the change and we left the pub with an air of injured dignity. Once outside, Frank shouted, 'We won't be back, HA!'

A shrill, raised voice from inside replied. 'We wouldn't have you back anyway.'

Laughing, we strolled slowly towards the station. The weather had taken a cool turn. The sky was the colour of slate, and spits and spots of rain hit us in the face in a squally wind.

We turned up our collars and ducked our heads into the wind as we walked. There was precious little shelter at the station. As it was Sunday, the only building open was the toilet block. We sat on a long, slatted, wooden bench and waited. Neither of us wanted to start a conversation in case the events of the night before came up, so we sat in a tense silence for the best part of an hour before boredom got the better of us.

'I spy with my little eye, something beginning with T,' said Frank.

'It isn't bloody train, that's for sure,' I said.

Frank laughed. 'No, it isn't train.'

I shivered in the cold breeze, cupped my hands and blew into them. 'Tracks?' I said, thinking it was an inspired answer.

'No, not tracks,' said Frank.

Sober, he was nothing if not a gentleman. Hesitantly, he wrapped an arm around my shoulder. I accepted the gesture gratefully, and snuggled in to his chest.

'Trousers,' I guessed, my face stared directly at them as I shivered again.

'No, not trousers,' he said.

I couldn't think of anything else, there were plenty of S's. Seat, signal box, sign, shoes, shivers, but no more things beginning with T, at least not that I could spot.

'Do you give in?' he asked.

'No,' I said, then two seconds later. 'Okay, yes, I give in. What was it?'

'Toilets,' he said.

'Toilets? You can't see the bloody toilets, they're behind you,' I said, more loudly than I meant to. The pensioner couple on the next seat looked at us quizzically.

'I looked around before I asked the question,' replied Frank.

I hit him in the chest. 'Oh, you cheat,' I said, and laughed along with him.

So, ice broken, we began talking about the farm and wondered how everyone had coped without us. It had never, to my knowledge at least, been left unsupervised before.

'Miriam won't take any nonsense. Not that I'm expecting there has been any,' I said.

'I bet Barney is clock watching,' said Frank. 'He'll be counting the minutes until you get back.'

'Why?' I asked. 'Barney can cope with any situation, work wise.'

'I know, but he'll be concerned about you, travelling all this way in your condition.'

'All this way? It's about thirty miles as the crow flies,' I scoffed.

'Yes, but to Barney, Sittingbourne is the other end of the country,' Frank replied. 'He's only been outside the town twice in all the time he's been alive, and both of those were visits to his father's house in the next village along.'

'You shouldn't laugh at him,' I scalded.

'I'm really not. That wasn't the point I was making.' He stretched his arm to ease a cramp, then wrapped it around me again. 'He thinks of you more as a daughter than anything else. He'll be worrying about you all the time you're away. Especially with a newcomer like me in tow. Anything could happen to you.'

I resisted the temptation to mention his drunken antics of the night before. 'He's a good man, Barney. I think a lot about him too. He's never once let my family down.'

'Nor will he,' said Frank. 'He's the best foreman you could ever get... apart from me of course, but that goes without saying.'

I twisted my neck to look up at his face. He was grinning.

'But you did say it,' I replied, 'so it doesn't count for anything.'

He laughed half-heartedly. 'I'll make foreman one day. Barney is in his late fifties now. He can't go on forever.'

I was about to tell him not to count on that, when we heard the tooting of the train as it made its approach.

The journey back was uneventful. As it was early Sunday afternoon, there were few passengers. The London based workers would get a later train, their truncated weekend at an end.

We arrived back at our local station to find Barney already parked up and waiting. He checked me over with his eyes before speaking.

'Welcome back, Missis, I hope you had a good holiday.'

'It was very nice, if brief,' I replied.

'The weather was decent enough too,' Frank added. 'Could you drop me at my mother's house please, Barney? She'll be expecting me to report in.'

Barney's eyes dropped to my left hand as I passed him my suitcase. He had seen the ring, I was sure of that, but he said nothing as he helped me onto the front seat of the truck. Frank pulled himself over the tailboard and found himself a seat on the oily tarp. He banged on the back of the cab, and Barney started the engine on the third attempt.

When we reached his mother's house, Frank climbed off the back of the truck and walked around to the side of the cab. I wound down my window.

'I'll be back later tonight, Alice. I just want to give my mother the good news.' He winked and turned away, walking briskly up the unevenly paved path, towards the gate where his mother was already waiting. I raised a hand to wave, but she turned away without acknowledging me.

Miriam, on the other hand, welcomed me like I'd been away for a month.

'Oh, it is good to see you got home safely, my dear. Your father's been his usual self... erm, there's nothing else to report. It's been very quiet here.'

She put the kettle onto the stove and tipped three spoons of loose tea into the tea pot.

I carted my case up to my room and unpacked it, leaving my used clothes on the chair in the corner.

When I returned to the kitchen, Miriam was making a sandwich.

'Have you eaten yet?' I asked.

'Not yet. I'll get something at home,' she said.

'Have half of that with me,' I replied. Miriam cut bread the thickness of railway sleepers, and as I was home again, that nauseous feeling was creeping back.

We sat and chatted about my day away while we ate and sipped tea. Miriam had already noticed the ring, but like Barney, she had said nothing. Her eyes kept looking across at it as I raised the cup to and from my lips.

'All right, Miriam,' I said, deciding to put her out of her misery. 'Frank and I were married at the registry office in Sheerness yesterday.' I held up my hand so she could get a good look. I hated having to lie to her but there was no real option.

She burst into a flood of tears.

'Oh, my darling girl, I'm so pleased for you. Frank did the decent thing in the end then? I wasn't sure he would and I wasn't sure you'd let him do it, if I'm honest. Shall I take his things up to your bedroom before he gets back?'

I was stumped. I hadn't thought about that. People would expect him to sleep with me if he was now my husband. I decided to think about it a bit more before I made up my mind.

'No, it's all right, Miriam, Frank can do it later. Maybe in a day or two, a week maybe. I've got to get used to the idea of being married first.'

Miriam looked at me with her head cocked to the side. I was certain she was going to ask about my wedding night, so I got to my feet, carried the dishes to the sink and changed the subject to something I'd been considering for ages.

'Do the kids visit you, Miriam?'

She seemed surprised by my question.

'They come when they can. They live miles away. They're all married with their own families, so they don't get much time.'

I knew she was making excuses for them. I'd caught her sniffling away to herself when she was in the kitchen, more than once. She always tried to put it down to her time of life, but I knew there was more to it than that.

'When was the last time you saw one of them?' I asked.

She was silent.

'Christmas? Last summer? Last New Year?'

Miriam held her hands, palms up. 'It's not easy for them, the buses are infrequent and they're not on the train routes.'

'How long, Miriam?'

Her face creased up and she began to sob. 'The... last time was... at my... my father's funeral.'

'Good God,' I said. 'That was ages ago, Miriam. You've been alone all that time, rattling about in that empty house?'

'It's not so bad,' she replied. 'I'm here a lot of the time.'

'Well, I think it's time you were here a lot more of the time,' I said. I got hold of both her hands and pulled her a little closer to me. 'Move in here, Miriam, we've got tons of room. You can have my father's old room. You'll never be alone here.'

Miriam burst into tears again. 'I couldn't, I mean, could I afford to, what sort of board and lodgings would I pay? I get the house rent free thanks to the generosity of your father.'

'You won't pay anything, and you'll get your food included.'

'I don't want to burden you like that,' she sniffed.

'Miriam, believe me, you'll earn it. First there's my father, he's getting more and more needy. Then there's the job you do here already.' I put my hands on my swollen stomach. 'Then, of course, there's the small matter of the new arrival, who will need your expertise when I bring it home. I have my work on the farm, I'll need a nanny, and I can't think of a better qualified one. You've looked after five already.'

Miriam did a little jig. 'Oooh, a baby to look after. I've not held one since our Rebecca was little.' She grabbed hold of me in a squeeze so tight that it nearly forced the baby out of me, there and then.

'Move in whenever you're ready,' I gasped. 'That bed will need airing though.'

And so it was agreed, Miriam was coming to live with us, Frank had already moved in. When the new baby arrived, the house would seem almost overcrowded. That was a bonus as far as I could see it. I used to feel so alone at times and now I'd have another woman to talk to in the evening, especially on bath night when Frank was at the pub. Miriam was an Agatha fan, like me. Two against one on the Monday night sleuthing.

As another plus, we now had a very nice three-bedroom cottage to rent out. I toyed with the idea of letting Barney have it, but he was settled where he was, and he would just see it as charity anyway. I could probably have persuaded him, but it would have been a long hard fight.

I decided to get in touch with the local newspaper and advertise the cottage. That meant a trip to town. I might also drop in on a solicitor if I could find one. I wanted to get my head around how a trust fund worked and whether I could get the farm added to one. I also needed to get my name changed before the baby was born. That was a must.

Lying in bed that night I made an executive decision. All the running backwards and forwards to town would soon become a real nuisance and I didn't want Frank getting wind of what I was doing, so I decided to get our farm put onto the local telephone network. We could afford it now, and after all, the two farms closest to us had had one for a couple of years. It made complete sense. The bloody council officials could telephone us instead of coming out to moan about the state of our yard and I could order stuff from the seed catalogue and farm suppliers without having to post order forms that took a couple of weeks to fulfil.

I heard Frank come in about midnight. He wasn't singing and he wasn't stumbling around the kitchen so I knew he hadn't been to the pub after his mother's.

He called goodnight to me before he went to bed. I didn't reply.

Chapter 46

Jess

Alice had only just settled back into her cushions to continue with her story, when her chest was convulsed by a fit of coughing. Jess was at her side in an instant, but no amount of rubbing, or patting her back, helped. She hurried to the kitchen, ran water into a glass and brought it back to the lounge. The coughing gradually subsided but Alice's breathing was irregular. Every few seconds she would tilt her head back and take three or four short breaths, but as soon as her lungs were partly filled with air, the awful, rasping, wheezing, noise returned.

Jess put the glass of water to her lips, and Alice sipped at it, gratefully. Another coughing fit followed, not quite as violent as the first, but it left her distressed, ashen-faced and struggling to get enough oxygen into her lungs.

Jess continued to rub Alice's back and give her occasional sips of water until she was able to breathe more easily.

'I'll call the doctor, Nana, his number is by the phone isn't it?'

Alice laid her right hand flat and waved it across her chest.

'But you need to see him, Nana. That cough was awful. You might have an infection of some kind.'

Alice shook her head. 'I'll be fine,' she spluttered, and began to cough again.

Jess rushed to the bathroom and came back with a bottle of cough linctus and a double ended medicine spoon. She measured out five mm into the larger end. Alice swallowed the syrup and leaned back into her cushion.

'I... really, don't feel-too-well,' she said. Her voice was weak, not much more than a whisper.

'Let me help you to bed, Nana, you're better off in there.'

Jess moved Alice's walking frame to the side, then she stood in front of her armchair, took hold of her hands, and stepped backwards, pulling Alice to her feet. When she was steady, Jess moved the walker in front of her and they made their way over to the bed.

At the bedside, Jess helped Alice remove her shoes and cardigan, then she pulled back the sheets, and eased her into bed.

Alice seemed to shrink into the pillows. Jess was amazed at how much her condition had deteriorated over the last twenty-four hours. Her face was ashen; she was still struggling to breathe properly, her eyes, usually so bright, now seemed grey and cloudy. Jess was dismayed. Why hadn't she noticed? Had she been more concerned with her own problems? with the story? Was this just what happened when you were close to the end? Maybe it was. Maybe the decline sped up dramatically over the last few hours. Jess gave herself a mental slap.

Pull yourself together, Jessica. Let's hear what the doctor has to say before you allow panic to set in.

She shook her head to clear her thoughts. 'I'll call the doctor now, Nana. No arguments please, he's coming out to see you and that's that.' She pulled her mobile from the pocket of her jeans and looked up the surgery number on Alice's emergency contact list.

After making the call, she sat by Alice's bedside, took hold of her hand and gently stroked it.

'The doctor will call round later today, Nana. He's in surgery at the moment and now that your breathing has settled down a bit, I didn't bother the emergency services.' Jess checked her phone for messages from Calvin, but there were none. She thought she had better let him know what was happening in case she got back late, so she sent him a text.

Nana's very poorly. Sitting with her while we wait for the doctor. Will let you know when I'm setting off for home. Xxxx

Jess slipped her phone back into the pocket of her jeans and settled on her seat. 'Would you like me to read from your novel, Nana?' she asked.

Alice shook her head. 'It's not...that...good, really.' She lifted her head from the pillows and pushed herself up onto her elbows. 'Jess...ica... my, stor...y.'

184

'Don't worry about it just now, Nana,' said Jess. 'There'll be plenty of time for that later.' She crossed her fingers and sent up a silent prayer that Alice would recover.

'Upstairs in... the... attic.'

'In the attic?' Jess looked puzzled.

'In the... cor...ner, past... the Dormer.'

'What's in the attic, Nana?'

'My story... all of it.' Alice took a wheezy breath, the air seemed to rattle about in her lungs.

'You kept diaries?' asked Jess. 'Oh, Nana, that's wonderful.'

'Not diaries. Memoirs,' Alice croaked. 'In box...files.' She began to cough again, but it was nothing like the earlier coughing fit. When she had recovered, Jess gave her another sip of water.

Alice took several gasping breaths, then pointed at the ceiling. 'In the... attic... nineteen thirty-seven... to...thir...ty...nine...just that...box... for now.'

Jess wondered what the urgency was. She could get the files down any time. 'I'll get them when I come back tomorrow, Nana.'

'Now...Jes...sica.' Alice was determined. She pointed to the ceiling again. 'In the cor...ner, past the...Dor...mer.'

Jess stood up. Alice was becoming stressed, and that wouldn't help with her breathing. 'All right, Nana, I'll get them now. I'll be back in a few minutes.'

Alice sank back into the pillows and once again, pointed upwards. 'Be...careful... lots of junk...'

Jess smiled. 'I'll be careful, Nana.'

As she turned away, she heard the front door open and a few seconds later, Gwen appeared.

'I was at a loose end, so I thought I'd just look in to see if there's anything that needs doing.' She suddenly noticed the white-faced figure of Alice propped up in her bed. 'Oh, my goodness, whatever's the matter?' She pulled off her coat, dropped it on the floor, and rushed to Alice's side.

'She's a little bit better than she was a short while ago. I've rung for the doctor; he's coming out later today. Can you sit with her for a few minutes, Gwen, I've been ordered to bring something down from the attic.'

Jess hurried across the lounge, feeling a mixture of nervousness and excitement. She had never been up to the attic before. When she was a child, sleeping over or staying for a week's holiday, the big white door leading to it had always been locked. She used to wonder what secrets were hidden up there. Now, she would find out.

Chapter 47

Jess

Jess climbed the stairs until she got to the first-floor landing, then she turned left, passed the room where she used to sleep when she stayed over as a child, turned right at the end of the corridor and opened the flaking, white painted door. She had never been in the attic before. She remembered her grandmother's stories about witches and demons as she began to climb. There was another, unpainted door at the top of the stairs. Jess hesitated before taking hold of the handle. Her heart was racing.

Come on, Jess, it's an attic, what could possibly be hiding in there?

She took a deep breath, turned the handle and pushed the door. It opened with a long, whining creak.

Oh my God. Why wasn't I expecting that? Get a grip of yourself, Jess, you've written ghost stories for pity's sake.

The light from inside came from the double, four-pane, Dormer window that had been built into the roof, way back in time. Jess stretched her neck to look what lay behind the door frame. As far as she could make out, the room was filled with old tea chests, thick cardboard boxes and dusty piles of old curtains and bedding.

Alice had said the box she wanted would be found in the corner, to the right of the Dormer. Jess took a deep breath, summoned up all of her courage, and stepped smartly into the room.

She stepped around the tea chest that sat in lonely isolation about three feet away from the doorway, and weaved around a maze of cardboard boxes containing crumpled newspapers, wrapped around what she assumed, from the shapes, were various items of crockery. Jess didn't bother to investigate them. As she passed the Dormer, she picked up a movement out of the corner of her eye. She looked across the attic to see a dusty, cobweb-covered mirror. Jess came to a halt and stared at the reflection that struggled to find its way past the dirt and grime. Staring back at her, was a young woman, little more than a teenager, her hair was light, almost flax coloured, and was swept back over her ears and rolled at the nape of her neck in a very similar style to Alice's. Her pretty face was heart shaped, her lips full, layered with raspberry red lipstick and her eyes were a deep shade of blue. As Jess leaned forward, she smiled. It was a warm smile, a smile that made her feel she should smile back. She took a step closer and the image began to fade. Jess hesitated, hoping that the friendly face would return, but when she reached out her hands to part the blanket of spider silk, only her own, familiar features were visible. Jess backed off to the Dormer and stared again into the murky mirror, hoping for another glimpse of the beautiful young girl, but whoever it was, had returned from whence she came.

'Pull yourself together, Jess,' she muttered. 'You're letting the place get to you.'

She picked up an old towel and wiped the cobweb residue from her hands, and after a quick look through the Dormer out over the old farm yard, she made her way to the right-hand corner of the loft.

Stacked on top of a badly splintered tea chest was a stack of old, brown-fronted, box files. Jess picked up the top one from the uneven stack, brushed the dust from the lid and used the torch from her phone to light up the gloomy corner. On the cover was a discoloured label; once white, it now sported a dingy, yellowy tinge. Written across it in a neat script were the words: Alice Mollison. Personal Memoir. 1943-1945.

Fighting back the urge to sit down and read, Jess took the next box off the stack. The label read: Alice Mollison. Personal Memoir. 1940-1942.

Jess sorted through the remaining boxes until she found the one Alice had asked her to retrieve.

Alice Mollison. Personal Memoir. 1937-1939.

The other boxes in the stack were labelled: Receipts, Farm Accounts, and Legal Papers, for all the given years. Jess decided to return at a later date, to collect the whole stack of boxes. There was a treasure trove of family history inside them.

She tucked the box file under her arm, made her way back through the maze of crates, boxes and fabric, and back down to the lounge.

Gwen was trying to persuade Alice to eat a little home-made broth, but she just turned her head away as the spoon neared her mouth.

'Leave the broth on the hob, Gwen,' said Jess. 'I'll see if I can persuade her to have some later on.'

'She's had nothing all day,' replied Gwen. 'No wonder she's got no strength left.'

As she passed Jess on her way to the kitchen, she whispered, 'I think she's given up.' She pulled a hanky from her pocket and dabbed at her eyes. Jess put a comforting hand on her shoulder.

'She's still with us and you never know, Gwen, her condition could improve. She's bound to have good days and bad days at her age. Keep the faith, she might surprise you yet.'

Gwen nodded her head repeatedly. 'You're right, we should never give up hope. I suppose we'll know more when the doctor gets here.'

As Gwen carried the bowl of broth carefully back to the kitchen, Jess pulled up a chair next to Alice's bed and sat down.

'I think I got the right one, Nana,' she said, lifting up the dusty old box file so that Alice could see it.

Alice tried to pull herself up into her pillows, but the effort was too great, and she sank back with a deep sigh. Her breathing had worsened since the morning. When she spoke, the words were broken and came between gasps for air.

'Look... in...side, Jessica. Just... che...ck.'

Jess lifted the lid slowly in case the file had suffered damage over the years. Inside were three volumes of foolscap notebooks. She lifted them out carefully, checking each one in turn, then she put the box on the floor and stacked the three volumes on her knee. She opened the volume for 1937 first and skimmed through the neatly-written pages, stopping to read a paragraph here and there.

'Nineteen thirty-seven. I think we've covered that one, Nana, but I'll read it properly when I get the time, to see if there's anything we've missed.'

'There's... nothing, impor...tant that I haven't al...ready told you in... that one.' Alice made a circular motion with her hand, encouraging Jess to move on.

'Okay. This one is nineteen thirty-eight, which is the year you had Martha. Is that the year you want me to concentrate on for now?'

Alice nodded. 'Give... me... the one for... nine...teen... thirty-nine.'

Jess passed her the volume, but Alice didn't have the strength to hold it, and the book slid off the bed and landed on Jess's foot. She picked it up and offered it to Alice again.

'Put... it... in... the dra...wer,' she stuttered between gulps of air. 'You don't... need... that... one, yet.'

Jess opened the draw and slipped the notebook inside.

'I'll catch up on nineteen thirty-eight this afternoon, Nana. You have a rest now. The doctor will be here soon.'

'Talk... to... me... Jess...ica... I don't want t...to sleep.'

'Shall I read from the memoir?' asked Jessica.

Alice nodded.

'Let me just get a cup of tea first, Nana, my throat is so dry after being in that dusty attic.'

As Jess got to her feet, the notebook slipped from her knee and fell to the carpet. When she picked it up, three photographs slid out from inside the back cover. The first was a picture of Alice holding a baby she assumed was Martha. The second was of a group of farm workers standing in front of a ramshackle barn. The third was of a young girl with fair hair and a heart shaped face.

'Who's this, Nana?' she asked.

Alice took the photograph in her shaking hand and held it up to her face. She smiled and her eyes became wet with a teary film. 'That's... my Amy,' she said.

Jess's mouth gaped. 'I've just seen her, Nana.'

'I... doubt... it... Jess...ica. Amy... died twenty years ago.'

'It was her, Nana. She was staring at me from the mirror in the attic. She smiled when I looked closer. It was definitely her.'

Alice kissed the photograph and held it to her bosom. 'So, she's... watch...ing over, you... too... Jessica. That... comforts... me.'

Ten minutes later, Jess set her steaming cup of tea on the bedside table, picked up the memoir, searched for the April chapters, and began to read.

Chapter 48

April 1938

On Monday, after I had finished in the piggery, I sat down to think about how to get in touch with the Post Office telephone department. I was going to call in at the next farm along to ask how they had gone about it, but in the end, I decided that I'd enquire at the Post Office in town. Knowing the way bureaucracy worked, I was sure it would entail filling in a form.

I had a wash in the sink to get rid of the piggery smell that used to stick to me like a coat of glue, put on my best coat, a pair of flat shoes, and walked at a brisk pace up to the town. Barney had taken the truck out to pick up a supply of ammonium sulphate fertiliser for the middle acre. Amy was at work at the mill, which was probably a good job, because a ten-minute chat with her could last for hours.

The Post Office official was very efficient and handed me the correct form which I filled in there and then. She told me that my request would almost certainly be granted, and because the two farms either side of ours already had telephones, the cabling would already be in place. Therefore, I should have my own telephone installed and connected to the system by the end of the week.

True to their word, on Friday morning, two Post Office engineers arrived and began the installation. Their names were Reg and Jack. Jack seemed to be the senior of the pair as he spent his time in the house, unpacking the internal equipment and finding the best position for the junction box to be placed.

Initially, I wanted it installing in the kitchen but Jack said that would be more expensive as the cable would have to be run all the way around to the back of the house. There was also the issue of steam getting into the wires. I wasn't sure about that, as we had electric lights and power sockets all over the kitchen and we had never had a problem with steam. I began to think that Jack was hoping for an easy installation so that he could get an early lunch. However, when he told me that if the box was installed in the front room, facing the lane, we could be on the network within an hour, I was instantly on board. I was so excited about getting the thing put in, I'd have agreed to have it in the outside lavvy.

An hour later, Reg joined Jack in the lounge and the telephone was ceremoniously connected to the junction box. The telephone itself was black, with a pyramid shaped body and a cradle on top that held the transceiver, which was the posh name for the bit you picked up to listen and speak with. On the pyramid was a rotary dial that contained both numbers and letters.

Jack informed us, proudly, that our newly installed telephone was a Bell system, model number 204. At the centre of the dial was our very own, three-digit, telephone number (in case we forgot it) and a 999 prompt which we would only ever dial to connect to the brand-new emergency service. Handy if we needed the police or an ambulance.

Most of this information went over my head, so I was glad when Miriam came in to see to my father. I asked Jack to go over it all again, so she could hear it too.

Thankfully, the telephone came with a directory containing the names, addresses and telephone numbers of every household that was connected to the network. In the front of the directory was a section that explained to the user, everything that Jack had just told us. I opened the thin book and searched for my name and address, but I wasn't listed although the farms either side of us were there.

'I can't see my name in here,' I said to Jack.

'That's because you've only been on the system for two minutes,' he replied, looking at me as though I had a screw loose. 'You'll be in the next edition; they update them every so often. Until then you'll need to tell people what your number is.'

I gave the engineers a shilling each, they touched their navy caps and returned to their Post Office van.

For the next hour, Miriam and I sat and watched the telephone, waiting for our first call. I picked up the transceiver thingy from the cradle twice, to see if I could hear a voice, but all I got was a buzzing noise. I was about to go to the Post Office to complain that the bloody useless thing wasn't working, when Miriam, who had more patience than me, read out a couple of lines from the front of the directory, explaining what a dial tone was.

Twenty minutes later we realised that no one was going to call us, so we went back to the kitchen. I decided to walk around the town in the afternoon and give the number to everyone we knew.

I wrote Spinton 134 out twelve times on a sheet of notepaper and tore the list into strips for the farm workers. None of them had a telephone, nor would most ever possess one, but we thought if they ever had a problem, they could walk to the Post Office kiosk near The Old Bull and let us know.

Later that afternoon, I walked up the lane to Farrow's Farm and told Iris Farrow that I was now on the telephone network. She eyed me with a look of distaste, said she'd save my pregnant legs and ring Mrs Cooper at the farm below us, and give them my new number.

'Ring any time,' I said, hoping she'd take the hint and give us our first call.

Iris nodded, said 'Good Afternoon' and with one last look at my bulging waistline, closed the door.

I dropped in at The Old Bull and gave the number to the landlord who was still providing my father with a bottle of whisky a day, down from the two per day he had been sending us until recently.

'How is he?' he asked.

'Dying,' I said, bluntly.

I stopped off at the greengrocer, who bought fresh veg from us at certain times of the year, the newsagent/tobacconist, the pharmacy, because I knew Geraldine who worked there and the Co-op where we bought our own food supplies.

When I reached The Old Bull on my way back, I decided to drop in on Frank's mother and give her our new number in case she ever needed to reach Frank in an emergency. She was only about fifty yards away from the Post Office telephone kiosk, so she could ring for a chat in the evenings if she felt like it.

I walked briskly up her front path, opened the wrought iron gate and knocked softly on her back door. She must have been in the kitchen because the door opened almost immediately. I took a deep breath and opened my mouth to greet her, but before I could get a word out, she stuck her head out of the doorway, checked the road to see if anyone was looking then, grabbing me by the front of my coat, she pulled me inside.

We looked at each other for a full minute before I broke the ice.

'Hello, Mrs Mollison, I'm—'

'I know who you are, Girl, the important thing is, what do you want?'

I ignored her hostile tone and spoke in what I hoped was a confident, but friendly voice.

'I just dropped by to give you our new telephone number. In case you ever need to get in touch with Frank. Call any time, if you want a chat, or if anything important comes up.'

She picked up a scrap of paper with a partly written shopping list on it, and a pencil.

'Well?'

'Spinton 134,' I replied and turned back towards the door. 'Sorry to have bothered you.'

'Wait,' she said. 'You shouldn't be rushing about in your condition.' She pointed to an open door that led to her living room. 'Go through and sit down. I'll make us a pot of tea.'

I wasn't sure where she meant me to sit, so I stood on the mat in front of the fireplace until she returned. She waved me to the sofa, then put the tea tray on the coffee table and sat down in an armchair opposite me. I expected her to say something like, *what do you have to say for yourself?* But she didn't.

'He's done the right thing by you then?'

I showed her my ring finger.

'Yes, we got married on Saturday.' I looked at my hands, trying to avoid her keen eyes.

'I have always looked forward to going to my son's wedding. Getting to know his bride beforehand. Help plan the wedding, the usual stuff.'

'I'm sorry about that,' I said, 'but there really wasn't time and... well, it would have been embarrassing for you anyway.'

'I'd still like to have been there, and I wouldn't have been embarrassed in the slightest.'

She poured tea into two delicate, china cups sat on matching saucers, added milk and passed one to me. 'I don't have any sugar,' she said.

I held onto the saucer with both hands, terrified of dropping it and trying to stop the cup rattling in my nervous hands.

She sipped her tea and swilled it around her mouth like a wine taster. 'I don't know how much Frank has told you, but... well, let's just say your situation isn't unfamiliar to me. The only difference is, Frank lived up to his responsibilities. His father, didn't.'

I decided not to let on how much I knew, and stared down at my unsampled, tea.

'How are you getting on together, Alice? I've only heard Frank's thoughts, and men don't see things like we do. All I got out of him was, *we get on fine.*'

'We get on quite well to say we haven't known each other long. I only met him the night... I mean, he was away for a while and he's only been on the farm a couple of months, so... we get on well enough,' I finished, lamely.

'You won't know him that much better in a year's time,' she replied with feeling. 'He's a man, and men never reveal much of themselves to anyone, not even to themselves.'

'I don't know much about men, Mrs Mollison, only what my best friend Amy and I learned from the boys at school, and from the novels we read.'

'Of course you don't, you're not much more than a child.' She thought for a while, her brow furrowed. 'Call me Edna,' she said, eventually.

I smiled at her. 'Edna,' I repeated.

'Seeing as I missed the wedding, and all the fun of helping to organise the reception, can I at least help out with the Christening celebrations? Maybe I could knit a little suit for the baby when it arrives. I can crochet too. What if I made a Christening shawl? I could do it in white, so that would be all right for a boy or a girl.'

I wasn't actually planning on having a Christening, but I didn't want to upset Edna after she had been so kind to me. I told her it was a lovely idea, and I'd let her know well before the ceremony so she could help organise it.

'Your mother is dead, isn't she?'

I nodded. 'She died last year. My father has never got over it.'

'Well, Alice, my dear. I'm not trying to replace her or anything, no one could do that. But, if you need any advice regarding the baby, before, or after the birth, then just ask. I'll be happy to help in any way I can.' She leaned forward and reached towards my bump. I just sat there, not knowing how to react.

She retracted her hand immediately. 'I'm sorry. I was just having a grandmother moment. The little one will have two grandparents at least.'

I thought about my father, the prospective grandfather. I doubted my child would ever get to know him well, if at all.

The wooden-framed mantle clock with its Westminster chime, struck five, and I got to my feet.

'It's been lovely meeting you at last, Edna. Give me a call sometime and we can have a chat about the baby. I'll bring it up to see you regularly... Or you can drop in on us... I'd better go now; my friend Amy will be home from work and I need to ask her something.'

Edna saw me out to the gate. As I opened it, she tapped me on the shoulder.

'Women never get anything but misery from men in drink.'

I walked the short distance to Amy's house, wondering why she had given me that particular piece of advice. I knew what drink could do to men. I only had to look at my father. Then there was Frank, I had only seen him drunk twice and both times I ended up in trouble. Was it a warning about men in general, or just her son?

Amy was as excited as I was about my new telephone system and demanded to be the first to call me on it. I insisted on giving her the tuppence the call would cost at the kiosk, and hurried back to the farm.

I had just walked into the front room, when the telephone rang. As I rushed forward to pick up the receiver, my father leapt out of his seat with amazing agility for a man in his condition. He ran through to the kitchen shouting, *FIRE!*

It took Miriam a full ten minutes to convince him that the house wasn't ablaze and there wasn't a fire engine waiting outside to put it out.

Meanwhile I picked up the receiver.

'Hello,' I said, in my poshest voice, trying desperately to remember the greeting suggested in the telephone directory. 'This is Spinton 134. Alice speaking.'

'I already know who you are,' shouted Amy.

I laughed. 'Don't shout, my ears are ringing.'

We spent the next few minutes discussing the merits of the new telephone, then I heard a series of quick beeps before Amy's voice came through again.

'The tuppence ran out, I had to put some more money in.'

'Don't spend any more,' I said. 'I'll come up for a chat in a bit.'

So, a few minutes later I walked back up to Amy's and we spent an hour reliving our telephone chat, playing records and chatting about my weekend away.

I showed Amy my wedding ring and told her most of what happened in Sheerness. I left out the bit about Frank's drunken attack. She would have hit him with something hard and heavy, had she known. She wasn't all that pleased when I told her the truth about still being single, but she accepted it and said she'd keep my secret until the day she died.

'At least he wanted to do the right thing by you, so he can't be all bad,' she said.

She was more than a little interested in hearing about my meeting with Edna. 'So, she wasn't the wicked witch you thought she might be?'

'She was a bit prickly to start with, but she was lovely after that. She wants to make a Christening shawl.'

'Christening! You in a church?' Amy was stunned, I'd only ever been inside one once, apart from the compulsory school visits. That was for my mother's funeral. Amy had to continually nudge me to keep me awake. Apparently, our vicar loves a long drawn-out send off.

When I got back home, Frank was at the kitchen table and Miriam was preparing to dish up the rabbit stew she'd made that afternoon. My stomach churned at the thought of it, so I excused myself and went to watch the telephone for half an hour.

After dinner, the three of us sat around the radio to see if we could work out who had done it this week. I articulated my thoughts while we waited to hear the detective's reply. Miriam didn't agree, nor did Frank. In the end, Miriam was proved right. It had been the maid. Frank complained that the scriptwriters must all be women, and Agatha Christie readers. I offered to let him borrow one of my books again, but as usual, he refused.

At nine o'clock, I bid them goodnight, and went up to bed. I had only just slipped between the sheets when there was a tap on the door.

'Yes?'

'It's me,' said Frank. 'I... err... wondered if I should bring my stuff up. Miriam wasn't sure.'

I thought about it for just a few moments. There didn't seem much point putting it off. I'd met his mother after all. I decided that it was time to play the married woman.

'Come in, Frank,' I said.

He stepped inside clutching his bag in front of him like a shield.

'Where would you like me to...'

I pulled back the covers on the empty side of the bed.

'In you get, but hurry up, I'm bloody freezing.'

He stripped to his long underpants and slipped in beside me. I asked him to turn over, so that his back was facing me, then I put my arm around his waist, snuggled my bump up against him and my knees into the back of his. I don't know why, but somehow, it felt right.

Chapter 49

April 1938

On Tuesday morning I sat in the front room with the new telephone directory on my lap and a cup of tea on the table at my elbow.

My father was in his chair as usual, snoring quietly. I couldn't see him lasting much longer. His clothes, that were once stretched across broad shoulders, now hung over his bones as if he was trying to hide in them. His hair and beard were long and unkempt. Miriam had tried to get a comb through it on numerous occasions but had given up when he began to wriggle about holding his hands to his head. The scarecrow in the top acre looked more human.

Most pages of the directory contained advertisements for local and, on occasion, national businesses. Some were in small, bold print running across the last two lines of the page. Others took up an eighth, a quarter, half, or even a whole page. The advertisements did look very professional, I wondered whether we ought to advertise our milk in it.

I flicked through the directory until I found a quarter page advert for Wilson, Kendall and Beanney, a firm of solicitors, whose offices were in Armskirk, which was only about five miles away.

I immediately thought of the comedy trio, Wilson, Keppel and Betty, who I had seen on the cinema screen performing the Egyptian sand dance. Still smiling, I picked up the transceiver and made my first telephone call.

I almost leapt out of my seat when the intermittent buzzing was replaced by a woman's voice.

'Wilson, Kendall and Beanney, solicitors, how may I help you?'

I forgot all about using my posh voice.

'Could I speak to Mr Keppel... I mean Betty, please?' I stammered.

'I'm sorry?' the obviously confused receptionist replied.

I wracked my brains trying to remember the names. 'Erm, a solicitor, it doesn't matter which one.'

'Mr Wilson is in his office, one moment and I'll put you through. Who shall I say is calling?'

'Alice M... Tansley,' I replied, almost giving her the surname I wanted my own name changing to.

'Mrs Alice M. Tansley,' the receptionist replied. 'Putting you through now.'

Her voice was replaced by more of the infernal buzzing, then a man came on the line.

'Good morning, Mrs Tansley, this is Godfrey Wilson, how may I assist you?'

'Erm, I err... well, I'm not Mrs Tansley, I'm Miss, but I'd like to talk to you about becoming Mrs Mollison.'

'You want advice on getting married? I don't think I—'

'No,' I interrupted. 'I'd like to change my name to Alice Mollison without getting married.'

'Ah, I see.' Mr Wilson cleared his throat. 'You want to change your surname by Deed of Name Change?'

'If that's the same as Deed Poll, then yes, that's exactly what I'd like to do.' I took a breath. 'I would also like advice on how I would go about putting our family farm into a trust, so that no one from outside of the immediate Tansley family would ever be able to take it away from us. Even if my name is Mollison by then.'

'We do provide that service. May I ask, does the farm belong to you?'

'My father is still alive, but I don't think he'll last for much longer,' I replied. 'This has to be done quite soon. The name change, especially.'

'Could you pop in for a longer chat, Miss, err, Tansley, isn't it?'

'Could you come to me instead?' I asked. 'I have the piggery to clean out this morning, and the slaughter house men are coming later. Then I have a crop planting meeting with my foreman this afternoon.'

'Oh, it won't be today, Miss Tansley, let me just check my diary.'

The line went quiet for a short time.

'Mrs... I mean, Miss Tansley... I can spare an hour or so tomorrow afternoon. Could you give my receptionist your address and telephone number? She'll ring you in the morning to confirm the appointment.'

Mr Wilson was replaced by a series of buzzes again, then the receptionist came back on the line. I gave her my details and waited for her to jot them down, but apparently, she had done it while I was talking.

'Mr Wilson will be with you at two PM tomorrow afternoon. Goodbye, thank you for calling Wilson, Kendall and Beanney.'

'You're very welcome,' I said to the dial tone.

By Wednesday lunchtime I had finished with the piggery, and dealing with the men the abattoir sent a day late, to pick up the latest lorryload of pigs that were the right size and weight for slaughter. I always felt a tinge of remorse when the time came for them to go. I understood the ways of the farming world but I always felt a real sadness inside whenever the bullocks and lambs went, but seeing the pigs driven away, always left me with a heavy heart.

The eighty sows we kept gave birth twice a year, and each one produced around twenty piglets during that time, so they were an integral part of the finances of the farm. The new pig shelter we had built would pay for itself by September when the first of the new sows would give birth.

I stripped down to my underwear and had a wash in the sink as there wasn't time to boil the copper for a bath. I couldn't really plan my future with a solicitor, stinking of pig shit.

As I stood at the sink, washing myself in the cold water from the tap, I happened to look across to the parlour, one wall of which backed onto the outside toilet. I suddenly had the brilliant idea of bringing that toilet indoors and maybe putting a porcelain bath in there too. Now that Frank wasn't sleeping in there anymore, it would hardly be used, and although it would mean installing a boiler of some kind, the thought of not having to sit in a tin bath in a draughty kitchen in winter, made whatever the cost might be, seem like a bargain.

I decided to call the local building firm I had seen advertised in the directory, to get a quote.

I dumped my dirty farm clothes on a seat next to the kitchen table and waddled upstairs to get changed into my newly altered trousers and one of my father's old woollen jumpers that hung on me like a sack. I came back downstairs just as the clock struck two.

Mr Wilson was a good-looking man with a medium build, dark hair and Clarke Gable moustache. He wore a dark blue pinstriped suit, with a white, spearpoint collar shirt, a navy coloured silk tie, black brogue shoes and a dark grey Homburg hat. He reminded me of a gangster in one of the James Cagney films. He carried a wide, tan briefcase.

He took off his hat as he stepped through the front door. My father stared at the wall and said nothing.

I led him across the room to a round table where he deposited his briefcase, offered his hand and a friendly smile. He also noticed my bump.

'Congratulations,' he said, nodding to my stomach as I shook his hand. 'How long before the little one is with us?'

'Early June,' I replied.

'A summer baby, the best time of the year to be born, or so I'm told.'

I waved a hand in the general direction of a chair, but Mr Wilson waited for me to sit first.

'So,' he said, opening his briefcase. 'Let's get this business started.' He produced a few pages of headed notepaper and a beautiful fountain pen that my mother would have killed for. He unscrewed the top and began to write, talking to himself as he went along.

I didn't understand half of the words he spoke as he wrote, but I did pick up, Deed of Name Change, which was what he had talked about on the telephone the day before. When he had finished questioning me and writing out the legalise, he asked me to provide my birth certificate and my parent's marriage certificate. I retrieved them from the tallboy drawer in the kitchen where we kept all our important papers.

He read the proofs of identity carefully, made a few notes, asked me to confirm my age and date of birth and then asked me to sign the document. He signed it himself before folding the certificates up in the sheet of paper he had been working on, and dropped it into his briefcase.

'This application will now go before a judge to authorise and countersign. Once that is done you will legally be known as Alice Mollison and the name change will be published in the London Gazette.'

'Published in the papers!' I repeated with alarm. 'Not our local one, surely?'

'The London Gazette is a newspaper published by the government,' Mr Wilson explained. Amongst other things, it lists new companies that have been formed, the names of newly appointed Lords and Ladies, or any other award granted by the King or Parliament. It also lists changes of name by any member of the public who has done what you are about to do. To be honest, I really can't see anyone around here getting it pushed through the letterbox by the paperboy. I have a regular copy delivered, but I need to have it for the business, and to make sure they've spelt your name correctly.'

When he smiled at me my knees went weak. He really was a handsome man.

'And now, we come to the matter of the legal trust,' he said.

Mr Wilson spent the next half hour explaining to me how a trust worked. Who could have one, who controlled it, how money was dispersed via the trust, and a lot more legal stuff that I couldn't remember ten seconds after I heard it.

Basically, I could set up the trust, but it would need my father's consent. The trust would need three trustees, one of which would be Mr Wilson himself, acting on behalf of his law firm. I couldn't be a trustee until I reached my majority at twenty-one, but the other trustees could act at my behest providing the actions stipulated, were both reasonable and legal. At twenty-one, I would have the final say on all matters, even dissolving the trust if I saw fit. The trust would protect the farm, and any money belonging to it, from any business or marriage partner, or anyone else who wanted to get their hands on the farm's assets. I could add children to the trust's beneficiaries at any time and pass the assets to them after my death or on the beneficiary coming of age. The farm would stay in the family trust, unless or until there were no surviving relatives. The assets would, in that case, be left to a farm worker's charity.

The only problem was, as I wasn't yet the legal owner of the farm, my father would have to set up the trust. Mr Wilson took one look at him and shook his head.

'As he's not fit to sign, I can't go through with the process. We can talk again if... anything, erm... remiss, should happen to the property owner.'

Mr Wilson tidied up his papers, shook my hand again and promised to get on with the matter of my Deed of Name Change.

He picked up his briefcase and walked towards the door. He stopped when he reached my father's side, he looked down sadly at the figure slumped in the chair.

'Such a shame.' He opened the front door, stepped outside and put on his hat. 'Goodbye, Miss Tansley. I'll see you in a couple of weeks.'

I looked across the drive to his Alvis car. It looked like the one I'd seen in the Cagney movie. I decided that Mr Wilson was a gangster at the weekends. I could have happily become his moll.

I watched him drive away then I sat down at the kitchen table to think about everything I had just learned.

Before the baby is born, I will have become Alice Mollison and my child would have the same surname, thus convincing any prying busybody that Frank and I are, actually married.

As a result, the child will have the Mollison name when we register the birth and later on when it attends school, thus avoiding any embarrassing questions about its parents.

The trust idea was a disappointment, but that didn't really matter. Frank didn't know that it hadn't been set up. I could tell him it was and he'd be none the wiser.

If I decided to marry him in the future, it could be a problem, but not if I waited until I was twenty-one. In essence, all I had to do was remain single for another three years. It sounded simple enough but, what if my handsome gangster, Mr Wilson, came calling?

Chapter 50

Calvin

Calvin walked slowly down to Tania's front door feeling as though he had been treated in a similar way to her druggy, low-life, ex-boyfriend. He didn't like the way he had been summarily dismissed a few moments ago, the only difference had been that he hadn't been thrown out, he could make his own way to the street.

He stopped in the hallway at the bottom of the stairs, and wondered why he had allowed himself to be treated like that. Frowning, he retraced his steps and marched into the bathroom.

Tania was in the shower, singing an old Abba song.

Calvin cleared his throat but she didn't hear. Deciding that he needed an excuse for being there, he lifted the lavatory seat and began to urinate.

Tania slid back the door of the shower, holding her exfoliating sponge, protectively in front of her.

'Calvin, what the hell are you doing here? I thought you'd gone. You frightened me half to death.'

Calvin shook his penis to release the last few drops, tucked it away and zipped up his jeans. He walked to the sink, ran the hot tap and lathered his hands with the soap from the dish before he replied.

'I needed to pee,' he said eventually. He rinsed his hands, then washed them again with scented, liquid-soap from the handwash dispenser.

'I can bloody well see that. Do you always take a piss when someone is in the shower?' Tania glared at him.

'Nearly always,' he said, then corrected himself. 'If I'm overnighting with someone, that is.'

'Well, you don't do it here. In my book, some moments should be private, and taking a piss, having a shit, and showering, are on the front page of that book, written in seventy-five sized, BOLD! Font.'

'No need for the vitriol,' Calvin replied, sulkily. 'Look, are we still on for tomorrow night? I can't wait to get you back in bed again. I'll bring more wine, and I'll pay for the takeaway.'

Tania thought about it for far longer than Calvin had imagined she would.

'All right. But, there are new rules.'

'Rules? What rules?'

'One, you don't ask me to rate your sexual performance, or compare you to anyone else. Two, you leave when I tell you to leave. Three, and this one is super-important, you don't take a piss while I'm in the sodding shower.'

Calvin's face reddened. He wasn't used to being ordered about by anyone, let alone a woman. He was about to give her a few alternative rules of his own when he noticed the scowl on her face and thought better of it. She was, after all, an excellent shag. He bit his tongue and forced a smile.

'Same time tomorrow then? I'll look forward to it.'

Tania relaxed, closed the shower door, and continued with the Abba song.

Calvin left the bathroom door open as he left. He muttered to himself as he stomped back down the stairs. When he reached the front door, he turned and gave the stairs a two-fingered salute.

She'll come around eventually, one way or another. They all do.

Back out on the street, Calvin checked his prized Bulova watch, and walked around to the University Campus offices, stopping to pick up a pale-blue folder and a portable hard-disk containing his work files, from his car. He hadn't been into the office for weeks. He waved to the Spanish receptionist, then blew her a kiss when she waved back. He took the lift to the third floor, and made his way to a small office at the end of a short, photo-print lined, corridor. As he was opening the door to enter, he heard his name being called, in not too friendly a manner.

'Calvin?'

He turned with a questioning look on his face.

'Hi, Darren, how are you?'

Darren Freedman was the head of IT. The main man. His boss. Calvin forced a smile.

'Could you step into my office, Calvin. I need a word.'

Calvin didn't like the tone in his voice. There was trouble ahead.

'If it's the report on the problems with the backup system, I've got it here. It took forever to work out what was wrong.' Calvin waved the folder at Darren.

'That report was due two weeks ago,' Darren said abruptly. 'It's irrelevant now; we paid outside contractors to sort it out. It took them less than an hour.'

Calving gulped. This was a little bit more serious than he had imagined.

In Darren's office, Calvin stood in front of his superior's desk while he searched through emails on his computer.

'Calvin. You were sent... five emails, asking you for that report. Did you read any of them?'

Calvin thought quickly.

'I didn't receive them; my laptop has developed a problem with the hard drive.' He showed the portable drive to Darren. 'I brought it with me to see if I can retrieve the data from it.'

'So, you didn't read any of the emails?'

'As I said, I—'

Darren held up a hand to silence him, selected an email and clicked 'print'. The laser printer on his desk immediately sprang into life. Darren removed the printed sheet from the printer's out-tray, and passed it to Calvin.

'It's a pity you didn't get this one, as it informs you that your services are no longer required by the university.'

'You, you, can't do that, I have a contract,' Calvin spluttered.

Darren picked up a file from his desk. 'Ah, yes, your contract. The contract that states that as a contractor, you will spend at least twenty hours a week on site. The contract that states that you will assist students with IT related projects and problems. The contract that you signed, stating that you possessed a Master's degree in Business Management and Information Technology when, in fact, you left university with just a basic degree. It begs the question, where did you get that Master's certificate from? We only found out about that little scam earlier this week. Now, I'd like you to clear your desk, and get out.' He pointed a Sir Alan Sugar style finger at Calvin. 'You're fired,' he said.

Calvin shrugged and tried to act as though he wasn't bothered in the slightest.

'I'll soon find something else. You owe me this month's salary. When can I expect it to arrive in the bank?'

Darren snorted. 'We owe you nothing, Calvin. You've done very little, if anything, by way of work this month. You haven't even visited the university. I checked. You made no attempt to contact us, or explain your absence. So, as I said. We owe you nothing.' He turned to his computer screen, then looked back across the desk. 'Are you still here,' he asked.

Chapter 51

Jess

The doctor came at two-thirty and gave Alice a thorough examination. When he had finished, he joined Jess and Gwen in the kitchen where he opened his bag, took out a pad and wrote out a prescription for antibiotics.

'She has an infection, but I don't think it's viral, so give her one of these, three times a day. She should hopefully pick up in a couple of days. Her temperature is normal and I'm not concerned about her general health. She's very weak so if you can get some food into her it will help a lot.' He made a few notes in a moleskin notebook, dropped it into his case and snapped it shut. 'I'll call back again in a couple of days. Let me know if she gets any worse.'

'Erm, Doctor, before you go, do you think you could give her another prescription for the sleeping tablets she had a while back? She's run out, and she's petrified of going to sleep without them. She has terrible nightmares. She dreams she's dying and being dragged into the afterlife by someone she's terrified of. She has the same dream every night. She's worried that if she allows this to happen, she won't wake up again. That's what's draining her, I think.'

The doctor thought about it for a few seconds. 'It won't do any long-term damage at her age. What was the name of the medication?'

Jess fetched the packet from Alice's bedside drawer and showed it to him. The doctor got his pad out again and scribbled another prescription.

'I'm only giving her half a dozen for now; let's see how the antibiotics work first. If she needs more, just ring the surgery for a repeat.'

When he had gone, Jess asked Gwen if she could hang around a while longer.

'I'll go to the pharmacy now, and I need to nip home to get some more clothes. I'll grab my phone and laptop chargers too. It looks like I'll be here for a few days at least. I'll see you're paid for the extra hours, Gwen.'

'Don't you worry about that, Jessica. I'll look after her any time you need me to.'

Jessica gave Gwen a hug. 'What would we do without you?'

The pharmacy was only a couple of hundred metres or so from Jess's flat. The shop had a queue of waiting customers, so she left the scripts with a staff member and told her she'd call back to pick up the meds when they were ready.

Jess drove the short distance home and parked up next to Calvin's car. She hoped he wouldn't take the news about her staying over for a few days with Alice, too badly. They had already agreed the Thursday sleep over, but he might not take too kindly to the idea of an extended stay.

Calvin was on the sofa, sipping coffee and skimming through Internet pages on his laptop. He lifted his hand and waved as she came in.

'Hi. How's Nana?' he asked.

Jess wasn't expecting that greeting. She dropped her overnight bag on the floor, walked to the sofa and kissed him on the cheek. 'She's very ill; she's got a chest infection. I'm picking up antibiotics for her in a few minutes.'

She waited for the inevitable response, but it didn't materialise.

'You're going back then?'

'I've got to, Calvin, she's so weak.'

'That's fine, I understand,' said Calvin. He patted Jess's hand. 'Look after your Nana.'

'That's very kind of you, Calvin. I'll just get some clean underwear and a change of clothes.' She walked quickly to the bedroom. 'How was your night, did you manage to last the pace?' she asked as she pulled open her knickers drawer.

'My night?'

'You were out with the lads, or have you forgotten already?' She grabbed a bra from the next drawer down.

'Oh that. It was okay, I was at it until the early hours,' he replied with a smirk.

Jess came back into the lounge carrying an armful of clothes. 'You look good on it. I'd still be in bed.'

'I wish I could be, but I've got stuff to do,' he said.

Jess removed the dirty clothes from her bag and stuffed them into the laundry basket in the bathroom. 'Could you put my stuff in with yours when you do a wash, please?' she asked.

'No problem. Anything else you need doing?'

'The bins need to go out tomorrow. It's recycled this week.'

'I'm on it,' he said.

'You might need to get a few bits in for supper. I'm sorry, but I haven't had time to do the shopping.'

Calvin waved away her apology. 'I'll see to it.'

Jess couldn't believe the change in him. There was almost always a row if she asked him to do something he considered to be 'women's work'. She wondered if being apart was having an effect.

She folded the clean clothes and put them carefully into her overnight bag, then she grabbed the charger cables she needed, put them in the side compartment and zipped it up.

Calvin got up from the sofa and walked over to her. Jess kissed him on the cheek again.

'Right, I'm off. I'm sorry, Calvin, but I don't know how long I'll be staying. If the antibiotics work, I could be back for Saturday afternoon. I've got a bit of running about to do on Friday, researching that article, but Gwen says she'll cover for that.' She kissed him on the lips. 'Thanks for being so understanding.'

She turned away but had only got as far as the top step, when he spoke.

'I won't be able to pay my share of the rent and utilities this month.'

Jess stopped dead.

'Why not? That's the third time in the last six months, Calvin. I can't afford to subsidise you like this.'

Calvin's mood changed in an instant.

'Ask your bloody Nana for the money if you need it. She's loaded for Christ's sake.'

'She already pays a third of the rent. I'm not asking her for more. It's your responsibility, Calvin. I've let you off with enough as it is. You haven't paid for a grocery shop for weeks.' She looked at him, puzzled. 'Why can't you afford it anyway? You earn enough.'

'I gave up my job today that's why. I'm sick of their demands on my time.'

'You hardly ever go in these days.'

'That's exactly the point. When I do, they overload me with work, that's why I was getting so stressed recently. Don't worry, I'll soon find another job. IT contractors are never out of work. I can do some agency stuff until I find something that suits.'

'I hope so, Calvin, I like this flat, I don't want to lose it.'

'I doubt your lovely Nana would let that happen,' replied Calvin. He returned to the sofa. 'There are a few temporary jobs advertised, I might apply for one or two this afternoon.'

'Good luck,' said Jess, still reeling from his revelation.

Calvin swiped his touch screen and lifted his mug of coffee. When he noticed Jess was still standing at the top of the stairs, he looked at her quizzically.

'What?'

'Nothing,' Jess replied. 'I thought you were going to say goodbye that's all.'

'Bye,' said Calvin, as he returned to his screen swiping.

The prescription was ready when Jess got back to the pharmacy. She signed the scripts on Alice's behalf and carried the bag of meds to the car. On the way back to the farm, she spotted Ewan coming out of the Tesco Direct. She wound down the driver's window and shouted to him.

'Do you live in there?'

Ewan laughed, and crossed the road to the row of marked parking spaces, where Jess had pulled up. He bent down to talk to her at eye level.

'This was meant, I was going to ring the Uni and ask them for your phone number. I was hoping to have a chat before you do the lecture on Friday,' she said.

'Great, you can come after all then,' replied Ewan.

'I'm sorry, I can't, my Nana is really ill and I'm looking after her. I can wrangle an hour before the lecture, if you can spare the time. I'd like to talk to you about women's rights in Africa. I've been asked to do an article on the changing roles of women on the continent, and you're just the man I need if I'm going to make a proper job of it. I'll give you full credits in the magazine. I wouldn't be able to pay you much though, just a token amount.'

Ewan grinned. 'I'd be delighted to help you out, and no payment is needed. It would be nice to get a credit for the charity at the bottom of the piece if you can sort that out. Tell you what? You provide the coffee and I'll provide the info you need.'

'Ewan, you're a star,' said Jess. She leaned out of the window to peck him on the cheek, but Ewan turned his face and kissed her lips instead. Jess recoiled.

'Sorry, I don't know why I did that. I shouldn't have. Sorry,' Ewan looked genuinely embarrassed.

Jess tried to make light of it. 'You'll have to get the coffees in now. You've already been paid.'

'What time on Friday?' asked Ewan, trying to move on.

'Twelvish, the café next to uni?'

'Perfect,' said Ewan. 'I'll be there. I need to leave for one o'clock though; I'll have to make sure the slideshow is working properly. I don't want to risk any disasters.'

'No, that would be awful. See you there.' Ewan straightened and backed off a pace as Jess pulled away. She held her hand out of the window and waved. 'Friday,' she called.

Jess gave Alice the first of her antibiotics and a glass of water to wash it down. 'These will soon have you back on your feet, Nana,' she said.

'That would be good, I wasn't on them much before,' Alice quipped. Her breathing had improved a little, but she still looked washed out.

Jess waved the packet of sleeping pills at her, then slipped them into her bedside drawer. 'No nasty dreams tonight, Nana,' she said with a smile.

'I had taken my last one,' said Alice. Her voice was still very croaky, but she could get more words out now without struggling.

'You're definitely improving, Nana. You look so much better than this morning. I really got a shock when you had that coughing fit.'

'I'm still a bit groggy, but I do feel a little bit better. I might have some of Gwen's broth later.'

'I'll bring it now if you like,' Gwen called from the kitchen where she had been listening in on the conversation.

Alice shook her head. 'Not yet. This evening, maybe.'

Jess settled down and picked up Alice's old notebook. 'Shall I read some more?'

'If you don't mind... I'm not really up to doing a session on your... recording, thingy,' Alice replied.

Jess opened the book. 'Now then. June nineteen thirty-eight...'

Chapter 52

June 1938

In the first week of June, feeling like a hippo and now unable to fit, or sit, comfortably in the galvanised hip bath for my Friday night dip, and becoming increasingly sweaty with the warmer weather and the extra effort I had to put in because of the state of my body, I made up my mind to make enquires into having the bathroom fitted in the parlour.

I had become quite an expert in using the telephone by now. So expert in fact, that at least two callers had taken me to be a receptionist and had asked to be put through to Miss Tansley. As I had based my telephone voice on my gangster lawyer's receptionist, who I now knew was called Miss Johnston, the confusion was understandable.

I did get caught out once or twice by Amy calling for no other reason than to hear my posh telephone voice. She used to get me to use it in her bedroom when we were having a catch up. She would be Lady Agatha of Christie, calling to speak to her literary agent about her latest novel. I would pretend to be the agent Blossom Flowers, and we'd spend hours laughing as we invented characters and absolutely horrendous ways to kill them off. My favourite being arsenic used as an enema.

I picked out a local building firm called M. Hart and sons, firstly because they were local, and secondly because of a recommendation from Frank who had done some labouring for them in the past. Mr Hart was a difficult man to catch up with and I finally got in touch by ringing in the evening. He sounded a nice man, who told me he always prioritised local customers and after hearing my heartfelt plea about the reason I needed the work doing as quickly as possible, promised to visit on Saturday morning to assess the situation, and price up the job.

I can honestly say I had never been so excited about anything in my life, even the telephone installation paled into insignificance. I could see an end to sitting in a draughty kitchen during a freezing cold winter, or taking a bath in summer when the lads worked late and my father, along with Barney or one of the other workmen, could just walk in while I was stark naked. I took to locking the back door before I got in the bath but they would just look through the window and tap on it asking to be let in. It was amazing how many important discussions had to be made on a Friday evening before the lads went home for the night. I couldn't bathe any later than nine, because it took an age to get my curls dry and I had to be up again at five the next morning. In the end I used to place four kitchen chairs around the bath in a square, and hang towels over them so that it was harder to see into the bath tub.

Mr Hart was a short, white-haired sixty-year-old with a broad chest, wide shoulders and a weather-beaten face. His jacket was daubed with old plaster and paint, he wore a similarly decorated pair of brown corduroy trousers. In contrast, his black boots looked relatively new and had been recently polished.

I had already hosed down the yard as I waited expectantly for him to arrive but he still picked his way carefully across the cobbles until he came to a halt next to the outside toilet. The building had been bolted onto the farmhouse back at the turn of the century, but the actual lavatory had been replaced in the twenties. The toilet had originally been part of a larger store house and my grandfather had divided it in two so as not to lose all of the storage capacity. We kept lengths of metal pole and fence posts in there along with rolled up, wire mesh fencing and barbed wire. Mr Hart, or Michael, as I was asked to call him, opened up the doors to both sides of the extension, then asked to see the parlour. He took off his coat and hung it on the gate post of the new piggery, and rolled up his sleeves, revealing thick forearms and standout veins.

Miriam, who was in the kitchen, whispered that he looked so fit and strong, he must even have muscles in his hair.

I pointed at him as he opened the door to the parlour and winked at Miriam. She blushed and rushed through to the front room to see to my father although she had only finished changing him half an hour before. We had now resorted to using terry towelling baby nappies on him instead of underpants.

Michael wasn't in the parlour long. He pulled out his measuring tape and asked me to hold one end as he took measurements and jotted the results down in a thick, well-thumbed notepad with the stump of a pencil he kept behind his ear.

He went back outside again and we did similar measurements on the old lavvy and wire-store. He carried a wooden ladder from the barn and examined the slate roof before removing his hat, scratching his head, and pronouncing on his thinking.

'We can do this job, one of two ways, Mrs Mollison,' he said.

I almost corrected the name but bit my tongue in time.

'We can revert this block back to its original size by knocking out the dividing wall, and build the bathroom out here, the drains and water supply are already in place, so that would save a big job trying to install them in the parlour.'

'But it's so cold in the lavatory, the pipes freeze up and the drains get blocked from time to time.'

'All drains do,' he said. 'It's what they do best.' He scratched his head again, then went back and looked into the parlour from the kitchen window. Miriam, who had just returned to the kitchen, suddenly found the need to be elsewhere.

He seemed to be having a mental debate with himself as he looked back and forth between the parlour and outbuilding. 'This way would definitely be easier, cheaper and a lot less disruptive, Mrs Mollison.'

'Call me Alice,' I said.

Michael gave me the thumbs up.

'Well, Alice, as I see it. Out here, we have good, strong, double brick walls, the dividing wall will only be single brick, so we can knock it down in no time. We can insulate the inside and plaster it up. We can even build in a window to help ventilate the place. The parlour would take a lot more sorting out. We'd need to fit drains, water pipes, and get ventilation through the wall to the outside, but we can't, because this (he pointed to the outbuilding) is in the way.'

'I understand, and I'm sorry to be a pain, but we don't really want to go to the expense of building a bathroom if we have to come outside to use it.' I was disappointed, and it showed.

'Ah, sorry,' said Mr Hart. 'I forgot to say, we'll also knock a door into the parlour so that you can access the bathroom from there.' He tapped his nose as though he was about to let me into a big secret and beckoned me to follow.

He led me back into the kitchen and stood by the sink.

'We'll fit a large Ascot gas heater in here and that will give you hot water wherever you want it. We can also replace this old sink and put in a new one with hot and cold taps. The town gas pipes run past here to the Cooper farm at the bottom of the lane. I know, because I fitted them out with a new bathroom last year.'

Talk about keeping up with the Joneses, we were keeping up with the Coopers. First the telephone, now the new bathroom. I wondered what else they had that we could copy.

Miriam, who had been standing by the front room door, rushed across the kitchen.

'You mean I won't have to boil that infernal copper for a decent amount of hot water. I can just turn on a tap?'

'That's exactly what I'm saying,' replied Mr Hart.

Miriam grabbed hold of him in her bear-like hug. 'Oh, thank you, thank you.'

When Michael eventually wriggled free, he straightened his hat and returned to business. He gave me his fee for the work, told me it could all be started within a week as he had two jobs that were finishing this weekend.

'Will I receive a written estimate? I'll have to put it on the farm's expenses sheet for tax purposes,' I said, sounding just like my father.

'If you agree the price now, I'll send the estimate and invoice with the lads when they start. It will probably be Wednesday.'

'So soon,' I said, getting excited at the prospect of instant hot water.

'I always try to put locals before outsiders,' he replied. He smiled at Miriam. 'I'll oversee this job myself.'

Miriam blushed twenty shades of red in as many seconds.

I grinned at her and winked again.

'I'll, err, just go and check on the Mister,' she said, hurrying across the kitchen.

Chapter 53

June 1938

Mr Hart was true to his word, and at seven-thirty on Wednesday morning he arrived with one of his sons and two other men. If you played a game where you had to guess their occupations just by looking at them, you'd choose builder, every time. Michael's son was, confusingly, called Michael, so I called him Michael Junior when I mentioned him. Michael himself didn't like the epithet Senior, so he just remained Michael.

'One of the lads I was going to bring with us today is called Michael too,' said Michael, 'but I thought that might make life difficult.'

Miriam came out of the kitchen in a fluster with a tray laden with mugs of tea. When Michael took his, he winked at her and complimented her on the brew. I lost count of the amount of times she stammered 'thank you' but it was at least six.

'Keep them plied with tea,' I said to Miriam as we stood by the sink watching the workmen offload wheelbarrows, shovels and sledgehammers from their open-backed truck.

The lorry was similar to ours but much newer, and as I found out over the next ten days, it started first time, every time. I thought about getting a new truck for the farm, but it would have to wait. The cost of the telephone and the bathroom had made a bit of a dent in our finances. The cottage that I had put up for rent a few weeks earlier now had tenants, a lovely Welsh couple with one child. Mr Owens had brought his family from Cardiff to take up a job as a pattern designer at the mill. The money they handed over every Friday would help pay for the cost of the building work.

We had money in the bank and money in the safe. We were due payment for a batch of pigs, a few bullocks and twenty lambs too. So, it wasn't like we were on our uppers, and our credit was good, we could get farm loans any time we liked. We never had though, and as far as I was concerned, we never would.

By the end of the first day, the dividing wall had been demolished; the space for a window had been knocked into the old lavatory wall, and a hole the size of a door knocked through to the parlour. The brickwork had been wheelbarrowed up long planks onto the back of the truck and driven away.

Mr Hart came in for a cup of tea and a progress report at five o'clock and informed me, and a flustered Miriam, that he would be bringing his plumber with him tomorrow to get the gas into the house from the main road. He would also check the drains from the lavatory and install the pipework for the water supply out of the kitchen wall and into the new bathroom.

Friday would see the Ascot and new kitchen sink installed.

I thought Miriam was going to faint when that news was announced.

On Friday lunchtime, Mr Hart ceremoniously switched on the Ascot and turned on the hot tap. A few seconds later, a torrent of boiling water splashed into the huge, white Belfast sink, which was easily big enough to bath twins in. Mr Hart thought of everything.

He held up a warning hand to stop us testing the temperature of the miracle hot-water supply and adjusted a thermostat controller on the pipework of the Ascot which lowered the water temperature to a safer level.

Miriam loved the new sink almost as much as the hot water system. Not only was it huge, so that she could do the washing in it, but it had a drainer built onto the side. Our old one, whilst large, was made out of sandstone and was built into the kitchen when the house was put up, some eighty years or so before. It took all three of the young men to carry it out.

Mr Hart was a businessman at heart, and it showed.

'You could get yourself a gas cooker next, or even a gas range if that's the way you like to cook.'

Miriam swooned. Our old range was heated by coal or chopped wood and the ovens were tiny.

My excitement rose by the day, I lay in bed at night, imagining myself soaking in the new bath and just topping the hot water up as the water in the bathtub cooled.

Miriam's excitement was at an even higher level than mine. Michael Hart, Senior, had shared his lunch break with her twice that week and she was now able to talk to him without blushing or stuttering.

He was a widower of some ten years, and since his wife passed, he had put all his efforts and spare time into the business. Miriam, a divorcee, was about five years younger, but looked more. She was trim, very attractive and had only a few grey hairs mixed in with the natural black. As she grew more confident, he seemed to go back into his shell. He almost ran out of the kitchen one afternoon when an over-zealous housekeeper pursed her lips, expecting a kiss, when he leaned towards her to whisper that he needed to use the lavatory.

Frank didn't seem too happy when he found out the Harts were doing the building work.

'You really should have told me, Alice. I might have been able to negotiate a discount for you. You could have let me work with them too, that would have cut costs. A building labourer earns more than a farm hand, so you could have saved a lot of money there.'

'I need you doing farm work at this time of year, Frank, you know that,' I replied.

He was still irritable; he had a bee in his bonnet about something. So, on the night before the work was due to finish, sick and tired of his week-long sulk, I decided to grasp the nettle.

'Come on, Frank, out with it,' I said as we lay together in bed. Me lying there like a beached whale, Frank clinging to the edge of the eiderdown to keep himself covered.

'It's just, well, I was hoping that when we got married, I might get a little more by way of recognition, a promotion if you like. I'm part of the family now, so the lads would accept it if I was given more responsibility in decision making and delegating tasks, that sort of thing.'

He still hadn't got used to the idea of being ordered around by a teenage girl – that was obvious.

'Two things, Frank,' I said. 'One, Barney is the foreman, and he'll remain the foreman until he retires. We've had this conversation. Secondly, and I hate having to remind you of this, but we're not married.'

'I know, and you never let me forget the fact,' he replied bitterly. 'Look, Alice, I'm not after Barney's job. I like him, we get on well. I just want the lads to give me a little more respect. They must be wondering why you haven't given me more responsibility. You don't want to let them start thinking something might not be quite as it seems.'

He did have a point.

'I'll think about it, Frank. I'll have a chat to Barney and work something out. We could maybe call you the charge hand or something.'

'Would there be a pay rise involved too?' he asked.

'We already pay you more than the other lads, Frank.'

'I know but, well, I don't get much, to say I'm part of the family, married or not. I don't get any say in decisions like I would if we were married. As I said, Alice, I know we're not married, but if we were living anywhere but here, I'd be boss of the house or I'd have a big say in how things are done at least.'

'Frank, my father is the owner of the farm, while he's alive at least, and you knew what the rules were before you agreed to all this. A good part of it was your idea I seem to remember.'

Frank sat up suddenly, hauled himself out of bed and began to pace the room, back and forth.

'I hope I haven't made a bloody rod for my own back,' he said, angrily.

'I was honest with you, Frank. You'll never get any part of this farm, even if we were to marry. The farm will always stay in my family. I'll pass it on in the future but it will be to a Tansley descendent. Mr Wilson, the lawyer who came to sort out my name change is working on setting up a family trust for the farm, so that it can never be taken over by any outside interest, and that includes spouses.'

I hoped I'd got all that right. Frank was a clever man and he might know about trusts.

He continued to pace back and forth. 'I can't say I'm happy about that, Alice. If we were to marry I ought to have some rights over money, the business, decision making, whatever, and I really don't like the idea of you doing things behind my back, like this trust thing, even the bathroom and telephone installations. It wouldn't have hurt you to discuss those things with me.'

'The trust has nothing to do with you, Frank. It's a Tansley family matter. As for the other things, it's the farm's money, not mine. I have my own savings account that I put a few shillings a week into, but that's mine, not yours. Do you have a savings account? If you did, I wouldn't expect to be able to benefit from it.'

'I do, as a matter of fact. But it has the princely sum of one shilling and eightpence in it as things stand. I've never earned enough to save anything regularly.'

I bit my tongue and decided not to mention how much he spent at the pub every Friday night. Instead, I listed a few of the benefits he had accrued whilst living here.

'You get free board here, Frank. You don't pay rent. You get your food, your laundry done, you don't have to pay for electricity, you don't pay for gas or water, and you get to keep every penny of your wages, none of the other lads can say that. They all have families to keep and rents to pay out of the money they earn. As for the new things I've just bought. You can use the telephone, free of charge, whenever you like, you can have a bath whenever you like... providing I'm not in it of course.' I laughed, hoping he would too. He didn't, he just pulled a face and let out a deep sigh.

'When you put it like that, I am better off than the lads I work with, but I still think we ought to discuss things like a normal, married couple would. We share a bed, we share our meals, by the end of this week, if your Mr Wilson has done his job, we'll share a name. Would it hurt so much to let me in on things, sometimes?'

'No, it wouldn't, Frank,' I replied, 'and if anything comes up where I think a joint decision needs to be made, anything to do with the baby, for instance, I'll ask for your opinion. If any issue crops up about the running of the farm that I'm unsure about, I'll ask your opinion, as well as Barney's, but that is about as far as I can go, for now at least. Think about it, Frank, you've got it good here, don't go and spoil it.'

He returned to bed and lay with his arms on the outside of the eiderdown. I patted his left hand.

'It will work out, Frank. We've hardly got to know each other yet. Let's not rush things.'

At lunchtime on the following day, Michael proudly showed me around the new bathroom. I'd had a sneaky peek a couple of days before, but since then, he had put a lock on the adjoining door from the parlour to give everything time to dry, and the fumes from the plaster, paint and lino glue, time to disperse.

He opened the door with a flourish, allowing me to step inside first.

The room had been tiled white to just above bath height with the top half of the walls painted hospital green. The lino was a light grey. There was a sink on a pedestal, with a shiny, oblong mirror on the wall above it. There was a porcelain toilet with a wooden seat, and a cistern with a flushing handle, built onto the wall at the back. Previously the cistern was a cast iron monstrosity, hidden behind a large wooden box, high on the wall, the flushing mechanism controlled by a rusty, pull chain. The bath, oh, my goodness, the bath, looked big enough for me to stretch out in. No more hunching up in the tin, hip bath, or stretching so that my calves and feet hung over the end. Best of all, it had a plug in the bottom, allowing me to empty the bath by merely pulling a thin chain.

I did a double twirl, grabbed hold of Michael and danced him around the bathroom.

Before he left, I went to the front room and opened a small safe in the corner cupboard. I took out six of the ten, five-pound notes that had been paid out by the National and Provincial Insurance Company on my mother's death, and took them through to Mr Hart with the invoice he had provided. He signed the bottom, wrote 'paid in full', and I handed over the money. Frank watched the transaction, rubbing his chin thoughtfully as each note was counted.

I could have attempted to withdraw the money from the bank, or have them prepare me a banker's draft, but that would have meant a trip to the next town where our branch was situated. It would also have meant me spending a frustrating hour at least, explaining to the bank manager why I needed to withdraw such a large sum, and why my father, the owner of the business, hadn't come in person. The chances were, I'd have come away empty handed. Bankers didn't believe women could be responsible with money.

So, at one PM. I eased into my first soak in the new bath. As I had promised myself, I stayed in it for an hour, topping up the hot water as needed. When I got out, I looked like a cross between a newly boiled lobster and a wrinkled prune, but I didn't care. I was clean, I had bathed in complete privacy, and I felt more relaxed than I had done in months.

As I stood on the damp lino, I noticed an envelope behind one of the sink taps. I picked it up to see it had Miriam's name written across it in a very neat hand. I fought off the almost irresistible urge to open it and instead, pulled a bath towel from the rack on the wall and once again looked around to admire my new, favourite room.

I dried off and walked back through the new door into the parlour, drying my hair.

'Who's next?' I asked. 'Run your own water, you can't jump in to share mine; it's all gone down the plug hole.'

Miriam put up her hand. 'Could I try it next? I missed my hip bath last night too.'

I knew she had; we were playing Gin Rummy with Frank for matchsticks until nine-thirty. She was almost as excited as me about the new bathroom, but that excitement had been tinged with disappointment when Michael left without saying goodbye.

'Try out the new sink first,' I said. 'The mirror will be all steamed up though.'

I waited until she had gone into the bathroom before tip-toeing through the parlour. I put my ear to the door and waited. Less than a minute later I heard a squeal louder than the piglets make when they get their heads stuck in the fencing. I held my hand over my mouth and returned to the kitchen to carry on drying my hair.

Half an hour later, Miriam walked back in the kitchen tapping the pocket of her house coat continuously. She had a smile on her face the size of a quarter moon.

'You look like you've found a fiver on the bathroom floor,' I said.

'It's better than that,' she replied. She took the letter from her pocket and kissed it twice before holding it over her heart. 'It's from Michael;

he's asked me to an afternoon tea dance next Saturday. Will it be all right if I have a couple of hours off? I'll make up the time in the week.'

I made out I was having to think about it seriously.

'Please,' she said. 'I'll clean out the piggery for you tomorrow.'

I burst out laughing and rushed forward to hug her.

'Of course, you can have the time off, my darling. Take the whole afternoon, go for a walk afterwards, or maybe he'll take you back to his house for...'

'Oh, my goodness,' she said, eyes wide. 'Do you really think he'll—?'

'He'd better bloody not,' I replied, laughing again. 'Just relax and have a wonderful time, Miriam. I hope it's the first of many afternoons out. You deserve this; you've been alone too long.'

Miriam burst into tears, so I hugged her again until she had quietened down.

'I don't know if I can remember all the dance steps,' she said with a worried frown on her brow.

'We could practice in here,' I suggested.

'What shall I wear, I've got nothing that would suit a tea dance.'

'It's not being held at Buckingham Palace,' I said. 'Have a look at my mother's wardrobe, you're about her size and she had clothes for all occasions.'

'I couldn't,' said Miriam, 'could I?'

When Frank came back at six, he immediately took off his shirt and began to run the tap in the new sink.

'Oi,' I called. 'You can't strip off in front of respectable, married women. Get yourself into the bathroom.'

Frank turned around puzzled.

'Married women?'

As Miriam preened, I told him about Michael's letter. Frank winked at Miriam and stepped towards her, bare chested.

'He's a decent bloke, Mike, but he's still in mourning and I doubt he'll ever come out of it. But he'll appreciate your company, Miriam, I'm sure of that.'

Frank picked up his shirt, slung it over his shoulder and headed for the bathroom.

'Don't mind him, Miriam,' I said as he walked away. 'He doesn't have a heart; he has a swinging brick.'

Later that evening, we sat around the kitchen reading novels. I had an Agatha Christie from the library. Miriam was reading Margaret Mitchell's Gone with the Wind, for the third time, while Frank sat on a kitchen chair with his back to us, engrossed in his book.

'What are you reading, Frank, is it any good?' I asked.

'Grahame Greene,' he replied, as though that was enough to say that it was.

I stood up to get a drink of water from our new sink and had to pass Frank to reach it. As I walked by, I glanced down at the book he was so immersed in. I tilted my head to one side and read the top line of the page.

Miss Jane Marple was sitting by her window...

I turned to Miriam with a big grin on my face.

'We'll have competition on Monday night for the sleuthing.'

Miriam didn't look up from her book. Frank looked up from his and shrugged.

'It was the only thing on the bookcase I hadn't read, except for that George Orwell, Road to Wigan Pier and that is so depressing.'

'My father got it from the library months ago, he's never read it. I'd better take it back; he must owe a fortune in fines on it.'

As if he had heard his name mentioned, a shout came from the front room. Miriam dropped her book on the floor and rushed through to him. I followed, with Frank just behind.

I gave Miriam a hand to pick my father up from the floor and get him back into his chair. I've picked up heavier piglets. Miriam checked his trousers for damp patches and I picked up the half empty bottle of whisky that he had knocked over. I was about to put it back at the side of his chair, when he snatched it out of my hands and held it to his chest protectively.

'I saw you,' he croaked.

'You saw what?' Miriam asked, 'What did you see?'

He looked at me from under his heavily lidded eyes.

'I saw you,' he said again, then he closed his eyes and hugged his whisky bottle.

I walked back to the kitchen puzzled. What had he seen? Then I realised he must have spotted me open the safe, or at least walk by him counting the money. I didn't feel the slightest bit guilty about it. The money would be paid back, and anyway, what use was it sat inside a locked, metal box for all eternity? I worked hard for this farm and I didn't feel I was being greedy by allowing myself a few luxuries. I wished to God I could somehow get my father into the new bath. He stank.

Chapter 54

Jess

That evening Alice managed to eat a whole bowl of Gwen's broth, and after a coughing fit which saw her expel a large amount of phlegm into a plastic bowl, she was able to sit up, propped on the pillows and speak without gasping for breath anywhere near as much as she had earlier in the day.

'Blimey, Nana. Those antibiotics work fast.'

'I don't think it's the pills, Jessica. I've been trying to clear that gunk for days. It just seemed to get stuck on my chest,' replied Alice.

Jess put her cup of coffee on the bedside table and ran a critical eye over Alice. Some colour had returned to her cheeks and her eyes were definitely brighter. 'I'm just happy you've recovered so quickly. I was really worried about you this morning.'

Alice took Jess's hand and smiled at her. 'I'm just happy that you're here with me and not stuck with that pig of a boyfriend.'

'He was great about the extra time I'm spending here, actually, Nana. He quite surprised me.'

'He'll want something in return,' Alice scoffed. 'Men always do.'

'Shall I read some more, Nana? I'm really engrossed in this. You should bring the book out under your own name. I'm sure it would sell well.'

'Oh, I'm not bothered about selling the story. I just wanted you to know what happened, and why things happened the way they did. You can have the fame and glory. I wouldn't want it anyway. I wrote the memoirs to remind myself what life was like back then, but as the years passed, I came to realise that I needed to share those events with someone who might show a sympathetic attitude, someone not likely to make a hasty judgement. I'm not really a selfish person, Jessica. Decisions were forced on me.'

'I don't think you were selfish, Nana. As you said, events determined your decision making. Attitudes are changing now, thank goodness.'

'They aren't changing fast enough,' replied Alice. 'Take your Calvin as a case in point.'

Jess sipped at her cold coffee and pulled a face. She picked up the first volume again and began to read.

Chapter 55

June 1938

On Friday mornings, Barney, and a random fellow worker, took a leather bag full of money, cheques, postal orders and any other payment the farm had received during the week, and deposited it at the bank.

The bulk of the money the farm earned came from the harvest and the sale of animals, but during the spring and summer, we catered for half a dozen shops and wholesalers who bought an assortment of vegetables from us. In winter we switched to broccoli, kale, winter cabbage and Brussels sprouts. We also sold raw milk to local people, but the bulk of it went to a dairy on the outskirts of the town, where our supply topped up their own. The milk was processed, bottled, and delivered to doorsteps in milk floats.

Barney had been nominated by my father as a trusted person before I was born, and in all his years of performing the task, he had never once had a problem with the officious manager, who had been at the bank longer than Barney had been at the farm.

When the bag of takings had been counted and entered onto the farm's account ledger, Barney would hand over a sheet of paper with a list of notes and coins that we needed to make up the wages. I used to sit at the kitchen table, work out what each worker had earned, and slip the money into four-inch, square, brown paper packets, with the employee's name written in ink on the front. I made up my own wages this way too, just so that the men could see we were all in it together. After making up the packets, I filed in our own cash ledger, adding the wages to any other outgoings we may have had during the week.

I used to enjoy filling in the incoming and outgoing columns and totting them up at the end of the week. I tried to teach Miriam how to do them once, but numbers were like a foreign language to her.

At twelve o'clock, the lads would form an orderly queue outside the back door and step inside one by one to receive their wages. They touched the peak of their cap as a mark of respect, then they would scan the front of the packet, open it, and check the contents before they left. Now and again there was a query regarding the amount someone had received, but the issue was always resolved quickly and without argument. I got my own wages wrong once and walked around all week thinking I'd lost a ten-shilling note. I found it in the cash bag as I loaded it up for Barney, the following week.

Every week, I would take five shillings from my wages and put in a porcelain piggy bank that had a slot in the top but had to be opened with key that I didn't possess, at the bottom. When it began to feel heavy, I'd take it up to the Post Office, where they would open it, count it, and pay it into my savings account. The cashier wrote the new total into my Post Office savings book, and I'd walk away feeling as though I had done something worthwhile. I had no idea what I was saving up for. I had no rent or expenses to pay out of my wages, so I mainly spent it on clothes, more recently, larger sized clothes. I didn't go for the actual maternity outfits as they were priced at ridiculous levels.

One Saturday afternoon, accompanied by Amy, we went to the Post Office to have my piggy bank emptied, before taking a walk through the town. As we were passing Stan's Bargain Emporium, Amy stopped dead and pulled me back by the collar of my baggy jumper.

'Look!' she squealed.

I looked, and squealed at an even higher pitch.

In Stan's window, was a beautiful, wind up, portable gramophone, in an almost unmarked, blue case. The lid was raised, showing the famous HMV terrier, Nipper, listening to a wind-up phonograph. It had a shiny, chrome plated, playing arm and a similarly finished winding handle which was sitting in its cradle, in the lid of the box. It was love at first sight. I didn't even notice the price tag that had been tied to the leather finished case handle, with string.

We rushed through the door and waited impatiently while Stan's assistant served a woman wearing a checked coat that was far too heavy for the summer. She was buying a bed, apparently for her nephew, who was paying her a visit. The assistant put the money in the till, wrote out a receipt and promised the woman that the bed would be delivered before ten o'clock the following morning.

I tapped my foot as I waited, then Amy spotted a pile of records on top of another wind-up gramophone. She sorted through them excitedly, passing some particularly well-known ones to me.

'Ahem. May I be of assistance, or are you just browsing?' said a deep voice behind me.

'Are these for sale,' asked Amy, before I could get a word in.

'They come with the gramophone,' said Stan.

We checked it out. It was priced at one pound fifteen shillings and eleven pence (even second hand dealers used the same eleven pence, trick). It wasn't a patch on the blue beauty in the window. The chrome fittings were dull, the black case was scratched and the carrying handle was coming away.

'How much is the blue one in the window?' I asked, trying to keep the excitement out of my voice.

Stan went off to check.

'That one is two pounds seventeen shillings and eleven pence,' he informed me, looking for all the world like he was wasting his time talking to us.

'Can I have a closer look at it?' I asked.

I could hardly contain myself when Stan returned carrying the musical box of my dreams.

Stan cleared his throat and began the big sell.

'This is the 1933, HMV model 102a with the advanced, model 16 receiver. That's the bit at the top of the playing arm where the sound comes out,' he added, helpfully.

I already knew that, as Amy had a similar model, in black.

'It comes with a pyramid of replacement needles, and I'll throw in a record stacker. He pointed to a leather box with a spindle inside where you could safely store your records.

I was about to say I'd take him up on his offer when Amy kicked the back of my ankle.

'Does it come with any records,' she asked.

'No, this one does not,' Stan replied.

'We might be interested in buying it if it did,' Amy said, looking at the pile of records next to the cheaper machine.

'I can't do that, I'm afraid.' Stan stood his ground. 'Can you really afford to purchase it?' he asked.

I produced my Post Office book, showing that I had in excess of fifteen pounds in my savings account. That may have been a mistake, as Stan suddenly smelled money.

'I'll let you have them for a pound,' he offered.

'A pound!' Amy stormed. 'You mean to say that this gramophone,' she pointed to the black model, 'is only worth fifteen shillings?' she turned to me. 'Buy that one, Alice, at fifteen bob, it's a bargain.'

I was about to say I didn't want the tatty black one, when Amy kicked my ankle again.

'It doesn't work like that, Miss,' said Stan.

'Well, we don't want it at all if it doesn't work,' replied Amy.

She began walking towards the door. 'Come on, Alice, we'll see if they have one at Harry's Home Furnishings.'

Harry's shop was on the far side of town. He sold everything from second hand mangles to radio sets.

Stan saw money walking away from him. 'Don't be so hasty. Maybe we can work something out.'

Amy stayed at the store while I rushed back to the Post Office to withdraw the funds required. I was so red-faced and out of breath when I got there that the woman behind the counter thought I was about to give birth. When I had assured her that I wasn't, she looked me over and ordered me to sit on a wooden chair while she sorted out my money.

'Just in case,' she said.

I did as I was told and sat impatiently while she recorded the withdrawal in my savings book, and stamped it with an inky, rubber, date stamp.

'Are you buying a pram, my dear?' she asked.

'Yes,' I said, in case she refused to hand over the money if she thought I was spending it on something else.

'Silver Cross, dear,' she advised. 'Even the second hand ones are worth buying. Mine lasted me for all three of my children.'

I thought she was going to give me the whole history of her pram, so I told her I had to rush in case someone else bought it before I got back with the money.

'Good luck, fingers crossed, or should I say, silver crossed,' she said with a little laugh.

I waved to her and hurried out of the shop. I rushed back to Stan's to find Amy guarding the gramophone as though her life depended on it. She blew out a sigh of relief and gave me the thumbs up as I rattled my purse at her.

Stan still didn't seem too happy with the sale. 'I'm robbing myself here,' he said as he counted my money into his till.

Five minutes later, we were walking home. Me carrying my beautiful, blue gramophone and Amy carrying the record stacker and an armful of records.

When we got back to the farm, we put it on the kitchen table, wound it up, and spent the next two hours dancing and singing along to Bing Crosby, Bessie Smith and Louis Armstrong.

Miriam came in from the front room as we were dancing a waltz to one of the slower tunes.

'Could you show me how to do that dance again, Alice,' she asked. 'I've forgotten already.'

I had been dancing with Miriam the day before, but we didn't have a lot of time to practice.

'Amy's the expert,' I said. 'Anyway, my bump gets in the way.'

Guided by Amy, Miriam learned how to Waltz and Foxtrot. By tea time she was doing well enough to dance with Michael on the Saturday.

'You'll be fine with those two dances, Miriam. Just stay clear of the Tango and Lindy Hop,' Amy said.

'What on earth is a Lindy Hop,' Miriam asked.

'Don't ask me to demonstrate in my condition,' I said, seriously.

On Saturday afternoon, at one o'clock, Miriam, looking stunning in my mother's navy, flared skirt, polka dot dress, left the house to find Michael waiting for her in his builder's lorry. I watched from the front window as he produced a spotless, white sheet and spread it out on the passenger seat. Miriam looked back at the house and waved. I had never seen her look so happy in all the years I had known her.

I waved back energetically.

'Have lots of fun, my darling,' I said.

At five o'clock, Frank came back from visiting his mother. He wasn't in the best of moods.

'What's this about a Christening? Going behind my back again I see.'

'The Christening was your mother's idea, not mine, Frank,' I replied.

'It doesn't matter whose idea it was. Once again, I'm the last to know.'

I thought I could smell stale beer. I leaned a little closer and then I was certain.

'You stopped off at The Old Bull on the way back then?'

'I don't have to consult you whenever I feel like a pint,' he said, his voice raising a level.

'A pint? More like five or six,' I replied.

'It's still nothing to do with you,' he said.

I bit my tongue and got to my feet.

'I'm going for a bath,' I said, more to myself than him.

'You had one yesterday,' he replied.

'I did, and I'll have one tomorrow, the day after, and the day after that if I feel like it. I'm paying the bloody gas bill, not you, Frank. If, and when, you decide to pay the bills, you can have a say in when I take a bath, until then... well, you know what you can do.'

I pointed out my new gramophone that I'd taken off the table and put beside the tallboy. 'I've been spending again, but, it's my own money, from my own Post Office account, and it's my choice of how I bloody well spend it. You throw yours away on beer, I spend mine on things that will give me pleasure for a lot longer than the fifteen minutes it takes you to drink a pint.'

He wasn't going to let an argument end with me having the last word. He wouldn't have even if he was sober. He got to his feet and shoved his face up close to mine. The stink of stale beer immediately brought on my nausea.

'One day soon, you'll fall off that golden perch of yours, Lady High and Mighty. You might even be knocked off it.' He pulled his sneering face away. 'Now get out of my sight. Go on. Piss off.'

I glared at him for a few seconds, but then I felt angry tears well up. I wasn't going to let him see he'd upset me, so I turned away from him and stomped off to the bathroom, blinking away my tears.

Chapter 56

Jess looked up from the book to see Alice had fallen asleep. Her breathing was shallow, but regular. She stood up, stretched and walked around the carpet in a circle in order to get her circulation moving again. She visited the bathroom and made another coffee before returning to her seat. The big clock on the wall read eight twenty-three as she walked back into the room. She watched Alice closely, ready to wake her on any sign of distress, but she seemed to be sleeping peacefully. Maybe that clock had something to do with her nightmares? She was always complaining about it.

Jess sat down again, sipped at her coffee and continued to read.

June 1938

My waters broke on the Sunday morning as I was working in the piggery.

I had been getting funny twinges in my stomach for an hour or two, but I put it down to wind moving through my bowels.

The waters broke with a gush, soaking me from the groin, right down to my ankles. I knew I hadn't peed myself because I had no control over it at all.

The pigs thought I'd brought them a watery treat, and all ten of them made a bee line, or should I say pig line, for me.

When they started snuffling around my lady parts I began to panic and I shouted for help, when that didn't work, I screamed for it.

I tried to make my way to the gate, but the weight of pork crammed up against my legs meant I couldn't move an inch. The panic switched to near terror as the two boars began to take an interest. They forced their way through the sows to get a closer sniff. One of the buggers butted me on the back of the knee and I went over, ending up sprawled across the backs of the sows.

I really thought I was a goner. As my father had warned me many a time; pigs will eat anything.

I screamed again as the big boar, Horace, started nibbling at the leg of my denim overalls.

Suddenly, the three overly excited sows I was lying across, decided to try to get around to the other side of the two boars, leaving me lying in shit on the floor of the sty, with ten pigs looking for a second breakfast. The boars began to fight amongst themselves over who would have the first sitting, Horace appeared to be winning that particular battle, his trotters pounding my legs as he bit out at Hector, his brother. I can't remember anything else, because I fainted.

When I came to, I was in Frank's strong arms, and he was taking me back to the farmhouse. He yelled at Miriam to open the back door, then he carried me inside and looked around frantically for somewhere to put me. He decided on our huge, oak kitchen table.

'Frank, I'm fine, just a little shaky, let me stand up.'

'Not until I know you're all right,' he replied and stretched me out along the full length of the table. My dungarees were in tatters from the crutch to the knees, and there were a few teeth marks and scratches on my legs, but apart from that, there didn't seem to be any other damage that we could see.

'What happened?' asked Miriam. She held both palms over her mouth, one on top of the other.

'She was on the menu for a pig's banquet, that's what happened,' replied Frank. He undid the straps of my overalls and slid the top down over my shirt. 'Lift your arse,' he commanded. I did as I was told and he pulled the dungarees down to the top of my boots leaving me showing off my soaking wet bloomers.

'Shit,' said Frank, realising his basic error. He pulled the slimy wellingtons off, one at a time, then he dragged the overalls over my feet and dumped them on the floor. He moved his hand towards a scratch on my leg but Miriam stopped him with a curt, 'Frank.' He looked up and she shook her head. 'Wash your hands first; you've got pig muck all over them.'

While Frank was washing his hands, Miriam moved to my side and stroked my hair. 'You must have been really frightened, Alice, you wet yourself. Hang on, there's a dry pair of your pants, on the clotheshorse.'

Frank came back, drying his hands on a towel. He had a close look at the nips and scratches on my legs, then turned away when Miriam reappeared clutching a pair of warm, clean knickers. I smiled at her gratefully, then clutched my stomach as a wave of pain shot across it.

'I didn't wet myself,' I said to her. 'My waters broke while I was in the pig pen.'

'Did you get any pain beforehand?' Miriam asked in a concerned tone. She opened the cupboard under the new sink and pulled out a clean flannel and an enamel bowl. She filled it with hot water from the tap, grabbed a bar of soap, and dumped the lot on the table at the side of me.

'Do you want to do it or shall I?' she asked.

'I'll do it, I'm fine, honestly.'

Miriam gave Frank a head flick to tell him to leave the room. He walked through to the parlour, and sat on a wooden chair that was in the same spot his foldaway bed used to be.

I lifted up my backside and pulled my pants off while Miriam wet the flannel and rubbed soap into it. I washed my bits first and then my legs, front and back then I lay on my side and let Miriam do my backside as I couldn't comfortably reach.

When I was dried off, I pulled on the clean knickers and struggled to a sitting position.

Frank came back into the kitchen and asked where the shells were for my father's gun.

'Why would you need bullets?' I asked.

'I'm going to shoot those bloody boars,' he said. 'They nearly had you for lunch. You don't know how close you were to being seriously hurt.'

'You'll have to shoot me first,' I said, dragging myself off the table. I staggered to the back door and stretched my arms out wide. 'I mean it, Frank, hurt those pigs and you're out on your ear.'

'I was only thinking of you,' he replied. 'You'll have to get back in with them sooner or later. What if they fancy a second course?'

'They won't,' I said, firmly. 'I'm in with them every day, Frank, and they've never come close to hurting me. It was my waters breaking, it got them excited. I'll make sure I'm drenched in Eau De Cologne, the next time I go in.'

Frank shook his head, wearing the slightest sign of a smile.

'All right, then, carbolic soap, the smell of that would stop anything wanting to get close.'

'You're right there,' he said, and a full smile lit up his face. He looked so different when he smiled. As the saying went, that smile could charm the knickers off a nun. I'm pretty sure it could too. It melted my heart as we stood facing each other in the kitchen. I thought back to the row we'd had earlier; I could even forgive him that.

Frank held out his arms and I walked straight into the softest hug. He wrapped those strong arms around me and whispered, 'I'm so glad you're safe.' *Not I'm so glad I got there in time. Not, I saved you from certain death, both of which were true, but, I'm so glad you're safe.*

Those whispered words went straight to my heart. Whether it was my heightened emotions or my shifting hormone levels, I don't know, but I felt I was beginning to fall in love with Frank. I knew I had to be careful, and let it evolve slowly, but the seeds of love were planted that day. I had never felt anything like it before. I hugged him closer and was about to tell him how I felt, when the next agonising pain shot through me.

My hands left his back and I clasped them together around his neck, as I bent forward to try to alleviate the pain.

Frank held me under my armpits to stop me collapsing altogether.

'Get her back on the table,' urged Miriam, who had been through this five times herself.

Frank sat me on the table and ordered me to lie down. I immediately slid off and sat in my favourite chair by the stove.

Miriam understood everything. 'Let's have a nice cup of tea. This could take a long time yet.'

She made a brew, and handed me a large mug with an extra two spoons of sugar, on top of the two I normally had.

'For energy,' she said.

The next contraction was a big one. As I was moaning, Frank went into flap mode and ran back and forth from the back door to the stove.

'Shall I go for the doctor? What about the midwife, is she coming? Do you need anything? Towels, hot water... anything at all?'

The pain lasted about ninety seconds. When I had recovered, I reminded Frank that we had a telephone and we could ring the doctor or midwife if we needed one.

'Can I use, it?' he asked. 'I'll ring The Old Bull and get them to bring my mother to the phone. I'd like to be the one to tell her she's going to be a grandma.'

'Of course, Frank, you know where it is,' I said. I sipped the super-sweet tea, pulled a face and tried to hand it back to Miriam, but she was having none of it.

'Drink it, it will do you good.' She sounded like my old teacher when I refused to drink the play time, runny, watery milk.

Frank came back, still in panic mode. He obviously didn't realise what he was saying.

'You haven't had it yet then?'

I patted my stomach. 'No, it's still in there.'

'I couldn't find your midwife's number,' he said.

'That's because I haven't got a midwife, and there are none listed in the directory, at lease none are advertising. You can run through all the names from A to Z to see if anyone has added 'Midwife' to their listing, but I doubt you'll find one, Frank.'

He raced back through to the front room again. When he came back, he looked full of himself.

'I've found one,' he said.

'One what?' I teased.

'A midwife,' he answered. 'I rang The Old Bull again. My mum was still there, she knows everyone in the town and she says we have a choice of three.' He listed them by counting on his fingers.

'One. Mrs Wallace.' Frank thought hard to remember what his mother had told him. 'She's quite old but she's delivered twenty or so babies in the town over the years. She'll charge fifteen shillings to see the job though.'

He ticked off a second one on his fingers.

'Two. Elsie Croggins. She lives at the back of The Old Bull. Mum knows her very well as she's only about a hundred yards away from her. She's quite a bossy woman, but she knows the job inside out.' Frank cringed as the unintended pun hit home. 'Sorry about that. Anyway, she charges a guinea and another ten bob for aftercare, she'll drop in for the next few days. She's got the new, midwifering... midwifing... qualification, and she has access to a doctor, should we need one.'

'It's Midwifery,' said Miriam, helpfully.

Frank stuck up a thumb to Miriam and then continued with his list.

'Three. Doris Bonner. She'll charge ten bob and not a word said to anyone about anything. She's probably delivered more babies than the other two put together, but she couldn't pass the midwifing... wifery, exam.'

I groaned as another wave of pain set about me. When I had recovered, I asked Miriam which midwife she had used.

'None,' she said. 'The old girl next door helped me with all of mine.' She tipped her head to one side, as she always did when she was thinking. 'Ooh! That was Doris. She's on Frank's list. What am I like?'

I made a decision.

'Can we get Elsie Croggins? I'm sorry, Miriam, but as it's my first time, I'd like to have someone with access to a doctor, especially after what happened to my mother.'

Frank hurried back to the telephone and returned with the news that his mother was going to call round to see if Elsie was available. 'She'll ring back from the kiosk near The Old Bull if she can't come. Elsie isn't on the telephone network either.'

Miriam made a fresh pot of tea and offered to make us all a sandwich, but food was the last thing I wanted and Frank didn't feel like eating either. She watched the clock like a hawk, counting the minutes between my contractions. We were down to eight.

'The shock you had in the piggery has done this, I'd stake my life on it. When I was having my first, I had contractions every twenty minutes for four days. Then they stopped and started up again two days later. I was in labour for thirty-four hours after that.'

I thought about my mother, and the life-changing labour she had gone though. I crossed my fingers and prayed to any god that might be listening, to spare me that horror.

We sat silently for a while, each of us deep in our own thoughts. We were dragged out of our group meditation, when the back door was flung open and a huge woman with her dark hair pulled back into a tight bun, burst into the room. Her face was red and her breath came in gasps. She was followed by Edna, who was looking mightily pleased with herself.

Elsie was a force of nature. She was an experienced midwife and knew how she liked things to be done. She also knew all there was to know about first time mothers.

'Right, Alice? It is Alice isn't it?'

I nodded.

'Good. Let's get down to business then. Where is the birth taking place?' She looked towards the open door that led upstairs.

'I'm not having it upstairs?' I said.

'Well, I can't see a bed down here?' Elsie strode to the parlour, then to the front room.

'There's a man in there who appears to be drunk,' she said, looking around as if we weren't aware of the fact.

'That's my father. He's been in there for months,' I said as though she ought to have known.

'So... where... is... the... bed?' she asked very slowly so we all understood.

'I don't know where I'm having the baby,' I said, quietly. 'I only know I'm not having it upstairs.'

'Why on earth not, child? You're being ridiculous. Are you seriously telling me you want to have your first baby on a dirty kitchen floor?'

'I'm not having it upstairs,' I insisted. 'My mother had me in the bed that I sleep in now, and it nearly killed her. She lost so much blood. She was never the same afterwards.'

'All right, I can understand that. Are there no other beds upstairs?'

'No, two of the bedrooms are empty and Miriam sleeps in the other, I'm not going to ruin her bed.'

'I don't mind,' Miriam said. 'We can always clean it up afterwards. I slept on the same mattress I had all of my babies on. There were a few stains, but they dried and...' Miriam went quiet after receiving a hostile stare from Elsie.

'Shall we put some sheets and pillows on the table then? It's huge, you could fit two people on it,' Edna suggested.

'It won't be the first time I've delivered on a table,' replied Elsie. She pointed at Miriam. 'You go upstairs and get some spotlessly clean sheets, a few pillows and a lot of towels.' She turned to Edna. 'You get me a bowl of hot water, some clean cloths and some disinfectant, if they don't have any, I have some in my bag.' She turned to Frank and seemed surprised to find him there. 'As for you, well, I don't know why you are here in the first place. A birthing room isn't the place for men.' She looked at me and tossed her head. 'Babies are women's business. Men shouldn't be allowed to interfere, and I include doctors in that statement. What would they know about it?' Her gaze returned to Frank. 'Are you still here?' she asked.

'I was hoping to make myself useful,' he said sulkily.

'The best way you can do that, is by clearing off.' Elsie pointed towards the back door. 'Be gone, and don't hang around outside either. You won't like the noises coming from in here, so, I suggest you go for a long walk and when you've finished that, go for another one. This will take hours.'

Frank blew me a kiss, wished me good luck, and walked to the door.

'Don't go to The Old Bull either,' said Elsie with a scowl. 'Drunken men and new mothers don't mix. She'll need your support, not your drunken efforts to stand up by yourself.'

Miriam came downstairs with a pile of sheets and pillows. 'Most of the clean towels are out on the line, I'll just go and get them,' she said, rushing to the back door.

Edna placed the enamel bowl that Miriam had used earlier, on the table, and tested the water temperature with her elbow. She tipped a capful of disinfectant into it and stirred it with her hand.

Elsie's eyes turned to me.

'Right, young lady. Up you get, and take your knickers off, you won't be needing them.'

Edna and Elsie spread a sheet on the table and stacked three pillows at one end.

I took my pants off and eased myself onto the table. Elsie put one of her ham-sized hands on my chest and with more gentleness than I was expecting, pushed me back until my head was nestled into the pillows. I smiled at her but she wasn't in the mood for pleasantries.

'Right, open up. Let's have a look at you.'

The last time I had been ordered to do that, had been by a dentist, but I did as I was told and she stuck her head between my knees. Something cold and metallic touched my bits and then I groaned as another contraction hit. Elsie fiddled about with whatever she had to fiddle about with, then her head appeared from between my open legs.

'You're further on than I thought, Alice. You'll be a mother before tea time.'

She backed away and allowed Edna to wash my legs with the disinfected water, then she leaned over to examine my battered thighs.

'What's been going on here?' she asked.

'Pigs,' I replied. 'They thought I'd make a nice change for dinner.'

Chapter 57

June 1938

The time went slowly.

Every so often, Elsie would get me to spread my knees and she'd stick her head between them for a while, and then her face would appear, calm and reassuring.

'Not yet, but things are moving on.'

I certainly wasn't moving on. I had been on the table for almost four hours. I felt useless, I wasn't allowed to do anything, I tried reading, but I kept dropping the book every time the contractions hit. By the time Miriam had picked up the book, wiped the cover down with a disinfected cloth and I'd found my place again, it was time for another one.

I almost began to look forward to the contractions, as at least they eased the boredom. I got severe cramp in my foot, twice and my right calf, three times, but Elsie was on hand to massage the painful limb for me. I wasn't even allowed to do that by myself.

Miriam suggested we play music on my new gramophone, but less than one verse into the first record, Elsie told her to turn it off as she considered modern jazz music, the work of the devil and she couldn't concentrate on what she was doing.

Miriam made tea, but Elsie only allowed me to have a quarter of a mug, even though I was thirsty.

'You'll only want to pee all the time and we don't want to be traipsing back and forth to the lavatory all afternoon, do we?'

I agreed that we didn't, but ten minutes later I found that it was either go to the bathroom or pee all over Elsie's head while she was examining me.

When I was back on the table, I suddenly remembered I hadn't asked Miriam about her date the night before. I say night, because she hadn't come home by the time I went to bed.

'Oh, it was lovely.' Miriam closed her eyes and a look of beatific joy spread over her face.

'And...' I said, having waited a full thirty seconds for the juicy details to be imparted. Patience wasn't on my list of virtues that afternoon.

'Oh, it was lovely,' Miriam oozed.

'You already said that,' I grunted, as another contraction made me arch my aching back.

'Well.' Miriam pulled up a chair and patted my hand. 'He picked me up at—'

'I know when he picked you up, I waved you off,' I said irritably. 'Come on, Miriam, get down to the nitty gritty. Did you get a smoochy kiss?'

'We had a few dances, waltzes mainly, although I did get to dance one foxtrot. He commented on how well I danced. He's a very good dancer. All the other women were staring at us. I think they were jealous of me.'

I thought about the square-chested, white haired builder with the weather-beaten face and smiled to myself. Beauty really is in the eye of the beholder after all.

'We had tea, lots of it, and cake. They had the daintiest tea cakes and the gateau, I mean, I can make cakes, but this was in a different league. It was like being at the Ritz.'

I thought about the village hall with its rickety old tables and the worn parquet flooring. My parents held their twentieth wedding anniversary celebrations there in 1936. It wasn't the Ritz by any stretch of the imagination. Then I remembered what a sheltered, lonely life Miriam had led, and mentally ticked myself off for being mean.

'The band was really good; Michael requested they play Blue Skies, just for us, and we had the floor to ourselves as we danced. They passed a hat around at the end and just about everyone threw some money in. Michael wouldn't let me get my purse out. He put five shillings in to cover both of us.'

'Most of the women were older than me, some didn't have dance partners so the men were eagerly sought out. Michael was asked to dance a few times, but he always refused politely, telling them he was with the only lady he wanted to dance with.'

She blushed at the memory.

'Careful, Miriam, he'll have you down the aisle in no time,' I said, grinning.

'I wouldn't mind,' she said.

'Miriam! Put up a bit of a fight at least. If you don't want to play hard to get, at least try to be enigmatic. You have to keep him guessing.'

'Never let a man think he owns you, because before you know it, he does,' Elsie said with a knowing look on her face.

'Don't worry, I know all about men like that. I was married to one for years. Michael's not like that,' Miriam replied.

I thought about Frank, he could be controlling at times. But this morning he had been the epitome of gentleness. Which one was the real Frank? I looked over my raised knees at Edna, who had spent her time crocheting the promised baby shawl. Was he his mother's son, or his father's? I'd find out sooner or later, that was for sure.

'Anyway,' Miriam continued. 'After the dance, we got back in his truck and drove over to Engleby, for fish and chips and we sat in the park to eat them. There was no one else there. It was like we were the only people on earth. We talked for ages. He told me all about his wife and I tried not to tell him all about my ex-husband, but he got it out of me anyway. He was so angry. He couldn't understand how a man could treat the mother of his children like that.'

'Nor can I,' said Edna and Elsie at the same time.

I gazed around the kitchen at the three women who were looking after me. All had picked the wrong man. I wondered how it happened. Why did so many of us choose the partner least suited to our personalities? Maybe we were attracted to the strong, silent type. Maybe we needed to feel we were being protected. In my case, and Edna's, we didn't really have much say in it. When I looked at the bitterness etched on Elsie's face, I wondered if she had been left in a similar situation. Was Michael the exception that proved the rule, or were these three women just unlucky? If Frank turned out to be the same as those three men, it would mean that we had a one hundred percent failure record. The odds on that occurring must be impossible. I sighed with relief at that thought.

When I came out of my reverie, Miriam was still talking.

'So, I took his arm and we had a nice stroll around the lake in the middle of the park, talking as we walked. We've got such a lot in common. He likes the same books as me, he likes the songs I like, he's even a Sagittarius.'

'What's that got to do with anything?' asked Elsie from between my knees.

'Well, I'm Aries, and we're supposed to be a good match... if you believe that sort of thing of course.'

It was obvious that Miriam did believe that sort of thing.

'My ex-husband was a Leo,' said Elsie. She straightened up as another contraction hit. 'Not long now, Alice.'

'What sign are you,' asked Edna.

'Taurus,' Elsie said, looking at her watch, waiting for me to groan.

'Taurus and Leo? That's a match made in hell,' replied Miriam.

'Tell me about it,' said Elsie, gruffly. My next contraction came long and hard. She nodded to herself and checked her watch again. 'Never marry a Leo. My sister used to tell me that all the time, but did I listen?'

'I never got to be married,' said Edna. 'I'm a Capricorn, he was a Libra. I never knew whether we'd get on or not because he cleared off when he found out I was pregnant. What sign are you, Alice?'

'Libra, just,' I said. (My birthday was the twenty-third of September.) 'Frank's a Pisces; his birthday was back in March.'

Miriam looked at me in horror, then she patted my hand and went to make more tea.

I didn't believe in all this astrology nonsense, but after Miriam's reaction, I made up my mind to look into my star sign's best and worst matches when I was up and about again.

About an hour later I felt the almost irresistible urge to push.

Elsie, who was by now more familiar with my nether region than I was, began a series of commands. She was so fearsome I doubt any soldier would have hesitated for a split second from going over the top, had she ordered him to.

'PUSH!' she cried.

I pushed.

'Well, that's a start but now put some effort into it,' she encouraged.

'PUSH!'

I screwed up my face and pushed again.

'Come on, let's have a bit more OOMPH!' she demanded.

I grabbed a lungful of air, gritted my teeth, and gave it my best shot.

'PUSH!' she yelled.

I looked over my bulging stomach at the bun on the back of her head.

'I am bloody pushing,' I yelled back.

'You can do better than that, Missy,' she said, without looking up.

'PUSH!'

Occasionally she would order me to pant, but I didn't even do that correctly.

'No, pant like a greyhound who's just done three laps of the track.'

And so, it went on.

The baby came quite unexpectedly in the end. I was tiring fast, but after half an hour of pushing, Elsie announced that the head was out. I tried to have a look myself, but Elsie must have felt me trying to sit up, and one of those huge hands arose from between my thighs and pushed me back again.

'PUSH!'

I don't know if it was the last big effort I could manage, or just the fact that I was sick of hearing Elsie's voice, but I managed the biggest heave I'd done all day, and the rest of the baby slid out.

'It's a girl,' Elsie announced.

She picked the slippery baby up like she'd been catching slithering eels from a bucket, all her life. She held her by the ankles and slapped her backside. The baby opened her mouth but refused to cry. Elsie tried again. The infant wriggled about in her vice-like grip, but again refused to cry.

'We might have a mute, here,' said Elsie, in a matter of fact way.

'She's probably just stubborn. I wouldn't cry when I was born either,' I said.

Elsie told me to bare my breasts. I wasn't going to argue, I was too worn out to raise a smile, let alone my voice.

Elsie introduced the baby to my left breast but she refused to suckle. My midwife tried the other one, but again with no real response. I thought I'd help her out a bit, so I squeezed my breast until a trickle of liquid seeped out. The baby licked at it, pulled a face, looked me in the eyes and screamed the place down.

And that was the start of my relationship with my firstborn. She wailed for fifteen minutes as she lay across my chest with Elsie trying to encourage her to feed. Eventually she gave up. The baby was scarlet-faced, I was falling asleep and Elsie's experience told her to give us both a breather. As soon as she lifted her from my chest, she stopped crying. Even when Elsie laid her between my legs and did the necessary with the umbilical cord, she was quiet as a mouse. Once the cord was cut, Elsie wrapped her in a towel and handed her to me. I looked down at my daughter with, I have to admit, a bit of indifference. She looked back at me with loathing. Before that day I wouldn't have believed a baby could do that, but she proved me wrong. She began to scream again almost immediately. Miriam took her from me and once again, she stopped her temper tantrum. All was quiet when Edna held her granddaughter for the first time, but when she was passed back to me, the inevitable happened.

'Will you take her for a while,' I asked Miriam, as Elsie began to clean up the detritus.

I lay back in my pillows and watched her walk around the kitchen rocking and cooing to my baby while an adoring Edna impatiently waited her turn.

'We'll have to get her to feed soon,' Elsie said.

I lifted my heavy breasts in my hands.

'Well, the pantry is well stocked,' I said.

'We may have to express the milk and feed it to her in a bottle. It happens quite regularly although I've never seen a reluctance to feed, quite like this before,' replied Elsie. She opened her bag and took out a box of powdered milk. 'I'll leave you some formula milk just in case. I'll show Miriam how to mix it before I go.'

'I suppose a wet nurse is out of the question,' I said, only half-jokingly.

Chapter 58

June 1938

My baby weighed in at five pounds and seven ounces. Edna told me that was a nice weight for a first child and as I hadn't needed stitches, I was a lucky girl.

'Frank came out at seven pounds,' she said.

Elsie chipped in with her first at six pounds even.

Miriam topped the weight poll. 'My first weighed in at nine pounds eight ounces.'

I winced. How could something that big ever squeeze its way through such a tiny place? Mine felt like a rugby player was trying to force his way out, and she was tiny compared to theirs.

In the early evening, I had a strip wash in the new bathroom, and hobbled back to the kitchen where I had unburdened the table of my presence, and had taken up my usual spot in the chair by the unlit stove. There had been no sign of Frank. He hadn't telephoned us, which surprised me a little. I wondered if he was staying away, in case I had a long, tortuous labour like my mother had suffered, or whether he was scared of coming back until the bossy midwife had departed.

Elsie left at seven, with a promise to return the following morning. The still unnamed baby was feeding well from the formula bottle that Elsie had provided. All I had to do was pump out the milk every few hours and try to persuade the baby to take it. I was happy with that solution, it seemed far easier than fighting with a baby that didn't want anything to do with my milk-laden breasts. Edna gave her granddaughter a kiss on the forehead and rushed off to catch up with Elsie.

At seven-thirty, Miriam came in from changing my father's nappy and set about changing the baby.

'It's cleaner than his, thank goodness. She won't poo for a day or two yet, so less smelly too,' she said, wafting her hand under her nose.

'I'd have done that, Miriam,' I said.

'You rest up, I don't mind changing her. I love the feel and smell of a new baby's skin.'

'You're looking after all three of us. It's like a hospital here. How's the front room patient, Nurse Miriam?' I asked.

'He's awake and quite lucid, for him at least. Now might be a good time to take the baby in to show him.'

'Let her go back to sleep first, Miriam. She'll scream the house down if I pick her up when she's awake.'

Miriam put the baby into the wicker Moses basket that she had brought with her when she moved to the farm. All five of her babies had slept under that hood, and she was reluctant to part with it. She sat on the floor with her hand on the baby's shawl and sang quietly to her. Within two minutes, she was asleep.

Fifteen minutes later, I lifted my daughter out of the Moses basket, and rearranged her shawl so that her face was completely visible. I waited for a few moments to make sure she wasn't about to wake up, then I tip-toed across the kitchen floor, Miriam opened the door to the front room, and I stepped through, being careful not to trip on the curled up edges of the faded carpet strip that lay on the bare boards, just inside the door.

My father didn't look up as I came in. He appeared to be concentrating on a large spider that crept along the skirting board in front of his chair. I crouched down as low as I could go without suffering too much pain, and held the baby in front of him. He seemed surprised by my presence. He twisted his neck and tilted his head, his pale blue eyes narrowed to slits. He scowled and made a growling noise at the back of his throat. I stood up and took a quick step to the side in case he made an attempt to get hold of her.

His eyes followed the baby as I pulled her away. His face became a mask of sheer hatred.

'You killed her,' he snarled.

'Mr Mollison!' Miriam came alongside me, and prepared to intervene if the situation got any worse.

'You killed her!' he repeated. 'It's your fault.'

I wasn't going to let him get away with that, sick as he was. I handed the baby to Miriam and once again tried to crouch in front of him. I tried to hide the anger that welled up inside me. I took a deep breath and when I spoke, it was in a soft, friendly tone.

'It's your new granddaughter. She only arrived today. Wouldn't you like to say hello to her?'

It was a real effort for him to raise his skeletal head on that scrawny neck. His eyes eventually focussed on me and once again his bony, yellow-tinged face, scowled at me.

'It should have been you,' he slurred. 'You should have died, not her.'

I refused to listen to any more. My eyes filled with tears of frustration. My emotions had been all over the place all day and his reaction hadn't helped them level out. I hadn't expected him to jump out of his chair and dance around the room at the news of his granddaughter's birth, but I didn't expect us to be greeted in such a hate-filled manner either. I thought he loved me. I had always thought he loved me, despite everything that had happened to my mother since my birth. Had it all been a cruel act? Or was it the whisky that had addled his brain, leaving him unable to think rationally. I decided that was his fault anyway. He didn't care about me or the farm when he took to the bottle. He had been so selfish. He didn't give a damn about me. He left me to run the farm on my own, with all the responsibilities that came with it. He didn't care about the workers either. What if I had messed up and they all had to be laid off? He didn't even care for the memory of my mother. She would turn in her grave if she could hear his accusations. She loved me, despite her troubled life. Terminally ill or not, he'd picked the wrong day to spit his venom.

'You miserable old swine,' I hissed. 'Her death was nothing to do with me. I wouldn't even be here if you hadn't got her pregnant in the first place. So, you're the one who should take the blame for everything that happened to her, not me. Think on that while you're sitting in your own shit, waiting to die.'

I turned on my heels and stormed out of the room leaving both Miriam and my father in tears.

At ten-thirty the back door almost came off its hinges as it burst open and Frank staggered into the kitchen. I groaned, not just because of the pain I was in either.

He swayed across the kitchen, arms outstretched.

'Where is she, where's my daughter. Let me see her.'

I picked up the baby and stepped away from the stove. I adjusted the shawl so that Frank could see her face. He leaned forward and put both hands on the table to support himself. Tears ran over his cheeks. He blinked twice, shook his head to help him focus, lifted an arm and wiped his sleeve across his eyes.

'She's beautiful.' He leaned forward again. 'Beautiful. She looks just like my mother.'

I thought he meant that she had a wrinkled face. I came immediately to her defence.

'All babies have wrinkled-up faces,' I said.

'Her nose and her eyes, not the screwed-up face.' He seemed to be insulted by my explanation. 'I want to hold her. Give her to me.' Frank straightened up and lurched towards me.

I moved across to the other side of the hearth. I held the baby in the crook of my arm and pushed the other one towards him, palm up. 'Frank. You're drunk, you'll drop her.'

'I just want to hold her, I'll be careful.'

I doubted he could safely hold a pint, let alone a new born baby.

'Tomorrow, Frank, hold her tomorrow,' I said, trying to calm him.

'But she won't be new tomorrow, I'm her father, I want to hold her, she's half mine.'

The baby decided to take Frank's side of the argument. She opened her eyes, realised who was holding her, and began to scream the place down. I rocked her ineffectively. When I tried to shush her wailing, she doubled her efforts.

'I only want to hold my daughter. She's as much mine as yours. I stood by you all the way along. I've done my bit, Alice.'

I almost asked what bit he was doing while I was writhing in agony on the kitchen table, but I doubted he would have heard me over the screaming baby.

'She's got some lungs on her,' said Frank, craning his neck to see into the shawl. 'Come on, Alice, let me see her properly.'

As I was trying to work out whether Frank should be allowed to hold my new baby after getting himself into such a state, Miriam came down the stairs to see if I needed any help. She saw Frank and waved. 'Hello, Daddy,' she said.

'See, I'm the daddy,' slurred Frank. 'Let me hold her, Alice. Come on.'

I felt a headache coming on. I'd had enough of the screaming.

'Sit in my chair, Frank. I can't give her to you while you're weaving around like that.'

Frank plonked himself down and held out his arms. I walked the short distance between us, motioned him to lean back into the chair, then I gently placed the baby into his arms. It immediately stopped crying.

Frank set his eyes on her and didn't look away for a good five minutes. When he did look up, his eyes were leaking again. He wept drunken tears as he rocked her. 'I promise you, that no one will ever hurt you while I'm alive. I'll protect you. If ever you need me, I'll be there in a heartbeat.'

He looked across the hearth and gave me that bloody smile again. 'Thank you,' he said.

The combination of the teary eyes and smile, almost made me blubber too, but I couldn't let him get away without at least a token ticking off.

'You shouldn't have got drunk, Frank. I needed you here with me this evening. I was worried about you.'

'I was only wetting the baby's head, Alice. I'm allowed to do that, aren't I?'

I sighed. 'I suppose so, but there's a difference between wetting the baby's head and drenching it. Hang on a minute, when you came in you already knew you had a daughter. Who told you?'

'My mother came into The Old Bull on the way home, I'd only had one pint by then. I'd been walking all afternoon, thinking about things. I walked round the town three times.'

'Didn't you think about coming home to see us?' I asked.

He became very defensive. 'Of course, I did, but the lads wouldn't let me leave, every time someone new came into the bar, they bought me more beer, and by the time I realised what time it was, the pub was closing.'

He leaned over the baby and kissed her on the forehead. 'What are we going to call her? Have you had any thoughts?'

'I was thinking about naming her Rosemary, after my mother, but I don't think my father would ever forgive me for it,' I said.

'We could name her after my mother,' said Frank.

I shook my head. 'I don't want to sound mean, Frank, but Edna is a bit old fashioned.'

Frank didn't seem to hear. 'Hello little Edna,' he cooed.

'She's not going to be called Edna, Frank, so stop that.' I crossed my arms over my chest and tried to look stern.

'What then? We have to call her something. I want to register her this week and she'll need a name by then.'

'I don't know, Frank. I've been thinking about it for weeks but I can't decide. I've narrowed it down to Rose, or Matilda.'

'What about Martha? That was my grandma's name.' Frank seemed determined to make the decision himself.

'Martha's even more old fashioned than Edna,' I complained.

'Toss you for it, then,' said Frank. 'You choose one from your two names, and I'll toss a coin.'

I was glad the responsibility of choosing a name was being taken out of my hands. I'd lost sleep thinking about it. I didn't trust Frank not to cheat though. 'Miriam can toss the coin. You can have heads for Martha and I'll have tails for Rose.'

Miriam pulled a penny coin from her purse and stood in the centre of the room. She tossed the coin in the air, caught it as it fell, and slapped it down on the back of her hand.

'Heads,' she said, showing us both the coin.

Frank grinned. I shrugged. It wasn't me that would have to live with the name after all.

Miriam dropped the coin as we heard a thud from the front room. She rushed across the kitchen calling to my father that she was on her way.

I sat in the chair opposite Frank and watched him whispering to his daughter. Once again, I felt a tug on my heartstrings. I leaned back in the chair and closed my eyes. The events of the day had finally caught up with me. I felt I could sleep for a month.

As it was, I didn't get as much as ten seconds. I almost leapt out of the chair as a blood curdling scream came from the front room. I got to my feet, thinking Miriam might have been attacked. My father had been in a foul temper when we left him earlier. Frank stood up, put Martha into her basket and followed me. I had only got as far as the table when Miriam almost fell into the kitchen.

'He's dead!' she cried. 'Mr Tansley. He's dead.'

Chapter 59

June 1938

My father had fallen out of his chair, Miriam found him with his head and right shoulder on the floor and his right knee bent over the arm of the armchair. The noise we heard was his head knocking over his whisky table as he fell.

He was definitely dead, there was no doubt about that. His unblinking eyes were still staring at the spider on the skirting board which had stopped dead itself to stare back with all eight eyes of its own.

Frank, who seemed to have sobered up very quickly, took charge of the situation.

'We can't leave him like that,' he said. He looked around the room but there was nothing we could lay him out on. The table was round, and not very wide, and if we pushed two chairs together, we'd have to sit him up, as he was a tall man.

We were all in shock, but in the end, it was Frank that came up with the solution.

'Let's get him into the parlour, we can get the old foldaway bed out that I used to sleep on. At least he'll be lying flat.'

The next problem was getting him in there. He weighed next to nothing, but picking up a man's body proved difficult to say the least. Frank managed to lift him at the third attempt, and Miriam went ahead to set up the bed, while Frank, still swaying a little, followed her to the parlour with my father's head and legs hanging over his arms.

Once he had laid the body on the foldaway bed, Frank crouched down beside him, said a few words that I couldn't make out, and crossed himself. I was quite touched by this show of respect, and not a little surprised, as apart from dragging me to the Catholic church on Sheppey, he hadn't showed the slightest sign of having any religious tendencies. I was agnostic at best but I did believe in some sort of life after death, just not with the angels, harps and St Peter's judgement.

When Frank had finished, I asked for a few minutes alone with my father. Frank left, closing the door quietly behind him and I sat down beside the shell of my former parent, and berated him for abusing me the way he had earlier in the evening. Then I had a go at him for being so selfish, for becoming a drunk, and for leaving me to sort out the farm. Then I burst into tears, took hold of his hand, put my head on his chest and sobbed.

Half an hour later I had run out of tears. The almost endless day had got the better of me. You couldn't make this sort of thing up if you were an author. No one would believe it. I let go of his hand and promised him that I'd remember the good times, and not the misery of his final months. I'd remember the piggy back rides, the times he carried me up to bed when I had fallen asleep playing with my dolls. The ticking offs for hiding in the cornfield when I should have been cleaning out an empty pig sty. I'd remember the way he looked at my mother when we were sitting around the dinner table. The way he kissed her every morning before he went out to work, the way he kissed her again when he returned for lunch. I remember being out in the fields for the harvest when she brought us sandwiches, cake and homemade lemonade and he said that Kings and Princes couldn't be served better fare. I'd remember the time I came down from my bedroom after having had a bad dream, to find them dancing to a song on the radio, their bodies so close, there wasn't room to slide a playing card between them.

But the time I remember most, is the day of the wedding anniversary at the Village Hall, where he made a speech, telling everyone in the room, why he was the luckiest man in the world. How he held both her hands, looked into her eyes and told her that he loved her with all his heart. There was no manly embarrassment, he didn't care who saw, or heard, when he said, *I love you with every fibre of my being. I have loved you from the moment we met. The first time you spoke to me I thought my heart was going to burst out of my chest. I have never looked at another woman since that day, and I never will. You own my heart. You are my world and everything in it.*

Before he was half way through that speech, my mother burst into tears along with every other woman in the room. When he finished, she kissed him on the lips and said, simply, *I love you too.*

I pulled a handkerchief from my pocket, dabbed my eyes and then blew my runny nose.

'Sleep softly,' I said, kissing him on the cheek. 'Say hello to Mum for me when you see her.'

Chapter 60

Alice

Jessica read beautifully, Alice thought. She really had a talent for it. If she wasn't able to make a living out of writing, she should consider narrating those new-fangled Audrey Books or whatever they were called. Alice had a few, but hadn't bothered listening to them for a few months. She had always preferred a paper book to any of the new ways of consuming literature.

She put her head back on her pillows as she listened to Jess read, her voice became quieter as a vision of the big clock came into her mind. The hands were just coming up to ten minutes to twelve, whether it was day or night, she couldn't tell. Jess's voice faded away into the distance, and suddenly she was sitting around the stove in her kitchen. Amy was there, and the two of them were laughing, singing and enjoying each other's company. Then the dream shifted and the awful tunnel appeared, though it seemed further away and less threatening than it had been previously. The mist wasn't as thick and the light was dimmer. She looked down to see that she was standing still, watching it from a distance. Then the clock reappeared again, the hands pointing to fifteen minutes to twelve. Alice blinked at the ceiling light and the sound of Jess's voice filled her head.

'Are you awake, Nana? I hope you didn't have any of those nasty dreams.'

'I saw the tunnel, Jessica, but it didn't seem so close, nowhere near as close, and I didn't see anyone in it. It was more like when I first started dreaming about it. The clock went backwards too. How can that happen?'

'I don't know, Nana, dreams are weird things. Maybe you don't dream so much about the tunnel when you can't see the clock. Shall I take it down for you?'

Alice was fully awake. 'No, I think I might miss it in an odd sort of way if it wasn't there. Leave it, my dear. It's been up there since before I started that book you have in your hands. It's like me, it belongs here.'

Jess made cocoa and they chatted about Jess's work for a while, before she bought up the subject of Alice's memoir.

'When you were sleeping, I read the chapter about Martha's birth and what happened afterwards. What a terrible day that was, Nana. I cried as I was reading it. A new arrival and a sad departure on the same day... and what about those pigs? I think I'd have dropped dead with fright if that had happened to me.'

Alice blew out her cheeks and expelled the air. 'The pigs! Oh, my goodness, I'd almost forgotten about them. Horace, Hector and their sows. They were gentle beasts really. It broke my heart when the time came to let them go.' She paused as she remembered them, then shrugged. 'It was a farm, sad things happened.'

Jess shook her head. 'As if you hadn't taken enough punishment for one day, you had Martha and lost your dad in the space of a few hours.'

'It was a very tough day, but, although it was a very sad time, I was relieved that my father had gone. It meant he wasn't suffering that dreadful, mental anguish anymore, and he'd moved on to wherever my mother had moved on to. I just hoped he was happy at last. The worst bit was seeing his coffin lid being screwed down. That really got to me.'

'I can understand that, Nana. Frank reminds me a lot of Calvin. You never know where you are with him when he's had a drink. At least Frank was better when he was sober, and he did care about Martha.'

'Did he?' Alice thought for a short while. 'Maybe he did. She always liked him; I know that much.'

'Do you want your sleeping tablet now, Nana?' Jess checked the big clock. 'It's ten o'clock.'

'No, I don't feel tired. Do you mind reading a bit more? The years have stolen parts of my story from me and I'd like to be reminded of what my thoughts were at the time.'

Jess opened the book again and read. June. 1938.

Chapter 61

June 1938

When I got back to the kitchen, Miriam was giving Martha the last bit of another formula bottle. She sniffled as she whispered, 'Good girl, drink it all up now.'

The bottle of expressed milk stood on the side of the sink. I picked it up, shook it and then sniffed it in case it had gone off. 'She wouldn't have it then, Miriam?'

'She had a sniff and turned her nose up, so I made some more formula. There's another bottle on the cold shelf.'

I sighed, as fatigue swarmed over me. I least I was spared having to squeeze out breast milk for Martha during the night. Elsie had given me a strict timetable that I was to follow unerringly. I had to get the baby into a routine. She had given me dire warnings about how my life would be ruined if Martha was allowed to dictate feeding times. My life had changed in so many ways over the last twelve hours. I needed Amy, she could help me through it all, she'd know what to say to ease my fears, she always did. I decided to take Martha up to see her tomorrow, then I remembered I hadn't bought a pram yet, and I probably wouldn't make it past the back door with Miriam and Elsie standing guard anyway.

'Where's Frank?' I asked.

'He went into the front room a while ago. I offered to let him feed Martha, but he said he needed a few minutes alone.'

I could understand that, we had all had a terrible shock. I stretched, rubbed at my aching back and eased myself into my chair by the stove. I was sore in all sorts of places, but that backache made it impossible to get comfortable. I stood up again and walked around the kitchen, but there was no relief. I needed a back rub and I knew just the man to administer it. He had performed miracles when I had almost seized up, getting out of bed during the week.

I looked at the clock. He'd had forty minutes on his own, that was enough, surely. I'd say sorry if it wasn't.

I made my way across the kitchen, bent over, thinking I must look like Quasimodo, the Hunchback of Notre Dame.

Miriam gave me her sad faced look. 'Can I do anything to help, my dear? I know exactly how you feel, it's the back ache isn't it? That was the worst part for me too. I'll give you a rub when I've finished feeding the little one if you like.'

'It's okay, Miriam, Frank can do it. He's got the magic touch.'

I tapped on the door as a courtesy, I was going in regardless. I was almost doubled over in pain as I stepped over the curled-up edges of the carpet strip. I forced myself to straighten up and found Frank sitting on my father's smelly old chair. He was holding a half-full bottle of whisky. He stared at me drunkenly.

'Can't let it go to waste. It's what the old bugger would have wanted.' Frank laughed a gravelly laugh, and I suddenly saw my father sitting there the day after my mother's funeral.

'Well done, Frank. You've managed to surprise me, and that takes a lot of doing these days.' I turned back towards the door. 'I expected better.'

'Better than what, or who?' Frank exploded. 'How could I be any worse than the old sot who used to sit here?'

'He was sick, he was mourning, he wanted to die. What's your excuse, Frank? It should be one of the happiest days of your life. You're a new father, you should be showing your daughter what a good one she's got. Not sitting in a dead man's chair, drinking yourself into oblivion.'

That hit home. Frank's head dropped and he became weepy again. I'd had enough of his drunken tears. 'Fuck you, Frank. Fuck you with a rusty old rod. You're not worthy of being called father. Mine was a great one, until he lost the love of his life. You've disgraced yourself on your first day. You ought to be ashamed.'

I stormed into the kitchen, if a bent-over stagger can be described that way. Miriam was rubbing Martha's back, hoping to get some wind up before putting her back in the basket. I was suddenly jealous of my own daughter. My back needed attention too.

'I've got some aspirin in my room if you'd like a couple of tablets,' Miriam said, soothingly.

'Miriam, I could kiss you,' I replied. I hadn't bought any since I became pregnant, I remember reading something about it thinning the blood, so didn't want to risk it.

Miriam nipped upstairs and came back with a small bottle containing a dozen pills. 'You can have them, sweetheart. I only take them when my own back plays up. I'll get some more tomorrow.'

'Get a triple supply,' I said, washing two tablets down with a glass of water. I walked over to the Moses basket and put my finger gently on Martha's cheek, the way I'd seen mothers do a hundred times. Martha opened her eyes, looked at me as though I was the scariest thing she had seen in her short life, and let out an ear-piercing scream.

'You really don't like me, do you?' I said to her.

'She'll grow to love you, don't you worry,' Miriam said.

I wasn't so sure. How could a new born take such an instant dislike to its own mother? I thought about the times I'd said that I didn't want her, and thought she had somehow understood. I put my finger back on her cheek and rubbed it softly. 'I'm sorry. I didn't mean it,' I whispered.

Martha quietened a little, so I rubbed her other cheek and she stopped wailing. I blew out a sigh of relief and leaned into the basket to give her a kiss. That was a big mistake, as before my lips got within a foot of her face, the squealing began again. I gave up. I'd had one small victory; I'd settle for that tonight.

Miriam smiled at me sympathetically. 'Why don't you go to bed, let those aspirin get to work. I'll sit up with Martha tonight.'

'I can't go up yet, I've got to get some more milk out.'

Miriam got up from her seat, I thought she was going to offer to help me express, so I held up my hand. I wasn't a cow; I could milk myself.

Miriam laughed at my concerned face. 'Don't worry, I'm just going to make a pot of tea.'

I joined in the laughter, pleased to have been allowed one lighter moment in my day of pain and sadness.

Twenty minutes of squeezing and swearing later, I fell into bed. My breasts were already sore, goodness knows what they would be like in a few days' time. I pictured them in my mind, red-raw and swollen, the skin flaking off, with rock-hard, sore, bleeding nipples. Elsie had rescued me by giving us the formula milk. When she arrived in the morning, I was determined to ask her whether Martha could stay on it full time. I wasn't being selfish; Martha was never going to feed from my breasts anyway. There was no point in rubbing and squeezing the poor things until they became too sore to touch. If I could give her powdered milk instead, it might fill her up, so there might not be so many feeds.

That made me feel guilty. I'd had Martha less than twelve hours, and I was already trying to push her away. I made up my mind to try a bit harder tomorrow. I could be a good mother, if she gave me the chance.

I was just drifting into a well-earned sleep when Frank appeared in the doorway of the bedroom.

'I've come to bed,' he announced, holding on to both sides of the doorframe for support.

'You're not bloody well sleeping in here tonight,' I told him.

'Where do I sleep then?' He looked genuinely puzzled.

'I don't care, Frank,' I said. 'Go and sleep with my father. You've got a lot in common.'

'But—'

'Go, NOW!' I yelled. 'I'm sick of the sight of you.'

Frank turned, though it took three attempts to face the other way. I heard his footsteps thump down the stairs and then a series of bumps as he fell down the last few. Miriam's voice was full of concern.

'Are you all right, Frank? Here, let me help you up.'

'I'll get my bloody self, up. Why can't bloody women leave men alone.' He was quiet for a moment then shouted. 'I was only wetting Edn... Rose's... whatever her bloody name is... Wetting her head, and I get all this shit. Is it my fault the old bastard died?'

I strained to hear him as he got further away from the stairs, but then he returned and shouted up to me.

'You want to know why men drink so much? Women, that's why.'

I turned onto my side and prayed for sleep. When it came, it was like an anaesthetic, and I knew nothing more until late morning.

Chapter 62

June 1938

The next day, I slept in. I was always up well before the sun, but the stress of giving birth and my father's death had taken their toll and I didn't stir until nine o'clock.

Miriam had Martha downstairs, so I lay in for an extra twenty minutes before the pressure on my bladder forced me to leave the bed.

'Morning,' Miriam had Martha draped across her shoulder while she rubbed her back. 'How's your back, do you need a rub too?'

I yawned. 'A lot better this morning,' I said with the back of my hand over my mouth. 'Sorry, Miriam, but I have to use the bathroom.'

I sat on the pan and admired my new bathroom, yet again. The lie-in had done me the world of good. I hadn't felt so fresh for weeks. When I returned to the kitchen, I found I was ravenously hungry. I cut two, Miriam-sized, lumps of bread and spread them liberally with butter. I topped them both with a thick slice of ham, then put the kettle on. I had eaten one sandwich and started on the other by the time it had boiled. I looked over my shoulder to the parlour door. *Shouldn't I be in mourning? But then, I've had months to prepare for the occasion, maybe I am all mourned out.*

'I'll have to find a funeral director today,' I said, more to myself than Miriam. 'I'll get the people who saw my mother off. They did a decent job. I'll ring them after breakfast.'

'I'll make the tea,' said Miriam who considered brewing tea part of her job. 'It's so nice to see you eating again.'

'I could eat a whole pig,' I said. Miriam looked up quickly. 'I'm just getting some revenge for yesterday,' I said, laughing.

Still chewing on the crust of my sandwich, I stood over the Moses basket and studied my sleeping daughter. I was tempted to stroke her cheek again but was wary of waking her up.

'We need to get a pram, soon,' I said.

'They'll try to sell you a Silver Cross,' said Miriam.

'The woman in the Post Office tipped me off about them. Apparently, they're the only ones worth buying,' I replied.

'They're beautiful, and they last forever, but they're so expensive. I could never afford one. I got a third-hand Pedigree pram and I had to pay that on the never, never. It took four years to pay off.'

'I don't think I'll buy new,' I said. 'There's bound to be a good second-hand one for sale locally.'

'That's the best idea. I'll ask around for you when I'm up at the market,' said Miriam.

'Are you going today?' I asked.

'As soon as I've washed your breakfast things. Is there anything I can get you?'

'Aspirin. Oh, and can you push a note through Amy's letterbox, please? She won't know about the baby yet. She'll want to meet her as soon as she can.'

I got a sheet of notepaper and my mother's favourite fountain pen from the tallboy drawer, and wrote a quick note.

Amy, come and meet Martha. She arrived yesterday. Alice. PS. I need your advice re: prams.

Amy's advice was the best. She ought to be a solicitor.

As if the word had summoned him. My handsome, gangster lawyer, knocked on the front door as I was folding the notepaper in half. He took his hat off as I opened the door and looked me up and down as he stood on the doorstep.

'Do I dare to assume that congratulations are in order?' he asked.

'Assume away,' I said. 'Martha arrived yesterday.'

I moved away from the doorway to allow him to enter. He passed my father's stinky old chair and placed his briefcase on the table.

'Is your father up and about today?'

'He's in the parlour,' I said. 'He fell out of his chair and died last night.'

Mr Wilson looked genuinely sad. 'My goodness, what a day you've had. If there's anything I can do to help?' He looked a little guilty. 'Not that I'm touting for business, but there will be legal issues that will need to be dealt with. We do provide those services.'

'I wouldn't go anywhere else,' I said, smiling.

'Have you contacted the doctor?' he asked.

'It's a bit late for that,' I replied.

It was his turn to smile, and what a smile it was. It made me smile a gooey, dreamy smile back, then I blushed when I realised what I was doing.

'You'll still need one to sign the death certificate,' he said.

'I'll ring him in a few minutes then, I've got to get the funeral director to call too. We can't leave him there much longer. It's summer he'll begin to...' I stopped myself saying, stink, just in time.

My dreamy, gangster lawyer, opened his case, took out a few sheets of paper and laid them on the table.

'You are now Alice Mollison. Here is your certificate.' He picked up a letterheaded sheet with the details of my name change. It was signed in two places at the bottom.

'It's a bit late for Martha though, she was born yesterday, so it's been a bit of a waste of time, really.'

'Ah, have no fears about that. She's a Mollison too. Your certificate is dated last Tuesday. I received it in the post from the judge who verified it on Friday, but sadly, I was too busy to bring it over.'

While I was reading my life changing document, he produced a few sheets of typed paper, written on his company's letterheaded paper, and my birth certificate and the other documents I had provided.

'I took the opportunity of detailing a typical estate-trust document. I've inserted your new name, so that you can see what a genuine one would mean for you and the farm. It's only a mock-up, it's not a legal document.'

I skimmed the papers. They looked genuine to me.

'Whenever you are ready to proceed, be it now or at a later date, we can use this as a basis for the real thing. You can keep that one, I have a copy.'

I put it back on the table with my Deed Poll sheet and my family identification stuff, and thanked him profusely.

He gave me that bloody smile again, and I blushed again, and started patting my curls into place. I dropped the dreamy-eyed look as his face suddenly became serious.

'Alice, I don't know the state of the farm's finances, but there will be quite a hefty tax bill to pay to the government. They have a thing called Estate Duty that is triggered whenever a landowner dies and the estate is left to a descendant. Sadly, there is no way around it.'

'How much are we talking?' I said, suddenly regretting the money I had spent on the new bathroom.

'I'll need the deeds, accounts, expenses sheets and anything relating to the business before I can work it out. We also have to transfer the ownership of the farm to you. Did your father leave a will?'

'Yes, he wrote it after my mother died. It hasn't been drawn up by a solicitor, it's just a single sheet of paper saying everything goes to me.'

'Could you get it for me, and the deeds, accounts, everything I just mentioned? I'll get them all back to you later in the week.'

I collected all the documents from the tallboy and took them back to him. He slipped them into his briefcase, snapped it shut, and fixed the brass clasp.

'I haven't even offered you a cup of tea,' I said, aghast.

'Don't worry about that, Alice. People treat solicitors like vicars. I drink so much in a workday that I can't face another drop when I get home.'

I walked him to the front door, he opened it, stepped outside, then thanked me again for the business, before donning his hat. Suddenly, James Cagney's gangster partner was on my doorstep again.

'I'll call you in the week,' he said.

'I'll look forward to it,' I said, giving him the goofy smile again.

He tipped his hat to me, turned on his heel and walked back to his gangster car. He climbed inside and waved to me from the open, driver's window.

'Bye, Bugsy,' I called out, much louder than I had intended.

When I had stopped daydreaming about running away to some dingy hotel on Sheppey with Mr Wilson, I picked up the phone directory and called the funeral directors that we had used for my mother. I explained the circumstances of my father's death, and the owner, Mr Jenkins, promised to pick my father's body up in the afternoon.

'Has a doctor seen him yet?' he asked.

I tried the same joke that had worked on my lawyer.

'It's a bit late for that.'

'Miss Tansley, this is not the time for brevity,' he said sternly.

'It's Mrs Mollison now,' I replied, refusing to apologise for my little joke.

'Well, Mrs Mollison, I'll see you around two o'clock,' he said, and hung up.

Next, I searched the directory for the doctor who had treated my mother over the years. My father always distrusted him because my mother never got any better, but at least he knew where we lived. He'd called here often enough.

Dr Philby wasn't available to call, but his partner in the practice, Dr Patterson, was. Because of the situation and the time of year, he promised to call before noon.

I suddenly felt incredibly weary, and went back to my seat by the stove, leaving the trust sheets and my Deed Poll document on the table.

Miriam had her coat on, and was ready to go. 'Are you sure there's nothing else I can get you?' she asked.

'Just aspirin,' I said. 'Oh, and did you pick up the note for Amy?'

Miriam waved it at me and set off for the market, leaving me in charge of my own child for the first time. Thankfully, she was asleep.

I wasn't alone for long however. Elsie arrived at eleven on the dot. After checking on Martha, she ordered me to take off my pants, get onto the table and spread my legs. Twenty seconds later her head assumed its usual position, between them. She had only been there less than a minute, when there was a knock on the window and a man in a black bower hat, got exactly the same view as Elsie, albeit from slightly further away.

I screamed, and closed my legs, trapping Elsie's head between my thighs. She must have thought I'd done it on purpose because muffled threats arose from my bottom end, and those great, ham sized hands took hold of my knees and forced them apart again. As she came up for air, red-faced and shaking with anger, I pointed to the window, where, thankfully, the bowler hatted man was still standing.

Elsie forced my legs closed, pulled my skirt over my knees, and stormed to the door.

'You disgusting individual, why the hell are you spying on a new mother, receiving her post-natal examination?'

The man in the bower showed his card as proof of identity, and said that he had come to remove a corpse.

'She's not dead, you moron, she's just had a baby.'

The man from the funeral director's tried to explain, but Elsie was having none of it. In the end I had to get off the table and join the fray myself.

'Elsie, my father died last night, he's in the parlour.'

Elsie stopped berating the young man and, red-faced, this time with embarrassment, hurried back into the kitchen.

'I'm John,' said the young man. He motioned to two other men who were standing by the back gate carrying a shiny coffin.

'You can't take him yet. The doctor hasn't seen him.'

'I thought he was dead,' said John.

'He is,' I said, cursing him for stealing my joke. 'The doctor has to write a death certificate before he can be moved.'

'Ah,' said John, looking at me as though I could sort out the problem myself.

'You're early anyway. You're not supposed to be here until two,' I said.

'We had a cancellation,' John replied.

'A cancellation?' I couldn't get my head around that.

Thankfully, a few minutes later, Dr Patterson arrived. He let himself in the gate, avoiding the men with the coffin, and strode purposefully up to the back door.

'I'm Doctor Patterson; I'm here to view the corpse.' He waved his doctor's bag at me as proof of identity.

I showed him through to the parlour, where he took one look at my father, and pronounced him dead.

'He's dead all right,' he said, as though it might come as a surprise to me. He lifted an arm and let it drop, it landed on the camp bed with a thud. 'Do you see?'

I nodded. 'I had an inkling.'

As if to prove that he knew what he was talking about, he produced a small mirror from his bag, held it in front of my father's lips, checked it for mist, then cleaned it on his tie, and put it back. He checked for a pulse, then pulled out a book of death certificates.

'How did he die?' he asked.

'He fell off his chair, drunk,' I replied, thinking that I seemed to be doing his job for him.

'He was a serious drinker then? I thought so, I could smell it on him, then there's the skin, the state of his body, it all points to that diagnosis.'

'He was an alcoholic,' I said.

'Such a shame. A grandfather should set an example,' he said, shaking his head.

I wondered how he knew I'd recently had a baby, maybe he had spotted the Moses basket.

'Deceased passed due to alcohol poisoning,' he said aloud as he wrote on the pad. I didn't know if that information was for my benefit or his.

He noted my father's name, place of birth and then asked for his date of birth. When I told him, he stopped writing. 'That would make him forty-eight,' he said.

'Correct,' I replied.

'My God,' said the doctor. I thought he was at least seventy.

I went to the kitchen, opened the much-used drawer of the tallboy, dug out my father's birth certificate and took it back to Dr Patterson.

He copied the details, announced that I owed him fifteen shillings, and issued me with my father's death certificate. I got fifteen, one-shilling pieces from the petty cash tin, and dropped the coins into his greedy palms. I was fed up with him. He'd been in the house less than ten minutes, and he wanted fifteen bob to write down the details that I'd given him for free, on a scrap of paper. I was in the wrong job, that was for certain. I began to wish I'd told him he'd died of an arsenic enema.

Once I was in receipt of his receipt, I showed him out, and allowed the funeral directors in. I let John see my father's newly-written death certificate, and the two porters removed the lid of the coffin and carefully laid my father inside. As they replaced the wooden cover and screwed down the brass fittings, it suddenly hit me that he was gone forever, and I sat on the empty foldaway bed, and sobbed my heart out as his remains were carried away.

Chapter 63

June 1938

At twelve-thirty, Frank came in, just as I was about to risk picking Martha up.

'I forgot to pack lunch this morning and I'm starving,' he said, trying to avoid my eye.

I said nothing, and stretched out a finger to stroke the tiny palm of her hand. She gripped it instantly. I got ready for more tears but the only ones that came were mine. Martha was awake, and she was allowing me to interact.

'Oh, my goodness,' I whispered, scared of making too much noise in case it set her off.

Frank put the kettle on and set about making a cheese and onion sandwich.

After a minute or so, I thought I'd try her other hand. She gripped that finger too. I was ecstatic.

'She's got hold of both my fingers,' I told Frank, forgetting that I wasn't speaking to him.

'All babies do that, they're born making fists, it's like they want to punch you for forcing them out.'

I didn't care. She was gripping my fingers and she wasn't crying. It wouldn't bother me if they were born wearing boxing gloves.

I eased my fingers out of her tiny fists and pondered whether to attempt to pick her up while she was in such a good mood. I checked the time on the huge, round wall clock. She wasn't due to be fed for half an hour, so I backed out, and stepped away from her basket, Miriam would be back by then, and I'd have help if the screaming started.

I sat on my chair by the stove, picked up an old magazine that I'd read every word of three times, and began to flick through it.

'I'm off the beer, Alice.'

I continued to flick through the pages.

'I mean it. As God is my witness, I'm done with drinking.'

'Have you been collared by the Temperance Society or something?' I asked. I didn't believe a word of it.

'I swear, Alice. I saw your father carted away this morning, and it made me think about last night in the front room. I just keep thinking, dead man's shoes.'

'Dead man's foul-smelling armchair, dead man's whisky bottle, dead man's daughter to yell at. You should have been thinking about that.'

'No, the phrase, dead man's shoes. It means stepping into a position of authority. A promotion, when someone leaves, or dies, you take their place.'

Alarm bells rang louder than the ones in the tower at a local church wedding.

Frank poured tea into two large mugs, added sugar and milk and brought one of them over to me.

I nodded my thanks and stood over the Moses basket, smiling down at Martha.

'I've got responsibilities now, Alice.'

'You had responsibilities before, Frank,' I replied, annoyed for allowing myself to be coerced into the conversation.

'I know, but now he's gone... Listen, Alice, I'm being serious here. There will be no more Friday nights with the lads in the pub. I swear to you, I swear on my mother's life, I swear on Martha's—'

'Don't you dare drag that poor little bugger into your fantasy, Frank,' I spat. 'Leave her out of it. If you want to condemn your mother to an early grave, that's up to you, but leave Martha out of it.'

'I don't say these things lightly, Alice.'

I had expected him to get angry, but he didn't. I shrugged and sipped my tea.

'You'll see,' he said. 'I really do mean it. I have respons—'

I bit that time. 'Responsibilities? Yes, Frank, I heard you the first time.'

'I know you're angry, Alice, and you have every right to be, but I'll prove I can be a good father. Isn't that what you asked me to do last night?'

I was amazed he could remember. 'Talk is easy. You've got a lot of work to do to get back into our good books, Frank.'

Just then the phone rang. I got up, but Frank was quicker. 'I'll answer it. You drink your tea.' He hurried into the front room before it stopped ringing.

I gave him a minute or so, then thinking it was more likely to be for me anyway, I followed him through.

He hung up the phone as I entered the room.

'That was the landlord of The Old Bull, asking if we still want the daily bottle of whisky now that your dad's dead. I told him to cancel the order from today. He wasn't best pleased. He asked me if I wanted it. I told him I'm off the drink now that I'm a father myself.' He looked down at the documents on the table as he spoke.

I rushed forward, scooped them up, opened up the safe, slipped them inside and locked it again, putting the bunch of keys back in my pocket.

'Your lawyer friend has been then?'

I bridled, and spoke too defensively. 'He's not my friend, he's a lawyer. He brought my Deed Poll name-change certificate round. Both me and Martha are Mollison's now, so you can register her any time you like, Frank.' I smiled at him, thinking he would be pleased at the news.

'What was the other thing? I saw the words Estate Trust and the name of the farm.'

'That's farm business, Frank. You know the rules on that.'

'But, I'm the man of the house now, Alice. I was speaking about responsibility and I think I should be given the chance to prove myself.

I'm part of the family now. You have my surname; we have our baby. Let's not spoil all that by being selfish.'

'I'm not being the slightest bit selfish, Frank. The farm is a family business, and it will stay a family business... A Tansley family business, no outsiders allowed.'

Frank thumped the table. 'I'm the man of the bloody house now.'

'Man? You should start to act like one. My father has only been gone a few hours and there you are trying to take his place. We haven't even buried him yet for God's sake.'

Frank decided not to argue the point and walked back into the kitchen to resume his lunch. When I walked in myself, I found Miriam cooing over Martha's cot, her bag of shopping still in her hand.

'I got the aspirin, and I posted your note to Amy,' she said.

I shot a glance at Frank. He was chewing his sandwich with a sulky look on his face.

'Thanks, Miriam. I'm so looking forward to seeing her.'

Before we had lunch, Miriam and I decided that it was time for me to attempt to feed Martha.

I sat in my chair and squeezed out enough milk for a feed into a bowl, then I transferred it to one of the three feeding bottles we owned. There was a back-up formula bottle on the cold shelf and a second, nestled in a pan of warm water, in case Martha refused the newly expressed breast milk. Miriam stood alongside me and made encouraging noises, while I summoned up the courage to pick her up.

Martha was making niggly noises as feeding time approached, so I bit the bullet and lifted her out of the basket. As I sat down with her, she took one look at me and screwed up her face. I panicked and stuffed the teat of the bottle in her mouth. She pulled a face like I had just tried to force-feed her lemon juice. Miriam tapped me on the shoulder and shook the warmed-up formula at me. We exchanged bottles and before Martha could work herself up into a fury, I shoved the teat in her mouth. It worked like magic. Martha looked me straight in the eyes and suckled at the rubber teat, as if it we had shared this moment forever. She drank every last drop of the milk and I waved the empty bottle at Miriam in celebration. Then I got too cocky and slipped her onto my shoulder. As soon as I got her into position, she started bawling. I was determined to finish off the feeding routine, and started rubbing her back. She gave one almighty burp, and then, as if she had been shocked into submission, she fell asleep.

I rocked her for an hour, refusing Miriam's offer to give me a rest. At two o'clock, I laid her down and took off the tea towel, covering the plate of doorstep sandwiches that Miriam had made while I was nursing the baby, and tucked in hungrily.

Amy came around straight after work. She squealed when she saw me, then she squealed again when she saw Martha.

She didn't even ask whether she was allowed to pick her up, she just grabbed her and walked quickly around the room singing Bye Baby Bunting to her, over and over again. Martha didn't make a peep.

When her excitement had died down, she put Martha back in the Moses basket, then slapped her forehead and looked at me, sadly.

'I was so sorry to hear about your dad, Alice. Brenda from the machine shop told me about it at break time. I should have said this when I first came in but I was so excited about Martha that it slipped my mind.'

'Blimey! If Brenda from the machine shop knows, I'm surprised it hasn't made the front page of the papers. Does everyone in the town know?'

'Probably. You can't keep a secret in a small place like this.'

For the next twenty minutes, I told Amy all about the events of the day before. She held my hand through most of it. I wasn't teary at all, and described the events of the day as though I was telling her about a suspense film I'd watched. Every so often she would say, 'Oh no!' or 'Oh my goodness'. I did tear up a bit when I told her about the undertaker screwing the lid down on my father. She gave me a hug and held me close for a few minutes.

'What a day, Alice. There's a novel waiting to be written there.'

'I didn't have time to worry about anything. Stuff just kept happening,' I told her.

Amy put her hand to her mouth and sniggered behind it.

'What?' I said, eager to be let into the joke.

'Did John, the undertaker, really see your bits?' she asked, wide-eyed.

'He couldn't have not seen,' I replied. 'My legs were spread so far apart; I had an ankle on each wall.'

Amy gasped, then doubled up in a fit of laughter.

'The only other people who have seen your bits are Elsie and Frank. Three is a lucky number isn't it? Or is that seven? Whichever, it was lucky for John.'

'Frank hasn't seen my bits, it was too dark when we were in the field and Elsie chucked him out before he got a glimpse, yesterday.'

Amy laughed again. 'Poor Frank, fancy being usurped by an undertaker.'

'I've got something to tell you about him. Frank that is, not the undertaker, but it can wait for now. Let's cheer ourselves up a bit.'

I set the record player up, and we sang along to a few songs. Miriam, worried about the noise waking Martha, took her out into the yard to give her a first taste of fresh, farm air. She obviously didn't appreciate the pig-poo smell, because she bawled the barn down. Miriam quickly brought her back inside, deciding instead to sit with her in the front room.

When we were tired of singing, we got to the girly gossip stage of the proceedings, and Amy filled me in on the doings at the mill, and our friends and acquaintances about the town.

'Do you know of anyone with a pram for sale?' I asked her suddenly, remembering that's what I wanted to talk to her about.

She thought for a minute.

'No, to be honest, I don't, but I'll ask around... Wait a minute! There's one in the wool shop. It's not a new one by any means. She uses it to show off dolls wearing some of the knitting patterns she sells alongside the wool and the other baby stuff. The right offer might persuade her to sell. It's my half day on Wednesday. I'll nip in to see her.'

She laughed suddenly. 'You didn't ask how I know about the pram.'

'How do you know about the pram?' I asked.

'Well, it's like this.' Amy looked up at the ceiling, then back to me. 'I was... I thought about... All right, I was going to learn to knit, so I could make something for the baby, so I went to the wool shop to see what she had by way of patterns for new-borns, but when I looked through the window, the shop was full of grannies. There must have been a dozen of them in there, chatting about whatever it is that grannies chat about. I sort of went off the idea, and decided to buy you something instead.'

'What did you buy me then?' I asked, teasing her.

'Nothing yet. I didn't know whether you would have a boy or a girl. I'll tell you what though, if it's coming from that wool shop, I'm sending my mum in. You won't see me in one of those places until I'm at least fifty.'

At seven o'clock, Miriam brought Martha back in, and settled her down in the Moses basket. 'We'll have to get her a cot soon,' she said.

'One of the lads can knock a cot up; we've got plenty of timber in the shed. Barney is wonderful with wood, and I think Frank is handy with a plane too. We will need a mattress and some bedding for it though. Still, she's fine in the basket for now. We've got plenty of time.'

'I'll buy the bedding,' said Amy. 'That can be my present.'

'That only leaves me with the mattress,' Miriam moaned.

'Oh, Miriam, I'll get the mattress, you can knit her some clothes if you like. Martha's only got the few bits of mine that my mother saved. She arrived before I could sort all that sort of stuff out.'

Miriam brightened. 'I'll nip into the wool shop the next time I'm up there. I saw a lovely new-born, baby pattern in there last week. I was looking for ideas. I didn't get a proper look at it because the place was full of grannies.'

Amy and I laughed riotously. Miriam looked at us wondering what we found so funny.

'Are you staying for dinner?' she asked Amy, when the laughter had died down.

'No, I'd better go. Mum will have made me something. I was only home long enough to read Alice's note.'

She whispered goodbye to Martha, and offered her arms to give me a hug, but I flicked my head towards the back door and we walked out into the yard.

We leaned against the gate, and I told Amy all about Frank's drink problem, and how he had sat in my father's chair, abusing me whilst drinking his whisky.

Amy ground her teeth as she listened.

'You have to get him off the drink, Alice. That, or chuck him out. He'll do you harm one of these days if you don't. The man next door to us went to prison for it. He nearly killed his wife. The silly woman had him back when he came out. They moved away because of all the gossip.'

'He says he's off the beer but we'll have to wait and see about that. The thing is, he thinks he's entitled to part of the farm now that my father isn't here. We had words about it earlier today. I told him I've put the farm in a Trust and he's getting nothing, but he can't accept it. Apart from that, and when he's in drink, he can be a really nice man. He's so warm and gentle when he's in the mood. Anyway, I owe him for rescuing me from the pigs, so I'll have to give him a chance to prove he means what he says.'

'All right, I'll give him that one. I won't forgive him for not knocking on our door when he passed by, yesterday though. He could have let me know you were having the baby; I'd have been down here like a shot.'

'He had things on his mind,' I said. I don't know why I defended him, nor did Amy.

'I don't trust him, Alice. I haven't forgiven him for what happened on your birthday, and I don't think I ever will.' She opened the gate and walked through.

'He's a bad sort, Alice. I know it.'

Chapter 64

June 1938

Frank came in from work at nine. I would normally be going to bed at that time but I didn't have to get up in the morning, the lads were taking it in turns to look after the piggery so I didn't have to worry about that. Barney and Frank had everything in hand.

Frank didn't mention the Trust at all. Instead he reported on the problems we were having with the drainage in one of the fields on the top acres.

I fed Martha without any tears from either of us, while Frank was eating the warmed-up stew that Miriam had made earlier. I made up enough formula for two more feeds, tipped it into the freshly washed bottles, and put them on the cold shelf in the larder. Then I picked up the basket and took Martha up to bed with me at ten. Frank sat up for a few minutes to allow his dinner to settle.

At one AM Martha woke up for her feed. I yawned and tried to summon the energy to drag myself out of bed, but there was no need. When I finally opened my eyes, I saw Frank walking to the bedroom door with Martha in his arms. I whispered, *thank you,* and went back to sleep. The next thing I knew it was four-thirty and Frank was shaking me gently awake.

'I'm off to work in a few minutes, Alice. Martha will need to be fed again at about six-thirty, but there's no milk left, so you'll have to make up some more. He sat on the edge of the bed. 'How long will it keep once you've made it up? If I bought a few more bottles could we get a bit in front.'

I scratched my head and blinked at the morning light. 'I'm going to get some more formula from Elsie this morning. I'll ask her if she can find me a couple of extra feeding bottles. She might have some spare.'

Frank kissed me on the cheek, and I thanked him for feeding Martha in the night.

'I do mean it about the drinking,' he said as he left for work.

Elsie arrived at eleven, as usual, and after checking me out and weighing Martha, she asked me if I had any questions.

'I have a few things I'd like to ask you. Could you get me a couple of extra feeding bottles and another lot of formula milk? She won't even consider taking my milk. As you can see, we're running a farm and we're up and about while the rest of the world are just turning over for the second half of the night. Poor Frank didn't go to bed until ten, and he got up to do both her feeds, if they need less feeds on formula, then I'd like to keep using it.'

Elsie leaned forward and pursed her lips. 'Firstly, I've got some spare bottles and teats in my bag, you can have a couple of those for three shillings. Regarding formula. I'd prefer you keep trying the breast milk, but I understand that for some babies, it's not an option. You can keep her on formula, Alice, I'll bring you some more tomorrow and give you a list of shops that sell it. You can also mix up condensed milk, but let's leave that for now.'

Elsie was as good as her word, and when she turned up on Wednesday morning, she bought a tin of milk powder and showed me how to mix it with a spoonful of condensed milk to bulk it up a little. I paid Elsie for the formula and the new feeding bottles, and we had a cup of tea. When Miriam came in, they had a long chat about toddlers, while I pretended to be interested. Martha loved the new mix, and the number of feeds over a twenty-four-hour period, was cut by a third

After dinner, I sat in my chair by the stove while Miriam fed Martha. I wasn't pushing my luck. I'd fed her twice that day without tears, but when I picked her up for a cuddle, late afternoon, she reverted to her petulant mode, and screamed until I handed her over.

At six-thirty, the telephone rang. It was my gangster lawyer, Mr Wilson.

'Hello, Alice. Apologies for the lateness of the hour, but I'm running a little bit behind today. I thought I'd ring you to give you an update on progress.'

I visualised his handsome face as he was talking. His voice was as smooth as ever and I found myself patting my curls into place as he spoke.

'I have some good news and some bad news for you. Which do you want to hear first?'

'The good,' I said.

'Right. The good news is, I have successfully transferred the farm into your name. Your father's will was very specific in that regard and you are now the legal owner. I have a couple of documents for you to sign, but that's just a formality. From today onwards, you are the sole owner of Tansley Farm.'

I did a little skip, and punched the air. 'And the bad news?'

'The bad news is, you owe the government ninety-two pounds and ten shillings, in Estate Tax.'

My jaw hit the floor. 'Ninety-two pounds...'

'And ten shillings. But you will have to add our company fees for the work done, and the total you need to find is, one-hundred and ten-pounds, thirteen shillings and ninepence.'

I was dumbstruck.

'I understand your shock, Alice. It's a lot of money.'

'I don't know how I'm going to pay it. I don't have that sort of money; it would wipe the farm out completely if I withdrew it from the bank. We just wouldn't survive. I've got my men's wages to find, Mr Wilson.'

'I wish I could help, but this is a government tax. You can't avoid it.'

'I've got thirty pounds left out of my mother's insurance money, and I can add another twenty from the bank without putting the farm's finances under too much pressure, but that's only half of what I owe.'

'Your mother's insurance money?'

'Yes, she had a policy worth sixty pounds, but I spent thirty of it on a new bathroom.'

'Was your father insured?'

I slapped my forehead with my free hand.

'OF COURSE, HE WAS!' I shouted. 'Wait a moment, please.'

I put down the handset and rushed to the safe. It took me three attempts to get the key in the lock.

I rifled through the old documents until I found a brown envelope with the word 'insurance' written across it in my father's scrawl. I tore it open and rushed back to the phone.

'I have it here. He was insured for...' I scanned the document quickly.

'One hundred and fifty pounds! We're saved,' I cried.

Mr Wilson sounded relieved. 'I'm so pleased for you, Alice. There will be a little extra money to play with now. You have to settle the bill before the end of August, so you have plenty of time to telephone the insurance company and get the claim settled.'

I was still in shock from discovering the amount that my father's life was insured for. I decided that I had better get my own policy in case something happened to me. I'd leave it to Martha.

'I'll telephone them tomorrow,' I said.

'Good. Now then, Alice. I'd like you to call into my office tomorrow and sign the inheritance documents. Your name will have to be on the deeds when it comes to paying the government their dues. It can get complicated if the handover hasn't taken place when the bill is paid. Could you call in at, let's see... twelve o'clock?'

'I'll get Frank to drive me up,' I said, without thinking. What would he make of me visiting my 'lawyer friend' again?

'There is one more thing, Alice. My brother recently lost his wife. Sadly, she was only in her thirties when she passed. Anyway, he's moving away to live in the West Country. The house he's moving to contains a lot of the appliances he already owns, so he wants to sell a lot of the things he's not taking with him. He's having an auction on Saturday.'

'What sort of things are up for sale? I have most of the stuff I need. I don't think I have the time to stand around all day at an auction and, I've spent a lot just lately, I really should slow down a bit.'

'Oh, I wouldn't expect you to come to the auction, Alice. You can have a private viewing after the appointment tomorrow. I thought of you because there are a few things that might be of interest. His children are now school age, so he's got a lot of things that they have grown out of. He's leaving a cot and all the bits that go with it, there's a pram, and—'

'A pram, Really!'

'Yes, really. There's a toddler's rocking horse too, then there's a gas cooker, and a lot of other household items.'

'How much does he want for it all? I'm interested in the cooker, rocking horse, cot, and of course, the pram.' I couldn't keep the excitement out of my voice.

'I'll talk to him tonight, but you'll get them at a good price. Auctions can be incredibly disappointing to the seller. I look forward to seeing you tomorrow, Alice.'

Had he been here, I would have kissed him. I'd have to fight off that urge tomorrow.

I walked back to the kitchen daydreaming about the gangster and his moll again.

Chapter 65

June 1938

On Wednesday, at nine o'clock precisely, I rang the parish vicar, Reverend Villiers, to see about setting a date for my father's funeral service, and burial in the grave next to my mother's. My mother had bought the plots, way-back in nineteen-twenty, following her health scare when she had me. The plot wasn't exactly centre stage of the churchyard. It was hidden away in a dark corner, beneath the branches of a huge oak that hung over the boundary wall. There was room for one more, if I ever fancied lying down beside them. No one else would want to be buried that far away from the church, unless they didn't want anyone to know they were there. It was a strange position to choose, but my mother was happy with it, and that was all that mattered. I think she felt sorry for the tree, stuck out there on its own like that.

Reverend Villiers checked his diary, and told me I had a choice of dates. I settled for eleven o'clock on the Friday of the following week. My father had been so keen to join my mother in the shady plot that he had drunk himself to death, so I wanted them to be side by side, as quickly as possible. Reverend Villiers marked down the date and time, and I said that I'd get on to Mr Jenkins, the funeral director, straight away.

At exactly nine-thirty, Mr Jenkins rang me to see if I had finalised a date for my father's funeral. I was beginning to think I had developed some sort of telepathic power; this was the second time in the space of a few days where I had mentioned a particular businessman and he had miraculously appeared on the end of a telephone line.

I gave Mr Jenkins the details of the funeral, and he checked his own diary. Thankfully, there was no conflict. When Mr Jenkins asked if I wanted him to arrange the floral display, I agreed. Apparently, he had a deal with the local florist. I ordered a simple wreath. My father wasn't big on flowers.

Next, I telephoned the local newspaper, and booked a slot in the obituary column.

Robert Tansley. February 18th 1890-June 26th 1938. Reunited at last. Funeral, St Wilfred's Church. Friday July 8th 11 AM.

After a cup of tea and an attempted cuddle with Martha, I went upstairs and pulled my favourite polka-dot dress out of the wardrobe. I laid it on the bed and sorted out my best heels and my one pair of silk stockings, then headed for the bath.

In the bathroom cupboard was one of my prized possessions. A box of rose-scented bath salts that Amy had given me for Christmas in 1937. I only used them once in the hip bath, and not at all since Frank had been sharing the water with me but, since the new bath had been installed, I'd poured a measure into the water, twice.

After the bath, I dried my hair and brushed it slowly, so that my chestnut curls were displayed at their beautiful, best. I dressed, then gave myself a spray with my mother's Tabu perfume, a gift from her well-heeled sister, who had married well and lived in London.

At eleven forty-five, Frank started up the old truck, and I clambered up to sit beside him.

'Who are you all dolled up for?' he asked.

'I've got to go to the solicitor's office to sign off the farm transfer and some other stuff. You don't go to those sorts of places stinking of pig shit.'

He leaned across and sniffed. 'You smell like a tart,' he said.

'I wouldn't know what tarts smells like, Frank. This perfume isn't cheap. I doubt even the most expensive tart could afford it.'

'You never wear it for me,' he complained.

'No, and I won't ever wear it now; you don't want me smelling like a tart in bed, do you?' I was angry, and he knew it. We drove in silence for the rest of the trip.

When we reached Mr Wilson's office, I waved Frank away and wriggle-walked across the forecourt just to piss Frank off even more. I stopped the tart act as I stepped through into the reception area.

'Miss Tans... Mollison,' said Miss Johnston, giving me a smile that was as fake as the necklace that hung around her neck. She pointed to the open door of an office to her right. 'Mr Wilson is expecting you.'

My gangster lawyer smiled his dreamy smile at me as I entered his office. I was tempted to do my wriggle walk again but thought better of it. He looked me up and down appreciatively. 'My goodness, Alice, what a vision of loveliness you are. He closed the door, and pulled out a padded chair for me to sit in. I crossed my legs in what I hoped was a ladylike manner, and fiddled with my curls. Mr Wilson stepped around to his side of the desk and smiled at me again. My heart flipped.

'Business before pleasure,' he said, pushing three documents across the desk. 'Please take your time to read, then sign them please, Alice.'

I couldn't understand a word that was written on the pages. The text was made up of words like herewith, forthwith, and notwithstanding, it was like a foreign language. I tried not to let on how out of my depth I was, and not wanting to drag things out, and because I trusted him implicitly, I just picked up the beautiful fountain pen from his desk, and scribbled my signature in all the marked places.

Mr Wilson blotted the wet ink and handed one of the copies to me.

'Congratulations, Alice. You are now legally the owner of Tansley Farm. Do you think you will change its name any time soon? Mollison Farm for instance?'

'Not while there's a breath in my body,' I replied. I folded the paper in half, then in half again, and stuffed it into my bag.

'Have you registered your father's death yet?' he asked.

'No, Frank's doing it just now. He's registering Martha's birth at the same time.'

'Was Frank the man driving your truck? I saw him drop you off. I must admit, I have been looking forward to your visit all morning.'

I bit my tongue before I could blurt out what I'd been thinking about, lying in my scented bath, and gave him my best smile.

Mr Wilson gathered up the documents, and stood up. 'Right, let's go and see what you fancy at my brother's house.' He looked at me as I got up from my seat. 'Did anyone ever tell you; you look like Rita Hayworth?'

We walked out into the reception area, together. Miss Johnston watching my every step. Mr Wilson dropped my documents on her desk. 'File these away please,' he said, before turning back to me. 'Right, Mrs Mollison, shall be go? My car is just outside.'

If looks could kill, I'd have been hung, garrotted, shot, stabbed and decapitated all at once. I gave her my wriggle walk as I left the office, then looked back over my shoulder and winked at her.

Mr Wilson opened the passenger-side door of the Alvis for me; I stepped onto the running board and slipped onto the seat as elegantly as I could. He slammed the door behind me and walked around the front of the car to get into the driver's side. He started the car, gave it a big vroom, and we pulled out of the parking space, onto the road.

I had a big stupid grin on my face as the gangster and his moll drove away from the heist. I resisted the urge to wave to everyone we passed and just concentrated on enjoying the ride in the powerful car.

After a mile or so we slowed, and turned right into a posh looking eatery called Café Blanc. It was a white building, with tables set out in a rose garden, facing the road. He parked up at the back, and we walked between the shrubs at the side of the building until we arrived at the dining area. There were a dozen tables occupied by ladies in summer dresses and wide brimmed hats. The men sported short sleeved shirts; their jackets thrown over the backs of their chairs.

Mr Wilson nodded to one or two people he knew, led me to a round, wrought iron table, and pulled out a seat while I sat down. No one had ever done that for me before, I looked around to see that many of the café customers were taking sly glances at me whilst nibbling crustless sandwiches or sipping at tall glasses of wine.

'White or red?' he asked me as I patted at my curls, looking out of the corner of my eye at a very handsome man who was giving me the eye in no uncertain manner.

'Pardon?' I replied.

'Wine. Would you like white or red? I'm happy with either.'

'White please, that bubbly stuff.'

'Champagne? You do have very expensive tastes.'

'No, not that,' I said, hurriedly. I put my hand to the side of my mouth and whispered, 'Is it called, Martina, Mr Wilson?'

'Call me Godfrey, outside of the office, Alice. I think you mean, Martini. So, you're a cocktail girl. Excellent.'

I didn't know I was a cocktail girl. I banked it in my memory in case I needed to impress anyone in the future... like Amy, for instance.

My gangster lawyer went into the café to order. As soon as he entered the building, the handsome young man who had been eyeing me up, weaved his way through the tables until he stood next to me.

'Hello, there,' he said.

'Hello,' I said.

'You're a pretty little thing, aren't you?' he said smoothly.

I blushed and said nothing.

'Out with your uncle, are you?' he asked.

'No, he's not my uncle,' I said, wishing he'd clear off before Godfrey got back.

'Oh, I see,' he winked at me and chuckled. He shot a glance at the café entrance where Godfrey was returning to the rose garden.

Romeo slipped a card into my hand. 'If you every fancy a spin with someone younger, here's my number. Slip it into your bag, there's a good girl.' He made his way back to his seat where two other men were waiting for his report.

Godfrey sat down and gave me that lovely smile.

'I hope you like cucumber sandwiches,' he said. 'What did that young man want?'

I tossed the card he had given me onto the table. 'He was trying to chat me up. He asked me if you were my uncle.' I was going to add, *I'm glad you're not,* but I managed to hold it back.

He picked up the card and read it before slipping it into his pocket. 'He's an assistant manager at the mill,' he said. 'With his surname, I'd guess his father owns it. I know him. The father that is, not the son.'

'I bet Amy has seen him. She works at the mill,' I replied.

'Were you impressed with him?' he asked.

'No, he's far too cocky for my tastes. He could get a part as the smooth-talking bad guy in the movies.'

Godfrey laughed. 'Ah, here are our sandwiches.'

The waitress loaded our table with a plate of tiny triangle sandwiches with the crusts removed, and another plate with thick-cut slices of strawberry gateaux. Then a man with a silver tray brought us our drinks. I took a sip of mine as soon as it had been put on the table.

'Ooh, that's gorgeous. I could drink that all day,' I said, licking my lips.

He laughed again. 'You had better not do that; we have to go to my brother's house yet.'

We chatted about his brother while we ate our lunch. I finished my Martini far too quickly, but I didn't really care. When we were done, we made our way past the table with the three young men sitting around it. The man who had spoken to me, winked. Godfrey dropped the card on the table. 'I'll tell your father we met when I bump into him.' He offered his hand. 'My name is Godfrey Wilson, I'm your father's solicitor, not this young lady's uncle.' The young man blushed while his friends laughed.

We got back into the Alvis and drove slowly up the dirt track path to the main road. As we waited to pull out, our farm truck came trundling along. Frank spotted us as he approached the turn off and slowed down to a crawl, to glare at us. Godfrey waved at him and nudged me, so I waved too.

Ten minutes later, we pulled into the drive of a large detached house. It was bigger than our farm house and barn combined. Godfrey got out of the car and walked around to open my door as his brother approached us. He was about five years younger than Godfrey, but you could see the family resemblance. His name was Norman. After the introductions were over, he took us to a garage where the contents of the auction had been set out. The pram was beautiful, the coachwork was navy blue, as was the hood. It had a long silver handle and silver wheels, with white tyres. It was love at first sight. The cot was nice, the mattress was spotless and the three sets of bedding that went with it were freshly laundered. The rocking horse had seen better days, but it didn't make a noise when rocked, and any child would love it.

But the thing that bought the biggest smile to my face, was the gas cooker. In my mind, I could see Miriam dancing around the kitchen with delight, as I looked at it.

I decided straight away not to try to barter over prices. I wanted the stuff, and I wasn't going to mess them around. Godfrey had been so kind to think about me, and I wasn't going to show him up.

'How much do you want for the cooker, pram, cot and rocking horse?' I asked.

'Would seven pounds, ten shillings be all right?' Norman asked.

I nearly choked. The cooker itself was worth a fiver, and the pram was in tip top condition, so that was probably worth the same. I was getting the bargain of the year.

'I'll make sure you'll get the money tomorrow,' I said, my voice shaking with excitement.

'Give it to Godfrey,' Norman said. 'He's already paid me.'

'I'll get someone to pick it all up in the truck this afternoon,' I said. I couldn't wait to show Amy the pram.

'I'll have them put on the forecourt in front of the garage,' said Norman.

I walked back to the car with Godfrey, still so excited about the pram. It could easily be passed off as new. 'Thank you so much for making sure I got everything I wanted, Godfrey. I really don't know what to say.'

I stood on my tiptoes and kissed him on the lips. I let the kiss linger much longer than I had intended to, but he didn't pull away. When I finally did, I heard the sound of a horn being pressed repeatedly. I looked around to see our farm truck parked at the end of the drive.

Chapter 66

June 1938

Frank said nothing when I reached the truck. I thought maybe he'd just pulled up and not seen me kissing my gangster, but if that was the case, how did he find us? I decided to brazen it out.

'Frank, good timing. I've just bought a pram, a cooker and a cot. Can you pull down to the garage so we can load it on.'

'I will, if lover boy there will get out of the way,' he replied.

I rushed back to Godfrey and asked him to move the Alvis, so that Frank could get the truck down the drive.

'Did he see?' he asked.

'I don't know, I don't see how he could have missed it. I'm so sorry, it was my doing.'

'Nonsense. I enjoyed it,' he winked at me and looked at his watch. 'I'd better get back to the office. Miss Johnston will think we've eloped.'

I waved him off, and Frank backed up so that Godfrey could get out onto the main road. When he pulled up to the garage, Norman's gardener was there to help Frank load up my purchases. Frank lashed them down on the back of the truck and covered them with the old tarp, then he turned the lorry around in the spacious forecourt, and waited for me to jump in. I hesitated, having spotted Norman waving to me from inside the house. When he came out, he was holding a rag doll.

'This was for my daughter, but, well, it wasn't to be, she died with my wife while she was giving birth.'

I immediately thought about my mother, and realised how close a call it was for both of us too.

'There are some baby clothes as well if you'd like them? I don't intend to marry again, let alone have more kids.'

This time, I thought about my father's devotion to one woman. I almost advised him to stay off the drink, but decided against. I'd only have to explain.

'I'd love to have the clothes,' I said. 'My baby is only a couple of days old.'

Norman nipped back to the house and returned with a cardboard box full of baby clothes in pink and blue, most of which were brand new.

'I'll have to pay for these, they're beautiful.'

Norman smiled a sad, smile. 'It's my gift to you. I'm glad they're going to a good home. My wife would have approved, I'm sure.'

I felt a tear ready to fall, so to hide it, I leaned forward, hugged Norman, and kissed him on the cheek.

'Take care, and I hope the move goes well,' I said.

I jumped in next to Frank, and waved to Norman out of the wound-down, window, Frank put the truck into gear and we set off for home. We had only been on the main road for a few hundred yards when his temper exploded.

'No wonder you got tarted up like that. Trying so hard to impress the posh boy, or should I say man, he's old enough to be your father for Christ's sake.'

'So are you, pretty much,' I spat. 'Talk about double standards, Frank.'

He wasn't expecting me to hit back like that, and he didn't know how to respond.

'If nothing is going on, why did you kiss him like that?'

'Like what, Frank? I was thanking him for setting me up with all this stuff, dirt cheap.' I waved towards the back of the truck. 'Do you know how much that lot would have cost, new, or even second hand if I'd bought them from a shop. I got the lot for seven pounds ten. The cooker alone is worth that.'

'That doesn't explain why—'

'That was a mistake, I'll admit that. I was just so excited about getting a pram and a cot.' I looked over at him as he gripped the steering wheel like it was about to fall off.

'There's nothing in it, Frank. He's married, he's in his late thirties, I just wanted to thank him for all he's done for me and the farm.'

'Paying him isn't enough?'

'He didn't' ask me to kiss him, Frank, I just did it on the spur of the moment. Haven't you ever done anything on the spur of the moment?'

'Not like that I haven't,' he snarled.

'Oh, what about my birthday night. That was more than a bloody kiss, wasn't it?'

Frank was silent for the rest of the way home. He parked the truck in the yard, called Benny Tomkiss from the barn, and grumpily ordered him to help him offload my purchases. They carried the cooker into the kitchen, then went back for the rest.

When Miriam saw the cooker, she clasped her hands together in a prayer like motion.

'Does it work, can I cook dinner on it... in it, tonight?'

'I'll have to call your friend, Mr Hart, to get his plumber to fit it. It shouldn't be too big a job, we've got a gas supply in here.' I put my hand on her shoulder. 'You can cook him a Sunday roast though. Invite him over.'

'Oh, I will,' she replied. 'I'm seeing him on Saturday. There's another tea dance.'

Frank came back in, carrying pieces of the dismantled cot. 'Where's this going?' he asked.

'Put it in one of the spare bedrooms for now, but leave the box of baby clothes, I want to show them to Amy, tonight.'

I wheeled the pram up the back steps, and into the kitchen myself. Miriam nearly swooned when she saw it.

'A Silver Cross, and in blue. I had my heart set on one of those when I was expecting my first, but I'd still be paying it off now if I'd bought it. How much was it if you don't mind me asking?'

'I got the lot for seven pounds ten!'

'Seven poun... the pram that I wanted was more than that and that was years ago. This one looks brand new.'

'It isn't new, but it's been well looked after,' I replied.

Miriam stroked the coachwork. 'It's beautiful.'

'Well, Miriam, seeing as how you've hankered for one for so long, how about you take Martha for her first walk in it.'

I thought Miriam was going to explode with pleasure. She rifled through the box of cot-bedding, found a nice, crocheted coverlet, a white cot sheet and folded them up so they would fit the pram mattress, then she picked up Martha from her Moses basket, laid her gently down in the pram and covered her with the crocheted blanket. I helped her down the back steps and she set off, talking constantly to Martha. She was gone a full hour.

At six, I decided to walk up to Amy's to show off my new pram, so I loaded it up with Martha, and a bottle, in case Amy and I got into super-chat mode. I had only just turned onto the lane when I saw her coming down from the opposite direction, pushing a pram, identical to mine.

We stopped, five yards apart. 'Snap!' we said, together.

Amy walked forward and examined my pram.

'It's as good as new, the same as mine,' she said, laughing.

I looked around hers, it was exactly the same model.

'What do we do now? Do we go for a walk, go back to yours, or mine?' I asked.

'I'll park mine up, then we'll walk Martha,' she said.

'Let's walk both prams, that will get people talking,' I replied.

'Not on your Nelly. I've got enough people gossiping about me as it is,' she said with meaning.

We parked Amy's pram in the porch of her house, and walked up the lane chatting about our individual days. Amy told my why she had the pram.

'I went there after work, as it was my half day. She said I could have it, straight away. She's selling the shop, so she's getting rid of a lot of stuff. Her name is Gloria Chambers, she said I could bring the pram to show you, but she wants it back by tomorrow if you aren't interested. She wants six pounds for it. She told me to leave it at the back of the shop after work if you don't want it, so I'll park it up there tomorrow night.'

I shook my head. 'Don't worry about that, I'll make sure it's taken back tomorrow. Leave it where it is and I'll get one of the lads to pick it up in the truck.'

I gave Amy the low down on my lunch appointment with Godfrey, how he had managed to wangle me the bargains and how Frank had suddenly turned up to ruin it all. Amy stopped and looked at me with her head tilted to the side. She sniffed the air twice.

'There's romance in the air. I can smell it.'

'Don't be daft, Amy, he's married. Frank reckons he's old enough to be my father.'

'So is Frank, just about,' said Amy.

'I told him that when he had a go at me,' I replied with feeling.

'Did he start on you again? Wait until I see the nasty... so and so.'

'He wasn't drunk or anything, he'd taken the truck to register Martha's birth and my father's death, which reminds me, the certificates are on the dashboard of the truck, I'll have to remember to get them out when I get back.'

'So, how did he know where you'd gone? You said he was there waiting, when you bought the pram.'

'I don't know, I think he must have followed us,' I replied.

'That's creepy. Remember that film we saw where the man was obsessed with the woman and he ended up killing her?'

'Frank's not like that,' I said, wondering why on earth I was defending him.

Amy leaned over the pram to make cooing noises at Martha.

'So, why was he angry, because you'd had lunch with your gangster man, or because he knows this Godfrey bloke, fancies the pants of you?'

I didn't answer.

Amy squealed.

'He does, doesn't he? He fancies you.' She skipped ahead of the pram singing, 'Alice has a gangster man, Alice has a gangster man.'

I laughed at her antics. 'It isn't like that, Amy. It's, well, I don't know how it is, to be honest.'

'He took you to lunch at a posh café, bought you Martinis—'

'Oh God, I called them Martina's. Like the girl's name, it was so embarrassing.'

'MARTINA'S!' Amy was in heaven. 'I'm going to call them that forever. Every time I order one, I'm going to say, could I have a Martina, please? Oh my God that is so funny.'

'It wasn't at the time,' I said.

When Amy had finished laughing, she went back to the subject of Frank.

'Why was he angry then? Was he jealous of this Godfrey bloke? Is he really that good looking?'

I pretended to wipe my brow and flicked away non-existent sweat.

Amy did a little dance. 'Ooh, I've got to meet him. Is he really dishy?'

'He is movie-star dishy, but he's married. We had lunch and we've only kissed once.'

Amy stopped dead and I ran into the back of her legs.

'You KISSED! Why didn't you tell me that? It's the most important part of the story.'

'It just happened. He's quite tall, so I just got on my tiptoes and kissed him.'

'On the lips!'

'On the lips.'

'You... kissed him. Oh, Alice, you hussy.' Amy's mouth opened wide enough to swallow a tennis ball.

'How long did it last? What did he taste like? Did he stop, or did you?'

'It lasted about ten seconds, his lips tasted of wine, and I broke off the kiss.'

'This is so good,' said Amy. She walked around in a tight circle and then faced me again. 'Sooo, Alice the hussy, when are you seeing him again?'

'Not until the end of August, early September. He's getting the estate death-tax documents ready. I have to pay the government money, because my father died, it seems.'

'Never mind that. Just think, your body will be back to it's usual, irresistible shape by then. He won't be able to keep his hands off.'

'He's married, Amy. Although, he did say that he'd been looking forward to seeing me all morning.'

'There you go then. Oh, this is so good, I don't think I'll sleep tonight. You lucky so and so.'

'He's married,' I repeated.

'Well, if he's that nice, and you don't want him, I'll have him. It's every young girl's dream to have an experienced, older man for a lover.'

'I've got an older man, it's not all it's cracked up to be,' I said.

'Have you and Frank... erm... done it again yet?'

'No, and I don't really want to either,' I replied.

'Good. Stick to your gangster for a while. Okay, you can't marry him... you could run away with him though... Anyway, you could have some fun. You deserve it after what's happened to you over the last year.'

'His wife deserves better too. Look, Amy, I kissed him, he didn't kiss me or even try to. I think this might be a one-way thing. Although... he did tell me he liked the kiss, and he did say that I look like Rita Hayworth... and he likes Rita Hayworth.'

'Just have a bit of fun, Alice, and if he's got a friend who's loaded and as good looking as him. Let me know.'

We turned back at the station; it was Amy's turn to push the pram.

'Oh, I know I meant to tell you something. I met your boss's son today, the mill owner's son that is.' I pulled a face as I thought of him.

Amy shuddered. 'That creep? He's like an octopus when he's on the shop floor. He's disgusting. We keep reporting him but nothing ever happens to him when we do.'

'It might now. Godfrey is the company solicitor. I might just have a word with him about that. He may have some influence.'

Amy nodded vigorously. 'He'll be the mill girls' hero if he could stop it.' She thought for a moment. 'You still haven't said why Frank got mad... OH MY GOD! Did he catch you kissing your gangster?'

'I think he saw every second of it. He had a bit of a go at me in the van over it, but I expected a lot more. I bet he's saving it up for tonight.'

Chapter 67

June 1938

By the time Frank got home, I'd fed Martha her formula bottle, and made up another one for the cold shelf. He didn't speak when he came in, but busied himself warming up his meat and two veg dinner that Miriam had left out for him.

I picked up the baby basket and walked to the stairs.

'Nothing to say for yourself then?'

'Nothing I haven't said already,' I replied before heading up the stairs.

I laid the Moses basket at the foot of the bed and slipped between the sheets, but I couldn't drop off. Worrying about Frank kicking off again, and the memories of what had been a lovely day, fought for dominance in my thoughts. The one thing I was certain about. I didn't love Frank, and I never would. Godfrey, although unattainable, had made me see that. I had allowed myself to be won over by Frank's smile, and his willingness to help with Martha, but he had a dark side to him, and that did concern me. I had been living with an abusive, uncaring, drunk for almost eighteen months, and I was determined that I wasn't going to spend the rest of my life with one.

Frank came up at eleven-thirty, and for once, didn't say goodnight to Martha. Instead he took off his clothes and dropped them where he stood, then yanked back the covers and threw himself into bed.

I was still in the middle ground between sleep and wakefulness, when you seem to know what's going on around you, but your mind is getting snippets of the dream you are about to fall into. Whichever dream that was, I was hauled right back out of it.

'You needn't expect me to feed Martha tonight. You can do it yourself, you lazy cow.'

His angry voice tore into my dozing brain, but I refused to reply.

He nudged me hard in the back with his elbow, when I didn't respond to that, he grabbed my shoulder and dragged me onto my back.

'I said—'

'I heard you, now shut up. I don't need a refrain.'

I regretted saying it the moment I closed my mouth. I tried to turn over again, but he was suddenly sitting astride me with his face so close to mine that I could smell the whisky on his breath, he must have discovered some of my father's stash. He used to hide it everywhere in the early days, before I finally gave in to the inevitable, I had tried to limit his consumption.

'You're a lazy cow, what are you?'

Frank straightened up and I put both my hands on his chest to try to push him off, but he grabbed my wrists, forced them onto the pillow either side of my head, and laughed at me. I felt salty tears of frustration in my eyes as I struggled to get my hands free. It was hopeless, he was far too strong. He leaned in again and sniffed at my neck.

'Why aren't you wearing your special, expensive perfume for me? I'm disappointed, Alice. Do you only wear it for that queer lawyer of yours?'

I remained silent. It wasn't an argument I wanted to get into with him in this mood.

My silence only made him angrier. 'I saw you kiss him, what else have you been up to behind my back?'

I had to answer that one.

'Frank, don't be stupid all of your life, have one day off at least. When am I supposed to have done all of this? I met him for the first time when I was nine months' pregnant, since then I haven't stopped bleeding. Is that the sort of thing you think a queer man might like to see?'

He eased his backside into the air, then slid back about a foot. He grabbed hold of my nightdress at the neck and tore it apart, exposing my leaking breasts. 'Did you show him these?' he shouted.

I felt totally humiliated.

'You call yourself a man, Frank. I've told you this before but obviously the message didn't get through that thick skull of yours. Men don't do things like this to women. They don't take advantage of them when they can't defend themselves. They don't abuse them; they don't get so insanely jealous that they lose every modicum of self-respect they ever possessed. Now get off me. If you don't stop this now, the police will get involved, and so will my lawyer friend, so think on.'

'The police will never get involved in a domestic,' he sneered.

I knew he was right. Our local sergeant was notorious for bragging about how he kept his wife in check. The threat of the lawyer becoming involved was a different matter though. I could see the doubt on his face as he thought about the ramifications.

Frank rolled off me, called me a disgusting tart, then turned his back and muttered himself to sleep. The row had woken Martha, she lay in her basket making niggly noises until I picked her up and put her to my shoulder, at which time, she wailed like a banshee.

'Take that brat downstairs, I'm trying to sleep here,' Frank moaned.

'Are you really? Well, Frank, I was trying to sleep when you came up, but that didn't bother you.' I walked around the room with Martha at my shoulder, the place she least liked to be. Her wailing continued until Miriam tapped on the bedroom door, to see if she could help.

'No, it's all right, Miriam, we're fine,' I lied.

Ten minutes later, Frank dragged himself out of bed, pulling the eiderdown with him. He yanked open the door, and went down the passage to one of the spare bedrooms. He must have slept on the floor, because there were no beds in either of them.

I sat on the end of the bed and put Martha to my leaking breast. She didn't bother suckling, but she licked at the wet nipple and quietened. Miriam went back to bed and I sat up for another ten minutes waiting for Martha to fall asleep, then I put her into her basket and climbed back into bed.

Miriam must have sneaked into my room to give her the three o'clock feed, because I knew nothing else until nine the next morning.

Chapter 68

July 1938

On Friday, just after breakfast, I telephoned my father's insurance company to make a claim. The company office was in Gillingham. I told the receptionist that it would be a difficult journey for me as I had a new-born. She immediately arranged for one of their insurance agents to visit me at home the following Tuesday morning. I told her I was interested in obtaining insurance on my own life and she said he would let me know my options during the appointment. I thanked her for her help and she wished me good luck with Martha.

When I returned to the kitchen, I found that Miriam had taken Martha out into the yard. I was about to go out myself, when Frank stepped out of the parlour. I hadn't seen him since Wednesday night because he was at work before I got up, and came back in after I had gone to bed. He had made no attempt to come into my room on the Thursday night. Miriam and I had shared feeding duties.

'Alice,' he nodded to me.

I ignored him.

He took a step closer. I took a step back.

'Alice,' he began again.

I tried to keep my voice calm and measured. I didn't want to set him off again.

'What do you want, Frank?'

'I shouldn't have said that about Martha, I do love her.'

'Okay... so, you are sorry for calling Martha a brat, but not sorry for calling me a tart, for ripping my clothes off and for scaring me half to death. I thought you were going to hit me, Frank.'

'I'd never do that, Alice,' he said.

'Never? You attempted it when we were on Sheppey. You came close the night my father died, and don't even think about denying you were closer still, on Wednesday night.'

'I wouldn't have, I was just angry about you and that posh bloke.'

'Because I gave him a kiss for helping me?'

'Because I was jealous. I can't give you the things that he can.'

'He hasn't given me anything, Frank. I paid for everything I've had from him.'

His eyes narrowed. 'Paid with... Never mind. The thing is, I'm thinking of leaving in a month or so. There doesn't seem to be a lot for me here, so I'm going away.'

'There's your daughter,' I reminded him.

'I know that, but, I mean, well, I can't take her with me, can I?'

'No. I don't suppose you can. But, what about your mother, Frank? Have you told her?'

'Not yet. I've told the lads I'll be gone soon, though. They didn't seem to care, either.'

'I thought they'd taken to you? Still, I suppose you know better than me. When are you leaving and what are you going to do, have you decided yet?'

Frank bridled. 'You see. You aren't even attempting to talk me into staying. You don't care either.'

'Oh, stop feeling so sorry for yourself, Frank. You know the reasons I won't miss you. If you had stayed off the drink, things might have worked out, but you're a different person when you're under the influence. I got sick of seeing it, day in day out, when my father had his problem.'

'I'm not feeling sorry for myself. I know what I've done.'

I nodded to him. 'So, what are you going to do?'

He sat at the kitchen table and pulled a scrap pf paper out of his pocket. 'I've applied to join the Merchant Navy. This advertisement was in the paper, yesterday. I'll get to see the world, have a bit of fun.'

'Have you told Edna?'

'Not yet. She's ill. I didn't want to upset her.'

'So, you're just going to leave without saying anything? Won't that hurt her more, Frank? What's wrong with her?' She had seemed fine when I was giving birth to Martha, though she had been a little quiet.

Frank shrugged. 'I don't know, I'm not a doctor, and she's used to me going back and forth anyway, she'll be okay with it.'

'When are you leaving? We've got the harvest coming up and I'll have to get a replacement, if only temporary.' We did get local men, their wives and even their kids helping out at harvest, but to be an experienced man down would be a bit of a blow.

'I'll give you a month's notice, Alice. I'll leave at the end of July. That should give you time to find someone else.'

I decided to talk to Barney about it at lunchtime, when he came for his wages. We were fine before Frank came. Maybe we'd be all right without the extra man.

Frank shuffled his feet and looked a little nervous. 'Will it be all right... I mean, can I still stay here until I leave? I'll put the camp bed up in the parlour again.'

'We have to get through the parlour to the bathroom now, Frank, so, put the camp bed up in the room you slept in the other night, but please, don't even think about coming into my room again. One more episode like that, and you're out on your ear. I'll tell Barney and the lads if you try anything.'

'You won't wash your dirty washing in front of the workforce,' he said.

He was right. The gossip about my private life would have reached Sittingbourne by nightfall.

'I might just surprise you, Frank. The offer of the camp bed is conditional anyway.' I looked at him sternly to make my point.

'Don't worry, I won't bother you again.'

'You had better not, Frank. It's Friday, you'll be out with the lads tonight, so think on. Don't even think about coming back here drunk.

You won't get in. The door will be locked and double bolted. Stay at your mother's if you're going to the pub.'

Frank looked as though he was going to argue, but in the end, he bit his tongue. He picked up his torn-out advertisement from the table and walked slowly out into the yard.

When he had returned to the fields, I searched the entire house to see if I could find any hidden bottles of whisky, but found nothing. Either my father had some truly imaginative places to hide the stuff, or I had found them all.

Frank didn't come back that night, and I didn't see him until lunchtime on Saturday. Miriam and I were chatting in the kitchen about her date that afternoon, when he knocked on the back door, and stepped in.

'Alice, Miriam.'

'Hello, Frank,' replied Miriam, who hadn't forgiven him for waking up Martha on Wednesday night. She had dealt with a brutal, drunken, husband and knew how quickly the abuse could escalate.

'I'd like a word with Alice, in private,' he stated, calmly.

Miriam looked at me questioningly, I nodded, and she went into the front room. 'I'm just through here,' she said.

Frank pulled out a chair and sat opposite me, across the kitchen table.

'I need a favour,' he said.

'I'm listening, Frank.'

'I telephoned the recruitment people for the Merchant Navy this morning, from the call box near The Old Bull. There are vacancies all over the country. There's a ship leaving from Hull in the next few days that is short on crew, and as I've had a bit of experience, they'll take me on. The first voyage is to Spain, then on to Tangiers via Gibraltar. I'll be gone about six weeks.'

'That's good news, if that's what you want, Frank. What's the favour?'

'There are two, actually. Firstly, could you lend me a few quid. I know I got paid yesterday, but I need train fare to Hull, then at least one night in a hotel and I'll need a bit of money for the voyage, not much, but I'll be going ashore in all the ports.'

'How much?' I asked.

'A fiver? I'll make it up to you.'

'A fiver? Blimey, Frank! It's only a few bob for the train fare, one way.'

'I don't want to look like I'm a shyster when I go out with the crew, that's all it is, Alice, and I won't be paid until the voyage is done. I could get a sub here and there throughout the trip, but that would mean I've got nothing left by way of wages to collect, when I get back.'

'Give me a minute to think about it. You said there were two favours?'

He sucked on his teeth. 'The other one... Look, when I talked to the guy on the telephone, he gave me a list of ports and destinations, from when I get back, right up until the first week in September. He told me how long the voyages are, the cargo, that sort of thing. Anyway, this first trip will see me back in mid-August. The ship then turns around and leaves a few days later, doing the same run. Now, in early September, there's a ship heading out to America. I've never been there, and I'd love to see New York, or Chicago with its gangsters. Anyway, I can't get on that ship if I sign up for a repeat trip on the first one. So, the favour is. Could I stay here from mid-August until the other boat sails in September. It will only be for two weeks, and I'll work for my keep. The other ship goes from Liverpool. I won't be any trouble, Alice, I promise, I swear on—'

'Don't you dare say, Martha,' I warned him.

'Okay, my mother's life then, I swear on my mother's life.'

I suddenly felt seriously worried about Edna's future. I thought about the money. It was a lot for him to ask for, but then again, getting a clean break from him might be worth it.

'When you come back, it's for two weeks, maximum, Frank, less if possible. Please let your mother know the name of the ships you're on, in case she ever needs you.' I paused, still reluctant to agree.

'Come on, Alice. I'll pay you back. Every penny.'

I came to a decision.

'I'll give you four pounds, Frank. You've still got the best part of your wages from yesterday. When you come back, you'll work for your keep, there will be no pay, I'll get it back that way. Are we agreed?'

I held out my hand. Frank thought for a moment and then shook it.

'Agreed,' he said.

'When do you leave?'

'I've got to meet up with the Nightshade, at six o'clock on Monday morning. My name will be on the ship's roll. If I leave this evening, I can get the late train from London to Sheffield and on to Hull from there tomorrow.'

I went to the safe and took out my own wage packet that I'd made up the day before. I counted out the money inside and topped it up from the petty cash tin.

'Here you are, Frank,' I said, dropping the money into his hands. 'Bon Voyage.'

'You won't regret this,' he said.

'I sincerely hope not,' I replied.

When Frank walked out, I felt a surge of relief, tinged with just a touch of sadness. I knew I was better off without him, but he had been a big part of my life for a good while. I shouted to Miriam to come back in and then put the kettle on for a celebration cup of tea.

Chapter 69

July 1938

It was the perfect day for a funeral, if you can have such a thing. In the films and in books, a funeral is always held in foul, wet, windy, weather, as though the deceased was playing a final practical joke on the mourners. My father, it seemed, had ordered wall to wall sunshine for his funeral. This made me happy for two reasons. One, I wouldn't have to stand around, shivering, while water dripped down my neck from the branches of the old oak, and two, the blue sky gave me the crazy idea that the sun was celebrating his reunification with the love of his life. This thought cheered me, and I clung on to it all the way through the service.

The funeral went off as well as we could have hoped, if not a little slower than I, for one, had hoped. The vicar spent so little time on my father's achievements and character and so much time on lecturing us on the temptations of life and the evils of drink. Had he gone on much longer I swear I would have stood up and asked him if he remembered staggering about in the garden of the vicarage with a bottle of best malt in his hands, the Christmas before last. My mother had sent me up with a Christmas card and a large home-made beef and onion pie. He was hardly able to see, let alone thank me for it, so I left it on his doorstep where I hoped he would tread on it.

I was on the front pew throughout. Miriam sat next to me, holding a very well behaved, Martha. The only thing she seemed to object to, was the hymn, Jesus wants me for a sunbeam, but Miriam quickly settled her. I almost laughed out loud as whenever my father heard that line of the hymn, he would sing, *and a bloody fine sunbeam am I.*

Amy couldn't be at the service because her foreman had refused permission, even though she'd offered to make the time up later. The foreman, who was Frank's age, and divorced, had asked her out earlier in the year and she had undiplomatically, refused, so he got over this perceived humiliation by stopping her going to her best friend's family funeral. She got her revenge immediately by telling everyone who would listen, how she had turned down his advances.

After the service, we trooped around to the grave site at the far end of the churchyard. The vicar apologised for the oak branch that hung over the two graves. He promised to get it cut back, but I told him to leave it. The tree was probably the reason my mother chose that spot in the first place.

When the coffin was lowered into the ground, I said my last goodbye to my father and tossed a handful of dirt into the grave as the vicar prayed. No one else did, in fact I was glared at across the open grave by the landlord of The Old Bull's wife, who had come to say goodbye to the man who virtually kept them afloat for the last eighteen months. Both she, and the vicar, gave me a sterner look when I dropped in my mother's favourite fountain pen.

'I hope you found her and you're happy again,' I whispered.

When the Reverend Villiers had done praying, we stepped away from the grave to allow the gravediggers to backfill the plot.

There were about thirty people at the funeral. I knew half a dozen by name and as many by sight. Some of the others might have been customers of ours that I never got to meet. Like the owner of the dairy that took the majority of our milk.

'I'm so sorry to meet you in these circumstances,' he said. 'I've been buying milk from your farm for years. I'm Maurice Hepplewhite and I own Middleton Dairies.'

'I hope you continue to buy it,' I said, wondering if he was about to impart bad news. I gave him my best Rita Hayworth smile, in case it helped sway the decision.

'I certainly will. In fact, I was hoping to persuade you to buy a few more cows. Your milk is of exceptional quality. I drink it raw myself.' He smiled and held out his hand. I shook it.

'I'll definitely think about it,' I said. We had plenty of pasture, but the overwintering facilities couldn't hold more than one or two more at best. The price we'd have to pay for buying in just two animals wouldn't be cost effective. I needed a bigger barn.

Martha began to get niggly, so I told Miriam to take her home for a feed. Barney and Benny, who were representing the workforce, tipped their caps to me and walked away with her. I sat around for a while on a seat just outside the church, thinking about how much my life had changed over the past year. I was so wound up in my own thoughts, that I didn't notice the man walking up the church path until he was standing right next to me.

'I hope everything went as well as it could, Alice.'

I knew that smooth as honey voice as he got the first two syllables out. I looked up into the midday sun, screwed up my eyes and tried to move my face into his shadow.

'Godfrey, what are you doing here?'

'I saw your announcement in the Births, Deaths and Marriages column the other day, so I thought I'd come down to see how you were coping.' He looked around. 'You don't have anyone with you?'

'Miriam was here, but she's taken Martha home for her feed. The farm lads went with her, they have a lot on at the moment. I just felt like sitting in the sunshine for a while to think about things.' I got to my feet. 'I've got an empty head now. All my thoughts have leaked out.'

Godfrey laughed. 'May I walk you home, I need the exercise, I'm always on my backside.'

'I'd love you to,' I said, smiling.

He offered me his arm, I slipped my own through it, and we walked through the church gates and onto the main road. His car was parked on the opposite side.

'I love your car; it reminds me of the ones in the gangster films. You know, Edward G. Robinson and James Cagney.'

'Little Caesar?' he asked.

'That's the one. Amy and I have seen it three times. We'll go again if they bring it back for the film festival this autumn.'

'I've only seen it once. Maybe I could join you?'

'Do you know a nice, handsome, gangster type, about your age?' I asked him.

'Not a gangster type, no. It wouldn't be good to hang around with gangsters in my profession. Why do you ask?'

'Because Amy wants to meet one,' I said.

Godfrey laughed again. 'Sorry, I can't help there.'

'Could I ask a favour?' I said when we'd walked a few yards further.

'Anything,' he said.

'I am enjoying the walk, but, well, would it be cheeky of me to ask for another ride in your car? I did enjoy it so much last time.'

He led me over the road to the Alvis, and opened the passenger door with a flourish. 'Your carriage awaits, Madame.'

I had to stop myself leaping into the seat. When I was safely installed, he closed the door and climbed into the driver's side.

'Shall I take you home or would you like a drive around the countryside for a while? I know which one I'd prefer but I also know what you've just been through, so, you choose.'

'I haven't been through as much as you think,' I said, quietly. 'I've seen this day coming for eighteen months. It just got closer every day, that's all. He hasn't really been my father since my mother died.'

'Home?' he asked, teasingly, knowing I'd say no.

We drove out of the town until we hit the narrow lanes, then we drove slowly along, admiring the countryside. It should have been a busman's holiday for me, looking at fields full of cows and sheep, but this was different. He talked to me as an equal, laughed at my silly little jokes and answered seriously when I asked a question. It was an adult discussion. When we had gone a few miles, we stopped at a country pub that I didn't know existed, and we found a table outside, in a shady nook. Godfrey took off his hat and placed it on the table.

'You look like a gangster when you wear that. Especially when you're in the car,' I said.

'You've got a thing about gangsters, haven't you?' He grinned as he put his hat onto my head. I ran my hands through my chestnut churls and struck a pose. 'Do I look like a gangster's moll?' I asked him.

'A perfect moll,' he replied with a smile. 'Now then, what would a gangster's moll like to drink. A Martina, perhaps?'

I blushed. 'I'm so stupid, I shouldn't have—'

'I found it amusing, not stupid. In fact, I might just make up my own cocktail mix and call it a Martina.'

'Can you do that? Make up your own cocktails? I thought they'd all been invented already.'

'One day, I'll show you how to make one, and it will be called the Martina,' he said.

I drank the Martini that arrived, far too quickly again, so we sat and talked about the ways of the world while he finished his wine. Afterwards, we took a long detour, and arrived at the farm at about three o'clock. Frank was just walking out of the yard with his bag of possessions as we pulled up.

'Wait here,' I ordered, then apologised. 'Sorry, I meant to say, please.'

Godfrey smiled and I got out of the car. Frank waited for me to walk over to him.

'Good luck, Frank. I really mean it. I hope the seas are kind to you.'

He leaned forward to kiss me but I stepped back and held out my hand instead. Frank shook it, took one hateful look at the Alvis, then turned away and spat in the dirt.

'See you in August,' he said and stomped up the lane.

I returned to the car and motioned for Godfrey to get out.

'Where's Frank going?' he asked.

'He's running away to sea,' I replied.

'Do you think I should offer him a lift to the station?' he asked.

'Not bloody likely, that's my seat, I don't want it getting dirty.'

I held out my hand to invite him into the farm yard. 'Would you like a cup of tea and one of Miriam's doorstep, cheese sandwiches?' I asked him.

He patted his stomach. 'I need to watch this; I'll settle for the tea.'

Chapter 70

July 1938

Godfrey was just leaving as Amy walked through the back gate. He tipped his hat to her, then turned to me and did the same.

'Goodbye, Alice, thank you for the tea. I enjoyed our afternoon. I'll ring with a progress report regarding the Estate Duty, in the early part of next week. Meanwhile, good luck with the insurance company.'

Amy had stayed silent while he was speaking. She looked at him, pretty much the same way I had when I first met him. She had a dreamy look on her face and her mouth opened and closed, but no sound came out. Eventually, she got her act together.

'Are you Alice's gangster lawyer?' she asked.

Godfrey chuckled. 'It seems I am,' he said.

'I thought so. You look like a gangster in that hat,' Amy replied.

'I'll have to remember to take it off when the police are around,' he said with a smile.

'I would,' Amy said. 'You have a gangster car too. Can I get a ride in it?'

I hid my smile behind my hand and tried to look serious.

'Not on the front seat, that's mine,' I said, trying hard not to laugh.

Godfrey looked at his watch, which was fixed to his waistcoat by a thick gold chain.

'I'm so sorry... erm, Amy, is it? I don't have time at the moment, but I'd be happy to take you both for a spin at a later date, if that is acceptable?'

'Only if you have a handsome, gangster friend to come with us,' Amy said seriously. 'I don't want to be a gooseberry.'

Godfrey shot a quick look at me from beneath the brim of his hat. He winked and turned back to Amy.

'I prefer strawberries.' He pointed to her fair hair. 'Blondes that is.'

While Amy tried to work out what he meant by that, he stepped through the gate and pulled it closed behind him. He tipped his hat again. 'Ladies,' he said, and set off up the dusty track that led to the lane.

Amy and I gossiped well into the late evening. I told her about my day, how my father's funeral had gone, how I dropped my mother's pen on the coffin and how Godfrey had been kind enough to think of me after the funeral was over.

'He can make his own cocktails and he's going to invent one for me, guess what he's going to call it?'

'Alice... no, Alice in Wonderland... no, Alice, erm, The Tansley, no, The Mollison, oh, I don't know, I give up. What is it?'

'Martina!'

'Oh, my God! Seriously? Doesn't that sort of take the joke out of it though?'

'Not really, no one serving you will know what it is, it's not like he's famous or anything. No one will copy it.'

'Good,' said Amy. 'I want to order one soon. Before the word gets out.'

Then I told her about Frank. How he'd attacked me again on the Wednesday night when he was drunk. When I told her that he'd joined the Merchant Navy, she whooped and gave me the biggest hug she'd ever given me.

'You're free of him. Oh, I hope his ship sinks, is that being too mean? I suppose it is as there will be others onboard. Maybe the navy will send him to Australia or on a ten-year tour of the Pacific Ocean.'

'It's the Merchant Navy, Amy. They sail around the world with cargo, you know, bananas, coal, anything really, they're usually gone a few months at a time.'

'That's not long enough for that swine,' she said with feeling.

Then I had to impart the bad news.

'He's... he's staying here for two weeks at the end of August, while he waits for a ship to America, then he's gone for good, I think.'

'ALICE!' Amy was furious.

'It's two weeks, Amy, and he's working for his keep, I don't have to pay him anything.'

'I assume he's sleeping in the barn. Why isn't he staying at his mother's?'

'She's ill by all accounts and to be honest, I don't think he can face her to explain what went wrong between us. I think he knows she'll accuse him of deserting me and Martha, but he knows I don't want him anywhere near us, so he's between a rock and a hard place really.'

'Good. I wish I was holding the rock,' said Amy.

'I don't know what's wrong with Edna, but she looked all right when she was here for Martha's birth.'

'I'll find out. I'll get the undercover crew on the case,' she replied.

Miriam flitted in and out, between upstairs and down. She had her Friday night bath, and sat with us while she dried her hair, then she set up the ironing board and pressed the clothes she was going to wear to the tea dance on Saturday afternoon. My mother's wardrobe was being well serviced. She watched over Amy as she fed Martha a bottle for the first time. Amy made coo and squee, noises all the way through the experience.

Our gas cooker had been plumbed in earlier in the week. It was green, with a white oven door and grill chamber. It had a plate warmer, drying rack at the top, and sported three burning rings with the grill underneath, and an oven with a thermostat that regulated how much heat the oven lost. You could set the temperature on the knob and forget it until the item you were cooking was ready. All you had to do was keep your eye on the big clock on the wall. Miriam was so used to the range oven, that it took her a while to get used to the idea, and she ruined three or four cakes by continually opening the oven door, to see if her creation had risen. She warned me on more than one occasion when I opened the back door, thinking that I was letting all the heat out of the room.

I fell in love with the cooker almost as soon as it had been connected to the gas main. It meant I could warm up milk for Martha, boil a kettle and make a slice of toast at the same time. How does that saying go? Something like, necessity is the mother of invention? It was surely a mother who invented this type of cooker. Men haven't got a clue how to do more than one thing at a time.

On Saturday night, after yet another tea dance and fish and chip supper by the boating lake, Miriam announced that she had been invited by Mr Hart, to accompany him on a weekend trip to Southend on Sea, over the late August bank holiday weekend. I was so excited for her. Things were moving on, it seemed.

'I won't go if you need me here. I know it's three days, well, it isn't actually as we won't be leaving until Saturday afternoon; because Michael has to sort out his work books in the morning. Would it be too long a break?'

I rubbed my chin as if I was thinking hard about it.

'Of course, you can go, Miriam. You can take the whole week if you want. You haven't had a holiday in years.'

'Would it, I mean… I know I only usually borrow your mother's clothes for the tea dances, but would it be all right to pack a few things. I promise to look after them.'

'They're no longer my mother's clothes, Miriam. They're yours. Use them whenever you like. My mother would be delighted, I'm sure. And…' I paused for effect. 'If you look in the drawer of my bedside cupboard, you'll find a little bottle of Orchidée Bleue, Eau De Cologne. That's yours too. Don't take the Tabu from my dresser though, that's my extravagance. Frank says it makes me smell like a tart so I wouldn't be without it now.'

Miriam looked at me strangely, obviously wondering why I'd want to smell like a tart, but after reassurance from me, she ran upstairs to find the spray bottle I had given her. She came down sniffing the back of her hand with a smile like she'd just won the football pools.

'Does it suit me? I've never had perfume before.'

I sniffed at her hand.

'It suits you perfectly, Miriam. It doesn't smell that good on me, I tried it.'

'What's it called again? In case anyone asks me?'

'Orchidée Bleue,' I said. 'It's French.'

'Oh, I say. Aren't I getting above my station? Me, in French perfume and fine clothes. My children wouldn't recognise me if they saw me out.'

'You deserve every bit of happiness, Miriam. I hope you have a lovely weekend,' I said, as she hugged me.

On Tuesday, the man from the Imperial Insurance Company arrived bang on time and by eleven o'clock, he had written and signed a cheque in my name, and set up my own personal policy that would pay my nominated next of kin, one-hundred pounds, on account of my death. My subscription would be collected by a local agent who would call to pick up the money, every Friday evening.

When he had gone, I asked Barney to accompany me to the bank, as he was on good terms with the manager. The cheque had been made out to cash and I know I, as a mere woman, would have had a problem cashing it. With Barney there to vouch for my identity (although the manager knew exactly who I was), life would be much simpler.

Once the formalities were dispensed with, I asked the clerk to write out a bank cheque to Messrs. Wilson, Kendall and Beanney, Solicitors, for the sum of one-hundred and ten pounds, thirteen shillings and ninepence. The rest of the money, I took in cash. It would go in the safe along with what remained of my mother's insurance money.

Back in the truck, Barney asked me whether I would be employing someone to take Frank's place.

'Do we need someone permanent, Barney? I thought Frank was surplus to requirements during the quieter times of the year.'

'He was a good worker, that was for sure. A bit up himself at times but he could do a shift with the best of 'em. The Merchant Navy has a grafter there. I was, err, surprised to hear he was leaving so suddenly though.'

'He's coming back for two weeks at the end of August; you can give him whatever work you decide on. There won't be any more of this charge hand, nonsense.'

Barney assessed the situation in seconds.

'We'll need someone full time for the harvest, plus the usual part-time locals.'

'Do you have anyone in mind, Barney? Frank will be working for his keep, so the finances will stand another full-time worker, for a while at least. I wouldn't want to have to pay out through the winter to have someone standing idle.'

'My brother is looking for some seasonal work, Missis. He does what Frank's doing, but he's getting tired of the sea. He's done harvest work before, so he won't be a burden to the rest of us.'

'Tell him he's hired for the harvest, Barney, don't let anyone else get him first.'

Chapter 71

August 1938

In early August I received a telephone call from Edna, asking me to pay her a visit. I assumed it was to give me a ticking off for not taking Martha to see her, but as it turned out, it wasn't anything to do with that.

Edna was dying. Ovarian cancer had gone undiscovered and untreated for too long. When she began to show symptoms, it was already too late. She had known about her condition for months, but hadn't mentioned it, because she didn't want to spoil the joys of Martha's birth.

We sat in her front room while I sipped tea and she held Martha. The change in her since late June had been dramatic. She looked even more washed-out and wasted than either my father or mother during their illnesses. When she was sitting with Martha, it was hard to tell where her breasts ended and her stomach began, but when she stood up, her bloated stomach was easy to spot, especially sat atop a pair of legs so spindly, it was hard to see how they supported her.

She told me that she only had a few weeks left, and when Martha fell asleep, I laid her on a chair, and Edna and I sat on the sofa where we hugged and cried until there were no tears left.

I was the piggy in the middle for sure. She didn't want Frank to worry about her while he was at sea, and Frank didn't want to see her wasting away. He always was a selfish man, but now I could see him for the coward he was too. Apparently, he had known about her condition for weeks. She had told him when she was first diagnosed, in early June. He had continued to live and work at the farm, and apart from the Friday night pub sessions he hardly went anywhere. She had to ambush him as he walked into The Old Bull, to tell him of her imminent death, but instead of wrapping an arm around her and taking her back home, he took the news like she'd just wished him a good evening, and left her standing at the door of the pub while he went inside for the night.

She pushed a few pounds into my hands and begged me to sort out her funeral when the time came.

More tears came from somewhere. I hugged her again and promised her that I would.

I never saw her again.

Chapter 72

August 1938

The wheat harvest started a week earlier than usual. Barney's brother arrived from Essex on the day he had promised he would, so we had a full complement of workers from day one.

The work went well, we employed a number of locals on temporary eight-week contracts, and in the evenings and the weekends, a lot of the local pensioners, wives and children, turned up to help for a few shillings pay at the end of the week.

The corn crop was coming on well, and it looked like being a September harvest for our main crop. That would only leave the root vegetables, which my own men could manage easily in October and November.

Frank came back, as promised, in mid-August. I can't say we didn't need him. During the first two weeks of the month we had suffered thunder storms and intermittent rain, but the sun came back with Frank at the start of the third week.

He slipped back into farm life as if he'd never been away. His skin had always had the brown hue of an outdoor worker, but the few weeks of sea air, had faded the tan and brought out a few laughter lines around his eyes and mouth. His skin looked rough, he had the beginnings of a sailor's beard, and his body, always so lean, looked a little fuller. They had obviously fed him well.

We worked into the darkness throughout the harvest. We lit lanterns around the fields so that the workforce could see what they were doing on the moonless nights. It was back-breaking work and the participants always celebrated when it was all over. The culmination came with a Harvest party at the farm, after the last ears of corn had been pulled in late September; we almost always finished in the middle of the week, before the Harvest Festival service at the church.

Bessie, our shire horse, worked hard during harvest. She was spoiled rotten at the end of every day by both our own men and the locals. She needed to plod those fields, to work off the amount of sugar lumps, dried apple, carrots and peppermints, she was fed.

The sun wasn't the only thing Frank's arrival brought back. The day he arrived; I started my first period since I had given birth. My monthlies were never a real problem for me. I didn't get particularly miserable, or moody like a lot of the girls I went to school with, I can't say I sailed through them like Amy did though. Nothing ever seemed to get to her.

My breast milk production had ceased in July. I wondered if I would bother even trying to breast feed another child if I had one. The formula milk had performed miracles with Martha.

Frank came in at midnight, and was out of the house again for five. We hadn't spoken a word since his return. I heard him muttering to himself as he crept up the stairs at night, but he didn't even hesitate outside my bedroom door for a second. I began to breathe easier. It looked like the Merchant Navy had done him some good.

I waited for my period to end, before I tackled my own job of feeding and cleaning out the pigs again. I was nervous of going in with the twin boars, Horace and Hector, so I spent a few minutes, three times a day, standing outside their pen, or sitting on the rails, scratching their hairy backs.
The acid test came on the Sunday of the third week in August. I donned my old dungarees only to find that I could have put someone else inside them with me, and they'd still be loose.

Miriam offered to take out all of the inserts she had stitched in over the months, while I searched my room for the spare pair that hadn't been altered for my pregnancy.

I finally found them stuffed under the bed with a couple of my father's checked, work shirts.

It was a strange feeling, sitting on a chair, in my unaltered overalls pulling on my rubber boots. It seemed an age since I had last done it. Benny, who had been looking after the pigs in my enforced absence, watched over me as I opened the safety gate to allow the pigs in the first sty to be corralled into the holding pen. When I began the process of the clean out, I worked too quickly, and had to go through the sty a second time to remove all the detritus. The stench was incredible, I knew I would get used to it again soon, but I wished to God that I'd put some scented cream on my nose before I set out.

By the time I'd done pen three, I was fully back in the swing of it. I was cleaning and sluicing almost as fast as I ever had. When I got to the last pen, the scene of my trauma, I told Benny to get back to the harvest, as I'd be fine. Benny was obviously under orders from Barney to do no such thing, and he hung around the fence of the new pen, as I tentatively opened the safety gate to the holding pen so that Hector and Horace, the huge brothers, could get at the whey treats, a by-product of Miriam's small butter and cheese operation. Not only did it give us as much fresh cheese and butter as we needed, it gave the animals some tasty, extra protein. My pigs loved it.

As soon as the gate was open, Horace led his brother and the sows into the holding pen. I stepped into the sty with my brush, disinfectant, hose and shovel, and began to clean. I was so engrossed in my work that I didn't hear the shout from Benny, until it was too late.

In my haste to get the boars into the holding pen, I hadn't shut the latch properly and both Horace and Hector were now standing directly behind me. Horace nudged the back of my thigh. I closed my eyes tight, expecting the worst, but all I got was another nudge. I turned around nervously, but the boars were just impatient for the daily back scratch I provided with the aid of the stiff yard brush.

I was in the pen with them for a good twenty minutes, making sure each of the twelve porkers got a hefty scrub with the brush. By the time I got out, Benny had gone. I punched the air with elation. My boars were the friendly, loveable creatures they had always been.

Frank came back early on the Friday with a cut across his forearm. Miriam washed his arm with disinfectant and put a bandage around it. Before he left, I asked him to spare me a couple of minutes in private.

'You do know what's wrong with your mother, Frank, don't you?' I said, more an accusation, than a question.

'I don't want to talk about it,' he replied.

'Frank, it's your mother, you only ever get one, and she's dying, you should at least see her before you go back. You might not get another chance.'

'Thanks for the advice, but I'd prefer it if you kept your nose out of my business,' he snarled.

'Frank, she telephoned me, she wanted to see Martha. She told me all about her diagnosis. Honestly, Frank, she's only got a few weeks left. Just say goodbye to her before you go back. It won't bloody kill you.'

He pushed my shoulder to move me away and walked out of the door.

'Bloody women. You're all more trouble than you're worth,' he said as he walked across the yard.

Because of the help of the locals, plus the added bonus of Frank, and Barney's brother, Raymond, the wheat crop had been cut on time and we were now ready for the threshing machine. We had beaten the bad weather at the start of the month, and caught up by the fourth week. It would cost me extra in payments to the part timers, but handing out a few sixpences to the children who were learning the value of work, was always a delight to experience. The look on their faces when they received their first shiny coins was a joy to behold. Most of them would have to hand their new found wealth over to a parent a few minutes after they were given it, but for those few moments, they felt as rich as Croesus. I knew that feeling, I had been in the position myself, the only difference was, I got to keep mine.

On Saturday I rang the Reverend Villiers to ask if he had been to see Frank's mum yet. He said he had been busy with other pastoral matters, but promised to visit her the following week. I reminded him that she had given me the money to cover her funeral, and said I'd drop in at the vicarage on the Monday evening. He said he was always busy in the evenings. I knew what that meant and I wasn't about to leave Edna's funeral money on his doorstep like I had done with the pie. We agreed that I should try to catch him at lunchtime instead.

We gave the locals the weekend off, while the retained workers prepared for the corn harvest which we would now start two weeks early. The wheat crop looked to have given us a higher yield than we had seen for many a year, and Barney assured me the same would happen with the corn harvest. The weather looked fine for the long weekend. Miriam had talked about little else all week.

On Thursday, I received an unexpected call from Godfrey. We had chatted on the telephone a couple of times since our outing, but he had been away on a family holiday for a week in the middle of the month, and since then I had been busy with the influx of workers.

'Hello, Stranger,' he said, in his soft as velvet voice.

'Hello, gangster man,' I said with a little laugh.

'I've got news for you, Alice. The government have agreed our assessment of your tax burden, so we can go ahead and pay them. The last time we spoke, you said you had a bank cheque made out to the practice. Do you think I could come over tomorrow to bring the liability form for you to sign? It's all done then.'

'What time?' I asked a little too eagerly. I couldn't wait to see him.

'I have a probate issue to sort out in the afternoon, and that will take hours, so, shall we say, ten-thirty?'

'I'm counting the minutes... To get this tax thing off my back,' I added, hurriedly.

'I'm looking forward to ending this nonsense too. I really can't think why the government treats small farmers this way. You are the backbone of the economy. Mind you, the way things are going abroad, you might see a change in their attitude soon.'

I hung up and did a little dance around the room, then I went upstairs to try on a couple of my best frocks. I stood in front of the half-length mirror to give myself a critical once over.

I'd done well, or I thought I had. The dress touched where it was supposed to, and when I turned sideways, my profile didn't look like the side view of a cottage loaf any more. I faced the wall, and looked over my shoulder at my backside, but I couldn't remember what it looked like before. The dress fell over it nicely, and that's all that mattered. The V neck of the dress was maybe a little revealing for that time of day, but I thought I'd risk it. I was feeling like a normal teenager again for the first time in ten months, and I was going to enjoy the experience.

Chapter 73

August 1938

The morning crawled by. I had my rose-scented bath, straight after seeing to the pigs. I couldn't face breakfast; my tummy was fluttering like a butterfly's wings. I resisted the urge to get ready too early, in case I was needed on the farm. Cornflower print dresses and farm muck, don't go too well together.

At ten, I decided I couldn't wait any longer, my hair was washed and brushed, my white, Oxford, shoes were wiped down and ready. I thought about wearing stockings, but as I wasn't about to go out anywhere, I left them in the drawer. I pulled the dress over my head and fastened the buttons from my waist to my bust, thought again about whether the quite dramatic V neck was a little too much, and deciding it wasn't. I dabbed my mother's Tabu on my neck, behind my ears and on the inside of my wrists. I checked myself in the mirror, back and front, and practiced my wriggle walk across the bedroom. By the time I got downstairs again, it was ten twenty-seven. I looked out of the window and waited for the Alvis to pull up.

Godfrey was Mr Punctuality, as he always was. At ten-thirty exactly, he knocked firmly on the door. I waited for what seemed an eternity, but was, in reality, more like thirty seconds, before I answered it.

'My, my, don't you look a picture,' he said, looking me up and down. 'Cornflower certainly suits you.'

My heart was racing, my mind, spinning. I stood at the door, desperately thinking of something to say. He was wearing a different navy suit with a thicker stripe. It made him look more gangster-like than ever. I smiled at him, and stood there, dumbstruck.

'Can I come in?' he asked.

'Oh, sorry, of course, come in, come in.' I rolled my eyes as he passed me. *Stupid, stupid, woman.*

He took three strides into the room and turned to face me as I closed the door.

'We've been blessed with a beautiful day again. How's the harvest coming on?'

I breathed a sigh of relief; the harvest was one thing I could find the words for.

'It's been really good so far. We had a bad start, but we managed to catch up this week. The wheat crop is cut, stacked and waiting for the thresher. We'll start on the corn after the bank holiday. Are you doing anything special this weekend?'

'I'm going down to Dover on Sunday. We have a businessman client who, unlike you, has got himself into a spot of bother over his government taxes.' He raised his briefcase and tapped the side of it. 'His case goes to court on Tuesday, and I need to be there to advise him throughout. It might be a couple of weeks before I get back, hence the urgency to get your Estate Duty taxes done and dusted before I leave.'

'I'll miss you,' I said, as though I saw him every day.

'And I'll miss you, Alice. You really are a breath of fresh air. My job can be quite dull at times, but you brighten my day whenever I see you.' He turned away, placed his briefcase on the table, opened the clasp and pulled out my tax forms. 'Sign where I've put the dots, please, Alice.'

He passed me his beautiful, gold-patterned, fountain pen, and I signed the bottom of all four pages of the document.

He wafted the papers in the air to dry the ink, then he slipped them back into the briefcase and pulled out another form.

'This is to say that the money has been paid in full. I filled it in as soon as you said you'd had the bank make the cheque payable to us. It's a bit naughty of me really, but I knew you wouldn't let me down.'

I went to the safe, pulled the key from the pocket of my dress, took out the banker's cheque and handed it to him. He scanned it quickly, dropped it into his case and snapped the clasp.

'Well, that's about it, Alice, our business is concluded. I do hope we will meet again soon.'

'Wait, please, don't go yet,' I almost begged.

He shrugged. 'I'm not in a rush. What did you want to discuss?'

'Dance with me,' I said.

'I'm sorry?'

'Dance with me, before you go. We've had lunch, tea, Martini's, but we've never danced.'

He looked around. 'Do you have a radio or something?'

'Much better than that,' I said. 'Wait here, please don't leave, I'll be back in two shakes.'

I rushed from the room and grabbed my beautiful, blue gramophone from its place next to the tallboy, then I picked up my record case, and returned to the front room, closing the door behind me with my heel. To my intense relief, he was still there.

I set up the machine and selected Fred Astaire, singing Night and Day. I lowered the arm onto the record, then turned around with my arms open wide.

Godfrey smiled at me. 'I love this song.'

We danced slowly, and properly to begin with, one of his hands in mine, one on the back of my shoulder, but as the dance progressed, I moved his hand down to my waist and put both of mine on his back. My breasts brushed against his chest and a tingle, like a tiny, electric shock, ran down my spine. My eyes sought his and I pressed even closer. He attempted to lose eye contact but mine must have contained powerful, eyeball-magnets, because his gaze only left mine for a millisecond.

'Alice. This can't happen,' he said, huskily.

I snuggled into his chest and laid my head against his shoulder. 'I know,' I replied softly.

'It's wrong. I'm old enough to be your father,' he said, brushing his lips against my neck.

'I know,' I repeated.

His hot breath breezed past my ear, then he kissed my neck gently, from the ear to clavicle.

I thought my knees were going to give way. I pulled my head back and looked him in the eye again.

'Alice... I'll hate myself...'

'I won't,' I said, truthfully. I moved my head forward hesitantly, then his lips found mine and my heart melted.

'Alice...'

He ran his tongue down my neck again, the song had finished, but we held onto each other like it was our last few moments on earth. He kissed me again, harder this time and his tongue found the inside of my mouth. What sorcery was this? I had never imagined people did this. His breath became hot, he pulled his face away from mine, and the next thing I knew we were on the carpet tearing each other's clothes off.

The sex was sublime. Sometimes gentle, probing, other times urgent, demanding. It was nothing like my only other experience with Frank. That had been brutal, incredibly short, and had it not been for the circumstance, utterly forgettable. With Godfrey, I understood where the term, making love, came from, because that's what we were doing. Afterwards, we lay on our backs, half-naked, cooling, still slightly breathless. He took my hand and held it to his lips.

'Alice,' he said, softly.

'Yes,' I replied.

'I'd just like to say... you... it... that was wonderful.'

I turned my face towards him. 'I'll never forget this day, Godfrey. I feel like a woman, a proper one, not just a flighty girl.'

'I've never considered you flighty,' he said, smiling back at me.

I rolled onto my side, put my hand on his chest and kissed him on the lips. When I pulled my face away, he lifted his head from the floor and looked over my naked breasts, towards the window.

'Alice?'

'Yes,' I replied, dreamily.

'Frank's at the window.'

I turned over, trying desperately to cover some of my nakedness with my hands.

Frank hadn't moved. He stood in the garden, about a foot away from the window, his face a mask of hatred.

I glared back at him and yelled with as much venom as I could muster.

'Get lost, Frank!'

Frank remained where he was. His eyes fixed on me.

I got up, my dress fell to the floor, I stepped out of it and wearing only my white heels, stomped across to the window, held out both my arms and pulled the curtains shut.

Godfrey pulled up his pants and trousers and got to his feet. I apologised to him as he fastened his shirt.

'That's typical Frank, trying to ruin the best thing that's ever happened to me.'

We finished dressing in silence, then Godfrey took my hands in his.

'Alice. I'm so sorry, I should have been stronger. This should never have happened. I take full responsibility for it.'

I shook my head. 'Don't spoil it please, Godfrey.'

'The thing is, Alice. In my job, we're supposed to act a bit like doctors. We're not allowed to have intimate relationships with our clients. It seldom works out well, when it happens. I feel bad about this, I seem to have led you on, and I really didn't mean to. I enjoy your company, you make me feel young again, but I was determined to leave it at that. You're a young woman with your whole life ahead of you. I'm a middle-aged, married man, there could never be a future for us.'

'I know that, Godfrey,' I said. 'I'm not looking for a happy ever after. I wanted a bit of fun after what's happened to me over the last year. I wanted romance, I wanted... I don't know... excitement... a bit of Hollywood... You gave it to me, it's something I'll never forget.'

Godfrey took a step towards me and held me tight. 'You are such a beautiful, person, Alice, inside as well as out. I really hope life gets better for you. You deserve every bit of happiness that's coming to you.'

I grinned. 'Well then. That means I deserved this. Please don't feel guilty about it, Godfrey, I want to enjoy the memory, and if I thought you were unhappy about what just happened, then it wouldn't be the same. It was perfect, the best moment of my life.' I pressed my lips onto his and let them linger for a moment, then pulled away, my eyes misty with a film of happy tears.

I walked Godfrey out to his car, and after checking we weren't being overlooked, I kissed him again.

'Thank you, my gangster lawyer. You made this moll, the happiest woman on earth today.'

He tipped his hat to me and smiled.

'I'll never forget you either. Goodbye, dear Alice.'

I watched him drive away, then walked, light of foot, back into the house. I put the document that Godfrey had left behind, in the safe, then, singing Night and Day, I danced a few steps across the carpet, looked up, heavenwards, then grinning like the Cheshire cat, I walked breezily into the kitchen.

Even the knowledge that Frank had seen us couldn't dampen my mood for the rest of that day. He was leaving to find his ship in Liverpool after the bank holiday and I sincerely hoped he'd never come back. I decided to call on Amy over the long weekend. If she didn't come to see me, first. I wasn't going to tell her about what had just happened, but knowing Amy, she'd smell something was in the air. She always did.

Chapter 74

August 1938

As if I'd sent a telepathic message, Amy stepped into my kitchen, still wearing her work clothes. She accepted the offer of a dance around the flagstones with Martha, then she sat down at the kitchen table and took hold of the mug of tea I'd just poured for myself.

'Thanks for this, I'm parched.'

'You're welcome,' I said, and got up to make another one.

'So, what's new?' she asked, looking me straight in the eye.

'Not much,' I said, trying to avoid her hypnotising stare.

'You can't fool me; I can tell by your eyes that you've been having fun without me. Come on now, out with it.'

'I haven't done anything.' I laughed nervously and tried to change the subject. 'The wheat harvest is cut and stacked, the thresher comes tomorrow, and we start on the corn nex—'

'I don't care about the bloody harvest. What's been going on? I arrived home from work, to a report that your gangster lawyer's car was seen driving up the lane this lunchtime. Now, what have you got to say for yourself?'

'Oh that,' I said, hopefully making it sound like a trivial matter. 'He came this morning to pick up the government tax cheque...' I hesitated, *why did I always hesitate like that? It's a dead giveaway.* 'He wasn't here too long.'

Her eyes lit up. 'Too long for what?'

My own eyes darted everywhere to try to avoid hers. 'Nothing, we had a dance, and—'

'You danced! You danced, and yet you say that nothing happened. Did you kiss again? What song did you dance to? ah,' she looked across the room to where the gramophone usually sat, 'WHERE did you dance? Please don't tell me it was upstairs... No, forget that, please tell me that is *was* upstairs.'

'You've seen my bedroom, there isn't enough room to swing a cat,' I replied.

'The front room then?' She got to her feet and rushed to the door. She threw it open and stepped inside, examining the room for clues.

I followed her in, my eyes searching for any bit of giveaway clothing that we might have left behind in our rush to get dressed. Thankfully, there was nothing.

The gramophone was on the table with the record storage box. Night and Day was still on the turntable. Amy wound it up and put the needle onto the record. She turned around and studied me again.

'So, Charlie Chan visits the scene of the crime. Tell me, Number One Son, what clues do you see?' Amy loved the Charlie Chan detective movies. She had seen them all.

'There are no clues to find because nothing happened,' I said defensively, too defensively, it seemed.

'Well, you danced a slow dance, so come on, show me how you danced. How did he hold you?' Amy held out her arms to me.

I blew out my cheeks and let the air out slowly. I held one of her hands and stupidly put the other on her waist.

'I see, this is much more adventurous than a normal dance hold, isn't it?'

I immediately moved my hand to her back. 'No, I got it wrong, it was like this. Proper dancing.'

Amy drew me towards her so that our breasts were touching.

'And did you pull him closer, like this?'

I didn't reply. I hated lying to her.

'Charlie Chan is closing in on the answer to the riddle,' she said, her eyes narrowing. 'Is this when you kissed?' she asked.

'Yes. All right, yes, it was when we kissed.' I looked away, thinking that was the end of the interrogation, but I was mistaken.

'Alice Hussy. Did it stop at a kiss, or did you...?'

I blushed; my cheeks were burning. I wouldn't have lasted thirty seconds under the frightful stare of the real Charlie Chan.

'YOU DID IT! YOU DID IT!' she cried.

'Shh. Don't let the whole world know,' I replied, pushing both hands down in a calming motion.

'Oh, my God, Alice. You sneaky little thing. You've done it with your gangster and you weren't going to tell me about it.'

'You'd have got it out of me anyway,' I said. 'You always do.'

'Because I am the master sleuth,' she replied. Amy looked me up and down as if the experience might have changed me somehow. It had, but not in a visible sense.

We sat down at the round table and I told her all about it, leaving out the bit where Frank caught us. I wanted to delete that grisly thought from my memory banks, and just remember the beauty of it all.

'How did it feel? Oh, Alice, it's usually me that gets to do stuff first, and explain to you how things are done, but you're one up on me now... two up, as you've had a baby too. I'm not counting the first time with that disgusting creature, Frank. What was it like with the gangster man?'

'It was perfect. You know when you have those dreams, the really explicit dreams, and you wake up wet through and red-faced? Well, it was like that, only better. He was slow, gentle, then quicker and harder, then slow and steady again, but it was never anything other than glorious. It felt like the entire energy flow of the earth was running through me. It was electric, it was poetic. You know how we used to laugh when we read someone say that the earth moved for them? Well, it doesn't seem that silly to me now. It didn't move, exactly, but I felt part of the universe, part of everything, all at once. It's hard to explain, Amy. It's like a tingle, that starts in the centre of your body and it just radiates outwards until it consumes you. You reach a point where you feel so tense that you don't think you can bear it any more, then a flood of contentment washes over you and you feel as floppy as a boneless fish.'

Amy had hung on to my every word. She sat, wide-eyed as she listened. 'Oh, I'm so jealous,' she said, eventually. Then she reached forward and grabbed both of my hands. 'I'm so glad you had this moment, Alice. You deserve it so much. You sound like you are in love. Are you?'

'No, at least I don't think so. I doubt it will happen again. He's working away for the next couple of weeks, and he is married, don't forget. I'd feel guilty if we went on to have a proper, lengthy affair. I'm happy with what I got. I know what making love should feel like now. I hope it hasn't spoiled me for anyone else. This will take some living up to.'

Amy went home at nine, and I fed Martha while Miriam made up the bottles for the night. I can't say Martha had taken to me, if I'm honest. She much preferred Miriam's company, or Amy's, if she came around. She was still liable to scream the house down if she wanted another shoulder to burp on, but by and large, we got on. I think she saw me as someone she had to put up with now and then. That never changed, even as she got older. There ought to be something special between a mother and daughter, an invisible bond that can stretch, but never break. I wondered if I'd ever have that with Martha.

Frank didn't go to the pub, none of them did. They were working late, preparing for the threshing machine, where the wheat seeds and chaff would be separated. The latter used for feed, and the stalks for bedding. Nothing was wasted. We didn't own our own steam-driven thresher, none of the local farmers did. We would all book the man who did own one, for certain dates, and hope the crop was ready when he turned up. Ours had been cut over the last couple of weeks and was stacked in neat piles to dry out thoroughly. The thresher would arrive on Saturday, at dawn.

This is where more extra sixpences would be earned by the local kids. We would have more people than animals on the farm by sun up and all the seed would be separated before sun down.

Frank came in at midnight and must have gone to bed without eating the meal that Miriam had left in the oven for him, as it was still there the next morning.

I was up at four to greet the thresher, when he arrived. He would not only be paid for his services, he would eat well and drink his fill, for the whole day.

Frank came downstairs while I was making a pile of sandwiches to keep our own men going over the long day. I had crates of ale stored away, and our workmen would receive those at regular intervals. Frank snarled as he passed me on his way out.

'Slut!' he spat.

Chapter 75

August 1938

At one o'clock on Saturday lunchtime, Michael arrived to pick Miriam up for their trip to Southend on Sea. She had been acting like a child, waiting for Santa Claus to turn up, all morning. She asked advice on which clothes she should travel in; did I think he would stop on the way for a toilet break and how to pronounce the name of the perfume I had given her. She got ready incredibly early, which meant that she had to wear a towel as a bib, in case she spilled tea down the front of her dress.

I was a little bit concerned about how it would look if they turned up at a posh hotel in a builder's lorry but Miriam didn't care. She'd have walked to the coast with Michael if it meant sharing a weekend alone with him.

As it turned out, the black Ford he had borrowed was both clean, and elegant. Amy came along to wave them off, and we stood together on the lane, whooping and cheering like we were sending a young couple off on their honeymoon.

Amy came back with me and we carried a bag of sandwiches and a crate of ale out to our lads in the wheat fields. Amy received a lot of attention from some of the younger men who wolf whistled and offered to show her the best night of her life as we approached. Amy took it all in her stride, as usual, and offered up her own banter in response. I let it go; the day had an end of term feel about it so we let the lads go a little bit further than we usually would.

Three of the local housewives helped out in the kitchen, making sandwiches and flasks of cold tea for their men, who had been invited to help with the threshing. We didn't need a lot of adults, but there were a dozen children; girls as well as boys, boosting the ranks. The kids had a rare old time, following the threshing machine around the fields, picking up the discarded stalks and tying them into small bundles for Benny and Bessie to pick up on the big cart. It was more fun than work for them.

At eight, it was all done. I paid the thresher, and he drove his machine out from the top field onto the lane and on to whichever farm had booked him next.

I paid the casual workers their day's pay, and gave the children a one-penny, packet of sweets each, so that they had some reward for the day's work after their sixpences had been confiscated.

My own men finished at nine. I thanked them in the yard, and handed out the few leftover bottles of ale. Frank refused to accept his, and walked past me without speaking. The lads dispersed a few minutes later, and I collected the bottles and loaded them into the empty crates. There would be a ha'penny refund on each bottle when they went back to The Old Bull.

Frank came down wearing a change of clothes a few minutes later.

'You can have a bath if you like, Frank, you've had a hard day out there.' I could smell the stale sweat from across the kitchen.

He sniffed under his armpits, then took off this shirt and washed, stripped to the waist. I picked up Martha and fed her a bottle, I didn't really care if he spoke or not but I would rather have kept things cordial if possible.

Frank was gone for nine-fifteen. On a normal Saturday, there wouldn't have been time to get properly drunk, but at harvest, the landlord used to break the law and continue serving until the last man left the pub. The police knew about the arrangement, but did nothing to enforce the statute, choosing instead, to sit in the snug and drink free pints. The landlord was happy to give away a few beers, as the two policemen were on hand, to break up the inevitable fights.

I went to bed at ten, thoroughly exhausted. It had been a long day and I was asleep almost as soon as my head hit the pillow. I was awakened by the sound of the back-door slamming, then heavy footsteps on the stair. I checked the alarm clock at the side of the bed. It was one fifty-five. I turned over just in time to see the door fly open and the shadowy figure of Frank stagger into my room.

'Get out, Frank!' I yelled, instantly awake.

He swayed drunkenly as he stood at the bottom of the bed.

'I've come for my pay,' he slurred.

'You've already had any wages due, Frank. You were paid early, remember? Now, get out please. Let's not go through all the nastiness again.'

Frank undid his belt and let his trousers fall to his ankles. 'I'll accept payment in kind,' he said. 'I want some of what your poncy lawyer had yesterday.'

I eyed up the door, and wondered if I could make it before he could get hold of me, but as soon as I lifted my knees to roll over, he was on me, pulling off the eiderdown with one hand and grabbling hold of my ankle with the other. I kicked out, catching him in the face, his head jerked back, but it didn't put him off, it just made him angrier. I tried again, feigning right towards the door, but rolling left at the last moment, landing on the floor with a thud. As I got up, he came around the corner of the bed with a sneer on his face.

'No way out, Alice.'

I picked up the clock and threw it at him, but it missed by a good two feet. He laughed and shuffled forward; his steps constricted by the trousers that were still around his ankles.

'I've waited a long time for this,' he said. His eyes narrowed, he licked his lips and moved forward again.

I backed off, but found myself pinned against the wall with nowhere to go. As Frank got closer, I used the only weapons I had at my disposal, and clawed him across the face with the nails of my right hand. He held his left hand to his scratched cheek, and hit me with a right hook. The blow hit me on the temple, sending me sprawling across the bed, I shook my head in an effort to clear it, but he was on me, forcing my head into the mattress with one rough hand, and pulling up my nightgown with the other. I tried to close my legs, but his knees were already between them, I yelled in frustration and kicked my feet ineffectively, then he yanked down the front of his pants, and he entered me. Spittle dripped from his mouth onto the back of my neck, the smell of stale beer and new sweat assailed my nostrils. I tried to wriggle free, I cursed him, I wished death on him, I promised to kill him myself, but my face was pushed so deep into the mattress, and my threats were so muffled, even I couldn't hear them.

In a repeat performance of our previous sexual encounter, the attack was brutal, but mercifully short lived. Less than a minute later, he groaned, stiffened, then collapsed on top of me, panting like he'd just run in the Olympic mile. I felt the pressure release on the back of my neck and I twisted my head to the side, taking in a big gulp of air.

'Get off me, you bastard,' I said, vehemently, and to my surprise, he did.

'You asked for that,' he said, as he pulled up his knee-length underpants, 'You bloody well asked for that.'

I was determined I wasn't going to cry in his presence, despite the severity of the attack. I reached down and pulled my nightdress over my backside while Frank sat on the end of the bed and pulled up his trousers. He stood up to fasten his fly buttons, managing to push two of them through the wrong holes, then, with his belt still hanging against his thighs, he got hold of my hair and yanked my head off the bed.

'Look at me,' he demanded.

I kept my face turned away, so he punched the back of my head and grabbed my hair, closer to the scalp, and jerked my head up again.

'Look at me.'

I thought I'd better comply while I still had some hair left. I twisted my head to face him, my eyes wet but defiant.

'I want you to remember tonight as long as you live. This is what happens when you shit on someone who has only ever tried to help you.'

I snorted at that, so he let go of my hair and punched me on the cheek. Lightning flashed in front of my eyes, my head bounced on the mattress as another punch rained down from above, this time hitting me with full force, on the ear. I curled up in a ball and waited for the next blow, but nothing came. I heard his footsteps as he stomped down the landing. He returned a few moments later with his bag thrown over his shoulder. I held my breath, holding back the sobs that were trying to break out from my throat, and waited for him to leave.

Martha, who had, incredibly, slept through the whole encounter, suddenly decided it was time to cry.

'You haven't seen the last of me,' Frank shouted as the back door slammed against the kitchen wall. I shushed, Martha, then curled up in a ball again as the tears fell, and the pent-up sobs escaped.

Chapter 76

August 1938

I desperately needed to talk to Amy. She'd know what to do. Why wasn't she on the telephone? Her parents had often talked about getting one. I thought about going up to see her, she wouldn't have minded, but it would have meant me suffering the extra pain and embarrassment of telling her parents why I was hammering on their door at three in the morning, so I ruled that out. Next, I thought about ringing Godfrey, but he would have to explain to his wife why he was consoling a sobbing woman, on the telephone, in the middle of the night.

The only thing I could realistically do, was to telephone the police. Frank couldn't have got far. There were no trains until the morning, and as it was Sunday, there wouldn't be that many running anyway.

I looked for numbers in the telephone directory and discovered the new, 999 emergency service. I dialled the three digits and after a few beeps and buzzes, a man answered.

'Emergency line, which service do you require?'

'Police,' I said.

'What is the nature of the emergency?' he asked.

'I, err, I've just been, err... attacked.'

'Where did the alleged attack take place?'

I gave my address and he told me to hold, while he tried to contact the police house in my local area. A few minutes later he came back on the line.

'I'm sorry, caller, but I can't get a response from the police house. Is the matter urgent enough for me to contact the Gillingham police, or would you prefer to leave it until tomorrow morning, when you should be able to contact your local police sergeant?'

I didn't want the Gillingham police. They came out to us a few years ago when someone stole some of our sheep. The theft occurred on a Wednesday night and they didn't even turn up until the following Monday, by which time the sheep would have been sold, butchered and served up on Sunday dinner plates.

I decided to contact the local police sergeant in the morning. He might have sobered up, following his harvest night in The Old Bull by then. I told the operator that I would deal with the incident myself, and he hung up.

I spent the rest of the night in the kitchen with Martha. She wouldn't settle at all; I think she was missing Miriam.

The next morning, at nine o'clock, I telephoned the police house. A grumpy police sergeant answered the call. I explained who I was, and gave a vague description of what had happened the night before. He agreed to come out to the farm later that day.

He actually arrived inside twenty minutes with a bored-looking police constable in tow. The collar of his uniform was too small for his flabby neck and it was chafing. He put his finger inside the collar to try to ease the soreness. He walked in without being invited, the constable followed suit.

I was wearing my polka-dot day dress as I was about to walk Martha up to Amy's house. The fat sergeant, who was in his late forties, looked me up and down appreciatively.

'So... Alice, is it? You made a complaint, regarding a late-night incident. What happened exactly?'

'A man raped me,' I said.

The constable suddenly became interested, he opened his notebook and began to jot down details.

'What time was this?'

'One fifty-five in the morning,' I replied.

'I see, and did this man break in?'

'No, he was staying here. He works on the farm and, well, he'd just come back from the pub and—'

'He was staying here? Where? In the barn, in the house?'

'In a room upstairs,' I said, wishing the officer would give me time to explain properly.

The constable sniggered.

The sergeant rubbed at his neck again. 'Right, let's take a few details. You are?'

'Alice Mollison.'

'And your attacker's name?'

'Frank... Frank... Mollison.'

The sergeant leapt onto that bit of information. 'Mollison, so, is this man your husband?'

'No, we didn't get married. I just took his name for the baby's sake.'

He looked at the Moses basket. 'So, the child is his? He is the father of the baby?'

'Yes, but... it's not how it looks. We had... we... It's really not how it looks. We were never... Oh this is so difficult.' I clenched my fists in frustration.

The sergeant preened as though he had the case solved. 'Did you live together as husband and wife, Alice?'

'No, well, yes, sort of.'

'Sort of?' The constable sniggered.

I began to feel that I was being interrogated as the culprit, not the victim.

'He slept in my bed but—'

'He slept in your bed?' The sergeant shook his head as the constable snapped his notebook shut.

'And there we have it, Constable Warren, it's obviously a domestic. She'll be all over him again by the end of the week.' He took a step towards me and put the back of his hand against my red, swollen cheek. 'I know you're only young, love, but take a little tip from me. Cook him a nice Sunday roast and he'll be whispering sweet nothing's in your ear, by bedtime.'

'He bloody won't,' I said angrily. 'Anyway, he's gone, if you check the station, you'll find him. He's on his way to Liverpool, he was only staying here while he waited for a ship. He joined the Merchant Navy in June.'

'He's gone eh?' He turned to his constable. 'Wait outside.'

When we were alone, he gave me a big smile and patted me on the arm. When he spoke, it was in the most patronising voice I had ever heard.

'Now then, Alice. This sort of thing happens all the time in families, and it can be a lot worse than this, believe me. You might be angry about getting a shiner, but there's nothing we can do about it, you see. It's what's known as a domestic incident. We wouldn't get a conviction, even if we were stupid enough to take the matter to court. You admitted that you sleep with him, that he's the father of your child, that he's been working on the farm and you've been feeding him.' He shrugged. 'A man is entitled to have his way with his missis, if he feels like it, you know? Any judge would rule that way. You'll be the laughing stock of the town if you try to take this further. Just be a good girl and forget the complaint was ever made.'

I walked to the sink to wash Martha's bottle out, mainly so I didn't have to look at his smug, fat face, any longer. I didn't hear him sneak up behind me, and the next thing I knew he'd slapped me on the backside.

'If you ever get lonely at night, just call the police house and I'll come around to keep you warm.' He gave me a lecherous look and touched his helmet with his index finger. 'See you around.'

Amy must have sensed that I was in trouble, because she turned up at lunchtime. She took one look at my swollen face, and gasped. She reached out and touched my cheek, so softly that I could barely feel it.

'That bastard, Frank. Where is he? Where's your dad's gun? I'm going to kill him.'

'He's gone, Amy. He's gone for good. He's on his way to Liverpool.'

'Call the police,' she said.

'I did, and they've been round to see me. Much good that did. They said it was a domestic incident, and that Frank had every right to do this to me.'

'He beats you up and they say no crime was committed? Where's the justice in that?'

'He didn't just beat me up,' I said, and burst into floods of tears.

Amy held me while I sobbingly described the events of the early morning. When I had recovered my composure, she held my hands and tried to think of a way of getting back at him.

'So, the police are as useless as we always thought they were. How about we get the farm lads to sort him out?'

'He's gone, Amy. He's on a bloody train. Soon he'll be on a bloody ship.'

Any rubbed her chin, deep in thought. 'Do we know anyone in the navy? Maybe we could get him thrown overboard, or used for shark bait.'

I shook my head. 'I don't know anyone in the navy; anyway, he's not in the navy.'

'Why is there navy in the bloody title then, it's so confusing. Wait a minute. What about your gangster lawyer? He must know a way of getting around the useless law. Surely there's something illegal in what Frank did?'

'I don't want to bother him with it, Amy... Anyway, he's away for the next couple of weeks.'

'Tell him when he comes back then. Promise me, Alice. Promise me you'll go to see him when he comes back.' Amy's eyes held mine until I gave in.

I nodded. 'All right. I'll go to see him,' I said.

Chapter 77

September 1938

Miriam came home on Monday evening. I expected her to be full of the joys of spring, but she was rather subdued. She made a fuss of Martha, and then spotted my swollen cheek. When I told her that I had walked into a door, she shook her head, looked around, in case the villain was hiding in the kitchen, and whispered, 'did Frank do that?' Miriam knew exactly what walking into a door, really meant. She'd walked into so many of them during her married life.

I admitted that he had hit me, but I didn't tell her the whole story, not wanting to spoil her moment. I was sure that Michael had whisked her away to propose. After she had taken her suitcase upstairs, I asked her how her weekend had gone. It couldn't have been worse than mine, that was for sure.

'We slept in separate rooms,' she said, sadly.

'Well, that's not much of a dirty weekend, Miriam. Did he sneak into your room after lights out, or did you sneak into his?'

'Neither, there was nothing but sleep after lights out. Nobody sneaked anywhere.'

'What was the point in the exercise? Amy and I thought it was a prelude to your nuptials.'

'He doesn't want to get married again.' Miriam looked crestfallen. 'He just wants to be best friends. Go out together, do stuff, dance, that sort of thing. He wants company, not another wife.'

'You wanted more, didn't you?' I felt so sorry for her, she had put all her hopes and dreams into this weekend, and it had fallen flatter than a boneless skate.

'He said he wants to honour the memory of his dear wife.'

'Well, that's a laudable sentiment, but why lead you on like that? It's just not fair.' I gave her a long hug. 'Did you enjoy the weekend apart from that?' I asked, hoping she got something out of the trip.

'It was nice. We had lovely meals, a few drinks, a couple of walks along the sea front. There was a dance band on at the hotel. It was all so romantic, except that it wasn't.'

I sighed with her. 'So, what happens now?'

'Nothing. I told him I'd think about continuing our relationship as companions, but I'm not going to. I want more out of life than that. I thought about it all the way home.' Miriam picked up Martha and kissed her on the nose. Martha stared back at her, refusing to 'goo-goo' as punishment for leaving her behind with me while she went off gallivanting.

'Have you told him that?' I asked.

'No, I'll tell him in the week, when he rings to invite me to the Saturday tea dance.' She sat down at the table and cradled Martha. 'There are plenty more fish in the sea, aren't there, little one?'

I thought about her ex-husband, Frank, the policemen, and the unobtainable, Godfrey. Maybe settling for companionship was the way to go. It would certainly be less painful.

On Tuesday morning, after a bank holiday nagging from Amy, I rang Wilson, Kendall and Beanney to book an appointment with Mr Wilson, when he returned. Miss Johnston was her usual bitchy self but she did have some very good news for me, even though she didn't realise it.

'Mr Wilson will be back in his office on Thursday,' she said, primly. 'Could you tell me what the matter is regarding? I thought our business was concluded.'

'It's a personal matter, I just need a little legal advice,' I replied, only just stopping myself from asking what the hell it was to do with her. And what was this 'our' nonsense, anyone would think she had personally sorted out my tax form, instead of just filing it.

'Mr Wilson will be back in his office on Thursday at nine o'clock sharp.'

'Does he have any appointments that morning?'

'Not as yet, but he is always in demand, I'm sure—'

'Book me in for nine,' I ordered her. 'Alice Mollison, that's M...'

'I know how your name is spelt,' she said in a surly manner.

'And I know how your name is spelt, Miss Johnston. I am the paying client; you are the secretary. Please remember that in future. Goodbye for now. I'll see you on Thursday.'

I arrived at the solicitor's office ten minutes early, wearing the same dress I had worn for Godfrey the week before. I ordered Benny to park the lorry a little way down the road so that I didn't give the scathing Miss Johnston, any more ammunition. As I entered the waiting room, she looked down her nose at me as though I had turned up wearing my shitty, work overalls. I walked to her desk, flicked back the curls from my shoulders, and announced that I had arrived. I gave her my wriggle walk across the carpet, sat down in a chair facing her, and crossed my legs demurely. I had seen many an actress do that in the films, and I was always impressed by the way they did it. I hoped Miss Johnston was impressed with my effort.

Godfrey arrived five minutes later, and annoyed Miss Johnston even more, by speaking to me before greeting her. She screwed up her nose and glared.

'Alice, what a pleasant surprise. Whatever are you doing here?' He smiled that wonderful smile, then noticed the bruise on my cheek. The swelling had gone down, and I had done my best to cover the mark with rouge, but it hadn't escaped his attention. He was a lawyer after all, he was paid to notice things.

'You're back early,' I said, as though I was surprised.

'My client decided to plead guilty on the first morning of the trial. He's in jail now. Attempting to defraud the government is never a good idea.'

He waved a hasty good morning to his secretary, and held open the door of his office, to allow me to enter first. Once inside, he closed the door, and offered me a seat.

'I don't want to keep you, I know you're a busy man,' I said, standing where I was.

Godfrey closed the gap between us and touched my cheek softly with the fingers of his right hand.

'What on earth happened here?'

I looked at the genuine concern on his face, and made an instant decision not to tell him the whole story.

'I walked into a door,' I said.

'Alice, do you know how many times I've heard that in my career? This was Frank's doing, wasn't it? Did he exact revenge for catching us the other day?'

I nodded. 'He's gone now. He's on his way to Liverpool. I called the police, but they said it was just a domestic incident and told me to cook him a nice dinner.'

'Things have to change, Alice. Women are beaten up every day of their lives by drunken, brutes of husbands, and the law does nothing to protect them even, though it is an actual crime.'

'He's gone,' I said again.

'But you shouldn't have had to suffer that, Alice. I'm not sure what we can do without getting the police to acknowledge it as an assault on your person, though. I don't fancy the odds; it will just be your word against his.'

'Leave it, Godfrey, I want to forget it ever happened. He's on his way to America now, and I doubt he'll ever come back here again. His mother will be dead by the time he returns, and he knows there's nothing for him at the farm. He's out of my life now. I want to try to forget he was ever in it.'

I thought about the rape, briefly, but it was so foul, so ugly, so horrible, that I didn't want it to get in the way of the joyous, lovemaking I had enjoyed with Godfrey. In future, whenever I thought about sex, I wanted to remember the beauty of that morning. I wanted to find a little room in my memory bank, and lock Saturday night away in there. I knew that dark attic would be opened in times of stress, but as long as I felt I had the strength to close that door on it again, I might just be able to manage the feelings of helplessness and revulsion.

'Well, if you're sure, Alice,' he said, without even attempting to try and persuade me to fight on.

He looked at the door, then at his watch. 'I have a client, soon.'

'You weren't in such a rush last week, Godfrey, and you have no clients this morning, I checked with Miss Perfect out there.'

Godfrey looked uncomfortable. He fiddled with his tie as he spoke.

'About last week. That was a mistake, Alice. It should never have happened.'

A mistake! It was the best day of my life and he was labelling it a mistake?

'That's not the way I see it. I gave you something precious, something, beautiful.' I smiled at him. The smile he offered back was more of a grimace.

'It can't go on. I've got too much to lose, Alice. My wife, my children, my partnership in the firm. Just think about that for a moment, will you? My life would be ruined if we carried on with this. I'm putting my foot down now. You'll have to stop contacting me. Our business is concluded.'

I was incandescent. It was all about him. He'd had what he wanted, and now he was going to throw me away like an old rag. I checked my impulse to shout at him. Instead I summoned up Rita Hayworth, the woman I had pretended to be so many times in front of my bedroom mirror. What would she have done up on the big screen? She'd have used her brain to win the day. She always got what she wanted in the end.

Men really thought they held all the aces. They held all the political power, but things were changing. Women now had the vote, there were female MPs, female scientists, soon there would be a lot of female doctors. Men used much of their power to subjugate women. That thing in their trousers made them feel invincible, but women were stronger than they ever imagined. They could suffer the pain of childbirth, the heartbreak of miscarriage, the cuts, bruises and humiliation of a beating, and still get back up for more. Women had a far more subtle power, if only they could learn how to use it. A power that men took to be their weakness. It was like a hypnotist's act at the music hall. All a woman had to do was flash those eyes and hint that she might be available, and the battle was over. Men were weak. I hid my anger, and let Rita perform.

I undid the top three buttons of my dress and stepped back until my backside bumped against his desk, then I brushed my arm across it, sweeping a pile of legal documents onto the floor. I placed both hands on the desk and pulled myself onto it, then I pushed my legs out and crossed them before slowly pulling my dress up to my thighs.

Godfrey began to sweat. He gulped and looked at the door again. Interestingly, this time, his watch was spared the interrogation.

I unhooked the front of my bra and pulled it aside, exposing my breasts, then I pursed my lips and blew out a kiss.

'Christ, Alice. What if she comes in?'

'She can bugger off back out again then,' I replied.

Godfrey took a step towards me.

'Alice...'

'I lifted up my backside and slipped my pants down to my knees.

'Now then, Godfrey, it's your turn, don't be lazy.'

Godfrey pulled off his jacket and dropped it on the floor. I pulled my pants over my ankles and let them fall.

'Oh, Jesus.'

'He's not going to help you now, Godfrey,' I said in a voice so alluring it would have made a monk think twice.

I grabbed hold of his tie and pulled him towards me. All resistance gone, he pushed his head onto my chest and began to suckle. I wish Martha had been as tempted.

I felt something stiff pushing against my thigh, so I dropped a hand down to it. Godfrey groaned.

'Oh, Alice,' he whispered, fumbling at his belt buckle.

Twenty seconds later we were at it. I leaned back on the desk, put my arms around his back and my feet around his backside.

The sex was much more hurried than it had been on my living room carpet, but it was still the second-best experience that I had ever had. When it was over, he tried to pull away but I held onto him until I was ready to let him go. He didn't put up too much of a struggle.

When I eventually slid off the desk to find my knickers, I felt jubilant. I had proved to myself that I had power over a man. I already knew that I was as good as any man when it came to strength of character, but now, I felt a sort of mental strength I had never felt before. Men were bullies, they had to resort to superior physical strength, or lies and deceit to beat a woman down, but women should always have the right to say no, or yes, if they felt like it. I owned my body, not Frank, Godfrey or any other man for that matter. Rita Hayworth taught me a very important lesson. Today I was in control. Godfrey was every bit as weak and helpless as I had been when under attack from Frank. I smiled at him as he straightened his tie. He smiled a genuine, but subservient, smile back.

'Would you like me to get you a taxi, Alice. I'll pay for it.'

'No, it's all right, Godfrey,' I replied. 'Benny is waiting in the truck. I'll be fine.'

He looked at his watch and cleared his throat. 'Well, it was nice to see you, Alice, but, honestly, we really can't do this again.'

I shook my head. 'No, we can't. I've had enough now. It's time to move on.'

He looked at me strangely.

'Alice, I don't know what's come over you. You were so innocent, unsure of yourself. You've changed, and I can't say I like it too much.'

'No? Ah well, never mind. I actually love the new me. To tell you the truth, I only discovered that person a few minutes ago, but I love her already. Let me tell you something, Godfrey. This young innocent has had to grow up very quickly, recently. You men always say you can't understand women, but you don't even try. You think a bit of flattery or a trinket or two will get them rolling over for a tummy tickle, but women eventually work you out, and when they do, they wonder why the hell they thought you were so complicated. You are the ones that roll over, and all it takes is the flash of a garter.'

I gave him a peck on the cheek and walked to the door. 'Don't let your wife smell the perfume on your collar, Godfrey, or you could still lose everything.'

I walked past Miss Johnston with the confident air of a woman of the world. 'He'll be out in a moment. Don't worry, there's no work for you this time. I've already filed it.'

With that, I tossed my Rita Hayworth curls and strode smartly out of the building. Half an hour before, I had stepped into Godfrey's office, an easy to please, walk over, but I left it feeling like a confident, powerful woman. I felt liberated.

The memory of Frank's attack would never leave me, but now I had a new weapon to fight the horror, whenever it surfaced. I had put Frank in a box and he would never be allowed out of it for long. Benny was catching up on some sleep when I got back to the lorry. I woke him by slamming the passenger door shut, and we drove back to the farm, chatting about the harvest.

Lying in bed that night, I felt I had been justified in my actions. Godfrey was just another Frank, albeit without the brutal instincts. I had now accepted that there would be no justice for me, so the best thing I could do was try to move on with my life. I made up my mind that I would always look for the positives, and that would start with the truth about me. I was more than just a pleasure doll for men; I had my own wants and needs. I felt helpless during Frank's attack, but today, I felt that I was in total command of the situation. Okay, I had taken advantage of someone myself this time, but I didn't feel guilty about it. We made love because I wanted to, not because some man or other fancied his leg over. Anyway, Godfrey could hardly say I forced him into it against his will. He didn't say no, did he? I laughed at that thought, as it was usually the accusation that was aimed at women. Today, had been my decision, my choice and that's how it was going to be from this day on. I would have sex when I felt like having sex, regardless of my relationship status. In future, men would play by my rules, or they wouldn't play at all. I felt a sort of release. I had to talk to Amy about it. Mind you, knowing Amy, she had already worked it out.

Chapter 78

Jess

Alice stopped Jess reading at eleven o'clock.

'I've had enough now, Jessica, I don't want to hear more of that part of my story. It's etched on my memory. I think I'd like to go to sleep now.'

Jess put down the book and gave Alice her antibiotic along with her sleeping pill, and by eleven-thirty, she was asleep.

No wonder she didn't want to relive it. Jess wept quietly for her teenage, great grandmother suffering an attack that ought to have meant prison for an uncaring, brute of a man.

She read on, starting the next chapter, hoping to clear her mind of the vile events for a while at least.

At twelve-thirty, she let the book drop to the floor, knelt by Alice's bed and kissed her on the cheek.

'Bless you, Nana, I never imagined I'd be reading these awful things when you first mentioned your secret. I thought it might just be about having Martha out of wedlock.' She fought back tears and sniffed to clear her nose. 'That Frank, I wish I'd have met him. I'd have told him what I thought. I might even have thumped him too, the nasty swine. To think Martha believes he was a war hero. He was nothing of the sort, was he?'

Jess crept out of the room, put their cocoa mugs in the kitchen, turned out all the lights except the small lamp at the side of Alice's chair, and went upstairs. She skipped the shower, got into her favourite PJs, and slipped into bed. Sleep didn't come straight away. She lay awake for an hour, going over what had happened to Alice all those years ago. Times were different back then and kids had to grow up a lot earlier than they did now. She tried to put Frank's attack out of her thoughts and concentrated on Godfrey, only the second man to come into Alice's young life, and the second one to take advantage of her.

Jess tried to remember what she had been like in her late teens. She hadn't known a man before Uni but she had been attracted to a lecturer who was pretty much the same age as Godfrey. He had been married too, although she hadn't known it at the time. To her, he was intellectual, enthusiastic, and amusing, he seemed caring, eager to please, he treated her as an equal intellectually, and took part in serious conversations about world events. Most of it was a sham. She found out, too late, that not only was he married, but he had a daughter about to take her A levels, so would only have been a year or two younger than her. The split had been tearful and emotionally draining, it had taken her months to get over him, and she had to suffer the ignominy of having to watch him try it on with girls studying alongside her. She was glad that Alice had her light-bulb moment. She had found her inner self, the Rita Hayworth personality that she could turn on and off when required. Jess wished she had a character she could use to similar effect. She fell asleep searching for one.

The next morning, she found Alice propped up on her pillows with an empty breakfast tray in front of her. Gwen had, once again, come in far earlier than her schedule dictated.

'She's had her tablet, Jessica. She clenched her fists and pumped them. She seems so much better today.' I touched clenched fists with her and walked over to the bedside.

'Good morning, Nana. Did you sleep well?'

'Like Rip Van Winkle,' she replied. 'I think I'd like to get back in my chair today, if that's all right?'

At seven-thirty, Gwen helped Alice to dress while Jess had breakfast, then, using her walker, better than she had for many days, she crossed the room, turned around by herself, and dropped back into the familiar confines of her armchair. She patted its arms as she made herself comfortable, then she looked straight ahead at the big old clock.

'It's good to be back,' she said.

Jess didn't mention the assault. Nana looked happier than she had done for a good while and she didn't want to risk making her ill again by bringing Frank or Godfrey's names up.

Later that morning, after listening to Radio Four news together Alice seemed eager to carry on.

'What's next? Is it October?'

Jess picked up the memoir and began to read again.

October. 1938.

Chapter 79

October 1938

On the thirtieth of September nineteen thirty-eight, our Prime Minister, Neville Chamberlain, came back from Germany waving a piece of paper whilst proclaiming 'Peace for our time'. On the same day, I received a letter from the Ministry of Agriculture and Fisheries, informing me that my application for a grant to help build a cowshed-come-milking parlour had been approved and the cheque would follow within a week. So, in true Neville Chamberlain fashion, I lined up the lads in the yard at the end of the day and waved my own piece of paper in the air, declaring, *Friesian for our time*. My little joke referred to the purchase, or breeding of, extra cows to add to our small herd. Maurice Hepplewhite, of Middleton Dairies, the man I had met at my dad's funeral, had planted the seed of an idea in my mind and after a couple of weeks thinking about it, I had applied for the grant. The new facilities would be a major upgrade on our old milking system and it would mean we could add a dozen or more cows to our herd. The new structure would be large, with the electric, pump driven, milking parlour at one end where we could milk up to four cows at once, and over-wintering stalls, running along both sides of the structure, giving us enough room to keep a couple of dozen animals, dry and fed in bad weather. I had to find some of the money myself, but the remainder of my parents' insurance money, and the good yields from this year's harvest, meant we could afford the expense without the need to borrow from the bank. The extra money from the milk and beef sales meant that it would pay for itself over time. We would also get all that extra straw and manure to spread on the fields.

I rang Michael Hart to ask his advice on whether we would need to hire a firm of specialist agricultural builders, but he said that as the winter was his quieter time, he could build it for us. He measured the ground at the back of our existing barn and marked it out with stakes. The work on the foundations would start mid-December, and the barn would be completed in late January. Miriam hid in the front room while Michael was here. She hadn't seen him since their seaside visit in August. He did ask how she was, which I thought was nice of him.

Edna died in the first week of October. A neighbour found her slumped on the kitchen floor when she went round to borrow her garden shears. On the shelf was a letter to Frank. The neighbour passed it to the vicar, who passed it to me. I burned it in the stove, unread.

Edna's funeral took place on a dreadful, wet, windy, day in the middle of the month. During the service, the vicar, once again, gave out a dire warning on the evils of the demon drink. I wondered if he was chastising himself in the speech, or whether he knew about Frank's temperament. There was no other point in bringing the matter up, as Edna had never been a drinker. Like Miriam and me, she had once lived with a man whose only concern in life was obtaining his next alcoholic fix. I sat in the church with five other mourners, two of whom were gravediggers who sat on the back pew just to get out of the pouring rain. The three genuine mourners were me, Edna's next-door neighbour, and a thin, sour-faced woman, who, it transpired, had only come to the service in case Frank turned up.

Just about all of the old folk in the town had a burial plot booked with the church. Most had lived in the surrounding area all of their lives, since the place was little more than a village. Middle-aged people tended to be buried in the council-owned cemetery, where the cost of burial wasn't as exorbitant. Most people described themselves as Christian, even if they had never been to church in their lives.

Edna's plot was at the back of the church, on the opposite side to my parents. The ground was prone to bogginess in winter, so the plots were much cheaper. The pile of soil at the side of the grave, oozed moisture. The diggers would have their work cut out shovelling spadesful of cloying mud, back into the hole. The rain, that had been heavy as we entered the church, had eased, and we were treated to a fine drizzle that got down the back of your clothes and sat in your hair until it formed enough of a raindrop to drip from it. My heels sank into the soggy ground on the perimeter of the grave site. The Reverend Villiers, who was obviously more important than us, got a strip of coconut matting to stand on. As I had done at my father's funeral, I took a handful of the soil and dropped it into the grave as the vicar was reaching the height of his graveside rant. He shot me a look of disapproval as he asked God to forgive Edna's sins. I doubt she had any, not real ones, although the church would consider getting herself pregnant, out of wedlock, as a biggie. Women, it seemed, always managed to get pregnant by themselves, I wondered what the Virgin Mary would have to say about that.

Reverend Villiers called to me as I stepped away from the grave, to make my way back to dry land.

'We have a problem with the payment for Edna's funeral, Mrs Mollison.'

'I gave you all of the money that Edna had given me,' I replied, wondering why he was telling me about it.

'The thing is... Oh, I hate it when I have to do this... The thing is, Edna's money falls fifteen shillings short.'

I shrugged. 'So, why did you go ahead with the service?'

'We thought one of our charities would make up the difference, but they just don't have the funds, so, sadly, as Frank isn't around, it means that you are her only surviving relative. I'm sure Edna would have been embarrassed by this oversight. It isn't the time or place to argue about a few shillings.'

I was about to tell him that I was no relation of Edna's at all, but I bit my tongue. The vicar had the ear of every nosy busybody for miles around and I didn't really want my private life discussed at every church event for the next ten years.

'Send me the bill, I'll make up the shortfall,' I said. It was the least I could do for Edna. She'd had a bad enough day as it was.

The skinny woman caught up with me as I walked out of the church gates. Her name was Gloria, a most unfitting name for such a miserable woman.

'You're Frank's wife, aren't you?'

I didn't reply.

'He owes me a pound from the bank holiday,' she said.

I shrugged and walked on, eager to get home and dry out.

Gloria grabbed me by the elbow.

'I said—'

'I heard.'

'Well then, what are you going to do about it? He said he was desperate and needed the money to buy baby milk and nappies. He was asking everyone who passed by. I said I'd help as I knew his mother, but I think he tricked me, because he went straight into The Old Bull a minute after I had given it to him. I can't afford to hand out pound notes like that. I'm not a rich woman.'

'I have no idea who you are,' I said, leaving it at that. The rain was picking up again. I turned up my collar and walked on. She had to almost run to keep up with me.

'I own the wool shop,' she said. 'You were supposed to buy a pram from me, but you let me down on that too. Deceit seems to run in your family.'

I stopped dead, and turned to face her; I'd had enough extortion for one day.

'Now, listen to me, and make sure you hear me properly because I'm not going to repeat it. One, your pram was overpriced, I got a better one for a few quid less, and actually, I never agreed to buy yours in the first place. The agreement was that I would consider it, which I did, for all of ten seconds. Two, I didn't borrow money from you, Frank did, so I suggest you stop bothering me and bugger off back to your shop, because I'm not paying for Frank's piss up. Do I make myself clear?'

'I've sold the shop,' she said, huffily. 'I'll have a word with the police; let's see what they make of it.'

'I don't care if you have a word with the bloody King, you're not getting a penny out of me.' I marched past the telephone kiosk and turned onto the lane that led to the farm. The rain got heavier, the clouds got blacker, but even the darkest of them couldn't match my mood.

That night, I told Amy all about it.

'Blimey! He left debts all over the place. All you need now is for some poor, unfortunate woman to turn up to tell you Frank got her pregnant and she wants you to support the baby.'

'Don't even joke about it,' I said.

'What if he's a murderer too, imagine that?'

371

'I don't want to imagine anything to do with that man,' I replied.

'I imagine him floating in the sea without a life jacket,' she said, her eyes lighting up.

She put on another Bessie Smith record and sat next to me on her bed. 'You haven't mentioned Romeo for a while? Is he too busy lawyering to look after your... needs, these days?'

'Oh, I don't think I'll be seeing him again. He was worried his wife might find out about us.'

'He should have worried about that before he started chasing you,' she replied.

'Possibly, but I don't regret what happened, Amy, it was really nice, but, well, we both got what we wanted out of it so, I'm not too bothered that it fizzled out.'

Amy clasped her hands together. 'Talking of fizzing. I wonder if he'll still invent that Martina drink. Maybe he'll think of you when he's in his dotage and he's sipping it on his terrace.'

I laughed. 'I think he'll have forgotten about me long before then.'

It was still raining as I walked home from Amy's. When I got in I shook my coat and hung it on the back door. Miriam had just made a pot of tea so we sat down and chatted about mundane, everyday things, until Martha woke up for her feed. Miriam always gave her the last feed of the day. It helped her settle for the night.

'Michael was asking about you when he came to measure up for the new cowshed,' I said, looking for a reaction.

'Was he now?'

I nodded. 'I think he's still interested, Miriam.'

'I know, he telephoned me while you were at Amy's. He wants to meet and have a chat about things. He won't change his mind on marriage though.'

'What are you going to do then?' I asked.

'Oh, I don't know. I did love the tea dances and I miss his company.'

'Give it a go, Miriam, you never know, he might come around to your way of thinking.'

She nodded and put the bottle on the table to give Martha a breather. 'That's what I thought. He is going to be here rather a lot over Christmas and New Year, I can't keep avoiding him.'

'It's back on then?' I asked, crossing my fingers.

'We'll see. I did say I'd go to the dance on Saturday.'

I patted her hand. 'You have a bit of fun, love.' I thought about me and Godfrey and smiled to myself. 'Just don't let him get off too lightly. Women should decide their own futures. Men get their own way far too much of the time.'

When Miriam had gone to bed, I sat in front of the stove in my dressing gown, thinking what a sad life Edna had lived, and what a sad ending she received as a bonus. I was determined it would never happen to me. I was worth so much more than that.

Chapter 80

Calvin

On Thursday morning, Calvin ate a late breakfast, showered and changed into a pair of loose tracksuit bottoms and a baggy t-shirt, and perused the online jobs. He wasn't particularly bothered whether he got one in the immediate future or not. Jess, for all her bluster, was hardly about to chuck him out, and when that precious Nana of hers kicked the bucket, money would cease to be a problem anyway. The old bitch was loaded, the sale of that huge farmhouse would buy this flat and five more like it. All he had to do, he worked out, was to hang around Jess for a year or so and put in a claim for a good wedge of her money, if and when they split up. Holidays and clothes wouldn't be a problem, so all he needed was something to keep the boredom at bay. He could even go into private tutoring. He could earn enough to keep the wolf from the door if the worst did happen, Nana lived on for a few more years, and Jess had to give up the flat. Tania had a nice little place herself. He was sure that she wouldn't see him on the streets. She was a bit of a challenge anyway. Jess had succumbed far too easily.

On impulse, he rang the two local independent colleges and asked for the IT dept. Both gave him short shrift. It seems that his ex-boss and been straight on the phone to warn the others off.

After lunch he went down to the driving range and hit a hundred golf balls, seeing that semi-pro arsehole, Jamie's face on every ball he hit.

In the evening he watched a recorded episode of Game of Thrones, then showered, dressed and prepared himself for another night with the passionate Tania.

He arrived at her flat, via the wine shop, thinking it was high time she provided the alcoholic stimulation for once, only to find a hastily scrawled note pinned to her front door. The note was folded in two and flapped about in the stiff breeze. He put down his shopping bag, pulled out the drawing pin that held the note to the door and read.

Sorry, babe. No fun tonight. Have been called into work. I'm in the café tomorrow at twelve if you want to catch up.

Tania

Calvin kicked the door in frustration and hurled a torrent of abuse at the note that was now in a dozen pieces, swirling around on the pavement.

He dropped the bag containing the wine into the back seat of his car and drove it to the rear of the Venetian, where he parked up, then he stood in the lobby of the restaurant and peered through the glass panes on the door to see if he could spot her. The place was busy, especially for a Thursday, then he spotted the two for one meal offer stuck to the wall and realised why it had suddenly become so popular.

Calvin strolled down past the Uni building to the Hand and Heart pub, where he downed several pints whilst chatting up a crowd of female students who seemed intent on extending Fresher's week into a month-long jamboree.

After collecting two or three mobile numbers for future reference, he left the pub at ten forty-five and walked back through the town until he got back to the Venetian. He had chosen his parking spot well, and sat with the air conditioning running to keep the windscreen free of mist while he kept his eye on the restaurant.

The last of the customer couples left at eleven-thirty. By midnight the lights were switched off one by one, and a small stream of waitresses, mostly students, supplementing their loans with poorly paid, hospitality work, left the restaurant. There was no sign of Tania. At twelve-fifteen the last of the lights went out, and two figures stood in the lobby while the taller of the pair locked the doors. As they walked out into the street lighting, Calvin spotted Tania, laughing and joking with an older man, who he recognised as the manager of the Venetian. He waited until they had turned the corner, then he got out of the car and ran to the point where the car park entrance met the High Street. He shielded his eyes from the glare of the street lights and watched them cross the road in front of the café where he had first met Tania. He sprinted to the safety of a bus shelter and saw them approach Tania's flat. She pulled the keys from her bag and opened the door, but instead of saying goodnight, she took his hand and led him inside.

Calvin waited for over an hour for him to come back out, but by one-thirty, the manager still hadn't surfaced. Admitting defeat, he walked slowly back to his car, seething about his wasted night. He visualised what the pair were doing inside the flat, and wondered if he was performing better than he had himself. The tight bastard hadn't even taken any wine with him. Maybe that was because it was a regular appointment on the nights that she worked. Maybe she got a bit extra in her pay packet for services rendered. He would tell the slut what he thought of her the next time they met. As he drove past the darkened café, he knew when that would be, and where.

Chapter 81

Jess

On Thursday afternoon, Jess gave Alice her antibiotic and settled down for another reading session.

'Where have we got up to now, Jessica?' Alice asked.

'We're just about to start December, nineteen thirty-eight, Nana. We're getting to the end of this volume now.'

'I don't really want to listen to that part at the moment, dear. Do you mind reading that alone, then telling me what you think afterwards? I'm rather tired.' She settled back in her cushions and stared at the clock.

Jess snapped the book shut. 'I'll read to myself later. Would you like the radio in the background while you have a nap? I'll do a bit of prep work on my new article before I go to see Ewan tomorrow.'

Jess switched the station to Radio Three, there was a Vaughan Williams concert playing. She turned down the volume, pulled the laptop out of her bag and set it up on the coffee table.

Women in Africa. Changing Aspirations.

Alice opened one eye, took in the situation, then closed it again and concentrated on the music. She had always liked Vaughan Williams.

After dinner that evening, Gwen washed up the plates while Jess got Alice into bed. There was no two ways about it, she had come on in leaps and bounds over the last twenty-four hours. She wasn't as worried about leaving her when she went to meet Ewan tomorrow. She might even spend Friday night at home. She decided to make up her mind after she heard what the doctor thought about things. He was due to call tomorrow morning, after surgery. She really would like to catch up with Calvin though. The poor man must have been feeling so alone recently. He had been really understanding yesterday. She smiled at the thought of him doing the washing on his own, and sent him a quick text message to say she'd probably be home earlier than expected. At seven-thirty, she sat down with Alice to continue the memoir.

Alice yawned and blinked a few times, as Jess opened the journal.

'I think being up and about today has caught up with me. I wouldn't mind an early night. Could I have my sleeping pill now, please, Jessica? I'll let you read the last part on your own. I'd like your opinion on it. Not tonight though. There'll be plenty of time, tomorrow.'

Jess gave Alice the pill with a sip of water and the pair chatted about Jess's new article for a few minutes. She was just getting to the heart of what she would be trying to achieve with the piece when she heard a light snoring, emanating from the pillows. She kissed Alice on the cheek, walked to the sofa and stretched out with the memoir opened to the final chapter.

Chapter 82

December 1938

On the sixteenth of December, Michael led his small team of men into the yard where four of our own lads were already waiting. He sent them out with shovels and barrows to dig a small trench around the marked off area. When they had finished, a diesel-powered, mechanical shovel, arrived and began moving the earth from inside the marked-out area. The shovel dumped the earth onto the back of both our own and Michael's trucks and they took the soil to the fields where it would be ploughed in later. Nothing was wasted on a farm.

By the end of the third day we had a four-foot pit dug, and the shovel was idle while lorry after lorry arrived to empty tons of hardcore and gravel around the sides of the pit. Snowy weather stopped work for a few days, but during Christmas week the shovel was at work again, dumping the hardcore into the pit. When the level of ballast reached around a foot from the top of the huge trench, the hired shovel was loaded onto the back of a huge lorry and was driven away.

We hit a cold spell during Christmas week and Michael was loath to start mixing concrete to finish the base slab until the temperature had risen a little, so he put off the work until after the festivities.

That morning, Miriam received a letter from her son, Harry, who lived about thirty miles away, inviting her to stay with him for Christmas. She was overjoyed at the news and hardly stopped crying for two days. There was a telephone number in the letter which meant that she could now keep in touch with at least one part of her family. She had never met any of her grandchildren and had never found out why she had been ostracised by her family, after all she had been through whilst bringing them up. After a quick call it was decided that her son, who was now also a car owner, would come to pick her up on the morning of Christmas Eve, and bring her back again on Boxing Day.

Miriam was concerned about Martha, but I told her that I would manage, even though there was a Christmas party to organise. Her absence would mean we were a woman down on Christmas Eve as we prepared for the workers' get together, but the wives and girlfriends of the workforce would be on hand to help out in the kitchen anyway. The only problem I could envisage was the last feed of the day, where Martha could sometimes kick up a fuss.

Amy would be at the party, as usual, but this year she had promised to sleep over until Christmas morning, so she could give both me and Martha our presents. I had bought her Artie Shaw's Begin the Beguine, which had been a hit in America in the summer. It was difficult to get hold of it in Britain, but Amy's uncle somehow managed to get me a copy. I was really looking forward to seeing her face when I gave her the record, she had only ever heard the song on the radio.

Christmas Day was going to be so much better than the previous year, which had been the first without my mother. It was also my father's first, and last, Christmas spent in a whisky enhanced, stupor. I was three months' pregnant and spent the bulk of the day, completely alone.

We woke up to a thin covering of snow on Christmas Eve morning but I knew that wouldn't deter the revellers. We would just light a fire in the middle of the yard and use it as a Yuletide centrepiece. Only heavy rain could really bring a halt to our outdoor festivities, and even then, we just moved the adults inside and let the kids run riot in the barn.

Miriam's son, Harry, was only a few minutes late. He was a nice man who gave Miriam a hug while holding back tears. He apologised profusely for not being in touch over the years, but there had been serious trouble within the family, and he had now divorced. To Miriam's delight, he had the addresses of two more of her children, who had always blamed Miriam for the separation of their parents. Since then, they had seen a far nastier, greedier, side to their father, and they were now keen to make a fresh start with Miriam.

I waved her off with a tear in my own eye. I had always been an emotional person, the first to cry at a reunion scene at the end of a movie, but my tear duct leakage had reached new heights recently. I'd sob at anything, remotely emotionally challenging and I didn't understand why. Perhaps my hormones hadn't recovered from having Martha yet or maybe it was a permanent change, brought on by childbirth. Whatever the reason, I was getting through more hankies than knickers.

Barney's wife turned up early, as she always did. Grace was a stout woman with rosy cheeks and arms that could hug a polar bear to death.

She arrived with Benny's fiancée, who I had never met, and Amy, who had caught up with them on the lane. The rest would arrive in dribs and drabs over the course of the morning, carrying baskets of sandwiches, mince pies, bottles of lemonade and handfuls of Christmas cards addressed to their recipients, even though they would never see the inside of a letterbox.

As usual, I had ordered up a barrel of ale, plus a few bottles of gin for the women who didn't drink beer. Most of them did, but it was nice to see them with a daintier glass in their hands as the night wore on.

By two o'clock, the lads were in from the fields, and the party was in full swing. In years past, we used to place the radio by the back door and set the dial to the National Service, where we could listen to the BBC Dance Orchestra. This year would be different, as I had my new gramophone, so the music wouldn't be interrupted by Tommy Handley or Arthur Askey performing funny sketches between the tunes.

When the sun went down, I switched on the outdoor wall lights while the youngsters dragged out bits and pieces of timber, and Barney lit a brazier fire in the middle of the yard. We'd had an open fire and flaming torches in the past, but as the quickening breeze was in the wrong direction, the barn was at risk. At six, the first snowflakes of Christmas began to fall and the children sat around the fire on old tree stumps that hadn't yet been cut up for firewood. It was a magical scene; we didn't often get snow at Christmas.

I only had two Christmas songs on record, Jingle Bells, and a nineteen thirty-five recording of Bing Crosby singing Silent Night. We played them over and over but no one seemed to get bored. As the snow got heavier and began to settle, Amy and I danced around the slippery yard to Bing on his seventh or eighth repeat. Some of the other women joined in, though, tellingly, none of the men.

At eight, John Postlethwaite brought out the accordion and the record player was forgotten. We sang along to a lot of old favourite songs and then, at nine, he began on the Christmas carols.

The women had demanded to take turns holding Martha, but as the accordion played, I wrapped her in an extra blanket and held her myself. I sang to her softly as we stood in a large circle around the brazier and sang God Rest Ye Merry Gentlemen, Oh Little Town of Bethlehem and In the Bleak Mid-Winter.

At ten o'clock precisely, as if someone had sounded a horn to mark the end of proceedings, the party began to break up. People hugged, promising to keep in touch, although they would see each other at the market the following week anyway. Over-excited children were shushed or clipped around the ear and told to behave, as they were ushered out of the gate where I stood, wishing everyone a Merry Christmas and pushing a little parcel containing a packet of sweets into the hands of the little ones.

When the last straggler had departed, I tipped a bucket of water onto the brazier and listened to the logs sizzle and pop as the fire was extinguished. Amy collected up the tankards, plates and empty glasses and took them back inside. Finally, having checked the fire was out completely, I turned off the wall lights at the switch near the back door, and went back inside to the warmth of the kitchen.

I produced a hidden bottle of gin, and two small bottles of Indian Tonic Water, and we took off our big coats and sat across from each other, warming our chilled hands in front of the stove.

Amy gave Martha a later feed than usual, but because it wasn't me providing it, she didn't kick up too much of a fuss, and drank the bottle in one go.

When Martha was settled in her basket, Amy and I got ready for bed. I took Martha upstairs, got into my nightie, then went down to check that the doors were locked and to switch off the lights. I was just about to go back up, when I heard a loud clang from the yard. I looked out of the back window, thinking the wind must have got up and blown the brazier over. What I saw instead, sent a shiver down my spine.

Standing in the snow, next to the fallen brazier, was Frank. He glared towards the house and took a swig from the half-bottle of whisky he held in his left hand. In his right, was the razor-sharp, long-handled axe that we used for chopping firewood. He slipped the whisky into his pocket and grabbing the shaft with both hands, brought the axe down onto the already broken brazier. A loud clang rang out in the night.

'Merry Christmas, Alice,' he shouted.

Chapter 83

December 1938

I froze.

Frank clattered the brazier with the axe head again. 'Come out, Alice, I can see you there.'

I walked to the back door and turned the key in the lock, picking up a large kitchen knife on the way. I opened the door about a foot, so that he could see the knife.

'What the hell do you want, Frank?'

'I want to wish my daughter Happy Christmas,' he slurred.

'She's asleep, Frank.'

'Wake her up then.'

I ignored the request.

'Frank, why aren't you in America. Wasn't that the big dream?'

'I missed the bloody boat. It went without me,' he replied.

'How can you miss a ship?'

'There are some good pubs in Liverpool,' he said.

I sighed. 'I might have bloody well known. You're hopeless, Frank. Clear off, go on.'

'MY MOTHER DIED!' he screamed.

'I know, I was at her funeral, unlike some people I could mention.'

Frank's face fell. 'You went?'

'Of course, I went. I liked Edna.'

'I was stuck on a stinking ship in Spain, I couldn't get back.'

'You didn't even know when she died, Frank, don't come it.'

'I would have been there, if... I've been at her house, all day. The landlord hasn't changed the lock yet. Did she leave anything for me?'

I thought about the letter I'd burned, but shook my head. 'Nothing.'

'Come out and talk to me, Alice. Please?'

'Not while you're carrying that bloody axe, Frank.'

He looked at the axe as though surprised to find he was holding it. He tossed it onto the floor, it slid towards me and came to a halt as it hit the back step.

'Wait,' I said.

I put the knife down, put my winter boots back on, and pulled my thick coat over my nightgown. Frank was still standing by the overturned brazier as I walked down the steps to the yard.

'I should have been there for her,' he whimpered.

'Yes, you should have,' I said as I walked towards him. 'Have you been to her grave yet?'

'No. I only got back in the early hours of the morning and I didn't want anyone to know I've been in her house.'

'Where did you get the drink?' I pointed to his pocket where the top of the half-bottle protruded.

'It was in my room at her house. I've already had one bottle,' he said, as if it was an achievement to be proud of.

'What are you going to do now? You know you can't stay here, not after what you did.'

His mood changed suddenly.

'What I did? You deserved every bit of that, and more. You treated me like a bloody skivvy for months, and all the time you were having it off with that sodding lawyer.'

'I wasn't, Frank, that was the first time, but that's irrelevant. What you did was both unforgivable and—'

I didn't get to finish my sentence; his hand shot out and grabbed me around the throat.

'Slut!' he hissed.

I struggled to get free, but suddenly his right arm drew back, and he punched me on the forehead. I staggered, my knees went weak, then he hit me across the face with the back of his hand. I fell into the snow and lay there, unable to move.

Frank stepped towards me, bent down, grabbed a handful of hair, and hauled me to my feet.

'It's time for that lesson I promised you,' he growled. He punched me hard in the stomach. I doubled over, gasping for air, but before my lungs could fill, he hit me on the back of the head, and I went down again.

'Stop that, you big, fucking ape,' Amy screamed at him from the back doorstep. I lifted my head and tried to focus.

'Amy, no,' I whispered.

Amy couldn't have heard me, but nothing was going to stop her anyway. She picked up the long-handled axe that Frank had dropped, and bare-footed, wearing only her nightdress, she ran across the yard with the axe held in both hands. When she got close, she swung it at him, but the axe was heavy and she didn't have the strength to land a telling blow. Drunk as he was, Frank easily avoided the weapon's arc. He grabbed hold of the shaft as Amy tried to lift it again, and snatched it from her hands.

'Now what are you going to do?' He laughed at her and tossed the axe towards the barn.

Amy wasn't put off; she lunged at him, fists flying. She caught him a good hard blow on the side of his head that made it jerk to the right. I tried to get up, but my head was still spinning and it was all I could do to stop myself from throwing up.

Amy let fly with her claws and drew blood from the same cheek I had scratched a few months before. Frank pulled back his arm and hit her with a crunching blow to the temple. She collapsed in the snow, her nightdress up around her waist. Frank leered down at her.

'Isn't that a sight for sore eyes? I always did fancy having a go at you.'
He got hold of a handful of Amy's hair and dragged her towards the
barn. 'Let's get comfortable,' he growled.

I got to my hands and knees as Frank yanked open the barn door and
dragged the still unconscious Amy inside. I crawled through the snow
towards them, shouting at him to leave her alone.

Inside the barn, Frank grabbed hold of Amy's shoulder and rolled her
onto her back. He lifted her nightdress up to her neck, and unbuckled
his belt.

'I hope you're a better shag than her,' he slurred, as his denim
trousers fell around his ankles. He bent over and parted her legs, just as
she was coming to. She shook her head and stared groggily up at him as
he pulled down his underpants.

'NOOO!' she wailed.

By this time, I was on my feet, albeit in an unsteady manner. I picked
up the axe that Frank had thrown into the snow, and moved forwards
with it held over my right shoulder. Unlike Amy, I was used to wielding
it.

'Leave her alone, Frank,' I yelled.

Frank took a quick look over his shoulder and straightened up. 'Fuck
you,' he spat and turned back to Amy.

'Fuck you, Frank,' I screamed, as I brought the axe head down.

The axe hit him on the right side of his neck and went in deep. A
fountain of blood spurted out from his severed jugular and formed a
black pool on the floor of the barn. A small cloud of steam rose from the
film of snow that had blown under the door. I shuddered and dropped
the axe. Frank looked up at me, stupidly, and tried to hold the gaping
wound together with his fingers. Thirty seconds later, he keeled over
onto the hen-shit-covered straw on the floor of the barn. I stepped over
his still twitching body, took hold of Amy's arm and pulled her outside
as Frank bled out.

We held onto each other for what seemed an eternity, then, as the
snow began to fall again, we staggered back to the kitchen and huddled
together in front of the stove.

I got a thick pair of socks from the clothes horse in the parlour, and pulled them over Amy's frozen feet, then I took her thick winter coat from the hook on the back door and wrapped it around her shoulders. I put the kettle on to make us a drink of hot, sweet, tea, and we sipped it, still shaking, both from the cold, and the shock.

Eventually, Amy felt able to talk. She rubbed my arm with her warming hands. I put my hand on hers and with tears streaming down my face, told her I loved her more than anyone else on earth.

'I'll be sent to jail for this, but I don't care, Amy. I couldn't let him do that to you.'

Amy was crying herself. 'The bastard got what was coming, Alice. He would have killed us you know? He couldn't have risked us reporting him over this.'

I nodded. 'I know. I was stupid to go anywhere near him. I should have stayed inside.'

Amy looked up at me. 'He would have got in, Alice, he had that bloody axe. I saw him from upstairs. I couldn't leave you alone with him.'

'You got there just in time. I think he was about to beat me to death,' I sobbed.

We were silent for a while. Then I got to my feet. 'I supposed I'd better telephone the police.'

Amy stood up too. 'No, you bloody well won't,' she said. 'Let's think about this first. There may be a way out of it.'

'How? What can we do? I killed him. I nearly cut his bloody head off, Amy.'

'He deserved it,' Amy said with feeling. 'Now, let me think for a minute.'

'The police won't believe any excuse I give them, Amy. They'll think I did this in revenge for what happened in August. They won't believe it was self-defence.'

'Well then, we won't tell them anything about it.' Amy replied.

'We'd never get away with it...would we?'

Amy had recovered her composure; there was no one better to have around in a crisis, even one as serious as this. It was amazing how she could think so clearly and precisely no matter how difficult the situation. I always envied her singlemindedness.

'Think Miss Marple,' said Amy. 'If she can solve a crime when no one else can, she can make sure no one finds out about one, too.'

'What do you suggest,' I said, beginning to feel a little more hopeful. I didn't regret what I had done to Frank, it was the only way I could stop him, but I didn't want to go to jail for the rest of my life, or swing on a hangman's noose either, if I could help it.

'I haven't got the whole answer yet but, let's just consider the facts of the case.' She held up her hand and began to count off valid points. 'One, who knew he was here?'

I thought about the conversation we had in the yard, before it turned nasty. 'No one. He sneaked into his mum's house in the dark, and came out of it in the dark too.'

'Two. Where does everyone think he is?'

'In America, he was supposed to catch a ship, but he missed it. No one else around here knows that.'

Amy smiled. 'Three. Did he go to his mother's funeral?'

'No. People will think if he couldn't bother coming back for that, he'd probably never come back.'

'Four. We're on a farm. A farm is a big place. How do we get rid of a body and make sure it's never found?'

'We feed him to the pigs!' I cried. 'Pigs will eat anything.'

An hour later, dressed in my old overalls, we dragged Frank's body around to the new pig pen.

'Horace and Hector will make short work of him,' I said. 'The sows won't get a look in.'

We had left a trail of blood in our wake, it glistened black under the sliver of a moon that peeked out from a gap in the snow-laden clouds.

We left Frank outside the pen while I got some whey treats from the store and tossed them into the holding pen. Horace and Hector, attracted no doubt by the metallic smell of Frank's blood, came barging out of the sty. I opened the holding pen and after sniffing the air, curiously, they led their sows into the safe area. I pulled the locking lever to shut them in, and we got hold of Frank again, me at the bloody, neck end and Amy at his feet.

'Will they eat his clothes, too?' she asked.

'I don't know, they've eaten fox fur and chicken's feathers before.' I thought for a moment. 'We'd better not risk it. Let's strip him; I'll burn the clothes on a bonfire.'

It took longer to strip him of his clothes than we thought it might. His boots came off easily, as did his trouser and pants. Amy pointed to his penis as she dragged them over his ankles.

'Is that it? Is that his fearsome weapon? I've seen bigger baby carrots.'

His coat, jumper and shirt were the hardest items to remove. By the time he was naked, we were both sweating profusely. After a quick breather, we grabbed hold of him again, and half carried, half bounced him into the sleeping block. We laid him out in the furthest corner, then backed out of the sty.

I blew out my cheeks and pulled the lever, allowing the pigs back into their pen. Horace and Hector moved remarkably quickly for such giant beasts, and raced each other back to their sleeping quarters, their snouts twitching as they ran. The sows followed, eager to find out what had been left for them.

'Enjoy your Christmas dinner,' Amy said. Then, carrying Frank's clothes, we walked back to the kitchen.

After a warming cup of tea, we went back out to the yard and hosed it down as best we could. We could hear the pigs snorting and snuffling as they tucked into their unexpected meal.

The snow began to fall in earnest again as we finished clearing the bloodied straw in the barn. I wasn't too worried if we missed a bit of the blood in the yard, as I could always say I had done what my father had done all those years ago, shot a fox and dragged it over to the pigs by its brush. That would also go to explain any chomping and snorting coming from the sty when the early milking crew came in on Christmas Day. Whatever was left of Frank, if anything, would go under the hardcore that had been dumped into the cowshed foundations. The builders wouldn't be back until the snow had cleared so I had plenty of time.

We returned to the kitchen and sat at the table munching on chunks of pork pie, left over from the party. The irony was not lost on us.

Chapter 84

Jess

At ten o'clock, Jess let the book drop from her hands. She looked across to where her great grandmother lay sleeping, then stared up at the ceiling, shocked to her core by what she had just read. Her mind was reeling. Alice had told her at the start that she had held a dark secret for all of eighty years but she never for a moment considered how dark that secret was. Her darling, sweet, great gran, was a murderess. There was no other way of looking at it. Alice and Amy had conspired to take a man's life, could there ever be a justification for that? She went over the events in her mind and then read it all again to make sure she hadn't missed any little detail that might have swung the jury in favour of the defence if they had been taken to court for the crime.

There was definite mitigation, but would they have been able to prove for certain that Frank intended to kill them. He was about to rape Amy, that was certain, but just as his anger had dissipated after the bank holiday attack on Alice herself, would he have just walked away this time too.

One thing was for sure. Alice had lived a long life whereas Frank's had been cut drastically short.

Frank was a detestable rapist, a bully and a woman-hater. That was indisputable fact. But did he deserve to die for it? She needed to think hard about that.

Jess sat up until three in the morning trying to work out what she would have done in the circumstances. She fell asleep at four, still undecided. When she woke, the sun was high and Gwen was shouting up the stairs to tell her the doctor was about to leave.

She got out of bed slowly, and still feeling the weight of the world on her shoulders, she went down to see what the doctor had to say about the health of her murdering relative but he had gone by the time she arrived in the kitchen. Gwen was drying pots at the sink.

'He's had to rush; someone has collapsed outside the railway station.'

'What did he say about Nana?' Jess asked.

'He said, keep on with the antibiotics until the course is finished. He didn't have a chance to examine her.'

Jess checked her watch, cursed and ran for the shower. She dressed quickly, grabbed her bag, and shouting 'Bye Nana' rushed out to her car.

Jess cursed as she drove towards the town. Why hadn't Gwen woken her when the doctor arrived? In fact, why hadn't she woken her at least an hour before the doctor arrived? She headed towards the Tesco Direct, driving at least ten miles an hour over the speed limit. She slammed on her brakes and hit the horn hard, as a woman with a pushchair, hurried across the road right in front of her. A film of sweat covered her brow, she wiped it with the back of her hand, and waved sorry to the furious woman, who had reached the safety of the opposite kerb. Breathing deeply, she took her foot off the brake, eased onto her accelerator and took her foot off the clutch.

She arrived in town at eleven fifty-nine, and parked her car in the Uni car park. She was risking a clamping, but time was pressing. She didn't want to miss Ewan, or find that she was a mere five minutes away from the best interview she had ever done, when it was time for him to leave. She looked around in case there was a warden lurking, but saw no one. As she pressed the button on her key fob to lock her car, she noticed Calvin's BMW parked up a few bays away. Thinking he must have called in to beg for his job back, or ask for money owed, she hurried around the side of the building onto the High Street.

The café was only a few yards further on, and she rushed past the front of the Uni block, pushed open the door of the café and breathed a sigh of relief as she saw Ewan standing at the counter, about to order coffee. They were the only customers, so they had the choice of tables. Ewen bought the coffee and pointed to a little private nook that couldn't be seen from the main area of the café. Jess sat down opposite him and still out of breath from the rushed journey, she pulled her laptop out of her bag and set it up on the table along with her recording device.

Chapter 85

Calvin

Calvin slept poorly and woke up in a foul temper as the memory of his perceived humiliation came back to haunt him. How dare that slag take him for a fool?

He showered and carefully shaved, not allowing his seething anger to transmit to the razor. He chose his clothes as carefully as he had shaved, wanting to look his best when he told the wanton bitch what he thought of her. He had rehearsed the scene in his mind, over and over again. He would be the man of integrity, she would be the craven, sullied creature, begging his forgiveness, claiming the Venetian manager was her uncle, or was gay... Yeah, right, like that scruffy, druggy bastard he bumped into at the foot of her stairs, was really her ex. She was on the game, part time at least. He was sure of it now.

At eleven forty-five he left the flat, climbed into his car and drove slowly into town, rehearsing her moment of humiliation, one final time.

He parked in the Uni building car park and at eleven fifty-seven, precisely, he walked through the ground floor of the Uni building and stood by the plate-glass entrance, ready to ambush his victim as she passed by.

Calvin had only just got into position when he heard a friendly, female voice behind him.

'Hola, Calvin.'

He turned to see the pretty Spanish receptionist waving to him. He took a quick glance out of the window and sauntered over towards her.

'Hello, Alana. It's lovely to see you.' Calvin flashed his best smile and rested a hand on her desk.

He wondered whether it was worth his while asking her out. She did wear an engagement ring, but sometimes women did, just to put off the men they didn't fancy. His thoughts were interrupted when her phone rang. With a shrug, she reached forward to answer it.

Alana was on the call for a good three minutes. She looked up at him twice and pulled a sad face as if in apology. As soon as she put the phone down, it rang again. Calvin gave her another two minutes before he waved goodbye to her, and walked back to his observation post. Five minutes after that, thinking he must have missed Tania, he left the Uni and walked the few yards to the café. Tania was sitting in her window seat, a steaming mug of Latte in front of her. She waved as she spotted him and patted the empty seat next to her. Calvin had used up the last of his pleasantries on the pretty Spanish girl, and with his anger rising, he stormed into the café to confront her.

Chapter 86

Jess

Jess had only just begun her interview when she heard the sound of the café door bang against the wall. It was followed by the voice of an angry man, hurling abuse at someone he was accusing of being a slut, a whore, and a bitch. Jess groaned and got quickly to her feet. She knew that voice, that temper, she had heard the same abuse hurled at her. She stepped out of the nook and saw Calvin standing near the window table of the café. Seated close by was a pretty woman, who seemed to be amused by his antics.

'Calvin, do one. I sleep with whoever I want to sleep with. I am not your property.'

'You're on the game, aren't you? I knew it,' Calvin stormed.

'Calvin, you're making a fool of yourself.' The woman was keeping her cool.

'You'll sleep with anyone, Tania, admit it.'

'I suppose you're living proof of that, Calvin,' the woman called Tania replied.

'You fucking bitch.' Calvin pulled back his fist.

Quick as a flash, Tania produced a can of Mace spray. 'It's yours if you want it, big mouth,' she said calmly.

Calvin backed off, as Jess stepped forward to enter the fray.

'Calvin?'

He spun around, his jaw almost hitting his chest. 'Jess... Jess, it's not what it looks like.'

'What is it then, Calvin? Because I'll tell you exactly what it looks like from where I'm standing.' Jess fixed him with a narrow-eyed stare.

'She's a student, she's pissed off with me because I won't sleep with her,' Calvin said, lamely.

'I wish to God that was true,' Tania said, laughing.

Calvin's startled face looked from Tania to Jess and back again, as if he was sitting in the front row at Wimbledon. His face darkened as Ewan stepped out from the corner nook.

'So, this is what you get up to behind my back, you two-timing bitch.' Calvin fixed his eyes on Jess accusingly and tried to lay off some of the blame.

'I'm here for an interview, which I told you—'

'LIAR!' Calvin yelled. He took a step forward, his fist raised.

Ewan leapt forward and stood in front of Jess. 'Come on, mate, have a go if you think you can do it, or are women the only people you hit?'

Calvin's bravado crumpled as the ex-rugby player made 'come on' motions at him. He thought about calling Ewan's bluff for a split second, but decided against it. A broken nose was all he needed today. He turned away, and with a final glare at Tania, he stomped out into the street.

'He wasn't much of a man in bed, either,' Tania informed anyone who wanted to listen.

'I knew he was married or something,' Tania said when Calvin had gone. She looked at Jess sympathetically. 'You're the woman who was in the foursome with him the other night. I'm a waitress at the Venetian.'

'I thought I'd seen you before,' Jess replied in a not too friendly a manner.

'Look, love, it's like this. He pulled me, in here, a couple of weeks ago. I quizzed him on who you were, but he swore on everything holy that he was only there to make up the four, because you had been stood up. I didn't know he had a partner, did I? When he came round, he stayed all night, that's what persuaded me more than anything else. I'm sorry but there it is. I thought he was single.'

Jess sighed. 'I should have seen it. He was too eager to get me out of the way.'

'He's a cunning bastard, that's for sure. He's far too full of himself. Men like that are always trouble. I was going to finish with him last night, or today at least. That performance was the cherry on the cake.'

Jess sighed again.

'I suppose I'd better go back and do the same. It's not his day, is it?'

Outside the café, Ewan offered to see Jess home but she politely refused.

'Thanks, Ewan, but this is something I need to do myself. I should have done it weeks ago if I'm honest.'

Jess walked back to her car. The BMW had gone already. She started up the little Toyota and drove back to the flat.

Chapter 87

Alice

Alice stared at the clock and closed her eyes. Yesterday's dream hadn't been so bad, the tunnel had seemed so far away, and there were no grasping hands trying to pull her into the fog. As she slipped into sleep, she found herself, once again, in the kitchen of the farmhouse. Miriam was there, as was Amy, and for some reason, Frank. Martha was, as usual, the centre of attention. Alice tried to look into the Moses basket to see what they were all staring at, but she couldn't find the right angle to see beneath the hood. The vision changed and suddenly she was looking down on herself in her armchair. The clock wall had vanished, and she could see down the lane, past the last farm and beyond. She began to float upwards until she was high above the farm. She looked across what used to be a hundred acres of farmland, but was now a large housing estate. In the distance, a train hurtled past the town's long-closed station. Children played in the fenced-off confines of the huge, twenty-year-old Academy school. Vans and lorries, drove in and out of the business park that had once been the top acres. So much had changed since she had been forced to take over the running of the farm, all those years ago. Alice saw it all. She saw Amy's old house, now sporting a new extension and greenhouse. She saw the cobbled farmyard and the piles of collapsed structures that were once pig pens. The cowshed was gone, now just a concrete slab that still hid Frank's indigestible remains.

'Alice, Alice...'

Alice felt a pull as though someone had hold of a kite string, and in an instant, she returned to her body. She sat bolt upright in her chair and slowly opened her eyes as Gwen tugged at her sleeve.

'My goodness, you gave me a fright then,' she said nervously. 'I couldn't wake you.'

Alice blinked a few times to allow her eyes to adjust to the light.

'I was just looking around, Gwen, so much has changed.'

Chapter 88

Jess

Jess drove home, still trying to take in what had just happened.

Calvin was a cheating, lying, pathetic excuse for a man, she knew that much. She wanted him out. Nana had been right about him from the start. Why did she always fall for the wrong sort of man? Why couldn't she be attracted to someone reliable, like Ewan?

She pulled into her parking space next to Calvin's BMW, turned her key in the Yale, took a deep breath and walked up the stairs to the lounge. Calvin was in the kitchen, making coffee. Jess dropped her bag on the floor and turned to confront him. She wanted to get the first word in but he beat her to it.

'So, you're back, you two-timing bitch,' he spat.

'Piss off, Calvin, don't try to lay off the blame. It won't work this time. I'm not the guilty one here. You're the one who's been having it off on the quiet, not me.'

Calvin left the coffee and walked purposefully into the lounge. He stopped two feet short of where Jess was standing and leaned forward until his face was so close, she could feel his hot breath on her skin. She stood her ground, which seemed to unsettle him for a moment.

'You've been shagging that bloody charity worker behind my back.'

'Bullshit, Calvin. Let's talk about... What's her name...? Tania. She had a few choice words to say about you.'

'She's mad, there was nothi—'

'Don't take me for a fool, Calvin, you've done that once too often. I want you out, and I want you out today.' Jess stood firm, refusing to be intimidated.

'You want...You want. It's always you, isn't it, Jess?'

She laughed. 'Oh, my God! You actually believe that, don't you, Calvin? The man who is never in the wrong, the little mummy's boy who never grew up. Well, I've had enough of your pathetic accusations. You're a bloody narcissist, Calvin, Nana was right about you from the start.'

Calvin slapped her across the face. 'Nana, fucking, Nana. It's all I ever hear. Well, I hope she drops dead... I hope she drops dead today and goes straight to Hell, the interfering old bitch.'

Jess took a moment to clear her head, the blow had come as a shock. She knew he could be verbally abusive, but she didn't think he'd resort to violence. She shook her head to help clear her thoughts and glared into his scowling face.

'Do that again and you'll bloody well regret it, you nasty little shit.'

He did it again, this time knocking her to the floor. Jess took a moment to get her breath back, then like some punch-drunk boxer, she tried to get to her feet. Calvin kicked her in the stomach and she went down again.

'Stay there, Jess. If you know what's good for you, you'll stay there.'

Jess got to her hands and knees, again. 'You lousy, disgusting—'

He kicked her on the temple. This time she went down and stayed down. Calvin stood over her for a moment, then walked slowly to the bedroom. 'I didn't sleep too well, last night. I'm going for a lie down.'

Jess lay curled up on the floor, sobbing tears of pain and frustration. She thought back to Nana's story, how Frank had beaten her, raped her, and tried to do the same to her best friend. She had been shocked by the revelation when she first read it, and she had tried not to think about it since. The taking of a human life was the worst thing anyone could do. But now, she asked herself what would have happened to her if she had fought back, how far would Calvin had gone? His mood could switch from dead-calm to tempest at the flick of a switch. When he walked away, leaving her on the floor, bleeding and in agony, he had spoken as if they had just had lunch and he wanted to sleep it off. She couldn't risk it happening again. Next time it might be far worse. As she got to her knees, her temper rose. She wasn't going to just take this beating as though it was a natural part of a relationship. She gasped and held her arm across her stomach as she forced herself to stand.

The bastard isn't going to get away with this. She closed her eyes and thought of the terrified Alice and Amy, fighting for their lives in the snow. She could call the police, but what would they do? Even in this enlightened age, it would take months, perhaps years to be rid of him. He could claim the flat was part his, as he had paid his share of the rent on odd months, but she had felt so secure in their relationship that she hadn't kept records. The rent always went out of her bank account and his share, when he did cough up, was usually handed back to him later in the month anyway.

Jess managed to pick up her bag and dropped it on the kitchen table. She pulled out her phone, rang her best friend, Sam and tearfully explained the situation.

'Jess, get out of there, I'll come around to pick you up in five minutes.'

'I'm not leaving, Sam. He is.'

'Jess, get out of there. Get the cops, they'll sort him out.'

'They'd let him go in an hour or so, Sam.' Jess thought about Alice's attempt to report her abuse all those years ago. What was the term they used? *A Domestic.* 'They'll just say it was a domestic, he'll promise not to do it again, and they'll allow him out without any restrictions. He'd have to do it a dozen times before it went to court.'

'I'm not sure you're right on that, Jess, but I'm coming over anyway. Don't do anything stupid. If he comes at you again, run.'

'He's just gone for a lie down,' Jess said. 'I want to sort this out, Sam. He's not going to get away with it.'

'Five minutes,' Sam promised.

It actually took six minutes by Jess's watch. They were six of the longest minutes of her life, as she looked repeatedly out of the window, then over her shoulder to see if Calvin had come back into the room. She got a sterilised pad from the first aid box and dabbed at the cut on her forehead, then, thinking she might need to wash a little more thoroughly she switched on the jug kettle to get some boiling water. Sam arrived just as the kettle switched itself off. Jess hurried down the stairs and opened the door before she could ring the doorbell that might alert Calvin to her arrival.

Sam took one look at her battered face, stormed past her and took the stairs two at a time.

'Sam, NO!' Jess called after her.

Calvin came back into the lounge just as Sam appeared on the top step.

'Well, well, if it isn't the lovely Samantha,' he said smoothly.

'You, lousy, low-life, scumbag,' she yelled. She rushed towards him stopping about a foot short. She stuck her face into his. 'You like to hit women, eh? Well try and hit me?'

Calvin gave a nervous laugh. He knew Sam did a version of Martial Arts, but wasn't sure which. He decided to tough it out anyway.

'And here's me thinking you've come round for that threesome we talked about.' He took a step back.

Sam laughed scornfully. 'I can't think of anything less stimulating than being naked in the same bed as you.' She took a quick glimpse over her shoulder to Jess. 'Did I tell you he asked me out, that night at the Venetian?'

'LIAR!' yelled Calvin, stamping his foot like a petulant two-year-old.

'Oh, but you insisted on giving me your number, Calvin. The number of the pay-as-you-go phone, that Jess knows nothing about.'

Calvin's face went a deep shade of crimson.

'LIAR!'

'I'll ring it shall I?' As Sam looked down to pull her phone from the pocket of her jeans, Calvin hit her, sending her sprawling across the carpet. The phone fell out of her hand and landed at Jess's feet. Calvin was on Sam in an instant. He sat astride her, lifted her head and slammed it repeatedly on the floor. Sam raised her hands groggily, and tried to fight back, but Calvin was too strong, suddenly his hands were round her neck and she was struggling to breathe.

Jess tried to pull him off, but he kept his grip on Sam's throat. Jess rained blows onto the back of his head as he sat astride her best friend, but her blows had little, if any, effect. She looked around the room for anything that might help her get him to release Sam, but there was nothing worth hitting him with. Then, from the kitchen, she saw the steam still rising from the jug kettle spout. She rushed into the kitchenette and grabbed the kettle, pulling the plug from the socket as she turned back. She stood over Calvin, grabbed his hair with her left hand, and yanked his head up. His hate-filled eyes held hers as he squeezed even harder on Sam's throat.

'Let her go, Calvin or you get this.' Jess allowed a few drops of boiling hot water to run from the spout of the kettle onto his upturned face. Calvin screamed, released his grip and held both hands to his cheeks.

'Not my face, please, not my face.'

'Get off her or you'll get the whole fucking kettle full,' Jess shouted. 'Off her, NOW!'

Calvin rolled off, and Sam, holding her neck whilst gasping for air, rolled the other way. Jess stood over Calvin while he writhed around, still clutching his face. 'I'll call the police; I'll tell them what you did.' He took his hands from his face and looked up pleadingly at Jess. 'Is it bad? Is it really bad? Tell me the truth.'

'Not as bad as it will be if you aren't out of here in ten seconds flat,' said Jess.

Sam wasn't about to take any more chances. She rushed to the kitchen and picked up the biggest, sharpest knife she could find in the knife block. She hurried back to Jess's side and held the knife next to Calvin's blistered cheek.

'You're going, you bastard. And don't even think about coming back. I'm staying with Jess tonight and the locks will be changed in the morning. Just think yourself lucky that I'm in a forgiving mood, or I'd run this blade so deep into your face they wouldn't be able to stitch it back together again.'

She pulled the blade away and Calvin got slowly to his feet.

'Keys,' demanded Sam. Calvin fished in his pocket and dropped his keyring on the floor. Jess removed his BMW fob from it and tossed the keyring onto the sofa.

'What about all my stuff,' he wailed.

'Come back at ten o'clock tomorrow morning. Your stuff will be outside. Make sure you're on time, Calvin, or the local kids are going to think all their Christmases have come at once.' Jess pointed to the stairs. 'Now, get out of my flat.'

Calvin meekly did as he was told. Halfway down the stairs he turned back. 'Where will I go?' he said. Tears welled in his eyes.

'I don't know and I don't care,' replied Jess. 'Try your mother's, if she'll have you.'

Calvin left the front door open as he left. Jess heard the roar as his car started, and she walked to the window to watch him drive out of her life, hopefully, for good.

Sam gave Jess a long, hug. 'You saved my life, there, Jess, I'm sure he would have gone through with it. Then again, I could easily have cut his throat with that knife, the only thing that stopped me was, what would we do with the body?'

'Feed it to the pigs,' said Jess. 'Pigs will eat anything.'

'Pigs!' Sam was confused.

'Never mind,' Jess replied. 'I'm thinking about someone else who got what they deserved.'

Jess insisted she would be all right on her own, convinced that Calvin wouldn't dare come back, so Sam left about an hour later. After waving her off, Jess went to the bathroom and stood in front of the mirror, checking the cuts and bruises. She touched the big swelling on her cheek and winced. Would she really have tipped that kettle over Calvin? The shock of the scalding may well have killed him, but if it was the only thing she could do to save her best friend, then she knew she would have done it, no matter what the recriminations. She remembered Alice and Amy in their struggle with Frank. She had wondered if their actions had been justified. She knew now that they were. She suddenly felt very guilty about rushing out of Nana's house like that. She should have told her she had every right to do what she had done, that people in such dire circumstances are entitled to do everything in their power, to survive. She turned on the shower and had just undone the top button of her blouse, when her phone rang.

'Jessica, it's Gwen. Please come quickly, I think Alice is dying.'

Jess pulled the keys from the pocket of her jeans and ran for the stairs. She hurtled down them, tripped on the bottom step and crashed into the front door. She dashed outside, slamming the door behind her, jumped into the little Toyota, reversed and turned in one movement, and raced out of the cul-de-sac, onto the main road.

She screeched to a halt on the farm's asphalt drive, and leaving the engine running and the car door open, she ran to the house. Gwen was at the front door, tears streaming down her face. She pointed to the lounge, as if Jess didn't know where to go.

Alice was in her armchair, staring at the big clock on the opposite wall, her breathing was shallow and irregular. Jess sank to her knees and took Alice's hand in hers.

'Nana, it's me, Nana, it's Jess. I'm here.'

Alice's hand twitched, and Jess let out a huge sigh of relief. She wasn't too late.

'Nana, I have to tell you that you did the right thing with Frank. I know that now, so please, if you're going, don't take any guilt with you. I would have done the same thing.' She laid her bruised face onto Alice's hand. 'You'll be pleased to hear that I chucked Calvin out too,' Jess snuffled, and warm tears fell onto Alice's fingers.

Alice tried to raise her hand, but found the effort too great. Instead, she rubbed her index finger on Jess's palm to show that she had heard.

As Jess sobbed, Alice fixed her unblinking stare on the clock, and breathed her last.

Chapter 89

Alice

As Alice stared, the wall began to shimmer, then it became translucent, before finally disappearing altogether. She looked for the lower farm that she had seen earlier that day, but everything beyond the room was shrouded in a thick fog. She looked back to see herself in the armchair with her beloved Jessica, kneeling at her side. She wanted to go back to her body for a moment, to tell her not to worry, that she would feel better in a few days' time, that they would meet again one day, but she didn't have the strength of will to do it. Instead, she allowed herself to float out of the house and into the mist. She strained her eyes to see what was coming up ahead, but the fog was so thick she couldn't even see her own arms that she had pushed out in front of her. Soon, the fog thinned somewhat and Alice could make out the shape of the feared tunnel, the focus of all her recent dreams. A white light pulsated from inside and she could hear the buzz of a billion conversations happening at once. She looked downwards to see that although she was levitating, her bony, vein-ridden feet, were moving, unerringly towards the tunnel. As she got closer, the light became more intense and she shielded her eyes from its glare. The mist thinned out further and Alice could make out shapes, figures moving around inside it. She heard Frank's cruel laugh and a feeling of dread overcame her. Grasping hands reached out from the fog, and his head, complete with gashed neck, shot out in front of her. Alice recoiled and tried to stop her forward movement, but her efforts had no effect. Frank reached out with those strong arms, that she once thought were so protective. Alice closed her eyes and begged for forgiveness. Suddenly, Frank's arms fell away and another figure appeared out of the mist. A figure she recognised instantly.

'You finally got here then, Alice Hussy.'

Alice gasped and then screamed. 'AMY!'

Amy laughed. 'We've been waiting for you for so long, we began to think you'd never get here.'

She took hold of Alice's hands and pulled her forward, away from the grasping arms, away from that broken neck, away from that hideous laugh which had now morphed into a beaten, howl of frustration. Alice didn't look back. All those nightmares were, literally, behind her now, and it was Amy, blessed, beautiful Amy that had come to claim her and lead her into the light.

She was dressed in her best white summer dress, the one she was so proud of. She wore her black patent, shoes, the pair she loved to dance in. Alice looked down at her own feet, to see her favourite Oxford heels. Her tatty old dressing gown was gone, and she was wearing her favourite polka-dot frock, and her famous Rita Hayworth, chestnut curls, hung around her shoulders. She hugged Amy and they wept tears of unbridled joy. Inseparable in life, they now had all of eternity to look forward to.

Amy pulled away from the hug, and still holding Alice's hands, she walked backwards, leading Alice on. 'People are waiting,' she whispered.

Alice looked past Amy, to see her mother and father holding hands, looking as much in love as they ever did. And there was Miriam, and Barney, Benny and the rest of her farm lads. They clapped and shouted to her. 'Nice to see you again, Missis.'

As she wiped away more tears, she heard music. Begin the Beguine was playing. Amy grinned and held out her arms. Alice took hold of one of her hands, put the other on her waist in her own, *adventurous*, style, and together they danced into the light.

THE END

Printed in Great Britain
by Amazon

34565653R00225